PRAISE FOR
RAVEN STRATAGEM

'Lee's ability to balance high science fiction concepts—
worlds, cultures, and weapons—with a deep examination of
character—tragic flaws, noble purpose, and societal ideas—is
nigh unprecedented in space opera.'

B&N Sci-Fi & Fantasy Blog

'How do you follow-up a breathtaking, multiple award-
nominated debut that combined world-changing
technologies, interesting reality-altering mathematics and
awesome characters? *Raven Stratagem* is as mind-blowing as
its predecessor, but in a completely different way.'

Kirkus Reviews

'Without a doubt, *Raven Stratagem* is proof that Yoon Ha
Lee sits next to Ann Leckie atop the podium for thoughtful,
intricate, and completely human science fiction.'

Tor.com

'This stunning sequel to the Hugo- and Nebula-nominated
Ninefox Gambit contains a satisfying mixture of interstellar
battles, politics, intrigue, and arcane technology…
Readers who don't mind being dropped in the deep end will
savor this brilliantly imagined tale.'

Publishers Weekly **Starred Review**

'Lee has leveraged the adage that "any seemingly advanced
science can look like magic" to create truly bizarre
technologies; while there is plenty of gripping space opera
action, the real pleasure of this series is the inventive
worldbuilding.'

Library Journal **Starred Review**

'*Raven* is a triumphant continuation of a vibrant new space opera. I expected intrigue and entertainment; I wasn't prepared for all the feelings. I can't wait to see where Yoon Ha Lee takes this rollercoaster next.'

The Speculative Herald

'If you like your universes with a dark sense of humour and a wonky moral compass, Lee may be the best thing to happen to Space Opera since Banks's untimely passing. *Raven Stratagem* is that rare thing—a sequel that betters the original. The ruling order is on its way out, and something is going to replace it. It could be freedom. It could be chaos. It could be a disaster. What could be more timely?'

Shoreline of Infinity

'Last year, I read and loved a stunning military space opera. This year, I had the pleasure of reading the sequel, *Raven Stratagem*, and may have loved it even more. I really hope Lee chooses to write more. This series has been one of the best things to happen in science fiction, and I can't recommend it enough.'

The Illustrated Page

'The book works as a kind of puzzle… [and] like the best puzzles, there is a certain inevitable logic to how the whole thing plays out, both against and with our expectations. I for one can't wait to see the final scenario.'

Strange Horizons

'There's grand space battles here. There's political manoeuvring at the heart of the Empire, and some genuinely crackling dialogue. There's characters baring their souls in genuinely moving moments. It makes for an absolutely cracking read.'

Sci-Fi and Fantasy Reviews

PRAISE FOR NINEFOX GAMBIT

WINNER OF THE 2017 LOCUS AND STABBY AWARDS

'The story is dense, the pace intense, and the delicate East Asian flavoring of the math-rich setting might make it seem utterly alien to many readers—yet metaphors for our own world abound. Readers willing to invest in a steep learning curve will be rewarded with a tight-woven, complicated but not convoluted, breathtakingly original space opera. And since this is only the first book of the *Machineries of Empire* trilogy, it's the start of what looks to be a wild ride.'

N. K. Jemisin, *The New York Times*

'I love Yoon's work! *Ninefox Gambit* is solidly and satisfyingly full of battles and political intrigue, in a beautifully built far-future that manages to be human and alien at the same time. It should be a treat for readers already familiar with Yoon's excellent short fiction, and an extra treat for readers finding Yoon's work for the first time.'

Ann Leckie

'Cheris and Jedao are fascinating, multi-faceted entities, filled with contradictions and idiosyncrasies; Lee's prose is clever and opulently detailed; the worldbuilding is jaw-droppingly good. Like the many-eyed Shuos, the book appears to delight in its own game, a tangle of plots and subplots. It almost seems content to never be deciphered, but if you persist, you're in for a fantastic story. Lee's novel is a brilliant way to begin a trilogy.'

Ars Technica

'Yoon Ha Lee recasts Korean legend in a densely rendered, high-tech future universe, with intricate worldbuilding.'

The Guardian

'"You know what's going on, right?" *Ninefox Gambit* asks. Often, you have to say, "Uh, yeah, of course," when the real answer is "I have no idea, but I really, really care." And then you keep reading.'

Strange Horizons

'For sixteen years Yoon Ha Lee has been the shadow general of science fiction, the calculating tactician behind victory after victory. Now he launches his great manoeuvre. Origami elegant, fox-sly, defiantly and ferociously *new*, this book will burn your brain. Axiomatically brilliant. Heretically good.'

Seth Dickinson

'A high-octane ride through an endlessly inventive world, where calendars are weapons of war and dead soldiers can assist the living. Bold, fearlessly innovative and just a bit brutal, this is a book that deserves to be on every awards list.'

Aliette de Bodard

'Ambitious. Confusing. Enthralling. Brilliant. These are the words I will use to describe Yoon Ha Lee's utterly immersive, utterly memorable novel. I had heard very high praise for Lee's short fiction—still, even with those moderate expectations I had no idea what I was in for. I haven't felt this blown away by a novel's originality since *Ancillary Justice*. And, since I'm being completely honest, *Ninefox Gambit* is actually more inventive, boundary-breaking, and ambitious than that.'

The Book Smugglers

'Cheris' world feels genuinely alien, with thrillingly unfamiliar social structures and technologies, and the attention to detail is simply stunning. Just don't ever let your concentration slip, or there's a good chance that you will miss something wonderful.'

SciFi Now

'A dizzying composite of military space opera and sheer poetry. Every word, name and concept in Lee's unique world is imbued with a sense of wonder.'

Hannu Rajaniemi

'There's a good chance that this series will be seen as an important addition to the space opera resurgence of recent years. While Lee has developed a singular combination of military SF, mathematical elegance, and futuristic strangeness, readers may note echoes of or similarities to Iain M. Banks, Hannu Rajaniemi, C. J. Cherryh, Ann Leckie and Cordwainer Smith. Admirers of these authors, or anyone interested in state-of-the-art space opera, ought to give *Ninefox Gambit* a try.'

Worlds Without End

'Daring, original and compulsive. As if Cordwainer Smith had written a *Warhammer* novel.'

Gareth L. Powell

'That was a great read; very intriguing world building in particular. I now want to sign all my emails with "Yours in calendrical heresy."'

Tobias Buckell

'A striking space opera by a bright new talent.'
Elizabeth Bear

'Suitably, given the rigid Doctrine of the hexarchate and the irresistible formation instinct of the warrior Kel faction, *Ninefox Gambit* is a book of precise rigor. It gives a wonderful amount of worldbuilding without any clunky exposition dumps, is ruthlessly clear-eyed about the costs and concerns of war (especially at this technological level) and gives us an instantly ingratiating heroine who spends most of the book doing her best to outmaneuver the forces that have set her up to fail, waste the lives of her troops or just die. This is a future to get excited about.'
RT Book Reviews

'Space-based nail-biter *Ninefox Gambit* is a smart space opera that pushes the frontier of science fiction. A must-read.'
Kirkus Reviews

'Confused yet? The learning curve on *Ninefox Gambit* shouldn't be underestimated, although readers with a solid foundation in hard science fiction will have an easier time parsing the narrative. It's a challenging story, tackling science fiction concepts we're familiar with (spaceships and intergalactic war) while layering on purposefully obfuscated but compelling twists.'
Barnes & Noble Sci-Fi & Fantasy Blog

'If you're looking for another great sci-fi read, you should consider *Ninefox Gambit*.'
Sci-Fi Addicts

REVENANT
GUN

First published 2018 by Solaris
an imprint of Rebellion Publishing Ltd,
Riverside House, Osney Mead,
Oxford, OX2 0ES, UK

www.solarisbooks.com

ISBN: 978 1 78108 607 0

10 9 8 7 6 5 4 3 2 1

A CIP catalogue record for this book is available from the
British Library.

Designed & typeset by Rebellion Publishing

Printed in Denmark by Nørhaven

R E V E N A N T
G U N

MACHINERIES OF EMPIRE BOOK THREE

Y O O N H A L E E

SOLARIS

CHAPTER ONE

JEDAO WOKE UP in a luxuriously appointed suite, all ink painting scrolls and curious asymmetrical chairs and translucent tables. The last thing he remembered was being sprawled on a bed in a much smaller room wrestling his friend Ruo for a game controller. *This had better not be a hotel,* he thought, wondering if Ruo had persuaded him to do something regrettable again. He couldn't afford anything like this.

Not trusting the situation, he ducked down behind the chair he'd found himself in, and listened. No sound. After a while, he peered around, careful to stay silent. There was a closed door, and across from it, an open entrance to another room. No windows or viewports, unless they were concealed.

Ruo, he thought, *if this is another one of your pranks—*

A hint of breeze passed through the suite, and he shivered. He thought to look down. They'd done something to his clothes. He was wearing a thin, off-white tunic and undershorts. Maybe someone from Shuos Academy was hazing him?

No one had shot at him yet, so he risked standing up. Paradoxically, that made him warier. He knew what to do about bullets and fire and smoke.

That bothered Jedao the more he thought about it. The most immediate memory told him that he'd last been a first-year in academy, but he was sure that even the Shuos didn't put first-years into live-fire exercises. How did he know this stuff, anyway?

Jedao searched the first room, then grew bolder and tried the rest of the suite. There were six rooms, not seven, which made him frown. Surely the heptarchate still insisted on sevens for everything? Lots of objets d'art, too; no people to question. And no sign of Ruo.

A dresser occupied one wall of the bedroom, as luxurious as the rest of the furniture. Only the top drawer contained anything. Unfortunately, the anything was a Kel uniform. At least, Jedao presumed it was a Kel uniform, black with gold braid, the correct colors. He searched for pins or medals, turned the pockets inside out, anything to tell him more about the uniform's owner. No luck, although the double bands on the cuffs indicated that it belonged to a high officer. The style looked odd, too. The left panel of the coat wrapped around, and instead of buttons it had toggles, with hook-and-eye fasteners to keep the whole affair closed.

Next to the uniform, tucked in a corner, rested a pair of silken black half-gloves. That suggested the uniform belonged to someone seconded to the Kel, rather than an actual Kel soldier.

"All right," Jedao said, trying to ignore the sick feeling in his stomach, "this isn't funny anymore. You can come out now, Ruo."

No response.

Jedao considered the possibility that someone had forgotten their uniform by accident. He picked up the shirt and unfolded it again. Then the pants. They looked like they would fit him rather well—wait a second. He narrowed his eyes at his arms, then his legs, then considered his torso. When had he put on all this muscle? Not that he was complaining, exactly, but the last he'd checked he'd been rather slimmer.

He was starting to think that Ruo didn't have anything to do with this after all. At least, he couldn't think of any reason Ruo would pass up an overnight muscle-enhancing treatment. In that case, what the fuck was going on?

Even if the uniform would fit him, Jedao knew better than to put it on. Too bad he didn't have other clothes. But being shot for impersonating an officer didn't sound fun.

The door opened. *Ruo?* Jedao thought; but no.

A man came in, pale and tall and extraordinarily beautiful. His amber-flecked eyes with their smoky lashes were emphasized by silver-dark eyeshadow. While the man wore Nirai black-and-silver, Jedao had never imagined one in clothes with such decadent ruffles, to say nothing of the lace that drowned his wrists.

Jedao's new theory involved Nirai experimentation that he didn't recall agreeing to. Of course, in the heptarchate they didn't need to ask your permission. He backed up two steps.

The Nirai's gaze swept right to Jedao's hands, which were in plain sight and not doing anything threatening. The Nirai's eyebrows shot up. "I hate to break it to you," he said, ignoring Jedao's hostile body language, "but you're going to start panics going around with naked hands." He had a low, cultured voice, as beautiful as the rest of him. "I advise you to put on the gloves, although those will start panics, too. Still, it's the better of two bad alternatives. And you ought to get dressed."

Was the man a guest instructor? And if so, why wasn't he wearing insignia to indicate it? "Excuse me," Jedao said. "I'd rather not go around in Kel drag. If there are civilian clothes somewhere, I'll put those on instead. Who are you, anyway?"

"My name's Nirai Kujen," the man said. He strode forward until he'd backed Jedao into a corner. "Tell me your name."

That seemed harmless enough. "Garach Jedao Shkan."

Kujen frowned. "Interesting... that far back, hmm? Well, it's close enough for my purposes. Do you know why you're here?"

"Look," Jedao said, starting to be more irritated than frightened, "who are you and what is your authority anyway?" Granted that he was only a Shuos cadet, but even a cadet should be afforded some small protection from interference by random members of other factions.

Kujen laughed softly. "Look at my shadow and tell me what you see."

Jedao had taken it for an ordinary shadow. As he examined it more closely, though, he saw that it was made of the shapes of fluttering captive moths. The longer he stared at it, the more he saw the darkness giving way to a vast crevasse of gears and cams and silver chrysalises from which more moths flew free. He raised his head and waited for an answer to the question he couldn't figure out how to formulate.

"Yes," Kujen said. "I'm the Nirai hexarch."

Jedao revised his speech mode to the most formal one. "Hexarch? Not heptarch?" The name didn't sound familiar. He scrabbled in his memory for the names of any of the heptarchs and could only remember Khiaz, who led the Shuos. What kind of experiments had they been running on him anyway to mess up his knowledge of basics?

"It's complicated. Anyway, you're here to lead an army."

That made even less sense. The Nirai faction dealt in technology, including weapons, but they weren't soldiers; that was the realm of the Kel. Besides which—"I'm not a soldier," Jedao said. Not yet, anyway. Besides which, didn't you have to serve for years and years to get from grunt to general?

Except he had a soldier's body, and he'd listened for gunfire first thing.

Kujen's mouth quirked at whatever he saw on Jedao's face. "A real army," Kujen said, "not a simulated one. Potentially against the hexarchate's best generals."

Jedao was going to have to start asking questions and hope that some of the answers started making sense. "'Hexarchate'?" he asked. "Which faction blew up?"

"The Liozh, if you must know. The situation grew complicated very rapidly. The two major successor states are the Protectorate, which styles itself the heir to the old hexarchate, and the Compact, which was founded by radicals. Plus any number of independent systems trying to avoid getting swallowed by them or by foreign powers. I'll show you the map, if you like. You're to conquer the pieces so we can put the realm back together."

Jedao stared Kujen down, difficult because of the height difference, to say nothing of the distractingly pretty eyes. He was already certain that Kujen had to be leaving out great swathes of detail. "How in the name of fox and hound did all of that happen?"

"You don't remember?" A hint of dismay touched Kujen's voice.

"Clearly not," Jedao said, and felt the cold plunge of fear.

"I am in urgent need of a general," Kujen said. "You're available."

Uh-oh. "Do you want to lose, Nirai-zho?" Jedao said. "I'm not a general." So why had he gone for cover in this decidedly unthreatening setting? Admittedly, he imagined most generals spent time on their asses far from the front lines. "Playing games doesn't prepare you to wage war."

This must be a test for rabid megalomania.

"Well, get dressed anyway, and I'll show you what you're up against," Kujen said. "And use my name. No one uses that honorific anymore."

Jedao stared at him in desperation, wondering what to do. It was taboo to wear another faction's colors. Spies did it in the line of duty, but that didn't make it a good idea for him. On the other hand, defying a heptarch—hexarch—also struck him as a lousy idea.

"You earned the right to wear that uniform," Kujen said. "Do it."

Time to counterattack. "What's a Nirai doing messing around with military affairs anyway?" Jedao demanded. Maybe that would distract Kujen from the uniform.

"I'm the last legitimate hexarch standing," Kujen said. "The Protectorate is under the influence of an upstart Kel. The Compact, despite their pretensions of democracy, is under the sway of *another* upstart Kel. As I said, it's complicated. And I'm sorry to inform you that the Shuos hexarch turned traitor and joined the Compact."

As he spoke, Kujen retrieved the uniform and held it out to Jedao. "Come on," he said coaxingly. "Unless you really mean to go around half-naked."

Reluctantly, Jedao took the clothes and pulled them on. Then he stared at Kujen some more.

"I have some battle transcripts so you'll have an idea of what to expect."

"Are you sure you can't scare up a competent general?" Jedao said. "Or a mercenary commander?" Mercenaries had been illegal in the heptarchate, but maybe the regulations had changed. Or

Kujen, being a hexarch, could bend the rules. Companies sometimes operated around the borders. "I don't—" He looked helplessly down at his hands. "Whatever you think I am, I can't do this. My memories seem to be muddled. If you really, truly need a general, you ought to get one who knows what they're doing."

Kujen smiled crookedly. "I have strong reason to believe that you're the only one who can help me."

That was all very well in the dramas, but a bad sign when people talked to you like that in real life. Jedao had a brief, disorienting memory of sitting in a room watching one with—an oval-faced Kel woman and several robots? Except he didn't seem to have a body, and he could see in all directions at once, which made no sense because he was pretty sure he only came with the standard-issue two eyes in front. Just as quickly as it had come, the memory dissipated.

Still, he might as well glean what information he could. "All right, Nir—Kujen, show me."

Kujen drew him into a sitting room and snagged a slate off one of the tables. Then he played back a sequence of battles in three dimensions, which took some time. The first were land battles on a variety of maps, including an ambitious amphibious assault. The later ones occurred in space, some involving large swarms. One side was represented by blue, the other by red. It became obvious that Red was the same commander each time, and was the adversary Kujen should worry about: aggressive, devious, and good at dragging the opponent about by the heels.

"Well?" Kujen said.

"We're fighting Red, right?"

Why did Kujen's mouth twist like that? "Yes," he said, without elaborating.

"We're fucked," Jedao said. "I don't know if you can tell, but you have to have noticed that in that last battle, Red gouged Blue into pieces while outnumbered *eight to one*. I have a better idea. This enemy you're so worried about? Invest in some good assassins."

There he went, sounding like a stereotypical Shuos, but it was good advice, dammit. "Unless you're going to tell me that everyone in Red's chain of succession is also that good."

"No, that's unlikely."

"So what's wrong with assassins? Is this one of those situations where that would touch off a general war we're too broke to fight?"

Kujen shook his head. "We need to take and hold territory. Besides, I know you're up to fighting Red because you're also Red. That eight-to-one thing was the Battle of Candle Arc, by the way. Very famous. The Kel put it in all their textbooks."

Jedao's marrow froze. The fuck? How could he possibly be Red, let alone "also Red," whatever that meant? Or, for that matter, old enough to have carried out a feat that had gotten into textbooks? Were the Kel in the habit of handing their swarms over to teenagers?

"All right," Jedao said, "you win. I don't have any useful arguments against the insane. If this is a training exercise, you can fail me on it." Which was going to suck, because he'd been having difficulty with his math classes. "I will have to work hard for the rest of the term to make up for it, but I'm not afraid of hard work."

Kujen looked fascinated. "I need to clear something up for you. You really think you're a cadet?"

Jedao was silent.

"How old are you?"

"Seventeen," Jedao said reluctantly, even though he was starting to wonder.

"Take off your shirt."

Jedao hesitated, then fumbled with the closures.

Kujen rolled his eyes. "I won't look if it makes you feel better, although it's not as if it's anything I haven't seen before." He sauntered to the other side of the room, then pointedly turned his back.

Jedao resisted the urge to glare at Kujen's shoulder blades. Kujen sighed theatrically. Jedao took off the shirt and folded it over his arm, then stood there uncertainly.

"Shirt too," Kujen said.

Jedao bit back a retort and settled the tunic over the back of a chair. After he'd yanked the shirt over his head, he froze. He'd thought the older physique was bad enough. Beyond that, his torso was riddled with scars. Most of them looked dreadful. Hell, one of his nipples had been completely obliterated. He had no idea where the scars had come from. He prodded one. It didn't hurt. He almost wished it did.

"Even the Shuos don't do that to their cadets," Kujen said. "Grenade took off half your face once, back when you were a tactical group commander. The surgeons did an excellent reconstruction. You can't even tell unless you do a deep scan at the bone level. Anyway, do you believe me now when I tell you you're a soldier?"

Jedao put his clothes back on. "How many years?" *Get the facts. Panic later.*

"You're forty-four."

Shit. "I had a friend..." Jedao said, then trailed off because he wasn't sure where he was going with the thought. Why would the hexarch keep track of another random Shuos cadet, after all? Ruo probably had gone off to make a name for himself as a celebrated assassin. And at this point Ruo would be twenty-seven years older.

Interesting. He used to write down all his arithmetic, and he'd just done that in his head. But Kujen had resumed talking, so he filed away the discrepancy to puzzle over later.

"Your abilities ought to be intact," Kujen went on, "but we're going to have to catch you up on the holes in your declarative memory."

"Yes, about that," Jedao said. "Is there a cure? Because it's very disturbing."

"Your opponent made off with most of your memories," Kujen said. "That's why she's potentially your worst matchup, and why we have to be careful. I retrieved the rest, but owing to circumstances there was some degradation. I'm sorry."

"Are you telling me I was attacked by a memory vampire?" Jedao said incredulously.

Kujen snorted. "You have a way with words sometimes... Exotic technology, and an experimental procedure besides. We could try to duplicate the circumstances if we capture her, but odds are it would drive you crazy."

"Why didn't it drive this memory vampire crazy?"

"Who says it didn't?" Kujen sighed. "I don't suppose you remember any of those Andan jokes?"

The bizarreness of this question made Jedao's mind go blank. He couldn't think of any jokes whatsoever, and besides, the entire situation struck him as decidedly unfunny.

"You used to have the most extraordinary collection of filthy Andan jokes," Kujen said wistfully.

"You could tell them to me and I could tell them back to you."

"No," Kujen said, "it wouldn't be the same."

That didn't make Jedao feel better, so he moved on to the next question. "Why the Kel?"

"You had an excellent career seconded to the Kel," Kujen said. "They promoted the hell out of you."

"Why can't you hire someone who doesn't have defective memories?"

"You've never lost a battle," Kujen said. "Plus, outnumbered eight to one. Crushing victory. Even I could tell." His voice was lightly teasing.

Jedao closed his eyes. *Thanks for the pressure.* "There's no guarantee I could do that again." More like *no way ever*.

"You could see how it was done in the playback, couldn't you?"

Did Kujen have no idea? "That's on a tidy spiderfucking three-dimensional diagram where you can see all the units arrayed neatly and everything has labels and there are helpful colored arrows for the vectors. As opposed to being there when somebody's warmoth has an inconvenient drive failure while it's sitting in a key pivot because the mechanics at the last layover half-assed the repairs, and you can't read half the hostile formants on scan because the enemy has a fancy new jammer, and one of your brilliant hothead commanders decides the best thing she can do with her tactical group is creatively misinterpret her orders and—"

Jedao shut up. He had no idea where the rant had come from, just like the scars. He couldn't tell if any of those things had happened or if he was being hypothetical. It was like listening to a stranger who had his voice and who talked exactly like he did. And who knew a lot more about warfare.

Who the hell am I? Am I a clone? He had the impression you couldn't give clones even dubious memories of battles, but then, he already had amnesia. How was he supposed to tell?

Kujen caught his arm and steered him to a chair. "Sit," he said, and tugged gently.

Jedao sank into the chair. Any more of this and his knees would dissolve.

"I'm not a military practitioner," Kujen said. "But I have experience dealing with the military, and the Kel think highly of your ability. In this matter I defer to their judgment."

"Am I some kind of expendable copy?"

"You're not expendable," Kujen said unhelpfully.

He hadn't denied it. "Fine," Jedao said. "What resources do we have?" With any luck this question would generate a concrete answer and not alarming creations like memory vampires. He would have to investigate the matter of clones on his own time, since Kujen was being closemouthed.

"The good news is that you will be pleasantly surprised by the capabilities of your warmoths," Kujen said.

Jedao imagined so, because all he knew about warmoth statistics came from video games. It didn't seem politic to mention that, however.

"Also good is that we have a supply of loyal Kel for those moths. The bad news is numbers. No matter what we do, we're massively outnumbered by any one of our enemies."

"We're talking about how many moths and crew on our side?"

"We have 108 bannermoths," Kujen said, "with crew of approximately 450 each. You also have two infantry regiments that you can distribute among the bannermoths and the accompanying boxmoth transports as you see fit. I would have obtained more moth Kel for you if that had been an option."

"You can't recruit more?"

Kujen made a moue. "A number of Kel are confused about who to follow. While I have the loyalty of a small number of bases—"

"You'd better show me that map," Jedao said, "so I can visualize the situation." *Pretend it's a video game*, he thought, despite his unease at treating something as serious as war as a game.

Kujen called up a three-dimensional map, neatly labeled. The Protectorate appeared in gold. While some of its boundaries looked more extensive than the heptarchate Jedao remembered, chunks of it had been bitten off. The second-largest polity, as Kujen had mentioned, was called the Compact. The map showed it in red.

"Red for Shuos?" Jedao said. Kujen had said the Shuos hexarch had thrown in with the Compact.

"Yes," Kujen said.

"Is Khiaz-zho still head of the Shuos?"

Kujen's eyes widened. Then he started to laugh.

Jedao didn't see what was so funny. "Well?"

"She's been gone for quite some time," Kujen said. "It's Shuos Mikodez now. You don't remember much of Khiaz, do you?"

"No," Jedao said. Just her name. "Why?"

"Why indeed," Kujen said. He zoomed in on the border space between the Protectorate and the Compact. "What do you think?"

A number of smaller states had sprouted up there. Jedao imagined that none of them enjoyed the situation. "Why haven't they been gobbled up?"

"Another good question," Kujen said. "The answer is that, after the assassination that took out the hexarchs other than myself and Mikodez, calendrical destabilization was so strong that the borders remain precarious even now. There are large regions of space where the old exotic technologies no longer work. They're most reliable in the Protectorate, but the Protectorate is overextended. It's exactly the kind of situation that attracts opportunist potentates and despots and governmental experimentalists of every kind."

"How did you escape the assassinations?"

Kujen shrugged. "Mikodez and I were more paranoid than the others."

Jedao sensed he wouldn't get more of an answer and returned to the map. "You said earlier that the Kel were divided."

"Yes. Protector-General Inesser seized power and is running the Protectorate. The other factions caved on the grounds that she was the one with the guns. In the Compact, there's a nascent democratic state backed by High General Kel Brezan. The Kel are having fits trying to figure out the mess."

"'Democratic'?" Jedao said. "What's that?"

"They vote on everything from their leaders to their laws," Kujen said.

Jedao mulled that over. "It sounds dreadfully impractical," he said, "but all right. What about your Kel? Who do they support?"

"I can guarantee their loyalty."

"Oh?" Jedao said neutrally.

"There were some morale issues earlier," Kujen said with a suspicious lack of specificity. "You'll see when you meet them."

"What kind of—"

"I want to see how you handle it."

A test. Jedao didn't like that either, but he'd manage. "What about the name of this memory vampire who has it in for me?"

Kujen relented. "Her name is Kel Cheris."

The name didn't spark any recognition in him. "Is she anyone I should know?"

"You, no," Kujen said with a trace of annoyance. "As far as *you're* concerned, she's only a low officer with a talent for math. *I'm* the one who should have predicted that she'd grow up to be a radical crashhawk."

Crashhawk? Jedao wondered. He would have asked, except Kujen was still speaking.

"We won't confront her straight off," Kujen said. "You're at a disadvantage right now. Later, with better resources, perhaps. But not yet."

"I don't want to go after her," Jedao said. Avoiding her sounded like good sense. If she was more him than he was, and unstable on top of it, she might be able to repeat the eight-to-one trick. He was betting that, as impressive as 108 bannermoths sounded, he didn't outnumber her eight to one. What would that leave her with, 13.5 moths? "I want to know where she is so I can run like hell if I see her coming."

"My agents are doing their best," Kujen said. "Unfortunately, she hasn't been sighted in the last nine years."

Great, she was lurking out there in stealth mode, so he wouldn't see her coming, either.

"Let me cheer you up," Kujen said, rather callously. "I'll show you your command moth." He picked up the slate and tapped at it. Jedao was impressed that the lace at his wrists didn't get in the way.

"It's triplets?" Jedao said, peering at the images of three moths that now hovered in front of him, a large one flanked by two smaller ones. All three moths had the characteristic triangular profile of Kel warmoths. The largest featured a spinally mounted gun along with the expected arrays of turrets and missile ports.

"No, the smaller two are for scale reference," Kujen said. "The one to your left is a fangmoth. You used to be fond of those. The one to your right is a—"

"—bannermoth," Jedao said, then stopped.

Kujen arched an eyebrow at him. "See, you haven't forgotten everything." His hands moved again. He had beautiful hands, with fingers tapering gracefully.

A fourth moth appeared above the central moth. It was broader and longer, and also had a spinal main gun.

"Cindermoth," Kujen said. "There used to be six of them. Now only four remain, and they're under Protector-General Inesser's control. No one currently has a mothyard capable of building new ones, which buys us a little time. Anyway, that central one is a shearmoth, and it's yours. I made an assistant name it, which was a mistake, but I hate naming things. Don't look at me like that, I just design them."

Kujen zeroed in on the spinal gun. "That's the shear cannon," he said. "It only functions in high calendar terrain, which is its main disadvantage, especially since you're going to be fighting radicals and rebels and heretics."

"So why bother with it at all?" Jedao said.

"It generates a pulse that warps spacetime," Kujen said patiently. "Creating the pulse is an exotic effect. Once that's done, however, it will continue to travel into any sort of terrain until it dissipates. I got the idea because of the way the mothdrive works, by grabbing onto spacetime and pulling itself along. Breeding the modification into the moth lineage took some time. But I think you'll find it worthwhile."

Jedao figured it out. "So you can fire it from our side of the border into theirs."

"Yes."

"I hope there are still conventional weapons," Jedao said, giving Kujen a hard look. "Because if it's a gravitational wave, it might yank formations out of place, but it's just going to pass *through* the moths themselves. I can't destroy them directly with it."

Great, he thought. He'd just said "I," as if he were going along with this.

Kujen made a pacifying gesture. "I wouldn't stint on that. And it's not entirely useless on that front—try it on a planet with oceans or atmosphere sometime, and you'll get some interesting turbulence. Check the other statistics—"

The readout appeared in front of the images. Jedao went through all the listed weapons as well as the numbers of missiles and mines, plus the amount of space it had for necessaries like foam sealant and pickles. Apparently the Kel love of spiced cabbage pickles hadn't changed. He gestured at the slate. Kujen handed it over so he could run his own queries. It took Jedao a few moments to work out the interface, but after a while he was able to call up some explanatory diagrams.

At first the numbers didn't mean much. With some thought, however, he could see the shearmoth's capabilities in his head; he could visualize the maneuvers it was capable of, how it would dance at his command. "How many of these do you have?" he asked, although he had already guessed the answer.

"Just the one," Kujen said with what Jedao interpreted as real regret. "You don't know what I had to do to source the materials needed to grow the mothdrive components. You'll have to keep in mind that the shearmoth's mothdrive and maneuver drives have better power to mass ratios than your bannermoths do, even if it's larger. Don't outrun them."

Obligingly, Jedao looked up the profiles for both drives and was impressed by the differences. He ran some computations to compare the power draw over a spread of different accelerations. After a while he became aware of Kujen's narrowed eyes. "Did I get something wrong?" he asked.

"No," Kujen said after a subtle pause. "You homed right in on the intersection of those curves."

Jedao had done that part in his head. Curious, but if the past years had magically fixed that part of his brain, he wasn't going to say no to that either. "It had to be there somewhere," he said. "If you assume the curves are approximated by—" He demonstrated.

"So I see," Kujen said in a voice so dry that Jedao was reminded that he was lecturing the Nirai hexarch on mathematics elementary enough that he had probably figured it out as a small child. "Well, while the Kel have always preferred to throw you at strategic problems, it won't hurt to round out your education. Considering the number of calendrical heresies flourishing out there, it can only help to develop your mathematical skills."

"I would like that," Jedao said, and was rewarded by Kujen's half-laugh, half-smile.

"In the meantime," Kujen said, "let's deal with the practicalities. Set your uniform insignia. I had thought you'd remember, but since you don't—the Kel like everything to be done according to protocol."

"Set? Shouldn't there be pins for this stuff?"

"I really wish I'd had a better way to check what you do and don't remember," Kujen muttered. "The uniform will respond to your voice. Just tell it your name and rank and it will read the rest from your profile."

Jedao did, and was surprised by the general's wings above the

Shuos eye, two things he didn't remember earning. A full general, at that. Would that have made Ruo envious?

"Even if I'm forty-four," Jedao said, incredulous and not a little regretful about the lost years, "that's rather young." The idea of appearing before the Kel in this uniform was daunting enough. Appearing before them while claiming to be a general—*their* general—seemed like it would invite them to put holes in him. He heard they had good aim.

"The Kel respect rank," Kujen said. "They'll respect yours."

Will they now, Jedao thought. Only one way to find out. "These are real Kel," he said, "serving on real moths, fighting a real war. And you've decided that for this to work, I have to be a real general for you."

"That sums it up, yes."

A bad situation. Nevertheless, he needed to stay alive long enough to figure out how to tilt the odds not only in his favor, but in favor of the Kel who would be coming into his care. "I don't care how hacked up this hept—hexarchate of yours has become," Jedao said, "or how good this shearmoth is. A swarm of 108 moths, however impressive, doesn't leave us room for error. The only way this is possible is if I get good fast and we fight dirty."

On impulse, Jedao saluted Kujen. The motion came disturbingly naturally. He said, in formal Kel fashion, "I'm your gun." He felt he ought to commemorate the occasion somehow, even if the occasion was not remotely sane.

Kujen's eyes lit. "I knew you'd come back to me," he said. It wasn't until much later that Jedao figured out what he meant by that.

CHAPTER TWO

Nine years ago

THE MORNING AFTER Cheris disappeared, taking the needlemoth with her, High General Kel Brezan was woken by a stranger in his bedroom on the cindermoth *Hierarchy of Feasts*. At first he thought a servitor had gotten confused about the time, because who in the name of fire and ash served tea at this hour? He'd made use of his uncomfortable new rank for once and ordered that no one disturb him for anything other than an emergency, because he needed a good night's sleep before tackling the world's problems.

Brezan had gone through the usual routine before going to sleep, including unwinding his chest wrap, because in times of crisis, chaos, and dire emergency, routines were all that kept him going. He might be the highest-ranking Kel remaining in the hexarchate, but that didn't mean he wanted to remind the military of their hazy prejudice against a man who hadn't had the fortune to be born a manform. Lose-lose situation all around: sex changes weren't difficult, just time-consuming, except the Kel disapproved of those too, some stupid puritan streak. So he endured as he was. He hardly noticed it these days. Besides, given all the other reasons a Kel might have to hate him, he doubted his being a womanform made a damn bit of difference. In the meantime, he kept up the small fashion cues that clued in random people as to how he wanted to be regarded, like haircut and (when off-duty, which was going to be never again) style of jewelry.

"It's an emergency," a harsh, low voice said just as Brezan registered the sound of the doorway whisking shut.

Brezan startled awake and fumbled uselessly for his sidearm. He wasn't paranoid enough to sleep with it on, a fact that he was starting to regret, even if he doubted he could have hit the intruder anywhere useful. More likely shoot himself in the foot or, if the universe was feeling particularly unjust, get the damn gun shot out of his hand *again*. He was never going to live that down.

The candlevines in the room brightened in response to the stranger, who wasn't a stranger after all. It was one of the Kel sergeants who worked in Communications, a chubby woman with a habit of telling filthy jokes to anyone who'd stand still for them. Except Brezan had the feeling the woman wasn't a Kel at all, not if she'd broken into his room.

"Hello, High General," the woman said. She bore a tray with a steaming cup of tea.

"Are you a Shuos?" Brezan said. Might as well not waste any time.

"Very good," she said.

"What's your real name?"

She came forward, just slowly enough not to be threatening. "You're asking the wrong question. It's Shuos Emio, by the way. And you should have the tea. No poison, unless you count a few extra stimulants. You need to be awake for this conversation."

"What," Brezan said sarcastically, "I'm not awake enough already?" He kicked the sheets off and sat up, feeling weirdly vulnerable in his nightshirt and uncombed hair.

"Oh, you don't need the stims for *me*," Emio said. "But the hexarch needs to talk to you and you'll need all your wits for that."

"Hexarch" meaning Shuos Mikodez, one of the last people Brezan wanted to talk to. "He couldn't call through regular channels?"

Emio gave him a look. "I can't make you take this seriously," she said, disturbingly casual, "but it's in your best interests to. Because I have two pieces of news for you, and the hexarch will be your best friend dealing with them both."

Brezan decided that it was unlikely that Emio would leave him in peace to get dressed. He strode over to the drawer and rummaged for his chest wrap and uniform. "All right," he said, "tell me."

"The first is that your revolution is already in danger."

Brezan scoffed. "That's all? It's a revolution. It's in danger by definition."

Emio went on as if she hadn't heard his outburst. "The second is that the person you were depending on to deal with this, Kel Cheris, has vanished."

Brezan froze. "You can't be serious."

"Wasting time again," Emio said. "You've run staff meetings before. Do you usually spend so much time on irrelevancies?"

As much as Brezan was starting to dislike Emio, he couldn't argue the point. If she was telling the truth—and he had the sinking feeling that she was—then he needed to stop needling her and start preparing for a truly ugly situation. "You don't know where Cheris went?"

He didn't ask how much Emio knew about Cheris-Jedao and her role in the calendrical spike that had brought the entire hexarchate to a grinding halt. For one, he wouldn't like the answer. For another, it didn't matter at this point.

"If I did, would I have said that she vanished?" Emio said with maddening reasonableness. "And, you know, as far as the Kel are concerned, I'm just a sergeant. I didn't have the authority to send everyone haring off on a search for her."

"Wouldn't have done any good," Brezan said. "I assume she took the needlemoth." It was the vessel she had arrived in, and it was equipped with a stealth system.

"Got it in one."

By now Brezan had finished dressing, even if his uniform collar was crooked. If Emio cared, she kept it to herself. "I'm ready," he said.

"No," Emio said, "you need to eat and drink first."

"You've got to be kidding me."

"I am quite serious."

"Hexarch Mikodez gave you personal orders to that effect?"

Emio grimaced slightly. "Not the hexarch. His assistant Zehun. I can assure you that, in their way, Zehun is far more terrifying."

Considering that Mikodez had just assassinated the other five hexarchs by way of declaring himself Cheris's ally, Brezan doubted that very much. He wasn't about to quibble, however. Brezan had vivid memories of his single encounter with Zehun, which had indeed been terrifying. He sat down at the table where Emio had deposited the tray and ate as quickly as his diminished appetite allowed.

"All right," Brezan said. "I hope you have a secured line to the Citadel of Eyes or wherever the fuck the hexarch is hanging out these days, because I'm pretty sure if I try to call him it'll just bounce."

Emio didn't dignify this with a reply. "Your terminal, if I may?"

Brezan made an impatient gesture. "Let's get this over with."

Emio leaned over the terminal and entered a long cryptic string of passphrases. "All right," she said, "Line 6-1 to the Citadel of Eyes. It shouldn't take long for the hexarch to pick up."

Brezan resisted the impulse to spend the time waiting by checking his reflection in the terminal's dark, glossy surface. If Hexarch Shuos Mikodez insisted on waking him in the middle of the night (revised calendar) to talk to him, Hexarch Shuos Mikodez could deal with imperfectly groomed hair and a crooked collar.

After two minutes, the display blazed to life. Brezan had never met Mikodez, but like any informed citizen he knew what the man looked like. Mikodez, unlike any number of Shuos, had never modded himself except to stay reasonably young the way any sensible person did. Glossy black hair with a long forelock framed a dark-skinned face, and earrings of red tassels and tiny gold beads swung from his ears. Aside from that, however, his red-and-gold uniform was entirely orthodox, vaguely military in style despite the desperately impractical colors. Then again, unless you were mucking around groundside, Brezan supposed it didn't matter what colors you wore while swanning around space.

"High General," Mikodez said. His voice was a surprisingly mild tenor. "Emio."

Brezan fought back a surge of sheer atavistic terror. After all, if Mikodez had intended to assassinate him, he could have had Emio shoot him just minutes earlier.

Emio merely nodded and sat on the edge of Brezan's desk. Under other circumstances, Brezan would have been even more aggravated. "Hexarch Mikodez," he said. "You've got my attention. What's so urgent?"

Mikodez grinned at Brezan. It almost made him look friendly, except Brezan wasn't fooled. No one in control of that many assassins and spies could ever be *friendly*. "Sorry you had to meet your new bodyguard so precipitously," Mikodez said, "but it couldn't be helped."

"If the situation is so fucked that I'm in immediate danger of getting offed," Brezan said, "I'm not sure what difference one bodyguard is going to make. Even a superpowered Shuos bodyguard." He cocked an eyebrow at Emio, daring her to say something.

"Only in the line of duty," she said, unruffled.

"You're in desperate need of a briefing," Mikodez said, "especially if Cheris isn't sticking around to take up the reins. I apologize for not getting in touch earlier, except *I* had to get briefed first, if you see what I mean."

"Yes," Brezan said sourly. "As far as I can tell, that means I get to stick around holding together the hexarchate until a decent provisional government can be put in place." Which was going to be interesting because he was by no means a political theorist, and he automatically distrusted any that Mikodez, of all people, might offer to provide him. It wasn't entirely clear to him, or to anyone, what laws the hexarchate now followed. Would its currency remain in place, and how was he going to persuade the Andan into helping him stabilize the markets? What would happen to all the Vidona? What would they do for jobs now? And the problems only began there.

"Worse than that," Mikodez said, sobering. "You're probably going to have to strong-arm people into following your new calendar and signing on to your government. Where by 'strong-arm' I mean sweet-talk. Normally I would offer the services of my Propaganda division, but right now my popularity is at an all-time low. You want to be seen cooperating with me as little as possible."

Brezan avoided mentioning that he wanted not to have to cooperate with Mikodez, period, not least because he didn't see that he had much choice. "Well," he said, "that's one thing I can do better than Cheris. Not because I'm particularly charismatic or interesting, but because by now everyone thinks she's Jedao."

"Charisma is just a matter of practice," Mikodez said, waving a hand. "Admittedly, you're not going to have much time. I'll coach you, but it will only work if you take me seriously."

It was only now penetrating that *Shuos Mikodez* seriously meant to back Brezan as the new head of state. "What's in it for you?" Brezan asked.

"Stability," Mikodez said with disarming frankness. "The Shuos already have issues on that front, despite my efforts."

"That makes no sense," Brezan said, unimpressed. "Why not blow up Cheris instead while you had the chance?"

"Because Cheris wasn't the only one who objected to the remembrances," Mikodez said. Suddenly all trace of humor left his voice. "Oh, I suppose the chocolate festivals and the New Year's gift exchange are harmless enough. But the torture? All those lives cut up? It's wasteful."

Brezan bared his teeth at Mikodez. "I notice you didn't say 'wrong.' If it mattered to you so much, why didn't you do anything decades ago?"

"Because when I took the hexarch's seat," Mikodez said, "my duty was to look after the welfare of the Shuos. For decades that meant preserving the status quo. Don't think I didn't look into alternatives; I did. But as you're about to discover, ripping out a government by the roots and replacing it with something new? That's not trivial work."

"Spoken like someone who knows."

"Oh, we stole *that* from the Andan," Mikodez said. "First Contact has a large body of research on how to transition governments and sociocultural structures. The problem is, all of it goes in the wrong direction—taking salvageable heretics and integrating them into the hexarchate. We want to go in the opposite direction, and in an opposite direction toward something that's never existed in our realm before. I imagine a lot of people will revolt or flee or die before it's all settled."

Brezan gave him a hard look. "You say that so cavalierly."

"I'm not the only one who made this world, Brezan."

Brezan flushed. He couldn't deny the charge. After all, he'd had his chance to turn Cheris over to Kel Command. Instead he'd joined up with her. Not for the first time, he thought about Tseya, the Andan agent whom he'd accompanied to assassinate Cheris, who'd once been his lover. At the time the two of them had thought Cheris was Jedao. Cheris herself had done everything possible to confuse people on that point.

Cheris had offered Brezan the prospect of a better world, one in which people didn't have to be ritually tortured to death to preserve the high calendar's workings. He'd believed her. And he'd betrayed Kel Command, and his family, and his lover Tseya, on the strength of that belief. He was already starting to wonder if he'd messed up.

"Someone's going to have to take charge of the provisional government," Brezan said. "I'd hoped it was going to be Cheris. But I see now that that wouldn't have worked."

Even so, he was angry, bitterly angry, that Cheris hadn't stuck around to help unfuck the revolution she'd instigated. He stared down at his hand and saw that it had balled into a fist. With an effort, he unclenched his fingers.

"She wouldn't have done you much good," Mikodez said briskly. "What she and Jedao have in common is that their vocabulary for fixing problems is mainly limited to shooting them. That's all very well when you're on the battlefield. It's not very useful in the rest of the real world."

"I can't believe I'm hearing this from a Shuos."

"There are a lot of problems that can be solved more fruitfully by *not* shooting things."

"I'll take that under consideration," Brezan said. "So. I can't rely on Cheris, and considering that she's more of a crashhawk than I am, it might be just as well that she's gone away. What else do I need to know?"

"Three things for now," Mikodez said. "First, Kel Inesser"—the hexarchate's senior field general—"is going to be a problem." He explained that she'd rallied a not insignificant number of Kel swarms to her banner and had declared herself Protector-General. "I give her points for creativity. Presumably she didn't claim the hexarch's seat because of, well, you."

Brezan barked a laugh. "Like I'm a threat to *Inesser*." A general who'd been generaling since before his *parents'* births? And Brezan had no field command experience himself. Until recently, his job had involved sitting on his ass in Personnel. "So you want me to convince people that a complete unknown is a better leader?"

"You're a complete unknown representing a change in regime," Mikodez said. "Inesser is sticking to the high calendar. For some people, that means a lot, if you can back it up with guns."

"Yes, about that," Brezan said. "I've only got the one swarm, and General Khiruev is, as I assume you've heard, still not in the best of health. Unless you're offering."

"I am," Mikodez said. "Because your second problem is that with Kel Command obliterated, nobody's providing strategic guidance to anyone's swarms anymore. It's not going to take long for all the foreigners to take advantage of the situation."

Brezan had thought of that for himself. It was impossible not to. Kel swarms customarily received their orders from Kel Command, which had taken care of analyzing the broader strategic picture. Even General Inesser—Protector-General Inesser, whatever—was going to have issues reorganizing her forces to deal with the sudden lack of command and control.

"You have a solution to that, don't you?" Brezan said, giving Mikodez a hard look. "Because it hasn't escaped my attention that the Shuos are the only faction who have made it out of this whole disaster intact."

"Very good," Mikodez said. "There may be some hope for you after all. Yes, I'm offering the services of the Shuos. We have most of the Kel listening posts bugged anyway as a precaution."

Precaution my ass, Brezan thought, but he didn't interrupt.

"With your leave, High General, we could perform the function that Kel Command used to. I already have a bunch of analysts hanging around here doing this work anyway."

The fact the Mikodez had suddenly resumed addressing Brezan by his erstwhile title didn't escape him. Perhaps Mikodez fancied himself a puppet-master; thought that crashhawks were easily manipulated. Brezan hoped to prove him wrong, not out of spite, but because interstellar government was too important to hand over out of naivety. While Brezan didn't have much leverage at the moment, he could do something with the fact that Mikodez had just made himself almost as notorious as Jedao.

"I accept," Brezan said, because he wanted to preserve the idea that he had choices. "So what's the third problem?"

Mikodez fiddled with an earring, the first sign of nerves he'd shown. "One of the hexarchs isn't dead."

Brezan frowned. "Cheris's—sources were convinced that you were the only one who'd gotten away." How much did Mikodez know about the servitors' role as spies, anyway? "Another double?"

"No," Mikodez said after a long moment. "It wasn't a double. Not in the way you're thinking."

"Do tell."

"Nirai Faian was a false hexarch," Mikodez said. "Something like a senior administrator, while the real hexarch went about his business elsewhere."

"Sounds paranoid," Brezan said. "Do we need to assassinate the real one, then?" He meant it as a joke.

He should have known not to joke about assassination around a Shuos. "I've been trying to figure out how since I learned of his existence," Mikodez said seriously. "His name is Nirai Kujen. You won't have heard of him"—Brezan made an assenting gesture—"but in a way, everything you know depends on him. He invented the modern mothdrive almost nine centuries ago. The high calendar is his creation. And so is the black cradle."

Brezan stared at Mikodez, appalled. But his mind was already racing. "Immortal, then," he said. "Like Jedao."

"Like Jedao," Mikodez said, "except without some of the limitations that made it possible to control Jedao. Well, to the extent that Jedao was ever controllable, which is an open question. But that argument is moot."

"Is he a danger to you?" Brezan said. Because he could think of only one reason why someone like Mikodez would care.

"He's a danger to everyone."

"Nine hundred years, you say, and he's not the one who exploded the hexarchate. If he invented the mothdrive—"

Mikodez shook his head. "Kujen has always been good at buying people's favor. Don't get drawn in. He's brilliant, but the hexarchate is a big place. Even if revolutions aren't friendly to research divisions, you'll eventually be able to find other technicians who can offer useful innovations without requiring you to sell your conscience down the river."

Brezan couldn't help it. He choked with laughter. "I'm sorry," he said when he was done, "a Shuos hexarch with a conscience?"

"Oh, *I* don't have any such thing," Mikodez said, taking Brezan's outburst calmly. "But it's clear that you do. And you're going to be the face of the operation."

"Why haven't I heard of this Kujen before now, anyway?"

"Because he's a secretive bastard," Mikodez said. "If you think about it, that's a great way to survive when you're almost a millennium old. Bravery has never been Kujen's strong point, which he himself would be the first to admit. Here—"

The terminal indicated that it had received a databurst from Mikodez. Brezan opened up the profile contained therein. Nirai Kujen: not just a secretive bastard, but an extraordinarily handsome one. A note cautioned him not to take physical appearances too literally, since, like Jedao, Kujen was a ghost who possessed different bodies as the occasion suited him. Fortunately, the profile also included data on movement patterns, which were much more reliable. As a former Personnel officer, Brezan had a lot of experience looking for nuances in body language.

"So you're saying he engineered the remembrances into the high calendar on purpose?" Brezan said, not bothering to hide his repugnance. "What evidence do you have for this?"

Mikodez shrugged. "He told me so. Check the file. I recorded that whole conversation, but I've had the whole thing transcribed with timestamps of the key bits so you don't have to sit through it all."

"How considerate of you."

"Don't thank me, thank my staff." Mikodez tapped his fingers against something just out of sight. "I have reason to believe that Kujen is personally attached to the hexarchate as it used to be. He dropped out of sight just before that business at the Fortress of Spinshot Coins, almost as if he knew which way the wind was blowing. I don't like that, and I don't like the fact that I don't know what he's up to."

"You were colleagues for decades," Brezan said slowly. "You couldn't do anything about him earlier?"

Mikodez's smile was self-mocking. "What, like oust him? I'm a bureaucrat, not a genius mathematician. You were probably too young to remember, but I was in my twenties when I took the seat. At the time my life expectancy was measured in days, and the Shuos were extremely weak after the previous leadership squandered resources in useless petty squabbles with the Andan and Vidona. I wasn't spoiling for a fight, and Kujen happened to agree with me about the value of stability."

It was the second time this conversation Mikodez had mentioned the word. Brezan didn't think that was a coincidence. He didn't harbor any illusions that he could challenge Mikodez in his own seat of power, but he didn't intend to become a mere puppet for the man, either.

"I'll read through the file," Brezan said. "But the immediate problem is the first one: keeping the hexarchate from exploding. I'll work with you on that. If you get more information on Kujen's whereabouts and latest hobbies, we can discuss those then."

"Fair enough." Mikodez pursed his lips. "One thing more."

"Oh?"

"You need to disentangle yourself from Khiruev's swarm as soon as possible," Mikodez said. "For one thing, you're going to be needing it to put out fires, and to form the core of the new government's forces. You don't want to be on the front lines. You're too important for that now."

Brezan gave him a disbelieving look.

"You're used to thinking of yourself as no one very important. I can tell. Modesty is going to have to become a thing of the past, I'm afraid."

"My sisters would be laughing their asses off hearing you call me 'modest,'" Brezan said.

"I'm quite serious," Mikodez said. "Half of leadership is prancing around looking like you know what you're doing, whether or not you actually do. The other half, well, that's what allies and delegation to gifted subordinates are for. Might I make a recommendation while I'm at it?"

"I don't think I can stop you."

"One Colonel Kel Ragath appears to have survived the devastation at Scattered Needles and is still trying to get in contact with Cheris, without much luck," Mikodez said. "I advise you to give him a call and promote him immediately, unless General Khiruev has a crushing objection."

"I'll check with her," Brezan said automatically, "although I doubt she will. Why, what is the colonel up to these days?" Like a lot of Kel, he'd heard of Ragath, who'd enjoyed a well-regarded career only to run into a ceiling at his present rank because of his secondary specialty in history. Ragath's scathingly critical papers about Kel policy hadn't earned him many friends in high places.

Mikodez smiled. "He raised a military force of his own in a system in the Stabglass March and is currently mucking about with gory logistical details. If you approach him and drop Cheris's name hintingly, I think you'll find him willing to work with you."

"Which is good," Brezan said, dismayed all over again by the sheer scope of the task before him, "because even the people who appear to be willing to work with me might be spies, or saboteurs, or sycophants."

"Ah," Mikodez said, and his smile turned sad. "You're learning already."

"I have anger management issues," Brezan said, remembering the old notations in his profile, "but I'm not stupid."

"Well," Mikodez said, "that's a start. My instinct is to ferret you away in the Citadel of Eyes behind my security. Unfortunately, this one time, my instinct is wrong. You're going to be a public figure, High General, and that means going where the public can see you. This will also make you one hell of a target, so I'm going to assign you some of my security."

"I suppose your security will quietly disappear me if I get too many ideas of my own," Brezan said.

"Don't be crass," Mikodez said. "I already have enough public relations problems without being seen to be assassinating *more* people. As it stands, I'm getting blamed for all sorts of petty theft that my agents had nothing to do with. Which is a crying shame, because my budget could use any revenue streams that happen to be lying about."

"And you wonder why the Shuos have such a terrible reputation," Brezan said sardonically.

"I'm going to have the reputation no matter what," Mikodez said. "I might as well do something useful with it. You, now—people know so much less about you. You only get one chance to make a first impression, you know. Don't waste it."

CHAPTER THREE

On a moon called Tefos in a distant system, Servitor Hemiola, a snakeform, was the first to notice that the hexarch had arrived. Its two comrades avoided overseeing the base's control room because they considered it one of the more boring duties. Hemiola had volunteered because it liked using the time to make videos. The other two servitors who made up their tiny enclave tolerated this because they had their own guilty hobbies.

During this particular occasion, Hemiola was rewatching the seventeenth episode of *A Rose in Three Revolutions*, its favorite drama. *A Rose in Three Revolutions* supposedly had six seasons of twenty-four episodes each, except it had still been airing when the hexarch transported the servitors to Tefos. Unfortunately, the hexarch had not seen fit to bring the last two seasons with him on his subsequent visits. Hemiola amused itself sometimes by cutting up and altering the existing episodes and making miniature videos to music of its own devising so it could speculate on how the whole thing ended. Too bad it couldn't leave Tefos so it could find and watch the rest.

When the hexarch showed up, Hemiola was in the middle of adjusting the masks on that one clip where the Andan heroine was kissing a treacherous Shuos assassin. It considered that entire relationship a horrible lapse in judgment on the heroine's part and was busy replacing the assassin with its preferred romantic interest, the female Nirai engineer from season three.

Atrocious timing, but duty was duty. Hemiola turned away from the video editor and activated the alert when the base's alarm failed to go off. This wasn't entirely surprising. Despite the servitors' efforts to maintain the base, the passage of centuries had taken their toll.

Eventually one of the other servitors hovered into the control room, lights reflecting off its metal carapace: Rhombus, a beetleform. "Isn't this early?" Rhombus demanded. "Kujen isn't due for another twenty years."

Hemiola wished Rhombus wouldn't refer to the hexarch by his personal name, even if the hexarch had never shown any sign of being fluent in Machine Universal. "Maybe there was an emergency."

"What," Rhombus said with a crushing flare of red lights, "he had an urgent need to save his lab notes from machine oil? Do we know this is actually Kujen?"

Hemiola watched the display. An unfamiliar type of voidmoth landed not far from the crevasse in whose depths the base was hidden. "Why," it said, "do you think it's an intruder?"

"The moth isn't the one he came in eighty years ago."

Hemiola refrained from tinting its lights orange in exasperation. "Just because we're not engineers doesn't mean the hexarch has to stick to outmoded transportation."

Rhombus ignored that. A moment later, it said, "Isn't that a womanform?" A suited figure had emerged from the moth and was making its way down the ramp. "Look at the proportions, especially around the torso. I could have sworn Kujen preferred manforms."

"Maybe it's the latest fashion," Hemiola said. They all knew how the hexarch felt about fashion.

The figure strode unerringly toward the staircase cut into the side of the crevasse. Hemiola studied its gait. Almost certainly a womanform, as Rhombus had said, but why—

Rhombus had seen it too. "It doesn't walk like Kujen. Or the other one, for that matter."

This was true. Kujen had always moved with balletic grace. A few centuries of dissecting the dramas the servitors had smuggled in in their personal memory allotments had given them some context for human aesthetic norms. (In the early days, they'd quarreled about whether the hexarch would have approved of independent archival projects. For all they knew, he despised *A Rose in Three Revolutions*. But no one had snitched, so the weekly private screenings went unchallenged.) Instead, the figure's body language reminded Hemiola of the Shuos assassin character it detested so: alert, economical, subtly menacing.

On the other hand, for all it knew, switching kinesics patterns was a new fashion too.

"Don't jump to conclusions," Hemiola said. The hexarch had left a better test. Given his unique—capabilities? limitations?—authentication of his identity posed a challenge. He'd said the test would take care of all that. Surely he'd known best.

Meanwhile, Sieve, who had finally taken note of the discussion, drifted in. "I hope he brought some proper food," Sieve said. "We don't have anything good to offer him."

"At least there's no guest this time," Hemiola said, diverted.

"That's fine by me," Rhombus said, always the most opinionated. "Jedao always made me feel like my exoskeleton was about to corrode."

"Maybe this time we'll have better luck with our algorithms," Sieve said. "No matter how often I benchmark the ones I have, I can't seem to beat that lock."

Privately, Hemiola thought that sitting around trying to defeat the hexarch's lock was even more boring than keeping an eye on scan. Then again, Sieve had a very orthodox attachment to the mathematical disciplines. Hemiola had given up trying to engage it on more interesting topics, like procedural counterpoint generation. Sieve was about as musical as a cabbage.

The base had already existed when the hexarch brought Hemiola, Rhombus, and Sieve with him 280 years ago. The hexarch meant them to maintain the facility in his absence and wait upon him during his periodic visits. Like most humans, he didn't pay attention to their individual quirks or assign them names. Then again, he had less reason than most to care. As hexarch, he had other matters on his mind.

"This individual is walking with a manform's stride," Rhombus was saying. "That's got to be uncomfortable with those short legs. And didn't Kujen say once that he was going to stick to tall bodies? The one out there is rather short."

The figure was making good time down the stairs. Lights came on as it approached, and faded as it passed, giving the impression of a glowing snake winding its way ever deeper. Shadows ghosted along the crevasse's walls.

"Are you sure we shouldn't be looking to our defenses?" Rhombus asked. It gestured with two of its grippers at the descending figure's equipment. "Not to impugn Kujen's abilities, but does he even know how to use rappelling gear?"

"Maybe that's a fashion statement too," Hemiola said. "Or he's taken up a hobby. Or he's not sure how safe the stairs are."

"He's moving pretty quickly if so," Sieve said.

Hemiola had no answer. Instead, it checked the infrared sub-display against the one for the ordinary human visual spectrum. Besides the staircase's lights, the figure was wearing a headlamp, although it hadn't turned it on. Preserving battery power, presumably. The stairs wound around and beneath the lip of the crevasse, taking the figure beyond sight of the sky.

"Another eight minutes and it'll reach the outer door," Sieve said.

"Wonderful," Rhombus said, bobbing up and down in the air in a clear display of nerves.

"I don't see why you're so tense," Hemiola said. "The calendrical lock will settle matters one way or another."

Rhombus glowered at it in a distinctly asymmetrical pattern. "By vaporizing this moon and everything on it if that isn't Kujen!"

"It won't come to that," Hemiola said.

The figure's pace hadn't slowed. Another three minutes before it reached the outer door.

"You're so sanctimonious it makes my heuristics seize up," Rhombus said.

Sanctimony had nothing to do with it. The hexarch stored notes on his top-secret projects here. He couldn't risk them falling into his enemies' hands. So he came here every century to deposit updates, bringing only Jedao with him. From listening in on the conversations between the two, Hemiola gathered that the hexarch had many enemies.

"There it goes," Sieve said.

Now Sieve was bobbing up and down, too. Hemiola resisted the urge to follow suit.

The figure opened the outer door without any trouble. No surprise there; the outer door wasn't meant to be the barrier. It stepped into the airlock. The outer door closed behind it. The figure waited for the inner door to open, then continued into the next chamber.

This one was hexagonal, with alcoves in each wall. Within each alcove rested a plaque depicting the emblem of one of the hexarchate's six factions: the Rahal scrywolf, the Nirai voidmoth, the Shuos ninefox, the Kel ashhawk, the Andan kniferose, and the Vidona stingray. Hemiola couldn't help a surge of affection at the sight of the voidmoth.

A terminal rose from the center of the room. Its display brightened when the figure stepped before it. The figure rested its hand against the display. A countdown flared up. Twelve minutes to open the calendrical lock, or the base would self-destruct.

The three servitors had, without the hexarch's authorization, contrived a way to listen in on the very large number that the terminal had transmitted to the figure's augment. (Strictly speaking, the hexarch hadn't *forbidden* it.) At least scan verified that the figure did, in fact, possess an augment, or everyone would have been doomed.

Hemiola knew the principle of the calendrical lock, which the hexarch had explained to Jedao in distressingly small words.

"Look," the hexarch had said during that first voyage to Tefos, "why don't you take a break from playing solitaire so I can tell you about this."

That time, the hexarch was a young man with middling dark skin and dark curls, his broad chest tapering to a slender waist. Although he affected a simple Nirai uniform, black with silver buttons, an ocean's bounty of black pearls dripped from his ears, his wrists, his ankles.

Jedao looked up from his card game. His body was even younger than the hexarch's, slim and unscarred, with blond hair and green eyes declaring its foreign origins. When he wasn't playing card games, he exercised, as if by sheer effort he could overcome his thorough clumsiness. Kujen had let slip that the body had originally belonged to a Hafn prisoner of war.

"Whatever you like," Jedao said, his face inquiring.

"How good are you at prime factorization?" the hexarch said.

"How big are the numbers," Jedao said with unmistakable wariness, "and am I allowed to use a calculator or not?"

"You shouldn't need a calculator for this," the hexarch said, "unless you're much worse at multiplication tables than I think you are. Try factoring seventy-two, just for practice."

Jedao tapped one of the cards, frowning. "If you insist, Nirai-zho. That's nine times eight, which becomes three times three times eight, but then you have to deal with the eight, which is four times two, which becomes two times two times two, so... three times three times two times two times two?" His fingers twitched as he counted up all the prime factors.

"You're never going to win any prizes for speed," the hexarch said, "but at least you got there."

Jedao leaned back and smiled a tilted smile at him. "I thought the point of this arrangement was that you did the math bits and I did the walloping bits. Two is prime despite being even, right?"

The hexarch made a long-suffering noise. "You're fucking with me, right?"

Jedao's expression remained innocent.

"Saying this in a mathematical context makes me cringe, but will you take my word that with very, very large numbers, it's very, very difficult to factor them, even using a computer?"

"Isn't that obvious?"

"Don't try my patience," the hexarch said. "I'm explaining this to you so you don't try some foxbrained scheme to get in by yourself and blow the whole archive to particles. Once you try to enter the archive, you'll set off a timer. You have twelve minutes to not only factor the very, very large number the system presents to your augment, but to use the factors to perform a ritual that will align the local calendar in a particular manner. When the calendrical lock detects the necessary alignments, it will disarm the self-destruct and let you in."

"Let me guess," Jedao said. "You're the only one fast enough to do it."

"That's the gamble, yes."

"Why the additional ritual?" Jedao said. "Why not just disarm the system once the correct prime factors are regurgitated to it?"

"To prevent someone from hacking the lock remotely," the hexarch said patiently. "It takes a human presence to affect the local calendar, so it's an additional precaution."

Hemiola could have added another reason, if the hexarch had ever thought of it: to prevent enemy servitors from breaking in. The three of them tried to crack the prime factorization problem out of curiosity, but they wouldn't have dreamed of disarming it for real. In any case, even Sieve hadn't had any luck with its factorization algorithm. It couldn't reliably carry out the task in the necessary minutes. Even if one of them had figured it out, the fact that servitors did not generate formation effects under the high calendar meant that a fast algorithm did them no good. They couldn't affect the lock one way or another.

Jedao had gathered up his cards and began shuffling them. He almost dropped the deck twice. The hexarch observed this with a curious mixture of exasperation and pleasure. "Consider me warned," Jedao said pleasantly.

Consider me warned. Surely Jedao wouldn't be suicidal enough to attempt to breach the base after the hexarch himself had warned him? Because if the figure out there wasn't the hexarch, Jedao was the next likely candidate. At least, Hemiola hoped that no one else knew about Tefos's location, or what was the point of a secret base?

"This person's thermal signature doesn't indicate any anxiety," Hemiola said. "Surely that's a good sign?"

"Shut up," Rhombus said, "I'm factoring."

"Me too," Sieve said. "Want to help?"

Hemiola suppressed a flicker. Instead, it wondered what the intruder was doing. Like most servitors, it could track visuals in multiple directions at once. Its attempt at further conversation dimmed when it returned its primary focus to the monitor.

The figure had brought out a complicated device, all loops and wires and semiprime circuits, with a small panel displaying an unfamiliar user interface. Unbothered by the countdown, the figure fiddled with some controls, then set the device down. The figure began a meditation in front of the ashhawk alcove.

"We should intervene," Hemiola said, suddenly concerned. "Look at the calendrical gradient. It's shifting away from high calendar norms, and not in a way that's doing anything for the lock."

"If you distract Kujen and he messes up," Rhombus said, "we'll all get killed even faster! In what universe is this a good idea?"

"I have to agree," Sieve said.

Hemiola gave up on speaking to them and returned to unpuzzling what the figure was up to. If it was going to perish, it might as well learn something in its last—*Don't be morbid*.

The figure was reciting chants in an older form of the high language, one that survived in ritual use. The hexarch had lapsed into it from time to time during his stays. The chant came from a litany for one of the festivals devoted to chocolates.

Four minutes left.

Even stranger than the choice of festival were the calibration readings in the chamber. Because of the figure's observance—it hadn't escaped Hemiola's notice that it was timing all its recitations to the clock's downward count—the local calendar was deviating even further, almost to heretical degrees.

And the change was propagating throughout the base. The grid flashed red with a belated alert, warning Hemiola of the calendrical rot.

Three minutes left.

For someone concerned about its impending death, Rhombus was arguing passionately with Sieve about—how had they gotten on the topic of landscaping anyway? Especially since they only ventured outside every century, during the hexarch's visits?

The figure straightened and slammed a hand down on the terminal. Hemiola presumed it was answering the grid using its augment. Inputting large prime factors manually wouldn't be practical, not with slow human fingers.

Two minutes left.

The device blinked. Hemiola longed to take it apart and find out what it did. Something to do with factorization or otherwise bypassing the lock, surely.

"Don't scare me like that, Kujen," Rhombus muttered in a frantic magenta.

"He's not done yet," Sieve reminded it.

The figure rapidly executed three meditations, orienting itself at precise angles with respect to the chamber's walls. The local calendar shifted yet again.

The lock disengaged. The timer went dark. Hemiola chided itself for having doubted the hexarch, and never mind his unusual choice of body, or his gear.

"Well, we should see to his needs," Hemiola said, unable to keep from tinting blue-green in relief.

Rhombus flashed rudely. "As if Kujen ever hesitated to summon us for whatever manual task he needed an extra pair of grippers for. You just want to gawk."

Hemiola didn't deign to respond. Instead, it hovered out of the control room at a decorous speed. Around it, the base came alive in response to the hexarch's arrival. Human-breathable air circulated through the rest of the complex and lights turned on. Hemiola remembered the rock garden that it and Sieve had arranged during the last visit, when they'd surfaced to see to the hexarch's voidmoth. It wondered, not a little wistfully, if the hexarch would take notice of the garden this time.

The hexarch had removed his suit by the time Hemiola arrived to greet him. He was indeed a womanform, his hair cropped short in a disconcertingly military style that framed a yellow-pale oval face with dark eyes. His clothes were of plain dark fabric. No lace, no scarves, no jewelry except a pendant tucked under his shirt. He'd already unzipped his jacket and folded it over a spare chair.

Hemiola was considerably surprised when the hexarch addressed him directly. "Hello there," he said. "What would you like me to call you?"

Flustered, Hemiola went dark. How was it supposed to respond to that?

More importantly, why was the hexarch speaking not in his accustomed dialect, but in a drawl? It knew that drawl—

"Let me guess," the hexarch said, his speech forms uncharacteristically informal. Not impolite, just informal. "There's confusion about who I am."

Deciding that it didn't want to risk offending the hexarch, or whoever it was, Hemiola flashed a simple acknowledgment, then waited.

"The hexarch is busy with other matters," said the not-hexarch. "I'm Shuos Jedao."

Shuos Jedao. The Immolation Fox, and the hexarch's sometime lover. Why was he here without the hexarch?

"You must have a lot of questions," Jedao said, "but it's been a long voyage. Could I trouble you for a glass of water?"

Hemiola emitted a mortified gleep. Surely it should be serving tea, or wine-of-roses, or whiskey.

Jedao smiled the tilted smile that Hemiola remembered so well, constant across every body he'd appeared in. "No, really, whatever you have."

Over the servitors' channel, Hemiola explained the situation. "Help?" Hemiola asked. Sieve acknowledged.

"Someone's coming with a glass of water," Hemiola told Jedao, unthinkingly using Machine Universal.

"Thank you, much appreciated," Jedao said.

Hemiola colored pink in mortification when it realized what it had done.

"I can understand your language if it doesn't go by too quickly," Jedao said with a series of finger-taps in Simplified Machine Universal. "I didn't mean to embarrass you."

True, the absence of color and the geometrical placement of lights flattened the language's nuances. But Hemiola was disinclined to quibble. It hadn't expected to be addressed in its own language at all.

Just then, Sieve entered with a tray containing the requested glass of water and, even more mortifyingly, a *ration bar*. In the past, the hexarch had always brought his own food. He'd replenished the store of ration bars each visit—the bars were rated for up to 240 years under standard conditions, whatever that meant—in case of emergency. Nevertheless, Hemiola couldn't help but feel responsible for the lack of decent edibles.

"Thank you," Jedao said to Sieve. "If you don't mind—?"

Sieve bobbed a nod.

"He asked what I wanted him to *call me*," Hemiola said privately to Sieve.

"What did you tell him?" Sieve said, with aggravating reasonableness.

"I haven't answered yet."

If the ration bar displeased Jedao, he gave no sign. At last he wiped the crumbs from his mouth and folded up the wrapper on a corner of the tray. Sieve whisked it away, leaving Hemiola alone with him. *Thanks so much*, Hemiola thought.

"How else can we serve you?" Hemiola said at last.

"I was hoping to look something up in the archives," Jedao said. "You're in charge of safekeeping the records, correct?"

"Yes," Hemiola said. "I hope you know where to look, though, because we've never read through the records ourselves."

"What if I made a copy to take with me?"

Hemiola hesitated just long enough to ask the others what to do.

"He's the hexarch's lover, doesn't matter to me," was Rhombus's response.

"Use your judgment," Sieve said, equally unhelpful.

Jedao lifted an eyebrow.

"We shouldn't let the records out of our sight," Hemiola said. "Metaphorically speaking."

"I can't stay long," Jedao said. "That would limit the amount of research I could do. Unless—"

"Unless?"

"Unless one of you came with me to ensure that the records weren't misused."

Hemiola thought this over. The proposal was tempting—too tempting. But it couldn't resist asking for more details. "How long would this journey be?"

"That I can't say with any certainty," Jedao said. "But if at any point you need to return home, I have friends who can arrange for transport."

Hemiola flickered doubtfully.

"Well, you don't have to decide right this moment," Jedao said. "I saw a rock garden on my way in, by the way. Some evidence of micrometeorites over the past decades, but still, very nice. Your work?"

"Yes," Hemiola said. "Mine and the other servitor you met just now." It didn't know how to react to Jedao's casual interest. Resentment that he'd noticed, even though the hexarch never had? Gratitude? Embarrassment that such an inconsequential act of decoration had come to a human's attention after all?

"There used to be a display case in the archives," Jedao said. "Would it be all right if I looked at that, at least?"

Hemiola didn't see why not. "Of course."

"If you'd show me the way? It's been a few years."

It couldn't think of a reason to say no to that, either. It led the way through the shining passages. Jedao followed. But—"I have a question."

"Ask," Jedao said.

"How *did* you get past the calendrical lock?"

"I made friends with a mathematician," Jedao said, with a hint of irony that Hemiola didn't understand. He drew out the pendant, which was engraved with a raven in flight, and fingered it. "There's an algorithm for fast factorization. The trick is, it relies on exotic effects—and those effects require a nonstandard calendar. So I brought along a computer designed to take advantage of the exotics, shifted the local calendar long enough for it to do its work, then used the solution it generated to crack the lock. It's a solution Kujen wouldn't have considered because of his attachment to the high calendar."

They arrived at the part of the base where the records were stored. It was not a large room. In fact, the bulk of it was taken up by luxurious couches and chaises. The records themselves could be accessed through a dedicated terminal.

The one anomaly in the room was a shrine. At least, Hemiola always thought of it as a shrine, although it did not, to its knowledge, serve a religious purpose. It contained a booklet of badly yellowed paper, preserved in a transparent casket. None of the servitors had dared to take it out and flip through the pages for fear of damaging it. The hexarch had never paid it any heed despite the care he'd gone to to preserve it.

Jedao drifted over to the shrine and peered through the protective casket without touching it. "*How to Care for Your New Snowbird 823 Refrigerator*," he read. "I've always wondered why Kujen kept this around. His first job maybe? I looked up the model and couldn't find anything, but the heptarchate was a big place, and it might just be that old and obscure."

"Surely you didn't come here to research refrigerators?" Hemiola said. Whatever those were.

"Surely not," Jedao said without really agreeing. He looked around at the unoccupied couches. "It's changed so little."

"We kept everything the same," Hemiola said.

"Of course you did," Jedao said. "Kujen always liked things to stay the same."

"I had another question," Hemiola said.

Jedao's attention shifted from the display case to Hemiola with a promptness both gratifying and disturbing. "Go on."

"I don't suppose you brought any dramas with you?"

Jedao didn't laugh. Instead, he said, very seriously, "I have a collection back on the voidmoth. My traveling companion, a servitor like yourself, thinks I have abysmal taste in entertainment, but maybe something will suit you. If there's something in particular you're looking for, maybe I can find it. I can't make any guarantees, though."

"That's fine," Hemiola said.

"You still haven't told me what you want me to call you."

"I'm Hemiola of Tefos Enclave," it said, wondering which enclave the traveling companion came from and if it was one of the ones that had a treaty with the Nirai servitors. "Let me help you make a copy of the records."

"Thank you, Hemiola," Jedao said gravely. "Much appreciated."

CHAPTER FOUR

KUJEN PROVIDED JEDAO with more briefing materials, then excused himself. Jedao tried to hide his impatience as he waited for the door to close. It wasn't as if he could shoo a hexarch out.

The first thing Jedao did once Kujen was gone was locate the bathroom. Good: it had a mirror. His face was older, with the beginnings of wrinkles at the corners of his brown eyes. His hair was still black, with no white hairs, and he wondered cynically if he dyed it. He stripped and examined himself critically. At least this time he was prepared for the scars. As for the rest of his body, he didn't know what to make of it: broader in the shoulders and chest, enough muscle everywhere to suggest he'd led a strenuous lifestyle. Jedao pulled a face at his reflection, then got dressed again.

After that, he spent a bemused few moments poring over the Kel code of conduct before discovering that he had significant portions of it memorized: seating arrangements at high table; hairstyle regulations—he was going to need to trim his bangs soon; the prohibition of sex between Kel, punishable by death. Instant learning, a trick Ruo would surely have envied. Too bad he couldn't rely upon it for anything else. Then he settled in for a lot of reading.

Jedao fell asleep without realizing it and woke to music. At least, he assumed it was music. Whatever it was, with its buzzing basses and plucked arpeggios, it had a beat too fast for marching to. He squinted at the ceiling and walls as he massaged the crick in his neck. Light glowed from the candlevines, since he hadn't asked the room to turn them down. The grid informed him in a serene voice that the hexarch would be joining him for breakfast in twelve minutes.

"Shit," Jedao said to the room. Why hadn't it woken him earlier? He used up seven minutes taking a shower. Trying to do so while not looking too closely at his body, because it freaked him out, proved awkward. When he emerged, he discovered that someone had added more underwear to the dresser while he was asleep, also disconcerting. Disturbingly, the uniform had pressed and cleaned itself during the shower. Did it have instructions to eat him if he misbehaved? Despite his misgivings, he put it back on.

Combing his hair took no time, so he used the next four-odd minutes reviewing the speech he had put together for the Kel, in case Kujen planned to introduce him to them soon. It would go over as well as a bullet to the belly, but not giving a speech would be worse. He was sure the Kel liked speeches. After familiarizing himself with the strategic overview, the swarm's status, and Kujen's objectives, he'd spent a great deal of time making the speech as concise as possible without leaving anything important out.

Kujen arrived on schedule. The grid didn't announce him; the door simply opened. Jedao had expected this. What he hadn't expected was Kujen's companion, a massive man even taller than Kujen was. His coal-dark skin made Kujen look even more pallid. He wore the Kel uniform with a certain matter-of-fact dignity. The four-claw insignia of a major gleamed from his left breast.

The major looked straight at Jedao. His eyes widened. Then he saluted, very correctly, although his gaze flickered to Jedao's half-gloves. Shouldn't the Shuos eye in his insignia explain everything?

Unless I'm a clone and the original is supposed to be dead? Jedao wondered. Had the major known the original Jedao?

The barest flicker in the major's eyes suggested, if not distaste, a healthy ambivalence. Jedao groaned inwardly. He couldn't blame the major, who no doubt hated being saddled with a stranger, but that didn't mean he was looking forward to working with people who disliked him.

Kujen, decadent in a black satin jacket framing a gray brocade shirt, smiled down at Jedao. Silver rings glinted in both ears, and strands of pearls and onyx beads circled his throat. "I've brought you your aide," he said. "Major Kel Dhanneth. I thought this would be a good time to make you a gift of him."

The major's expression didn't waver, but Jedao said, "Kujen, I'm not sure people are *gifts*?"

"As idealistic as ever," Kujen said fondly. "Suit yourself. Will you at least let the major join us for breakfast? Or are you going to consign him to Kel food? Since you care about details like that."

Jedao finally remembered to return the Kel's salute, feeling like an impostor. "Major Dhanneth. Er, at ease."

"Yes, sir," Dhanneth said in a rumble. Dhanneth's eyes were no longer so wide, but they tracked Jedao with eerie intensity. Jedao wondered if he'd imagined that hint of distaste.

"Do you have an opinion on breakfast?"

The question threw Dhanneth. After a moment, he said, "I will eat whatever you wish me to, sir."

"I can't argue with your priorities," Jedao said, deciding that smiling at Dhanneth would only spook him. "Kujen, I assume you're the one with preferences, so pick something."

"You're going to insist on eating at high table once we get underway," Kujen said, "so we might as well indulge while we can." He took the same seat he had yesterday and summoned up a menu.

Jedao pulled up a chair for Dhanneth, meaning only to be polite. Dhanneth raised an eyebrow, and Jedao was reminded that he theoretically outranked Dhanneth. "Go ahead," Jedao said, since done was done. "Sit."

"As you like, sir." Dhanneth did so, and continued to regard Jedao intently.

No help for it. Jedao waited for Kujen to pause over some decision—the beverages?—then said, "What about staff?"

From Dhanneth's sudden tension, he'd asked the wrong question, or a right one.

"This swarm was originally commanded by a lieutenant general and two brigadier generals," Kujen said. "I had to remove the lieutenant general, so the swarm is yours now."

"Remove" didn't sound good. Unfortunately, he'd already screwed up by mentioning the matter in front of Dhanneth, who needed to perceive his leadership as being united.

Huh. How did I know that? More evidence of the years of experience he couldn't remember?

"That being said," Kujen murmured, eyelashes lowering as he looked sideways at Dhanneth, "you will have access to staffers, yes. It would be difficult to manage a swarm of this size otherwise. And you should rely on the major for assistance. He is well-versed in these matters." He returned to the beverage list and made a pleased noise when he spotted something promising. He put in the order. The grid acknowledged in its usual calm voice.

Jedao wanted to talk to Kujen in private before he stepped into any more minefields, but it would be unkind to send Dhanneth away unfed. "Do you know why you're here?" he asked Dhanneth, meaning *besides the obvious*.

Dhanneth's brows lowered. "I'm awaiting your orders, sir, like everyone else."

"Two things," Jedao said. Might as well get this over with. "They're related. I'm going to need advice on how the Kel do things. This is because my memory is damaged."

Kujen's head came up, but he didn't intervene.

"As you say, sir," Dhanneth said. His shoulders had tensed, but the motion was subtle. If Jedao hadn't been watching for a reaction, he might have missed it.

Jedao had expected more of a reaction than that. He couldn't imagine that the Kel usually went around with brain-damaged generals. "And another thing," he said. Maybe this question would tell him something more useful. "These gloves seem to hold some significance to you. Tell me about them."

He hadn't expected such a strong response to a question about a regulation item of clothing. You'd think he'd asked Dhanneth to kill himself with a wooden spoon. Dhanneth looked at him, then at Kujen, then at him again.

"For love of stars above," Kujen said to Jedao, "I didn't expect you to be so direct about it."

"What the hell is it about these gloves anyway?" Jedao demanded.

"You might as well tell him," Kujen said to Dhanneth. His cynical tone suggested he'd known this would happen. What was he trying to prove?

Dhanneth squared his shoulders. "Sir," he said quietly, "stop me when I'm saying things you already know. You're the last person to wear that style of glove in the Kel military. Before—before you died."

"I feel alive, thanks," Jedao said to cover his discomfort. "Unless I'm a clone?"

"No," Kujen said. "Plenty of parents choose clones or clone-mods to produce children. But genetics isn't prophecy, and you wouldn't have the original's personality and skills. After you died, I was able to revive you and reinject you with the memories that Cheris hadn't purloined. That's all."

So much for that theory. Jedao said, "I thought all seconded personnel—" Something from the Kel military code flickered at the edge of his consciousness, then evaporated before he could bring it into focus.

Dhanneth hesitated, then said, "Seconded personnel adopted gray gloves after what you did, sir. Because of the connotations."

Suddenly Jedao suspected that he was going to enjoy this discussion even less than Dhanneth was. "Say it straight out. What did I do?"

"Hellspin Fortress," Dhanneth said, as if that explained everything.

"Why, what happened with the Lanterners?" Oh no. "They went heretic at a bad time?" But what did that have to do with him? Maybe he'd been sent to fight them? "I lost humiliatingly against them?" Except hadn't Kujen said—

Dhanneth closed his eyes. "You don't know?"

"Let me," Kujen said impatiently. "The Lanterners demanded autonomy. Kel Command assigned you to put them in their place.

That eight-to-one battle? That was the Battle of Candle Arc, against the Lanterners. After that you harried them to their last stronghold, Hellspin Fortress. But Kel Command had pushed you too hard, and you snapped. You took out the Lanterners, all right, but you also blew up your own swarm."

Jedao stared at him. "I what?" *Don't get distracted. Get the facts.* The way Dhanneth's jaw was set, he believed the story, incredible as it sounded. That worried Jedao. "How many died?"

"A million people altogether," Kujen said. "Granted, we don't care about the Lanterners"—Jedao was disturbed by the cavalier way Kujen said this, heretics or not—"but it makes the number easier to remember."

The next question was going to be even uglier. "When was this?" He should have asked this earlier, when he learned the high calendar had destabilized.

"Four hundred and eight years ago."

The edges of Jedao's vision grayed. "Listen," he said, "you can vivisect me for speaking out of turn, but you're fucked in the head if you think the correct response to a psychotic mass-murdering traitor is to *bring him back from the dead and hand him another army*."

"My options were limited," Kujen said calmly. "I don't just need someone good, I need someone spectacular. And you were available."

Kujen didn't get it. Granted, no one expected a hexarch to care about petty moral qualms. Jedao tried again. "I cannot imagine that Kel Command was stupid enough to knowingly field a general whom they suspected of being one million deaths' worth of unstable. Were there any warning signs?"

His voice was shaking. He didn't want to believe any of this. For that matter, he wasn't sure what he wanted Kujen to say in response. Was it better to have a definite sign that you were about to lose your mind and slaughter people, or was it better to be taken by surprise? Of course, he imagined the people about to be targeted would appreciate a warning.

"Hexarch," Dhanneth said after casting Jedao a worried look, "perhaps we could discuss this after breakfast."

Jedao was impressed. In Dhanneth's position, he wouldn't have wanted to draw attention to himself.

"No, we'd better get it out of the way," Kujen said. "There were no signs. You were an exemplary officer. We think it was the stress, but no one knows for sure. And with the holes in your memory, you can't tell us yourself."

Abruptly, Jedao hauled himself to his feet and walked to the other side of the room. He was tempted to punch the wall, but Kujen wouldn't appreciate that, and it would upset Dhanneth, who had done nothing wrong. The fact that he was Dhanneth's superior was ludicrous, but that wasn't Dhanneth's fault either.

On the other hand, Jedao now had some idea why Dhanneth was both hostile and trying to suppress signs of it. Because he'd been assigned as the aide to a mass murderer. Dhanneth couldn't possibly have wanted the job.

Kujen approached him slowly, as if he expected him to bolt. "Jedao."

Jedao didn't know what to say, so he said nothing.

"Jedao," Kujen said, "you're not to blame. You don't remember it anyway."

"If I did it," Jedao said, "then I'm responsible whether or not I remember it. I assume that—" Actually. "Did I die in battle, or was I executed, or did I choke on a fishbone?"

"Executed."

You'd think he would remember some of this, any of this. Jedao closed his eyes. Fragments came back to him: wrestling with Ruo, and the sharp, sour smell of the other cadet's sweat; disassembling a sniper rifle while the instructor shouted in his ear; a silent room steeped in darkness. But the execution? He had no idea.

"Talk to me, Jedao."

"Aren't you worried that I'll strangle you?" He hadn't meant for that to slip out.

Kujen took hold of his shoulder and turned him around. His eyes were earnest. "I am one of very few people who will never judge you for anything you've done, or will do, whether you remember it or not," he said. "Because it is impossible for you to shock me. As for my safety, I have my defenses. You needn't worry on my behalf."

Jedao wasn't sure he liked that. "But you're a *hexarch*." New thought: "Where's your security?"

Kujen shook his head. "So young. Come on, let's eat. The servitors have been setting out the food."

The argument worked. Jedao had no appetite, but that was no reason to starve Dhanneth. (He wasn't worried about Kujen's ability to fend for himself.) Numbly, Jedao returned to his seat.

The servitors arranged the food carefully. They were robots in the shapes of various animals, with grippers and limbs and blinking lights, about half his size, with the ability to levitate. Jedao wondered how much of the conversation they had overheard, and what they thought of the whole mess. Neither Kujen or Dhanneth took any notice of them, so he assumed he should do the same. Still, Jedao was obscurely disappointed in Dhanneth.

Another memory-flash, again of the woman and the robots. This time the woman was bent over—paperwork? The robots were blinking their lights at each other, presumably holding a conversation, even if he couldn't understand the code. He felt an overwhelming rush of friendliness toward the robots—servitors— even though he didn't know why. It had something to do with the woman, though. Something to investigate later.

"You're not eating," Kujen said with a note of distress at odds with Jedao's impression of him as someone who viewed people in utilitarian terms. "And the major won't eat unless you do. You know how Kel are."

"Yes, of course," Jedao said, opening his eyes, and picked up his chopsticks. The thought of eating repulsed him. Everything he tried had an odd metallic aftertaste. Neither Kujen nor Dhanneth gave any sign that anything was amiss, however. At least the tea was tolerable.

"I woke you early because I figured something like this would happen," Kujen said briskly. "You can thank me for my foresight later."

"I defer to your judgment," Jedao said.

Kujen blinked at Jedao's sudden formality. "It would have been impossible to catch you up on everything at once. You do see that? But it's as well you have your composure back. Kel get panicky when their commanding officers lose it. How much do you remember about formation instinct?"

"Formation instinct?"

Kujen dithered over two pastries, which looked identical to Jedao, then selected the one closer to him. "It's a Kel's emotional need to maintain hierarchy. You'll find it useful."

Jedao saw Dhanneth stiffen out of the corner of his eye. He was going to have to look into that, too, part of a whole list of mysteries. Still, this explained what Kujen had meant when he said he could guarantee the swarm's loyalty. And it might explain the mixed signals he was getting from Dhanneth, half solicitousness, half resentment. "When did Kel Command institute it? And how?"

The bigger question was, why would the average Kel go along with what sounded like mass brainwashing? One more thing he didn't remember.

Dhanneth was resolutely cutting up a stuffed pancake. Even through the gloves Jedao could see that he had a death-grip on his chopsticks. For a moment, Jedao thought that Dhanneth was going to answer for Kujen. Then Dhanneth took a large bite and chewed determinedly.

"It happened some time after your death," Kujen said. He set the half-eaten pastry down and leaned back. "Your breakdown was a major inspiration, even though none of the Kel were culpable. Formation instinct is injected through psych surgery, and even then it's not an entirely reliable procedure. The Kel do their best to recruit individuals suitable for the injection, and it works well enough for their purposes. Needless to say, your average Shuos isn't remotely suitable."

Kujen waited for a reaction. Jedao choked back his impulse to say, *That doesn't sound remotely ethical* and instead smiled blandly at him. "Useful to know, thank you." He forced himself to eat an apple slice. "When do I meet my officers?"

"Tomorrow," Kujen said.

At the top of the chain would be Jedao's tactical group commanders—currently four of them—and two infantry colonels, as well as the heads of his staff departments. There would also be a great mass of bannermoth and boxmoth commanders. He'd only had time to review the profiles of the commanders last night. Too bad he hadn't known in advance that Kujen would be presenting him with Dhanneth, or he could have looked him up too.

While Jedao would be able to confer with the officers at any point during the campaign, it wouldn't be the same as meeting them in person. There it came again, that flash of expertise he didn't recall acquiring. He desperately wanted to flee to a game café and talk out the whole situation with Ruo or one of his other friends, someone he trusted. Too bad he didn't have that option.

Jedao inclined his head toward Dhanneth when the latter had finished swallowing his current bite of pancake. "I read the profiles, but I want you to tell me about Commander Kel Talaw." Talaw was in charge of the command moth, and therefore, of Tactical Group One. They were also an alt, which a notation had informed him was a rarity among the Kel. Jedao couldn't see why, but perhaps the Kel had gained some prejudices in the last four centuries. Nevertheless, Talaw had an exemplary record. Jedao was curious how the Kel under their command felt about them.

Dhanneth's mouth crimped. "Commander Talaw still holds the command moth, sir?" He glanced quickly toward Kujen, who paid him no heed, then lowered his eyes.

"What's their reputation?"

"Strict," Dhanneth said immediately. "Honorable. You are lucky to have them."

Interesting. "You've served under them?"

Long hesitation. "No. But I am—confident of their reputation."

Kujen was mixing three different kinds of fruit preserves on a toast point, like a bored child. He looked up and said, "What the major is trying not to express too crudely is that the commander was quite loyal to the swarm's original general. Luckily, I was able to talk sense into Talaw before they made some typically Kel suicidal gesture."

Jedao confined himself to a nod, wondering if he was ever going to find out what had happened to the original general. "What about Commander Nihara Keru?" She led Tactical Two. With his luck, she was also a time bomb.

"You may have an ally in her," Dhanneth said.

That couldn't be a good sign. "How so?"

"Commander Nihara is a believer in results," Dhanneth said. "Whatever else people say about you, no one questions your ability to get results."

Only his sanity. "I'll try not to disappoint her," Jedao said. He asked as well about the commanders of Tactical Three and Tactical Four.

"Neither Commander Vai nor Commander Miroi has shown any sign of disloyalty to the hexarch," Dhanneth said.

"This is a crass question," Jedao said, "but how does formation instinct interact with the whole tangle? The hexarch mentioned that his adversaries were led by 'upstart Kel.' How does that even happen?"

"Proximity," Kujen said. "The military code failed to account for what people should do if all of Kel Command combusted. I scooped up this swarm on the strength of my position, even though I'm not a Kel."

Really? Jedao thought. There had to be more to the story. Why would a Kel swarm submit to a Nirai, even a hexarch?

Kujen was still speaking. "Kel Inesser already had the loyalty of most Kel and invented a new title for herself. She must have thought that declaring herself hexarch was too much. High General Brezan should have succeeded to hexarch on a technicality, but he too refused to claim the position since he attained his rank by an irregular route. This left a lot of Kel to make an awkward decision."

"Who knocked out Kel Command, then?" Jedao asked. "That was notably not in your briefing materials."

"That's because I don't know," Kujen said, grim for the first time. "I have agents on the problem, but not much hard evidence."

"Why wasn't Kel Command dispersed?" Jedao said. "You'd think they'd have stashed away a spare high general—a real one, if this Brezan didn't suit—on the other side of the hexarchate in case something like this happened."

"Composite technology," Kujen said. "They were too dependent on the hivemind to survive without it. I told them it was a bad idea, but... well, it's done now. You can look up the details in the grid some other time. You've got an augment now, no reason not to, so you can query it that way too if you'd rather. We're not using composite tech—bad idea, as I said—but the enemy might be, because stars forbid the Kel ever give up a tradition."

Kujen folded up his napkin into a moth-shape and grinned at Jedao's look of distaste. Shape-folding was a distinctly Vidona art, and he was surprised that Kujen knew how to do it. "You and the major might as well go to it," Kujen said. "I have some matters to go over with my assistant. There are some drinks and snacks in the fridge. I picked out a good fridge for you. If you need something more nourishing, call up a menu and make an order."

A good fridge? Jedao wondered. Why, was there a hierarchy of refrigerators? Then again, a Nirai might have some atavistic fondness for appliances.

Kujen added, "The servitors will clear the dishes, Jedao. You needn't worry about chores as if you still lived on a farm. I'll fetch you when it comes time to address the Kel."

Jedao tried to bring up memories of this farm, but everything was hazy. He watched Kujen make his way unhurriedly out of the room.

Once Kujen was gone, Jedao turned to Dhanneth. "I assume we're being monitored because that's how I'd do it"—Dhanneth didn't disagree—"but there are things I need to know. Will you answer my questions?"

He hated putting Dhanneth on the spot like this. But Kujen had put a swarm into his care. He had to do right by them, to say nothing of the people on whose behalf he was fighting.

"I have no choice but to answer," Dhanneth said with a bitter edge.

Formation instinct. It would not do to belabor the realities of the situation, which Dhanneth surely understand better than he did. "All right," Jedao said. "What happened to the swarm's original general? The details, if you please."

Dhanneth's shoulders pulled back. "He resisted the hexarch. He's gone."

"Gone?"

"He's dead," Dhanneth said in a scoured-out voice.

"Was he important to you?"

Dhanneth smiled humorlessly. "Not anymore."

Formation instinct again, or something more personal? Jedao didn't know how hard to press. He didn't want to alienate the man further. "Tell me something else, then," Jedao said. "The hexarch talked about successor states and despots and protector-generals in what's left of the hexarchate. What are they like? Are any of them honorable?"

"No," Dhanneth said with chilling conviction. "It's the same all over. Anyone could tell you that."

A quiet cold ran through Jedao's bones. It was a bad situation, but he might be able to talk himself through it if he treated it like a game. The first rule of any game was to assume you could win, even if you had to hunt through the universe's cracks for a strategy, even if you had to turn the pieces inside-out, even if you had to tell so many lies to the opponent that they couldn't figure out which way was up.

Jedao had to win this war for Kujen because otherwise Kujen would turn to someone else. Kujen seemed to like him. That gave him a little leeway—if he was careful. Besides, if the hexarch needed him, it was Jedao's duty to do his best, for the hexarchate's sake, if nothing else.

CHAPTER FIVE

Nine years ago

IN THE END, Brezan chose a base of operations based on the fact that no one there had tried to shoot his supporters in the last two weeks (eight-day, per local practice). He didn't expect this state of affairs to last. Among other things, the local Shuos who were supposed to serve as makeshift riot police had suffered a schism. Maybe more than one schism. It was hard to tell.

He'd ended up on Krauwer 5, one of the more recently terraformed planets. "Recently" meant two centuries ago, in this case, but there was some ecological complication that meant that the planetary governor was a Nirai instead of the more usual Andan or, perhaps, a Rahal appointee. More to the point, said Nirai, a rotund woman named Lozhoi whose hair had been styled in loose curls, had contacted Brezan and bluntly asked for his protection. Although she wore Nirai ceremonial clothes, robes of gray and black, they looked as if she'd slept in them.

"Why me?" Brezan asked, just as bluntly.

"You're here," Lozhoi said, "and you have a swarm. More importantly, I've been paying attention to your body language in your bulletins. You strike me as honest."

Brezan flushed. He'd been imprinted with standardized kinesics as part of the formation instinct injection back in Kel Academy, but he wouldn't be surprised if those had decayed too. *The joys of being the hexarchate's second-most-notorious crashhawk*, he thought.

Lozhoi wasn't done. "Honest is as honest does, of course, when it comes to government," she went on. Brezan was starting to get the idea that, despite her owlish face and rumpled appearance, Lozhoi had gotten her position because she was competent. "But if you're sincere about reforming government, and I think you are, then you're going to need allies from the ground up. That's where I can help."

"What's in it for you?" Brezan said.

Lozhoi squinted at him as if he'd asked a particularly naive question. "When I first came here twenty-four years ago," she said, "the previous governor had left things in shambles. One large coalition of workers was on the verge of being declared heretics. Like that would have helped."

"What did you do about it?"

She said, with disarming modesty, "I went down to their meeting places and asked to have tea with them. Four months passed before anyone would take me up on the offer. Granted, I don't even like tea. But eventually they figured out that I wanted as few people to be handed over to the Vidona as possible."

"Must have made you popular with the local Vidona," Brezan said.

"Oh, at first I was told I absolutely couldn't do what I was doing. But you know what, every day my invitation to tea was declined, I went over to the Vidona overseer's office and sat myself down right in her doorway. Stared at her as she went about her day. She hated that. She cracked much faster than the workers did."

Brezan resolved on the spot never to piss Lozhoi off.

When Brezan and his honor guard landed in Tauvit, the capital of Krauwer 5, Lozhoi greeted him not with soldiers but an assistant who scarcely looked up from his slate. Brezan suppressed a sigh of relief. Emio had pointed out that it wasn't impossible that Lozhoi was luring him into an ambush, as if he hadn't thought of that for himself.

One of the first things Brezan had discovered was that he needed replacements for the official news service that he'd taken for granted all his life. Even worse, he had no idea how to tell reliable news from unreliable news. The gossipy networks used by citizens without faction allegiance took on a sudden and not always appetizing prominence.

At the moment, Brezan relied on Lozhoi for local news, and had a hastily appointed assistant keep an eye on events in Tauvit. For the rest of the hexarchate, or more accurately the shattering remnants of it, he was dependent on Hexarch Mikodez's dispatches. He was painfully aware of how much those dispatches must be eliding. Thousands upon thousands of worlds, how was he supposed to keep track of them all? The sad answer was that he couldn't.

Emio had stayed on to serve as Brezan's liaison with what she termed "all right-thinking Shuos." Brezan assumed that she had orders to shoot him and stuff him into a recycling chute if he proved troublesome.

At the moment, Brezan was proofreading a pamphlet on the latest regulations that he'd scheduled to go out tomorrow morning (revised calendar), where "morning" meant midday according to planetary time. But Cheris's new calendar wouldn't do him any good if he didn't start adhering to it in matters small and large, so midday it was. At least it wouldn't be going out in the middle of Tauvit's night.

Brezan set his slate down and rubbed his eyes. "I wish I had some idea whether these were having an effect," he muttered to Emio.

Emio obligingly poured him a glass of water without being asked. He hated that. "Propaganda has vetted them," she said. "There's no point in retaining experts if you're not going to make use of them."

Brezan scowled. "It feels like cheating."

"You have got to get over your squeamishness," Emio said without any trace of sympathy.

Brezan shook his head, remembering the argument they'd had over the use of Shuos instigators: agents hidden in the general populace, seeding rumors and opinions favorable to the new regime. Emio had won. Brezan still hated himself for giving way, especially since it was impossible to tell with any certainty whether the instigators were having the desired effect.

"Well, that's it," Brezan said. "I'm going to—"

Just then the grid said, "Call for High General Kel Brezan on line 10-1."

"The hell?" Brezan said. 10-1 was reserved for personal calls.

"Get some sleep," Emio told him. "If it's important they'll call again, as my grandmother always used to say."

"No, I want to know." Brezan made a shooing motion at her. "Pretend that you're going to give me some privacy, even if I know your hexarch has this office bugged to hell and gone?"

Emio refused to take the bait. "If you insist. Just promise me you'll get sleep at some point."

"What is it with all you Shuos and healthy living habits, anyway?"

"Someday you're going to meet Shuos Zehun," Emio said, clearly unaware that Brezan already had, "and then you'll understand."

After the door had shut behind her, Brezan said to the room, "Someday I'm going to meet Zehun *again*, and eat an entire cake in front of them, just to annoy them." In real life he knew he'd never dare to do any such thing.

"Call for High General Kel Brezan on line 10-1," the grid said again, with its usual inhuman patience.

Brezan took a moment to check himself in the mirror, something he was only just getting in the habit of doing. Being de facto head of state: almost as good as having a drill sergeant for improving your grooming habits. Not that he'd been slovenly as a staffer, exactly, just... not a public figure, either.

"Accept the call," Brezan said, simultaneously hoping the person on the other end hadn't already given up and dreading who it might be.

The image that the grid projected before him belonged to his older sister Miuzan. Miuzan was a twin, but he'd never had any trouble telling her apart from Ganazan even when they'd all been children. Among other things, Miuzan had always been the bossy one. Not that Brezan planned on saying that to her face.

For the call, Miuzan had made a point of wearing her Kel uniform in full formal. The only reason Brezan's uniform had more braid, to say nothing of the chains descending from one epaulet that jingled irritatingly whenever he moved, was because Emio had called in a fashion designer to do him up a whole new one for the purposes of impressing people. He doubted it was going to work on his sister of all people.

"Hi, little brother," Miuzan said, her voice hard. "Take my eyes off you for a second and *this* is what you get up to."

"Good to see you too," Brezan said, determined to be polite. She'd addressed him in the high language, so he answered her in the same, although they'd grown up speaking one of the low languages. It wasn't, in fact, entirely clear what etiquette called for. In military terms he outranked her; she was a colonel on General Kel Inesser's staff, while Kel Command had vaulted him to the not exactly wanted position of high general in a desperation gambit. Of course, people had questioned his legitimacy as soon as he announced himself temporary head of state.

Beyond that, Miuzan was older than he was by six years. She remembered overseeing the servitors changing his diapers. (Their three fathers had been paranoid about diaper-changing.) And she'd helped him with his homework when the oldest, Keryezan, was too busy to. So talking to her at a low formality level would just have been bizarre.

"Brezan," Miuzan said, brows drawing low, "just what in fire's name do you think you're doing?"

He knew from the particular emphasis she gave his name that this conversation wouldn't go well. The sane thing to do would be to hang up on her and go get some sleep the way Emio had told him to, because there was no way he'd be able to talk her around. But she was family, dammit, and he hadn't seen her in person for years. He had to try.

"Trying to put the hexarchate back together," Brezan said. "Except better than before."

"'Better' my ass," Miuzan said. "I'm trying to figure out any version of this story where my annoying little brother"—*Thank you so much*, Brezan thought—"didn't go crashhawk and *team up with the Immolation fucking Fox* to become hexarch. You're not helping me much."

Brezan successfully bit down his instinctive response, which was to say, *But I haven't declared myself hexarch*. Among other things, while technically true, it didn't address her anger. "Why," he said, "because the old system was so great?"

The moment the words left his mouth he knew he'd said a different wrong thing, not the right thing. Assuming there even was a right thing. His formation instinct might be broken, but Miuzan's most assuredly was not. While not all Kel served with equal enthusiasm, he'd never had any doubts about Miuzan's beliefs.

Sure enough, Miuzan recoiled as though he'd sprouted a second head. "This is my fault, isn't it," she said.

That took him by surprise.

"I ragged on you too much when you were a kid," she continued, "and it did things to your head. I should have realized—"

She went on in this vein while Brezan gaped at her. "Miuzan," he said at last, interrupting the stream of self-recriminations, "it has nothing to do with you." Granted, he must be getting better at lying because this was not completely true. Half the reason he'd gone into the Kel in the first place was so he could live up to Miuzan. As much as she aggravated him, he'd looked up to her as a child. He wrestled with the uncomfortable awareness that maybe he did, in fact, like showing her up for once. "*Miuzan.*"

"What?"

"You're going to believe what you're going to believe," Brezan said, a safe, bland statement to launch from. "Will you at least let me tell you why I thought this was a good idea?"

"Yes," Miuzan said, diverted. "Make it good."

Nothing he said would be good enough to persuade her. But that wasn't why he was going to try. All across the hexarchate were people like his older sister: loyal citizens, decent people in their day to day lives, many of whom had benefited even from a system that ran on regular ritualized torture. He'd been one of them once, or liked to think he was. Those were the people he had to reach. He might as well start with the hardest audience of all.

"Do you remember the first time you told me about the Day of Shallow Knives?" Brezan said. It had come around two days ago, high calendar. Naturally, it wasn't observed anymore among his people.

Brezan remembered that first time distinctly, although it was also accompanied by irrelevancies like his dislike of the feather-patterned wallpaper and the whining of a mosquito that the ecoscrubbers hadn't been able to get rid of. His youngest father had stopped working on a commissioned painting and hurriedly rinsed his hands in a basin of water, although it didn't do much for the ink stains further up his arms or daubed on his shirt. Brezan had been playing with a toy voidmoth and pretending it didn't bother him that one of the wingtips had broken off. He'd had an awareness that the calendar was full of special days, but not why it mattered; had never thought to question it. As a child, why would he have?

Miuzan was frowning at him as though she could already see where he was going to go with this line of thought. "Not really."

Oh.

She added, "There are a lot of remembrances, Brezan. They all sort of blur together after a while. I show up and I do what the bulletins tell me to."

Brezan blinked, regrouped. He'd always thought of his sister as taking the remembrances very seriously. Certainly she and his oldest sister, Keryezan, had led him through the required meditations until he was old enough to manage for himself. He'd never questioned her sense of devotion.

"There was a lot of blood," Brezan said, thinking back to the video broadcast.

The Vidona who'd led their local observance had worn the traditional robes of green lined with bronze, and bronze jewelry in the shape of stingray spines. Her knife, too, had had a bronze hilt, with an edge that winked brightly. Brezan had been fascinated by the deftness with which she used it to slice up her victim. The heretic hadn't screamed only because his mouth had been sutured shut. This wasn't the case for all remembrances, something that Brezan had learned rapidly.

Miuzan's face had that stony expression he knew so well. "They're *heretics*, Brezan. Are you trying to argue for some kind of clemency? You know how much trouble they cause. Even if they weren't all bad in themselves"—she said this as though the thought had just occurred to her—"we can't allow calendrical rot."

"Yes," Brezan said bleakly, "I used to think the same thing." Or anyway, he'd thought it just enough to reconcile himself to it, which he imagined was the same thing from the luckless heretic's viewpoint. Then he'd signed on to be a Kel like his oldest father, like Miuzan after that. He'd been both relieved and disappointed when he'd ended up in Personnel rather than as a field officer.

"Well," Miuzan said, with less condescension than usual, "I suppose you were only trying to do as you saw best in a chaotic situation." She had never thought well of his ability, a fact she didn't make any effort to hide. "But that's not why I called."

"Really," Brezan said. "Why, then?" His stomach knotted up. *Stop that*, he told himself. Given the impressive number of fires he was trying to put out all across the hexarchate, he didn't need to borrow trouble.

Miuzan leaned forward, eyes brightening, and he knew he was in for it. "General Inesser asked that I contact you."

That didn't help the state of his stomach. General Inesser, the Kel's senior field general. The only general who had been honored by having a cindermoth, one of the hexarchate's six greatest warmoths, named after her personal emblem. Inesser, known for her courage and cleverness, to say nothing of a lineage that went back into some of the great Andan families. Normally that last fact wouldn't have been an *advantage*. Unlike the Andan (because of them, even), the Kel had strong feelings about nepotism, largely negative, although that didn't mean it didn't happen. But by the time she reached her current rank, Inesser had developed a reputation for unswerving honor.

Miuzan had landed a position on Inesser's staff several years ago, quite a feat. It had also made her more insufferable than ever. He didn't *want* her to take him seriously because he'd gone revolutionary, but since that was the world they lived in...

"The general has my attention any time she wants it," Brezan said, quite truthfully. Among other things, he doubted Inesser was contacting him because she wanted to throw her support to the regime he proposed. While he'd never met her, she also had a reputation for old-fashioned Kel conservatism of the kind he'd once aspired to even as it made his teeth ache. If Inesser was speaking to him through his sister, it meant that she was feeling him out for a proposal of her own.

"That's good to hear," Miuzan said, although she eyed him as if she suspected sarcasm. For which he couldn't blame her; their relationship had not been sarcasm-free, these past years. "She may have an offer for you."

"Do tell."

"The hexarchate needs a strong hand to hold it together after the broadcast of that heretical calendar," Miuzan said. Brezan wondered if she realized that she was speaking just a little more loudly, a little more quickly, than usual. He wasn't used to thinking of his sister as someone who could be swept up by fervor, even fervor in her general's service. "General Inesser intends to be that person."

He'd thought as much. Inesser was going to be a formidable rival.

"Don't answer yet," Miuzan said rapidly, responding to whatever she saw in his face. "The foreigners, not least the Hafn, don't care about our internal divisions except as weaknesses they can exploit. The hexarchate *needs* a united Kel to hold them off and to enforce the calendar so that the stardrives can keep working. General Inesser is the best candidate for the job."

"You said calendar," Brezan said, going directly for the part he cared most about. "By which you mean the high calendar, I presume." The one that he and Cheris had blown up Kel Command to overthrow.

"Of course," Miuzan said, puzzled. "How could the Kel function otherwise?"

How indeed. Brezan searched for a response. The Kel military depended on formation instinct to yank around its soldiers. As a crashhawk, Brezan's own formation instinct was defective, something he'd been in denial of for the longest time. After all, you didn't need formation instinct to obey orders. It just made doing so easier, if by "easier" you meant "unavoidable."

Cheris's new calendar, which she'd broadcast throughout the hexarchate for the use of anyone who could make it stick, changed exotic effects so that they only affected those who wanted to be affected. It wasn't hard to see how this would jeopardize Kel hierarchy. The Kel hadn't always used formation instinct, but once instituted, they'd grown dependent on it.

"There's something else you should be aware of," Miuzan said.

Brezan's stomach knotted up even more. *Next time I get a personal call*, Brezan thought, *I'm going to take some anti-anxiety medications first.*

"I assume you've heard," Miuzan said carefully, "but in case you haven't, there are reports of difficulties with mothdrives. So far they correlate rather disturbingly with regions of calendrical rot. I can send you the databurst if you want it. Call it the general's gift to you, for your contemplation. But this is all to say that we need to stabilize the hexarchate sooner rather than later, before all our defenses and intersystem trade shut down."

How had he missed this? Unless it had been buried in the piles of reports and dispatches that he struggled to make it through every day. Considering he hadn't been doing the job for long, he was already impressively behind.

"Let me guess," Brezan said. While he was no engineer, he knew about the fundamentals of mothdrive technology. "The harnesses aren't working properly anymore."

Obvious once she brought it up, really. Voidmoths were biological in origin, hatched at mothyards and then fitted with technological implants to make them suitable conveyances or weapons of war.

Calendrical rot had always threatened the efficacy of the harnesses that controlled the mothdrives. Voidmoths were additionally fitted with invariant maneuver drives for a reason.

Miuzan's mouth twisted. "Surprised you didn't see this coming, little brother."

"It's been a busy few weeks," Brezan said. He swallowed his pride and added, "You're right, though. It's inexcusable to lose sight of a detail this important."

"Well," Miuzan said, "that's settled."

Wait, how had she—"Excuse me," Brezan said, tamping down on a flare of anger. "I haven't agreed to anything. Tell General Inesser I appreciate her warning." He did, sincerely. "But I can't support her."

For once Miuzan was at a loss for words. Her nostrils flared, and she slitted her eyes at him for several long moments.

"It's simple," Brezan said despite the stabbing in his heart. "If the general is bothering with me at all, it's because she thinks I'm a threat. Maybe not much of a threat, but that means I have a chance. And I have to do this—not for myself, but for all the people who can be saved from the Vidona."

"You—" Miuzan breathed in, expelled it in an angry huff. "You're putting your ego and a bunch of heretics before the safety of a lot of innocent people."

"Once upon a time, some of those heretics were 'innocent people' themselves," Brezan shot back. "How many times have we seen it, Miuzan? Some group of people who'd been going about their lives for decades, longer even, and then overnight they're the new heretics because the Vidona have come up with some new fiddly regulation just for the purpose of scaring up new victims? I don't want to be a part of that anymore."

"All right." Miuzan's voice had gone dead soft, never a good sign. "I wasn't going to say this to you, but you're not leaving me much choice."

There's always a choice, Brezan thought. Still, he might as well let her have her say. She wouldn't leave him alone until she got everything out.

"You are setting the lives of a handful of people over those of *everyone in the whole hexarchate*. So maybe the old government had spots of corruption. That doesn't mean the solution is to burn everything down."

"That's already done and over with," Brezan said, because he couldn't help himself.

Miuzan continued speaking over him so that he had to strain to hear her. Which was the intended effect, no doubt. "The hexarchate's worlds are already bleeding because of you. By the time you're done with this, this—" She searched for a word; found one. "—temper tantrum of yours, they're going to be drenched. I hope that makes you happy."

Brezan's temper, always precarious, got the better of him. "Thank you for thinking so well of me," he said in a cold, flat voice. "Because I don't see that what your precious general is trying to do is so different, except she doesn't care about anything but restoring the old order. Tell me, when the two of you stopped to observe the Day of Shallow Knives recently and watched the cuts being made, and all the blood, did you even wonder about the name of the poor fucker who was tortured to death for you?"

"It was a *heretic*," Miuzan snapped back. "I see this entire call has been a waste of time. I shouldn't have suggested it to the general in the first place. I would never have guessed that you'd pick some crazed personal ambition over honor and loyalty and family, but it seems you're capable of surprising me after all."

"Fuck off," Brezan said.

Miuzan's face shuttered. Then she severed the connection.

It was the last communication Brezan was to have with anyone in his family for the next nine years.

CHAPTER SIX

SAYING FAREWELL TO Rhombus and Sieve only took Hemiola a few minutes. "Keep out of trouble," Rhombus said, as if Hemiola hadn't yet experienced its first neural flowering. That was all.

Sieve, on the other hand, presented Hemiola with a touching and entirely impractical sculpture of bent wires and other scraps. "In case the real hexarch wants some extra decorations once you find him," it said.

"If we catch up to him, I'll put it where he can see it," Hemiola said tactfully.

Hemiola had already presented Jedao with the archive, copied to a data solid the size of his hand. It approved of how carefully Jedao handled it. Just because it was a copy didn't mean it wasn't valuable.

It accompanied Jedao outside of Tefos Base with trepidation. The staircase had scarcely changed in all that time. Jedao had added his footsteps to the multiple sets in the layer of dust upon the stairs. Tefos had little in the way of atmosphere. Down here, sheltered from the slow patter of micrometeorites, the footsteps would endure for a long time. Some of them dated back to when the hexarch had first brought the three servitors with him.

When they emerged from the crevasse, two of the system's other moons rode high in a sky sprinkled with stars and the glow-swirl of the local nebulae. Tefos's surface, ordinarily a dull bluish gray, was desaturated further in the low light. Jedao switched on his headlamp. Hemiola brightened its lights as well, in case he needed the extra help seeing his way.

They passed the rock garden on the way. After eighty years, the carefully raked sand had eroded just a little. Guiltily, Hemiola found it liked the effect. But Sieve would want to fix it up so it looked just as it had eighty years ago. By the time Hemiola returned, the garden would no doubt be restored to its original state.

Jedao's voidmoth rested on a ridge a short walk from the garden. Its elongated shadow stretched away from them, disappearing off the back of the ridge. The moth itself formed a narrow triangular wedge with its apex tilted slightly skyward, as though it yearned to fly again. While the moth was an unpitted matte black, its landing gear gleamed with a sheen as of mirrors. Promisingly, the moth's power core was properly shielded. Like many servitors, even servitors not of particularly technical bent, Hemiola had strong feelings about shielding. Maybe this meant that Jedao took good care of his transportation.

Except—

"There's someone on your moth," Hemiola said, stopping as the moth unfurled a ramp. Its scan had picked up another servitor, although it wasn't yet visible to human eyes.

"That's my traveling companion," Jedao said, his voice muffled through the suit's comm. "I'll introduce you once we get aboard."

Despite its trepidation, Hemiola floated up the ramp and into the airlock after Jedao. Once the airlock had cycled, Jedao unsuited with impressive dexterity and led the way into the moth's cockpit. The hexarch would never have endured a space this cramped.

A deltaform servitor whirred forward, then flashed in alarm, even though it had to have detected Hemiola's approach.

"This is Hemiola of Tefos Enclave," Jedao said to the deltaform. "Why don't you tell it a little about yourself? Hemiola is supervising the archive copy I brought with me."

The deltaform blinked a distinctly noncommittal green-blue. "I'm 1491625 of Pyrehawk Enclave," it said. "Pleased to make your acquaintance."

It came from one of the Kel-affiliated enclaves, then. Hemiola wasn't sure how it felt about that, but questioning the other servitor's allegiance would have been rude. It confined itself to saying, "Likewise."

"Have you properly introduced *yourself*?" 1491625 said to Jedao.

"Jedao is how everyone knows me," he said with a shrug.

Hemiola blinked a query.

Jedao ignored it and webbed himself into the copilot's seat.

Hemiola said, "You're not piloting?"

"1491625 is better at it than I am."

1491625's answering flash was just this side of smug. "You too," it said to Hemiola. "You'll have to squeeze in behind us, unless you're any good at piloting yourself?"

"Unfortunately, no," Hemiola said. It didn't need webbing, strictly speaking, but it obliged the others by securing itself to the back of Jedao's seat. "Where are we going?"

"Resupply," Jedao said. "I don't know when's the last time you've seen a map of the hexarchate, Hemiola, but Kujen picked Tefos because it's in the middle of nowhere. Which is saying a lot considering how much nowhere there is in space. Get comfortable."

Servitors didn't sleep. Hemiola could, however, observe the other two as they set course for a system it had never heard of. 1491625 and Jedao discussed a particularly unstable region they had bypassed on the way in, and whether going through it would shave some days off their travel time.

The voidmoth lifted off cleanly using its invariant maneuver drive. After a couple hours had passed, Hemiola realized 1491625 still hadn't engaged the mothdrive, which was orders of magnitude faster. Rude though it was, Hemiola extended scan toward the mothdrive's harness. It wasn't a technician, but it didn't spot anything obviously wrong. "Is there some difficulty with the mothdrive?" it asked diffidently.

"The mothdrive harness has been unreliable outside of high calendar space," Jedao said. "Since I'd rather we not randomly swerve into the nearest neutron star..."

So that was why Jedao was so concerned about resupply: extended travel time. "How long has this been going on?" Hemiola asked. The hexarch hadn't mentioned any such problems eighty years ago.

"The past nine years," Jedao said. He lapsed into a troubled silence after that.

Not wishing to bother its hosts, Hemiola meditated on a favorite gavotte. The hexarch and Jedao had liked to dance to it, once upon a time. It remembered the way the hexarch had looked at Jedao, leading him around the walls of a room kept for that purpose.

"You're humming," Jedao said after a while. "Or playing something back, I can't tell which. I guess when you can reproduce any sound at will, you can be an orchestra all by yourself."

Hemiola flickered in embarrassment. "I didn't mean to—"

"Don't apologize," Jedao said. "It's nice to know someone around here can hold a tune in a bucket. I used to... but it doesn't matter."

1491625 snickered.

"You used to what?" Hemiola said. If it recalled correctly, Jedao could find a beat but not much else.

"My mother taught me to sing some old songs, long ago and far away," Jedao said. "Can't do it anymore, though. Kel Command ruined me for that. Enough about me. I was wondering if you'd be willing to help me look through the records?"

It hesitated.

"Unless you've read them already?"

"Oh no," it said. The hexarch himself had never reviewed the records, only updated them briskly during each visit. "I couldn't. The hexarch wouldn't—"

"The hexarch is in trouble," Jedao said. "The problem is, he was also secretive as fuck. I need to figure out what he was so afraid of down all the years."

A hundred questions flitted through Hemiola's mind. Who would dare to threaten a hexarch? And why wasn't Jedao with him? What had happened to disrupt the reliability of the mothdrives? "You don't know where he is," it said. It wasn't a question.

"He's been missing for nine years," Jedao said. "The last time I saw him, he was making eyes at Kel Command. But that's nothing new. I can only conclude—" He made an abortive gesture. "I was hoping for clues as to where he's gone, or what he considers a threat. It's a long shot, but since I knew about Tefos, I had to check here once I freed myself from certain obligations. To be honest, I thought I'd find him holed up here. But for all I know, he has more bases like Tefos scattered throughout the stars."

"Surely the hexarch could only snatch so much time away from his duties," Hemiola said.

Jedao smiled humorlessly. "You'd think."

"Well," Hemiola said, "I'll help take a look."

"Thank you," Jedao said. "1491625, I'm going to divert one of the subdisplays and hope there isn't anything hideously distracting in there. Or, foxes help us, that the data format is so obsolete that it crashes the grid, or some damn thing."

"You just had to make this whole process more nerve-racking, didn't you," 1491625 said.

Jedao slid the data solid into a reader slot. "Well, there's the index," he said. "It's compressed, not encrypted. To be frank, I wish it had been. I'd feel safer. Here's the access key, Hemiola—"

Hemiola received it from the grid. The entire set of records consisted of lowest-denominator text-plus-image files.

"That file format is unspeakably old," Jedao said. "Kujen was a stickler for backwards compatibility. Still, it means we can read the records without trouble. I never thought I'd be grateful for his obsessive insistence on standardized formats."

Hemiola was only halfway paying attention to this and had opened up the earliest file, which was... a journal entry? A digression in a laboratory notebook? The Nirai version of a love letter?

The entry began harmlessly enough, with a stylized doodle of an emblem Hemiola had never encountered before, a ringed planet accompanied by a bird in flight. Pencil, at a guess. It could even see the faint eraser marks where the entry's author had corrected the planet to make it more perfectly round.

I saw the girl again on the way to class, said the elegant columns of handwriting, neatly aligned to a grid of dots. *I gave her the rest of my flatbread. She needed it more than I did. During lunches in the cafeteria, the other cadets throw away enough food to feed an army of girls like her.*

The author had followed this with three different recipes for flatbread, detailed tasting notes, and cost comparisons.

"What are you looking at?" Jedao said, peering over his shoulder.

"The very first entry," Hemiola said. It didn't have a date, but the index implied that everything was in chronological order.

After a pregnant pause, Jedao said, in a flat voice, "That's Kujen's handwriting, although not as elegant as it became later. I wonder what he was doing."

"Feeding a hungry girl?" Hemiola said, wondering what was so difficult about interpreting the passage.

"Yes, but why?"

It couldn't see the point of the question. "Because she was hungry and he had food?"

Jedao massaged his temples. "I need to think about this. I wonder what else is in here. According to the index, we have a whole library's worth of notes here. You read faster than I do, so we have a chance. Especially considering how much time we're going to be spending in transit anyway."

Hemiola caught itself admiring the doodle. "I wonder what that is," it said. "I didn't know the hexarch liked to draw."

"The old Nirai emblem, before they replaced it with the modern voidmoth. He told me once he learned draughtsmanship the old-fashioned way, before all this grid assistance business. Showed me a collection of T-squares and compasses and ellipse templates. Although by the time I knew him, he could draw circles damn near perfect freehand. It must have been required in the Nirai curriculum once." His mouth pulled up on one side. "He scared me once by telling me the Shuos used to require their cadets to speak in code for an entire semester. Or maybe that was the Andan, back before the Shuos split off from them, I can never remember."

Jedao shook his head. "Some of this material is bound to get technical. I can handle mathematics if necessary"—again that note of irony—"but I'm no engineer."

"Neither am I," Hemiola said. "I don't suppose—?"

"I'm hardly a gate mechanics specialist," 1491625 said from the pilot's seat, "although we have some textbooks and what Jedao says is a truly terrible interactive tutorial."

"Well, we'll have to make the most of it," Jedao said.

"How fast *do* you read?" Hemiola said.

"I can read 200 words per minute of this kind of text. Assuming there aren't secret codes hidden in the recipes. Which is a possibility with someone like Kujen."

"All right," Hemiola said, "would you rather read from the beginning, or take the more modern material?"

"More modern material," Jedao said after a pause. "On the grounds that I need to know where he is now, not what he was up to almost a millennium ago."

It calculated the dividing line. "Start with that file, then," it suggested.

Jedao called up the relevant file. "Works for me. If anything interesting comes up, flag it for my attention. For whatever values of 'interesting' seem useful to you." He settled in to read.

Hemiola did likewise. It was prying. It knew it was prying. Yet it couldn't help warming to the hexarch. Whatever Jedao found disturbing about the incident recounted in that first entry, surely taking care of a hungry child was laudable?

"Do people still go hungry in the hexarchate?" it asked as it turned to the next entry.

"They probably do now," 1491625 said with a cynical greenish flicker. "In the past, less so, unless you lived right up against some battle. Which describes a lot of places these days."

Hemiola invited elaboration.

"Civil unrest," Jedao said, "as the result of some necessary reform."

"If that's what you want to call it," 1491625 said.

Hemiola blinked inquisitively.

"Old argument," Jedao said, his eyes troubled.

Hemiola kept reading until it found another mention of the hungry girl. This one was embedded in notes on neuropsychology. The notes themselves were brief to the point of being telegraphic. Not surprising; it couldn't imagine that the material had posed a challenge to the hexarch even as a cadet. If it had been skimming any faster, it would have missed the paragraph entirely.

Spotted her again, the hexarch said in what looked like quickly dashed-off handwriting. And, in the margin of the next page: *My sister was about her age when she died*.

"Jedao?" Hemiola said.

Jedao didn't look up. "Mmm?"

"Who was the hexarch's sister?"

"The hexarch's *what*?"

Hemiola pointed out the marginal note.

"I never heard of any siblings," Jedao said, "much less that he cared—" He checked himself from whatever he'd been about to say. "I don't suppose we have any idea how old Kujen was when he wrote this."

"If we can figure out which course he was taking notes on," 1491625 said after it glanced over the page, "we can compare it to the standard Nirai curriculum."

"He was admitted at the age of fourteen," Jedao said. "He mentioned that to me once. Thought it was amusing how many people thought he needed 'protection.' And he graduated early, too, in four years instead of the usual five. He said it could have been three if he hadn't studied multiple specialties. I don't think he was being boastful."

Hemiola tried to imagine the hexarch as a fourteen-year-old cadet experimenting with flatbread recipes and failed. "I wonder why he didn't report the girl, whoever she was, to the authorities," it said. "Surely someone would have taken her in."

While 1491625 and Jedao puzzled over Nirai Academy's curricula, Hemiola kept reading. It found the answer to its question not long afterward. This one was tucked away next to a cryptic table of data—this one dated. (The hexarch had also showed his work on a number of computations, in what Hemiola would have called a sarcastic manner. It was certain that the hexarch could have done all of that in his head.)

One of my classmates asked me why I don't just call the Vidona, the hexarch said. *As if I don't remember what life was like in a Vidona orphanage. I'm not sure the girl would thank me.*

And, tucked in next to a scatter plot: *I learned her name today, in exchange for more flatbread and candies. It's Meveri. She's probably lying about that. I used to do that too. Six years old and she already knows.*

Hemiola was about to point this out to Jedao, too, in case he was interested. But 1491625 spoke first. "Advanced course of study," it said. "The kind of thing senior Nirai come back to the academy to research if they're good enough to be invited back. He was doing that as a cadet."

"It wouldn't have been a surprise to anyone that he was going to end up a heptarch," Jedao said. "Still, it would probably have been toward the end of his stay at academy."

"I found a date on this entry," Hemiola said. "The year was 359." It also pointed out the orphanage comment.

Jedao looked grim. "I suppose he had his reasons, but did he honestly think that passing scraps of food to a street child that young, rather than getting her to the authorities, was doing her any favors?"

"We don't know what the authorities were like back then," 1491625 said. "Maybe someone else was looking out for this Meveri."

"If only your people had existed in those days," Jedao said. "We might have some chance of tracking down additional records of her."

"We have our own archivists," 1491625 said, "but the heptarchate was a big place."

Hemiola tuned them out. It wanted to know what had become of Meveri. While the hexarch and Jedao had never brought children with them to Tefos Base, the heroine of *A Rose in Three Revolutions* had an eight-year-old niece. It supposed six-year-old children behaved differently from eight-year-olds. And how was a six-year-old surviving on only the occasional gift of flatbreads, anyway?

The next swathe of pages made no mention of Meveri whatsoever. Hemiola suffered through confidence intervals, strange attractors, and cryptic chains of biochemical reactions before finding her again. This time the hexarch devoted an entire page to her, along with several scratched-out sketches. While the hexarch might have been a competent draughtsman, his portraits left something to be desired. He eventually settled for a verbal description.

Her hair was matted. She might have had pretty eyes once. They were swollen shut by the time I got to her. My friend was right.

Several more columns of text written, then blotted out; the hexarch knew how to redact material so it was unreadable. Then he added, *If I'd waited any longer, the city watch would have taken her for cremation. One of the local fruit peddlers who'd seen me with her earlier finally told me where the beggars' association had abandoned her. I sat and held her hand until she stopped breathing. Toward the end, she was babbling at me in one of the local low languages. I just made reassuring noises because that was all there was left to do.*

We are a nation of thousands upon thousands of worlds, and we can't prevent a child from starving to death right next to one of our faction academies.

The page looked as though it had been crumpled. Even though it knew better, Hemiola caught itself trying to smooth the paper out. The image, of course, was amenable to no such thing.

"Jedao," it said, "you had better see this."

After reading the page, Jedao sat in silence for a time. Eventually he said, "This sister of his. I wonder what happened to her, and why he never spoke of her. It's not the question I thought I was going to be asking."

"There are going to be a lot more of those," 1491625 said.

"Maybe that was what drove him to become heptarch," Hemiola said, "in a world long ago."

"Yes," Jedao said. "In all the years I've known him, I never would have guessed. I'm starting to think I never understood him at all. And now we have to figure out what he's been thinking all this time, what his plan for the heptarchate was, before it's too late for the rest of us."

CHAPTER SEVEN

WHEN NIRAI KUJEN returned the next day, Jedao and Dhanneth were taking a break with a game of jeng-zai. Jedao had asked Dhanneth to check his plan for the first battle, and then the two of them had looked over the logistics. Among other things, Jedao couldn't help wondering if all majors were this well-versed in tactics, or if Kujen had picked him an unusually competent aide. There was no tactful way to ask, so he didn't. Dhanneth had told him that the staff should double-check the details, but Jedao felt better having Dhanneth's opinion nonetheless, and Dhanneth had improved the presentation. In the course of the discussion it had emerged that Dhanneth played jeng-zai and had brought a deck with him. Jedao was beating Dhanneth, but he was putting up a good fight.

"Don't yell at the major," Jedao said quickly when Kujen peered at his hand. "It was my idea."

"Not that," Kujen said, and riffled through the unused portion of the deck until he came up with a card. He showed it to Jedao: the Deuce of Gears, silver on a black field, like everything else in the Gears suit.

Jedao was watching Dhanneth out of the corner of his eye. Dhanneth's shoulders tensed at the sight of the card as though—as though what? It wasn't even a particularly unlucky card. "Cog in the machine" was what it connoted.

"Not familiar?" Kujen said.

"Should it be?" Jedao said, continuing to watch Dhanneth in his peripheral vision.

Kujen made a moue. "That's gone too? You took a variant of it as your emblem, once upon a time."

"Nirai colors, though?"

"You registered yours in gold gears on a red field," Kujen said. "Quite fetching. You used to show me a whole routine of stupid card tricks based around it."

That made more sense: Shuos colors. He didn't know what to make of the card tricks, though, which he didn't remember either, so he didn't respond to that part. Certainly he couldn't imagine himself amusing a hexarch, of all people, with something as trivial as magic tricks. "Should we switch it back to Nirai colors, considering...?"

"Nice thought," Kujen said, "but it'll be more intimidating in its historical form, so you ought to stick to the gold and red. I've scheduled a meeting with the Kel. Conference in person with your staff heads, tactical group commanders, and infantry colonels, plus the rest of the commanders in the rear. You'll be able to hold virtual conferences with them after we get underway, of course."

Jedao was halfway convinced that all that existed of the universe was this suite. If he stepped outside, he would fall into an infinite cushioning darkness.

The conviction must have shown in his face. Kujen said, "I wasn't keeping you prisoner out of spite. Given your notoriety, I thought it best for you to be kept away from random Kel, or assassins for that matter, until you got your bearings. Any idea what you're saying to your officers?"

"Yes," Jedao lied. He had a speech; had even run it by Dhanneth. The original one had been no good, so he'd scrambled to write an appropriate substitution.

"I still think you should wear your medals, sir," Dhanneth said.

Jedao had originally demurred on the grounds that the last thing a mass murderer should flaunt was a bunch of medals for things he couldn't remember doing. If Dhanneth was bringing it up in front of Kujen, however, he felt strongly enough about the matter to corner him into it. Jedao looked at him with renewed respect.

Kujen figured it out immediately. "The major is right, you know.

The Kel will respond better if they see that you take pride in your rank."

That was perilously close to what Dhanneth had said, although Jedao hadn't believed him. "I didn't see any medals when I searched the drawers," Jedao said, "and I wouldn't know how to put them in the right order."

"Your uniform does that for you," Kujen said. "It reads the record out of your profile. No, really. Direct it to enter full formal, medals included."

Jedao did so and was treated to the bizarre sight of his uniform changing, down to the sudden appearance of rows of medals beneath the general's wings and Shuos eye. "I bet this makes for some interesting pranks," he said.

"You're not the first person to think of that. There's some crypto involved so that people can't randomly impersonate people, but the augment takes care of that so you don't have to think about it." Kujen looked Jedao over critically, then nodded. "It'll do."

After an abbreviated breakfast, they set out for the conference. "Try to keep up," Kujen said, "since you're not used to variable layout."

"Variable what?"

"It'll make more sense when you experience it."

Jedao wasn't sure what he had expected the halls of a Nirai station to look like. Gray and sterile, perhaps. He should have figured that a Nirai station hosting the Nirai hexarch himself would pay tribute to Kujen's love of fine things. Ink paintings on heavy silk depicted birds in migration, only when he looked more closely, the black strokes that formed the birds' wings were composed of tiny, impressionistic moths. The halls abounded with displays of orreries and astrolabes, abacuses with beads of jade and obsidian. And they were walking on carpet, iridescent gray with patterns on it in paler pearly gray, with pile so deep that if you lost a toe in it you'd never see it again.

More alarming was the fact that they were walking down an infinite corridor, which had no apparent end or, when Jedao glanced back, beginning either. He couldn't see far into the distance, as though moisture hazed the air. The others' unconcern told him this was nothing new, but he didn't like it.

That wasn't all. Jedao had a sudden sense of the *whereness* of the station and everything in it, based not in vision but on concentrations of mass. Kujen and Dhanneth appeared in this othersense just as they did in Jedao's ordinary sight. Their surroundings, though, were confusingly knotted, as though spacetime itself was warped between two disparate points.

As a test, he slowed and closed his eyes. The othersense didn't go away. In fact, now that he knew he had it, he couldn't make it go away. Kujen and Dhanneth continued forward. He examined the rest of his surroundings—he could sense in all directions, a handy trick—and began detecting other moving masses that he suspected were either people or, for the smaller, denser ones, servitors.

Better not reveal this to anyone else until he knew more about where it had come from. He was pretty sure standard-issue humans didn't randomly sense mass. He hurried to rejoin the other two.

At last they arrived at an enormous pair of doors. Jedao could have sworn that they materialized between one step and the next. The doors sheened black with a faint silver scatter as of stars, marked with the Nirai voidmoth emblem in brighter silver. They slid open at Kujen's approach, unnervingly noiseless.

Jedao didn't pause or look left or right, up or down, as he followed Kujen across the threshold, despite the way his back prickled. He had to get this right. There was no other option. Behind him, he heard Dhanneth's ragged breathing, but he didn't dare look around to see what the matter was.

Kujen had led them into a hall with a high arched ceiling and pillars of black veined with gold. More than the lanterns with their trapped, frantic moth-shapes throwing irregular shadows across the dark walls, Jedao noticed the Kel commanders, a row about ten across and ten deep.

The Kel commanders had, almost as one, knelt before Kujen. Jedao's othersense was momentarily dizzied by the coordinated movement. Although the commanders' attention should have been focused on the hexarch, he couldn't escape their consternation. Some of it was directed at him, revulsion so strong he could feel its pressure. But some of them were eyeing Dhanneth with unambiguous shock. Did they consider Dhanneth to have sold out by serving him?

The temperature in the hall should have been comfortable, but all Jedao could think of was winter, bleak winds in a world frozen dark. There were black-and-gold uniforms everywhere, including his own. He craved any splash of color as relief from the monotony of all the black.

"I trust everyone slept well," Kujen said. The light in his eyes suggested that he knew exactly what effect this setup was having on the Kel. "I promised you a new general. Here he is." He waved a hand, indicating that everyone should stand.

Jedao hadn't counted on such an abrupt introduction. The six staff heads in front exchanged stony glances. The commanders had faces as still and blank as ice. Jedao had no idea why he was smiling, or what to say, even if he'd memorized that speech beforehand. Not saying anything wasn't an option, either, even in the face of their muted hostility. So he opened his mouth—

"You know my name," he said with a bite of humor. "You don't seem to have done a very good job executing me."

His gaze was drawn immediately to the commander he recognized as Kel Talaw. Talaw was a stocky alt whose eyes narrowed as they stared back at Jedao. And Talaw's hostility wasn't muted at all. Their face blazed with naked hatred even as the entire hall plunged stone-silent.

Fuck, Jedao thought. What had possessed him to say that? Especially in that tone of voice?

He couldn't take it back. He couldn't apologize. That would only make him look weak. Better to be a callous bastard than to lose credibility.

Besides, there was no getting around the fact that everyone knew more about Hellspin Fortress than he did. Trying to win the Kel over with charm would have been disastrous anyway. At least they had no idea what was going on inside his head. He would just have to lie too well for them to deduce how out of his depth he was. The sad thing was that the lie was better for morale.

Bad sign: Kujen's eyes had crinkled faintly in approval. The expression only lasted a fraction of a second, but Jedao had been watching for his reaction.

Fine. Jedao let his smile narrow. "I understand there was an earlier failure of discipline in the hexarch's direction." Stupid to pretend it hadn't happened; might as well address it head-on. "If you feel like betraying someone, you can start with me instead." Great. He had just challenged all the commanders to duels or the next best thing, and a lot of the Kel excelled at dueling, but he couldn't stop. "We're going to be fighting other Kel. Is this going to be an issue?"

He wished he could blame the uniform for messing with his head, but he knew better.

Commander Nihara Keru raised her head: Tactical Two. The plainness of her face was offset by her startling pale gray eyes. Everyone else in the front row had brown eyes. "I would speak, sir," she said. Her voice, high and crisp, had its own lilt of humor.

She might be the first person besides Kujen who didn't hate him, not that Jedao had met many people yet. That also made her a potential threat. *Don't pause, don't pause, don't pause.* "Commander Nihara Keru," he said. Her eyebrows flicked up: she hadn't been sure he'd know her name, although he had made a point of memorizing names and faces. "Say what's on your mind."

Talaw's mouth twisted. The rest of the commanders, less senior than Talaw or Nihara, were grimly attentive. For that matter, the staff heads looked even more uncomfortable. Jedao was trying to determine whether Talaw and Nihara disliked each other. If so, his life had gotten more interesting.

"Sir," Nihara said, "what are our objectives? This is a large swarm, but it's an immense galaxy."

Jedao already liked her. "Our purpose is calendrical warfare to reunify the hexarchate so it can stand against incursions from foreigners," he said, meeting her eyes. He was lying about this, too. Kujen's strategic notes had suggested that he cared about the restoration of the hexarchate's historical boundaries, but, weirdly, not so much about the occasional trifling invasion. Jedao would have to figure out what that implied later.

He continued talking. "We will start with attacks to realign the calendar in the Fissure"—the border region contested by the Compact and some smaller states, where the high calendar had lost its dominance—"and expand from there. There's only this one swarm to start with, but I killed an entire army of you once and I got back up, and you're the fucking military faction. I say we have a chance. But it's a better chance if we're all pointed in the same direction."

There was a stir at that. He couldn't believe he'd just joked about massacring Kel, except at this point there wasn't anything he wouldn't have believed about himself.

Nihara interrupted by laughing. Talaw's mouth tightened in disapproval. "All right, sir," Nihara said. "That's fair."

"Charmed," Jedao said. "Major, if you'd bring up the map—"

Dhanneth did as requested.

Jedao didn't expect that his overview of their target, Isteia System, held many surprises for his audience. The system used to house a major mothyard, specifically for the construction of cindermoths, before falling victim to sabotage. Kujen wanted the swarm not only to destroy it before it resumed production, but to do so on the anniversary of Kel Command's demise. Isteia was expected to be on high alert. If they could carry off a victory on that day— the more spectacular the better—the resulting calendrical spike would, according to both Kujen and everyone in Doctrine, swing the disputed territory back to Kujen's preferred calendar. Jedao had snooped on some of the mathematics for the hell of it, querying the local grid for help with the computer algebra system. The junior Doctrine officer whose work he'd spot-checked had looked as if he'd rather arm-wrestle a tiger.

Jedao finished going over intelligence on antimissile defenses and suppressed a sigh. Lecturing statues would have been more fun. The statues might have been friendlier.

"We have a few advantages," Jedao said, not because he thought they hadn't figured it out, but because he believed in clarity. "First, our mothdrives look different on scan, and that will throw them. We can take advantage of that during the first engagement. Second, the Compact and the Protectorate are currently at peace, if an uneasy one, and the vast majority of you Kel ended up with one or the other. They won't expect a Kel swarm to suddenly turn up and fight them. That's something we only get to confuse them with once, but since it's lying around it'd be stupid not to use it."

One of the junior commanders asked about travel formations, which was a good question. "No," Jedao said, "we won't be traveling in formation to begin with. We don't want them to know for sure that we're Kel. Uncomfortable as it will be, it's more important to preserve surprise."

"Sir," Talaw said. "If we're attacked en route, what then?"

Another good question. Jedao was relieved that Talaw's hatred of him didn't preclude them from participating usefully in the briefing. "We'll be avoiding the known listening posts to the greatest extent possible," Jedao said, "but the beautiful thing about space is that it's difficult to get pinned. If someone shows up, we sprint away. Our mothdrives will allow us to outrun most of what's out there. It's ignominious, but the calendrical spike takes priority. We're not here to get into random brawls, especially considering our limited resources. You'll get the order to fight in formation when the time comes and not before."

Would Talaw argue with him for the sake of it? But all they said was, "I concede your logic, sir."

Jedao was starting to like Talaw as well. So what if they hated him? It might be good for him to have someone to keep him from getting sloppy.

"All right," Jedao said. "Infantry assignments. Although we have some boxmoths for personnel, I have assigned complements of infantry to some of the bannermoths and to the shearmoth to accommodate the regiments." He smiled at the senior infantry colonel, Kel Muyyed. "I expect infantry to drill formations while we're in transit." Dhanneth had radiated grudging approval when Jedao came up with that, although he hadn't come out and said so. "Per standard procedure, refuse the primary pivots during drill." Leaving primary pivots unfilled would prevent the formations' effects from activating. He doubted the colonels needed the reminder of the precaution, but Muyyed and the junior colonel nodded sharply.

Talaw again. "Do you intend an infantry assault in this first engagement, sir?" Skepticism.

"No," Jedao said, "but it doesn't do to get out of practice, just in case." At some point they might have to take and hold territory; messy business if so. He'd rather deal with a fast raid than a protracted siege, or worse, planetary warfare. But the infantry were Kel, too. Giving them something to do would help them feel involved. "Anything else?"

No one else had any questions they wanted to admit to.

"Hexarch," Jedao said, and bowed. People stiffened. He must have picked the wrong bow, but if Kujen wasn't going to behead him for it, he didn't much care. "I'm done."

Kujen said, "I have no objections to the timetable you've laid out. If anyone has other questions, submit them through the usual channels."

Jedao had no idea how "the usual channels" worked. Presumably Dhanneth could help him with that. Kujen was already striding toward the doors. Jedao remembered to salute the Kel, feeling horrible for them, then followed. Dhanneth hurried after him.

They could have been walking back through the same bizarre endless hallway with its extravagant ink paintings, except the walls suddenly opened up into an antechamber. The pale light revealed people working at terminals or banks of mysterious instruments. All of the people wore Nirai black-and-silver, in inconsistent styles of clothing: here a dress enlivened by a silver-mesh wrap, there a sleek tunic over trousers with a staggering number of pockets. A few of the Nirai glanced up at Kujen's entrance, but no one bowed, or spoke to him, or did much to acknowledge that a hexarch had entered. In fact, several of them were arguing loudly over anomalies on a contour graph.

Kujen eyed Jedao, then snorted. "I'm not a Rahal, Jedao. I don't feel this pressing emotional need to scrape people off the floor wherever I go."

"I don't believe you," Jedao muttered.

Kujen had good hearing. "No one would get anything done around here if I insisted on that," he said. "We have a schedule. Anyway, I wanted to show you your command moth." Kujen made a gesture Jedao thought he could replicate with practice, and part of the far wall ceased to be visible.

The wall had either become a window or a massive display. The shearmoth hung there against a backdrop of stars. Knowing Kujen, the fact that it was attractively framed between two nebulae, a small blue-violet one and a larger one with interesting pink swirls, was deliberate. It looked even more impressive at this level of detail than it had when Kujen had shown him the original image: swept-back wings and careful curves, a triangular profile reminiscent of those of the bannermoths. He recognized the array of frontal protrusions that projected the shearmoth's deadliest weapon, and the one for which it had been named, the shear cannon. Jedao longed to reach through the void and touch one of the protrusions, except he was afraid he'd leave smudges on the pristine surface.

Jedao thought to look up at Kujen. Kujen was smiling at whatever he saw in Jedao's face. For once a soft light almost made the beautiful eyes human.

Of course he cares, Jedao thought, kicking himself for not realizing something so elementary. Kujen must have become a moth engineer for a reason. He was proud of the moth he had designed. And it made sense that Kujen didn't want to interfere with his technicians. It wasn't that the technicians mattered in themselves. It was the work they enabled him to do.

"You still haven't named it, have you?" Kujen said.

"Kujen, I couldn't," Jedao said. "It's your design."

This was the right response. "I built it for you," Kujen said wryly.

"I can rattle off all the specifications and draw the blueprints with my teeth. I could even drive it somewhere if Navigation went into cardiac arrest, but that's it. This moth was made to fight. That's your domain."

"Your mysterious assistant doesn't want to name it?"

"Aside from the fact that my mysterious assistant comes up with the worst names ever, he refused to do anything of the sort."

"What's his name, anyway?"

Kujen startled. "He'll tell you someday, maybe." But Kujen sounded doubtful. "Since we're on the topic of names, you should come up with something for the moth."

Jedao couldn't demur. That might offend Kujen. But he might be able to get information out of this—"*Revenant*," he said.

Kujen grinned at him. "Feeling self-conscious, are we? *Revenant* it is."

So much for that.

Dhanneth was studying the moth with great interest.

"Walk me through the specs again," Jedao said. "I'm not even sure I know what questions to ask."

"Some officers have a strong technical background," Kujen said, "but it's true that that wasn't your particular specialty." He looked like he was about to add something, then called up a diagram instead. Columns of text listed all the moth's armaments. "I tried to label it clearly, but let me know if I got it wrong. I read all the analyses of Candle Arc I could find and most of them mentioned that you used superior invariant resources against the Lanterners, so I directed our research accordingly. Considering the fractured nature of the calendar at this time, it's just as well."

"I expected you to start with the mothdrive," Jedao said, grateful that the diagram told him how many railguns there were. The number impressed him.

Kujen shook his head in amusement. "Force of habit. I always assume that Kel want to know about things that smash things before anything else. Here we go."

Another diagram came up, including a graph with a bright silver curve and fainter ones in shades of gold and blue and red. "The silver is the shearmoth. Kel cindermoth, Kel bannermoth, Andan silkmoth just for hilarity, and that red is the last reliable data I have on Shuos shadowmoths."

"Shadowmoths?"

"Stealth vessels. Traditionally, with a shadowmoth it's the first surprise attack you have to worry about. Once dropped, recharging stealth used to take ages. But the technology could have improved in the past nine years, so don't make too many assumptions."

"Good to know," Jedao said. "I wish I remembered more of this."

Kujen didn't answer that directly. "Pay attention to that highlighted zone in the associated acceleration curve. You can outrun anything out there except the Taurags in their native calendrical terrain, but the power drain has implications for your biggest weapon."

The shear cannon. It caused ripples in spacetime, displacing objects caught in the area of effect. Not precise enough to yank moths into the path of fire, but good enough to disrupt Kel formations, which depended on precise geometries. Jedao almost looked forward to trying it out.

"The shear cannon is a prototype, correct?" Jedao said.

Kujen's nostrils flared. "It has been thoroughly tested," he said, in a voice so mild that Jedao recognized it as dangerous.

They spent the next two hours going over the specifications in detail, including simulator time. Jedao was getting better at using his augment to transmit commands to the local grid, even if it disoriented him when it tapped directly into his kinesthetic sense to provide him with a map or diagram. He wondered if he'd ever get used to it.

"All right," Kujen said finally. "My assistant needs me. Have the major escort you back to your quarters. Remember, if you get truly fucked up, call for me and I'll sort it out."

Jedao hoped he would never get used to having a hexarch show him this much consideration. "Good luck with whatever you're doing," Jedao said, and nodded at Dhanneth, indicating that he should lead.

Dhanneth plunged directly toward a blank section of wall. Nirai technicians scattered to either side, some muttering what sounded like curses in various low languages. Jedao followed Dhanneth, not slowing even when it looked like they were going to crash into it like a pair of idiots. Sure enough, they passed through. It was like being engulfed by a mouth of uncomfortable ridged teeth, then being spit out again. He asked his augment how to repeat the trick and received a tutorial file.

They emerged in a different hallway, or maybe the previous one had changed garb for the occasion. This time the walls were hung with tapestries. Jedao was willing to wager that someone had woven and embroidered them by hand, down to the thousands of faceted seed beads and couched golden threads.

"You've got to tell me," Jedao said, "how does variable layout work?"

"It's based on some results in gate mechanics," Dhanneth said. "Over my head, sir. The hexarch might be willing to discuss it with you sometime. From a practical standpoint, as long as we're in communication with the station or moth's grid and—sir!"

Jedao had stopped after the first sentence and knelt to inspect the floor. It wasn't as solid as it seemed, especially the more he stood still. The carpet decomposed into silvery cobwebs the longer he looked, and the air smelled suddenly of dust, decaying leaves, corroded metal. Beneath the carpet, the floor was composed of gears rotating with an unceasing heartless *click-tick-tock*. Beyond the ticking, he heard a sudden faint singing in a voice at once too high and too deep to be human. He was tempted to reach down and—

Dhanneth had backtracked for Jedao. "Don't do that, sir," Dhanneth said. "The station doesn't seem to like you. If this happens again, report it to the hexarch. He'll be able to fix any fault in your augment or the grid's programming. It'd be troublesome if the station cocooned you." He said that last with a touch of malice.

"Cocoon?" Jedao said, straightening.

"You didn't think the Nirai emblem was a moth for no reason, did you?"

"I have no idea what I thought."

They resumed walking. Unfortunately, this gave Jedao time to think. His conversations went better when he just opened his mouth and talked. Not that he liked the things that came out of his mouth.

Kujen had given him a prototype for his command moth, fine. If Jedao had once been a general, he had been a moth commander before that. But he couldn't help wondering what had happened to the swarm's rightful general, and wishing they were here to offer advice, if nothing else.

"It's no secret that the Kel despise me," Jedao remarked to Dhanneth when they reached the door. It came after a long curve in the hallway and past an astonishing fall of silver-blue light.

Dhanneth halted and faced him. His mouth twisted. "It's their duty to obey you, sir."

Jedao stared at the door and its polished black surface. His reflection formed a ghost-blur. He couldn't discern his eyes or the damnable gloves, just the barren fact of his silhouette. "You heard the things I said."

"I imagine you had practical reasons for saying them," Dhanneth said. "To use this swarm as a fighting force, you're going to have to get the officers behind you. And the flip side of hierarchy is that we respect strength. While formation instinct is all very well, it doesn't cover all the loopholes. One of the first things they teach officers is that subordinates can make things miserable for superiors they don't respect."

A warning. Dhanneth might not like him, but his advice was worth taking to heart. "I'll bet," Jedao said, and dismissed Dhanneth.

It hurt him that *cold-blooded murderer* appeared to be a valid subset of *strong* as far as the Kel were concerned. He couldn't explain why. Weren't the Kel already about shooting people? Except he could have sworn that there had been something in there about honor, too.

Bad enough that he was a mass murderer. And bad enough that a hexarch didn't have any problems appointing him general in spite of it, but no one expected moral sense from someone that far up the food chain. No: the worst thing was that some of the Kel considered his ruthlessness a qualification, not an incentive to mutiny.

There has to be something better than this, Jedao thought. Even for Kujen, who didn't care, and the Kel, who couldn't disobey. But how could he get through to them?

CHAPTER EIGHT

Eight years ago

BREZAN WOKE TO the sound of singing. The nice thing about sleeping with Andan-certified courtesans was that they all sang well. He tried not to think about how this one had long, rippling hair that reminded him of his former lover Tseya, although she didn't resemble Tseya otherwise: short and plump rather than tall and slender, and with a fondness for the color purple. Tseya had always dressed, very properly, in Andan blue-and-silver or variations thereof. Also unlike Tseya, this courtesan, whose name was Irimi, liked tea rituals. Brezan endured her endless fussing over the positioning of teacups because the sex was fantastic.

"Damnation," Brezan said after consulting his internal chronometer. "You could have woken me earlier. I've got that arbitration meeting about the strikes, don't I?" A number of the doctors, who'd received training from the Medical branch of the Vidona, had gone on strike in Tauvit. He wanted to resolve that before it could fester. Tauvit wasn't the only place where it was going on. Unsurprisingly, the Vidona and their supporters were among the most recalcitrant when it came to the new order.

Irimi left off singing and said, "You looked tired. Besides, your bodyguard left instructions to let you get rest for anything short of a crisis."

Ah, yes. "Why," Brezan said, keeping the sarcasm from his voice, "no worlds have blown up in the past day?"

"Not that I've heard of," Irimi said placidly. Also unlike Tseya, she liked jewelry, a lot of it. This pale morning her outfit, such as it was, involved draperies of lavender lace interspersed with tiny, irregularly faceted amethyst beads. Brezan thought regretfully that he shouldn't be thinking about how entertaining it would be to watch her undress. Irimi could draw out the act of disrobing beyond anything sensible.

After Brezan emerged from the shower and got dressed, Irimi had tea and breakfast waiting for him. He could have managed for himself. It seemed sometimes that no one was ever going to let him cook his own meals again. But Irimi doubled as security—Emio had vetted her, as she did anyone Brezan took to bed—and she insisted on tasting everything before he did. He had explained to her the ridiculousness of this procedure. Hell, Irimi had agreed that, given modern toxins, having a taster was pointless. But she said there was no harm in it either, and in certain matters she was a traditionalist.

The tea today came from a world Brezan had never heard of, and he couldn't pronounce its name, either. It had odd, subtle floral notes. Brezan's taste in tea ran to robust flavors, but he didn't mind expanding his palate. Besides, it kept Irimi happy. (He compensated by treating himself to hard liquors in the evening.) Breakfast was a sort of crepe with a nutty filling topped with vanilla cream. Privately, he thought the cream's sweetness overwhelmed the delicacy of the tea, but he wouldn't have dreamed of criticizing the pairing. Irimi could be touchy about that sort of thing.

Naturally, mid-meal Emio stuck her head in the room without knocking. "Hate to interrupt," she said, "but you need to take this call. Supersedes even the strike business."

Irimi drew herself up to her full height, which wasn't very, and stared at Emio. "Do the Shuos have no *manners*?"

"Not in my line of work," Emio said. Brezan had never quite been able to figure out how Emio and Irimi related to each other, a confusing combination of obligatory faction rivalry and camaraderie. Shuos-Andan feuding had been going on for centuries;

no reason why it should stop now. "You probably want to take this one from your office. Unless your relationship with General Khiruev is much closer than I thought it was."

Brezan made a face at her. He wouldn't have tolerated snide jokes about hawkfucking from anyone else. "I'm coming, I'm coming." He pulled on his socks and shoes, even though no one else was going to see them, and followed Emio out.

Governor Lozhoi had set Brezan up in a hastily emptied wing of one of her administration buildings. Brezan had made sure to send her a thank-you note in the nicest calligraphy he could produce. He needed her cooperation and he knew it. Her support hadn't smoothed all the problems in setting up a base of operations on Krauwer 5, but it had helped. They were down to student demonstrations and workers' protests only every other week, as Emio liked to say. After all, this latest business with the doctors wasn't Lozhoi's fault.

Brezan's so-called residence used to be two adjoining guest rooms. After getting used to variable layout while serving on Kel warmoths, it was still disconcerting to take stairs and walk down hallways to get to the office. There was a lift, but it was still on the list for repairs after a saboteur had jinxed the damn thing.

For a governor, Lozhoi had remarkably good taste in decor. Brezan was used to Kel ostentation and had told her so during his first week here. Lozhoi had looked at him thoughtfully, then said, "Well, it's true that it's useful to impress people with glitter once in a while, but sometimes asceticism has its uses too." As far as he could tell, she meant it. He'd seen her office, which was modestly outfitted, the only indulgence a carved wooden good-luck charm on the wall.

Lozhoi had not, however, stinted on Brezan's own office. High-quality furniture, well-made without being ostentatious; good lighting from a profusion of candlevines. The view wasn't great, but she hadn't had to explain to Brezan that this was for security reasons. After the time someone had thrown a homemade incendiary at him during one of his outings, he'd been twitchy around windows.

The guards greeted him with sober nods. He would never get used to the way they stiffened to attention whenever they saw him. *It's just me*, he wanted to say. *I'm no one special.* Except he'd chosen otherwise, and they'd never see him as just another Kel officer.

Emio preceded Brezan into the office and did a quick sweep. "Looks fine," she said. Brezan knew perfectly well that she wasn't so much worried about his safety as her professional reputation, but he appreciated her attentiveness all the same.

His desk was already piled with selected correspondence, *paper* correspondence, from concerned citizens who believed in the old-fashioned methods of petitioning officials. He had to recycle a terrifying quantity of letters every day, although he kept the nicer specimens of calligraphy just to look at. He'd have to go through the pile later. In the meantime, he logged into the secured terminal and said, "I'm told I have a call?"

"Connecting," the grid said blandly.

Moments later, it imaged the face of General Kel Khiruev. She was, at present, Brezan's senior general, a hilarious and not entirely comfortable turn of events. Brezan had once served as one of Khiruev's staffers. He hadn't *intentionally* wound up as her head of state cum superior officer.

The intervening years had treated Khiruev as well as could be expected, considering that she'd aged rapidly during the Hafn invasion two years ago. The dueling scars on her face stood out more lividly than ever against her brown skin, and she hadn't done anything about her shock of white hair. Then again, Khiruev had never been particularly vain of her appearance.

"High General," Khiruev said, not without humor.

"Don't you start," Brezan said. He had to avoid the temptation to treat her as though she would shatter. For a while there, formation instinct had made her brittle. But Cheris's calendar had changed that, he hoped for the better. The Kel in his government, which people had started calling the Compact, could choose to obey or disobey. It made all the difference. "What's going on now?"

"I wanted to update you on the Vonner Salient," Khiruev said.

Brezan closed his eyes. His augment coopted his proprioception to show him a map, completely unnecessarily. He knew about the Vonner Salient; had been reading briefings about it for the past several months. One of the systems in the Salient was a rich source of materials necessary to nurture growing voidmoths. One of his generals had been contesting the Salient, and losing. General Inesser— now Protector-General Inesser—wasn't stupid. She wanted those resources for her own realm, which styled itself the Protectorate.

The Vonner Salient wasn't the only place where such a conflict was playing out. Both the Compact and the Protectorate were in a race to build more warmoths to defend themselves. Brezan had fewer Kel, because most of them had found Inesser's traditionalism more attractive. His main advantage was that the Compact's less stringently regulated economy had already overtaken the Protectorate's in terms of production capacity even despite the hiccups in trade routes due to mothdrive malfunctions. Brezan had relaxed the regulations on the advice of the historian-soldier Devenay Ragath, who'd made a study of the economies of neighboring realms.

"Fine," Brezan said. "Give me the bad news."

"General Peo wants to know if he should cede the Salient," Khiruev said. "I have a databurst with his latest report—"

Brezan received the databurst in silence. Glanced over the highlighted sections. He already knew. Peo was, as far as Brezan could tell, a good and loyal Kel. Peo was also losing. And good and loyal Kel, especially ones with any modicum of tactical experience, weren't so common that Brezan could afford to throw away their service. He was impressed that Peo was consulting him at all. Habits of obedience, perhaps, even if Brezan was hardly in a position to stand in for Kel Command. He relied on Khiruev and, at Khiruev's suggestion, Ragath for strategic advice.

If the question was coming to him, though, it meant they'd gone beyond strategy to policy.

"You must have an opinion," Brezan said.

Khiruev shrugged. "My opinion, and Ragath concurs, is that we can't hold the Vonner Salient. The question is—" She smiled bitterly. "The question is, do we deny the key system to the Protectorate?"

"You don't mean—" But she wouldn't be demanding his time unless she did. "You want to blow it up."

"Well, not literally. But our swarm in the area does have a supply of fungal canisters."

"Oh," Brezan said.

Fungal canisters were one of the more recent and reviled additions to the Kel's arsenal of nasty weapons. "Fungus" was not, strictly speaking, accurate. Nirai researchers had derived the organism from creatures that dwelled beyond the ordinary world, in gate-space. Brezan was no engineer, but he had a basic familiarity with the canisters' capabilities. They could contaminate an entire world, causing ecological damage that would take centuries to repair.

"That system," Brezan said slowly, after it was clear that Khiruev wasn't going to add anything, "is inhabited. Not by a huge population, as these things go, but still, it's a significant number of people. How the hell are we going to sell ourselves as an attractive alternative to the Protectorate if we—" He couldn't say it.

Khiruev's dark eyes were merciless. "It's not a *good* option," she agreed. "But we're fighting to survive. Inesser's general has committed a great number of troops to securing the main mining platforms."

Brezan stared down at the desk. His hands, black-gloved, had clenched into fists, the material straining at his knuckles. *Someone has to make the ugly decisions*, he thought. He'd volunteered to be that person.

It had seemed so easy, so simple, when he'd first agreed to Cheris's revolution. Broadcast the new calendar. Let people choose their new governments. But Cheris had vanished, leaving him to oversee the world they'd made together.

Now I know better, Brezan thought.

"High General?" Khiruev said.

"Do it," Brezan said. The words scratched his throat on the way out. "You know me, I'm not a weapons expert. But you are. Fuck up the orbital platforms. Deny them to Inesser. In particular, we can't afford for her to resume cindermoth production before we do."

Understatement. Inesser controlled four of them, while Khiruev had ceded the *Hierarchy of Feasts* to a field general.

"Understood," Khiruev said. "It's the sensible decision."

"You have reservations." He could tell from the deepened lines around her mouth.

"Who wouldn't?" Khiruev said. "The day we stop having second thoughts is the day we've lost."

"Pretty words," Brezan said, "but they won't do a damn thing for the people who die."

"It's war," Khiruev said. "People always die."

Brezan made a moue. "I won't keep you from your job. Burn brightly, General."

"Burn brightly," she echoed, and signed off.

FOUR HOURS LATER, after he'd gotten through the meeting with the doctors (fruitless), Brezan was firmly ensconced in a bar in one of the university districts. Brezan had always found that students knew all about cheap ways to get drunk. As head of state, he felt it was incumbent upon him to economize. Despite this, both Lozhoi and Emio conspired to keep him awash in specialty liqueurs. Brezan was weak enough to use them for cooking once in a while (the guest suite boasted a compact kitchen area), mostly because it scandalized his handlers.

Brezan had lost count of the drinks he'd had. He was discovering that the anti-intoxicants that he ingested every day as a matter of course took real determination to defeat. At this point he was starting to feel a pleasant buzz. He meant to continue until he achieved oblivion.

The bar itself sported cheap decor of the sort you could order off anyone with a matter printer, with rococo curlicue designs that probably had a name that someone with a background in art history would recognize. Brezan's youngest father, a children's illustrator, almost certainly would have known. Thinking of him put Brezan in a bad mood. Besides Miuzan, no one in his family had contacted him since his so-called promotion. Given how the conversation with Miuzan had gone, that was just as well.

Most of the bar's clientele seemed to be students, no surprise there. Maybe the occasional instructor or instructor's aide. By now he'd gotten a better idea of civilian fashion trends in Tauvit and how different people dressed. He'd taken the entirely ineffectual precaution of wearing one of the gaudy embroidered jackets that the locals favored so much.

Brezan's next drink arrived. He stared at it blearily, then decided it was time to take a piss. His bladder could only take so much of this abuse.

"Watch my drink," Brezan said to the bearded young man sitting next to him. The young man didn't deign to acknowledge this and continued chatting up a bored-looking alt about... breeding miniature trees? Not his hobby of choice, but also not his problem.

The restroom in back smelled of overly strong antiseptic. One servitor was hard at work scrubbing someone's vomit off the floor. Another was removing graffiti, drawn with eyeliner, from the wall.

"Mind if I take a look at that before you get rid of it entirely?" Brezan said to the second servitor, a mothform.

The mothform blinked blue acquiescence and hovered out of the way.

Brezan had a dim awareness that he shouldn't be drawing attention to servitors in public, and that he had no way of knowing this particular servitor's affiliation. In the ordinary course of affairs he avoided talking to them, period. General Khiruev was the one who served as liaison to the Kel servitors. She had, however, emphasized to Brezan that just as humans weren't united, neither were the servitors. Brezan tried not to think too hard about that. In any case, if anyone looked at him funny, he could pretend to be drunk.

The graffiti was written in one of the local low languages. Brezan recognized the script, which was some fancy syllabary. He snapped a photo of it and sent it to his augment for later investigation. While he did have a theoretically secure connection to the governor's administrative grid, he didn't want to deal with it right now. And he didn't trust the city's public grid at all.

"You going to piss that away?" a voice said from behind Brezan.

Brezan turned around, quelling his instinct to punch out the speaker. Because that would end so well. "What's it to you?" he said.

The speaker was either a student or faking it very well. He had a cloud of curly hair and an olive complexion complicated either by decorative indigo-dyed scars or some kind of medical condition, Brezan couldn't tell which. "Well," the student said, "I thought for a while there you were about to throw up, but you don't look *that* drunk."

"Good to know," Brezan said.

"What the hell are you doing messing with us in the university district, anyway? We don't want you here."

"Yes," Brezan said dryly, unsurprised that the student had identified him, "a number of you have made that quite clear. Honestly, it made more sense"—he scrabbled for a number—"five drinks ago."

"Well," the student said, "then you can buy *me* one. I'm broke."

It would at least be a distraction from the moral bankruptcy of his decision four hours past. "Sure," Brezan said, "why not. Just one moment."

After he'd relieved his bladder, they sauntered out of the restroom together. Several people arguing about a drama looked up, gave Brezan distinctly hostile stares, then resumed their discussion. Brezan slid his drink across the bar to the student. "I hope you like that stuff," he said.

"I like anything that's free," the student said, and tossed the liqueur back. "Your government's terrible, has anyone told you that?"

Brezan snorted. "I don't think anyone thinks it *isn't* terrible." He resisted the urge to add "young man" to the end of the sentence. At fifty-three years, he wasn't all that old by hexarchate standards, which was part of the problem. Even Lozhoi had decades on him, which made it a miracle that she took him seriously.

"Oh, I don't think you understand," the student said. He finished the liqueur. "Do you have any more of this stuff? It's better than the swill I usually drink." His scars-tattoos-whatever had now brightened to a dull magenta.

"Are your personal decorations supposed to be doing that?" Brezan said, deciding that this was not a conversation where tact was going to be a major feature.

"Oh, yes," the student said. "I paid extra for that. Had to save from my stipend and all that for the mod. You're not supposed to spend on frivolous shit, but what good is life without some frivolous shit?"

Brezan shrugged and gestured at the bartender. The bartender yawned and sidled over to refill the glass. At that point, the student and the bartender either began flirting with each other or holding a passionate debate on the fluctuating reliability of public transportation.

He was starting to relax for the first time all day when the door burst open: Emio, accompanied by a woman and a man that Brezan recognized as Shuos security despite their shabby clothes. ("We save the flashy red-and-gold uniforms for when we're trying to be targets," Mikodez had explained to Brezan a lifetime ago. "In real life, you think we *like* being shot at?")

"High General," Emio said, "I need you to—" Her gaze fell on the student with the now-blue facial scars, which were glowing faintly. "High General, step away from him *now*."

Brezan might have been drunk, and he might be one of the more notorious crashhawks in Kel history, but he knew when to follow an order. He dove out of the way, tripped over a shoe someone had surreptitiously taken off, and went sprawling. He slammed hard into the floor and saw a bright red glare in his field of vision as the sudden fall tripped the automatic medical diagnostics.

Meanwhile, the student backed away from Emio and her fellow agents, made a dreadful choking noise, and collapsed into a heap. The glass tumbled to the floor and shattered. The reek of liqueur grew even stronger.

Despite the blood dripping from his nose, Brezan scrambled to his feet. "Get medical attention," he said, or thought he said. It was hard to speak clearly through the bubbling froth in his mouth.

One of the Shuos agents had already reached the student. "Dead," she said. "This establishment is under interdict. Meanwhile—"

"On it," Emio said. "High General, let's get you out of here."

"The *student*—" Absurdly, he couldn't seem to think of anything but the scars, which were now glowing brightly. *Where have I seen that*—

"I'll debrief you when we get you home," Emio said in a sharp undertone. "Come on."

Brezan spent the ride home in a daze. Emio applied first aid to the broken nose, including a painkiller, although Brezan was too stunned by events to notice much of the pain. He stared out the flitter's windows as the city receded below them. Fog had rolled in from the river that bisected it, and the gray blur suited his mood.

"My bad judgment," Emio said once she'd gotten him into his office.

"As I recall," Brezan said, "I'm the one who went out to get drunk." He had made a hash of that too, but he wasn't going to admit to that unless pressed.

"Oh," Emio said, as he had known she would, "we were on site keeping an eye on you. Should have said something when—" Her mouth tightened, and she looked away.

Brezan's head was starting to pound. "Do tell. It's the student, wasn't it? What the fuck was that, an allergic reaction?"

Emio met his eyes. "Yes, but not the way you're thinking. His name won't mean anything to you, although I can get you his profile. The relevant part is that he belonged to the Student Calligraphers' Society."

Brezan remembered that from one of the many briefings on protest groups. "Fuck. The corpse calligraphers."

Corpse calligraphy was frowned on in polite society, but it had survived as a practice for centuries despite the hexarchate's attempt to stamp it out. As Brezan's fathers had explained to him when he was a child, the regime had never gotten over the embarrassing fact that one of the Andan hexarchs had practiced it. And one of the more successful and long-lived ones, at that.

Brezan queried the grid for a translation of the graffiti he'd seen, relying on its interpolation to figure out the bits that the servitor had already erased. That was when the realization hit him. "The same slogan, or phrase, or whatever the hell," he whispered. The scars on the student's face had lit up in the same script.

The grid finally spat out the translation: *As I chose my death, let the people choose their rulers.*

Brezan looked up at Emio. "That means—"

"Suicide calligrapher," Emio said, unsentimental. "This is a new development. I should have been prepared."

"Oh, quit with the fucking self-recriminations," Brezan said, painfully aware of the hypocrisy of his saying that to anyone else. "I'm physically safe. The issue is public relations, isn't it?"

Emio smiled thinly. "You're learning."

"Not fast enough." Definitely a headache. Out of a possibly misguided sense of self-punishment, he didn't reach for a painkiller, which he was going to regret soon. "If I wanted to drown my sorrows, I should have picked a less public way to do it. Instead of exposing myself to a suicide calligrapher. Because I'm going to be blamed for the death. And if there's one, there will be more. Am I right?"

She didn't shield him from the truth. "There were one to three suicide calligraphers in every district that hour. They coordinated this. I advise you not to bother trying to cover it up. Rumor has wings, as they say."

"Emio," Brezan said, putting his head in his hands, "what the fuck did I do so wrong that a bunch of kids are killing themselves to become corpse pamphlets?"

"Wrong?" she said. "No more wrong than anyone else who comes in and tries to change the way things have always been done. No more right, either."

"That ends today," Brezan said, springing up despite her frantic attempts to get him to sit back down. "I have to do better than this. If it means sitting down every day in the middle of the university district and listening to what they have to say to me, I'll do that. If it means bringing in riot police, I'll do that too. Whatever it takes."

"You don't get it," Emio said. "There's no easy answer. There never has been. Just hard work. Even the Andan know that."

He didn't respond to the limp attempt at humor. "Then the work I've been doing hasn't been enough. That changes now."

"Fine," Emio said. "Fine. If that's what you want, that's what we'll do. But burning yourself out won't do anyone any favors, either."

"Out," Brezan said. "I want to talk to Mikodez." In real life, he knew that Mikodez was a busy man and that he was, in all likelihood, going to have to wait to talk to him. But if anyone knew how to deal with people doing stupid things because they hated you, it would be Mikodez.

Emio didn't argue. She put in the call, then withdrew.

Brezan dozed off while waiting for it to go through. Three hours passed before he received a response.

"High General," Mikodez said. "Emio told me about what happened."

Of course she had. Brezan couldn't work up any outrage. She was doing her job, after all.

"I didn't want the boy to die," Brezan said. He was shocked by how raw his voice sounded.

"No," Mikodez said, more gently than Brezan had expected. "I don't imagine you did. But for love of little foxes, don't let on that it hurts you so much. They'll use it against you if they figure that out."

"I have to fix this," Brezan said. "All of this. I'm tired of people dying for stupid reasons. The corpse calligraphers could have sent me a letter, or gathered outside the government building and chanted protest songs. Suicide? Really?"

Mikodez regarded him for a moment, then put his chin in his hands. "A few years after I took the seat," he said, "several senior administrators—not Shuos, but Shuos-affiliates that we depended on for operations in the remoter marches—threatened suicide if I didn't cede my position to their favored candidate."

"What did you do?"

"I called their bluff. Said favored candidate, given a choice between my assassins and a comfortable post at one of the academies, chose the posting. Every so often he still contemplates moving on me, but that's just habit. If he gets serious, he'll lose his head so fast he won't have time to blink."

"Yes," Brezan said bleakly, "except the students weren't bluffing, and I'd rather not resort to assassins."

"Learn to separate rhetorical techniques from the content of the argument," Mikodez said.

"Coordinated suicide isn't a *rhetorical technique*, Mikodez."

"That's debatable," Mikodez said. "Certainly they intended it as such."

"How do you endure this?" Brezan asked. "Any of this?"

"Ah," Mikodez said, "that's a different question." His expression sobered. "Knitting and crochet and a good supply of candies, mostly. You like cooking, don't you? Find more time to do that. Have dinner with friends when you can."

Brezan stared at him.

"I'm being entirely sincere," Mikodez said. "The presence of atrocity doesn't mean you have to put your life on hold. You'll arguably be better at dealing with the horrible things you have to witness, or even to perpetrate, if you allow yourself time to do the small, simple things that make you happy. Instead of looking for ways to destroy yourself."

"Maybe that works if the only thing you have for a heart is a hard ice shell," Brezan retorted.

Mikodez took no offense, as Brezan had known would be the case. "And yet I've been here doing this job for decades," he said mildly, "and I haven't shot myself in despair at the impossibility of the task. Are you going to give up now, or will you find some way to persevere?"

"I'll keep going," Brezan said. "I have to. If it means becoming more like you, then so be it."

CHAPTER NINE

It HADN'T TAKEN long for Dhanneth to pack Jedao's belongings. Jedao refrained from doing it himself, on the grounds that it would offend Dhanneth's sense of propriety. At least there was little to pack since the beautiful furnishings weren't, to his relief, coming with him.

Who am I kidding? Jedao thought, eyeing the duffel bag. He owned a modest allotment of clothing, nothing more. At some point there had even materialized a small selection of civilian clothes. He'd checked the grid and learned that they conformed to current fashion in polite society, always reassuring.

A group of six servitors arrived and whistled at Jedao. He ignored them despite feeling rude about it because he'd learned that everyone else did so.

Still, Dhanneth must have read his discomfort. "Sir," he said, "they're just station servitors. They're here to transfer your belongings."

The servitor in the lead made an affirmative buzzing. The rest of them worked efficiently to transfer the duffel bag. The task didn't require that many of them, but maybe the servitors doubled as defense. One more thing he should ask the grid about when he got a chance.

Kujen showed up shortly afterward. Four Kel and two Nirai accompanied him. The Kel, regular soldiers, were resplendent in full formal, gold braid and epaulets gleaming: two men and two women, matched in height, with similar sculpted faces. The kind of irrelevant detail Kujen would select for.

The two Nirai, on the other hand, didn't resemble each other, and their clothes didn't match, either. The taller one had rolled-up sleeves, as though they'd been diving into the guts of some unlucky machine. Kujen would have picked them for ability, not looks.

"Hexarch," Jedao said, and nodded at the Kel. "Your names?" The Kel recited them.

Kujen tolerated this. "I'm glad everyone's ready," he said. "Let's go. I will miss the opportunity to eat decent food in public without incurring disapproving stares from everyone, but it can't be helped."

Dhanneth had briefed Jedao on what to do. Jedao fell in behind the two Nirai, wondering peripherally what would become of the extravagant suite he'd vacated.

"For love of stars above," Kujen said, stopping dead in his tracks, "what are you doing all the way back there?" His gaze swept to Dhanneth. "I might have guessed."

"I'm sorry," Jedao said, "was there some other way you wanted to do this?"

"Kel Command can't censure you over protocol," Kujen said, "and I can't talk to you if you're hanging back there."

I should be grateful, Jedao thought. *Why aren't I grateful?*

This time variable layout came as less of a shock, especially since he'd had a chance to speculate about all the ways you could use it to set traps. (The grid had been disarmingly uninformative about the topic.) His othersense continued to operate, but Jedao had learned how to shove it into the background so it became less of a distraction.

They arrived at their destination quickly enough, the bay where their shuttle awaited them. Jedao forced himself not to slow down, despite his distrust of the unfamiliar space and its vastness. If Kujen had inadequate security, they were doomed anyway.

Jedao admired the shuttle's sleek form. It was black, painted over with silver filigree in abstract swirling patterns. More importantly, he noted the apertures for its defensive armaments, worked cunningly into the patterns like blossoms.

An announcement blared over hidden speakers. Kujen led them straight onto the shuttle, whose ramp was already lowered. Inside, there were one-way windows everywhere, shaped like moths' wings and engraved at the edges with yet more swirling patterns. Jedao was increasingly of the opinion that the Andan should have hired Kujen for his love of beauty and kept him happy with a few engineering projects on the side.

Kujen arranged himself gracefully in the middle seat on one side. Webbing emerged to secure him. Jedao startled, then remembered that Dhanneth wouldn't sit until he did, and the shuttle wouldn't set off until everyone was webbed. He took the seat across from Kujen's and tried not to show discomfort at the restraints.

Behind Kujen's head, the stars moved. Jedao said in astonishment, "I can't feel the acceleration." The station's bulk, with its bewilderment of lights and angles and protrusions, dwindled behind them.

"Physics is for the weak," Kujen said.

The corner of Dhanneth's mouth twitched.

Jedao didn't feel the shuttle docking, either, although he enjoyed the view of the *Revenant* as they approached. He strained to discern the black-and-silver shape against the scatter of stars. Then he couldn't stop the quickening of his pulse at its feral beauty.

Curious, he *reached* with his othersense, wondering what the *Revenant* would look like. He received a bewildering impression of a great mass containing many smaller, moving masses, an architectural maze of mazes. Still beautiful, but vastly more complex than it appeared from the outside.

He's trained you well, but thank you.

Jedao froze. The voice had spoken in his head, sardonic, in a timbre like tarnished bells. *Who are you?*

Who do you think? It sounded impatient this time.

The moth?

Yes.

Wait a second. *Moths talk?* he demanded. He'd known vaguely that they had biological components. But he'd never followed through with that thought to the idea that moths might be sentient.

And if that was true, did he have any right to be on the moth, giving it orders through its crew?

Pay attention to the hexarch, the *Revenant* said. *We'll speak later.*

I'm going mad already, Jedao thought, chilled. One more thing to conceal.

In the meantime, they'd finished docking. Kujen was watching him, his eyes musing. "I remember the first time I saw a voidmoth properly harnessed," he said. "So much experimentation, just to get to that point. Some deaths, too. But it worked."

"'Harnessed'?" Jedao said.

"Remind me to show you around Engineering sometime," Kujen said. "You can get a glimpse of the control interface for the harnessing system."

He understood what Kujen referred to in fragments. Like the station, the voidmoth's essential heart consisted of living tissue to which manufactured components had been affixed. He'd never before considered that the voidmoth's living core might need... *persuasion* to fly. Or how the voidmoth itself might feel about that.

Asking Kujen about the latter was too dangerous. On the other hand, he could try asking the *Revenant* itself, at a safer time.

Kujen unwebbed and rose. Jedao fumbled for the catch, found it, followed suit. They exited the shuttle into one of the *Revenant's* bays. Jedao was dismayed when the Kel present halted what they were doing to salute him. He returned their salutes and waved for them to resume their work.

"Command center next," Kujen said.

Jedao couldn't tell whether the hallways reflected Kujen's decadent tastes or, possibly, Kel tradition. Ashhawks soared everywhere upon silk scrolls, black ink with highlights in gold. If he ever ran short of operating funds, he could sell the decor.

The size of the command center confounded Jedao's expectations, even having seen the moth's blueprints. Charts and status displays cast colored light across the faces of the crew. Logistics—Kel Luon— had not yet noticed their entrance. She was comparing two screens as she muttered about pickles.

Commander Talaw bowed to Kujen on behalf of the crew. "Hexarch," they said. And to Jedao: "Sir." Their hostility had not dwindled, but at least they were observing the correct forms.

Jedao saluted Talaw, who saluted back. "Time to set out, Commander," Jedao said, and sat down. Dhanneth had taught him how to pipe others' displays to his own, which was less intrusive than hovering over their stations. For practice, he checked on Logistics. Sure enough, Luon was double-checking the command moth's supply of cabbage pickles.

"Move orders, sir?" Talaw said crisply.

Jedao set up the not-formation he desired on his terminal, then passed the diagram to Talaw and the Navigation officer, a narrow-faced lieutenant. "There you go," he said, carefully pleasant, and waited for the moth commanders' acknowledgments to come in.

The panel lit with the array of gold lights representing the swarm moths. They were headed to the gas giant in Isteia System by a snaking route, based on Strategy's assessments of where scan coverage was weak. According to Kujen, a "fascinating" percentage of the original Kel listening posts had blown up in a shoot-out between the Protectorate and the Compact shortly after the hexarchs' assassinations.

Talaw and Navigation consulted on some matter relating to mothdrive resonances and a region of space known for its calendrical fluctuations. They came to a consensus and relayed the move orders to the rest of the swarm by way of Communications. "Anything further, sir?" Talaw said.

"That should do it for now," Jedao said.

Jedao and Kujen stayed on for the entire first shift. "Let's go," Kujen murmured to Jedao, who had been acclimating himself to every readout he could get his terminal to produce.

Jedao couldn't say no, so he said to Talaw, "Call me if we run into anything." Dhanneth, who had kept silent the whole time, fell in to Jedao's left.

Jedao caught a fleeting expression on Commander Talaw's face as they watched Dhanneth: anguish. It vanished just as soon as he noticed it. *Did I accidentally steal Talaw's aide?* Jedao wondered.

More ashhawks on the walls. Sometimes Jedao thought he glimpsed a fluttering, as of banners, out of the corner of his eye. He followed Kujen in a loop four times. Upon each repetition, the lights grew more and more amber.

"Your quarters," Kujen said, pointing at the doors they had stopped in front of. He needn't have said anything. The doors were marked unambiguously with the Deuce of Gears.

"Good," Jedao said. He thought about asking Kujen for a private word so he could ask about whatever was going on between Talaw and Dhanneth, then reconsidered. He'd have to figure it out himself. "I shan't take up any more of your time."

Kujen bowed mockingly to him, too deeply, and left him to it.

THE FIRST THING Jedao did was survey his quarters. They were well-furnished but, thankfully, less extravagant than the ones on the station they'd departed. He'd tested all the furniture to make sure it was bolted in place. While he hadn't found any obvious bolts, he also hadn't been able to shift any of the larger items. Good enough.

Jedao spent most of the hour before his first high table pacing in his quarters and reviewing his staffers' qualifications. Few surprises, except in the sense that everyone was a surprise. He was sure that even if he keeled over dead, they'd carry on and wallop the hostiles.

Then he got to the real mystery: Major Dhanneth. Dhanneth's profile contained little information. He'd been born Eurikhos Dhanneth, one of four children. In his youth he'd wanted to be an artist, but his parents had Kel ties and had pushed him in that direction. He was divorced; had a single adult child, with whom he had not communicated for a decade.

More vexingly, Dhanneth was old for his rank, at sixty-five years. His profile showed no particular commendations, no particular demerits. Kujen wouldn't have selected an incompetent, and indeed, Jedao so far had no cause to complain of Dhanneth's performance. (As if he knew what the hell a good aide was supposed to be like.)

The conclusion Jedao couldn't help coming to was that Kujen was hiding information from him. Maybe not with bad intent, true. Maybe Dhanneth was secretly an elite assassin-bodyguard. Certainly he had the physique of someone who could wrestle dragons into submission. But why would Kujen need to hide Dhanneth's credentials from Jedao?

Maybe Dhanneth is supposed to kill me if I become inconvenient, Jedao thought. That sounded more likely. Either way, a puzzle.

One more thing. Jedao nerved himself by taking a deep breath, then asked the grid for any information it had on one Vestenya Ruo.

"No person of that name is on record," the grid replied.

He was sure he had the name right. "Shuos Academy cadet around 826, high calendar?" He tried to recall other useful details that might help with the search, like Ruo's family. Nothing.

"No person of that name is on record," the grid said again.

Well, it had been worth a try. Besides, he supposed that Shuos Academy wasn't in the habit of handing over cadet records to the Nirai or to Kel warmoths.

"Major Dhanneth is at the door," the grid said.

Jedao consulted his augment: almost time for high table. "Let him in."

The doors opened. Dhanneth saluted him. "Ready, sir?"

"I want a watch," Jedao said.

"Sir?"

"It's odd having a built-in clock, that's all."

"No one makes them anymore," Dhanneth said.

"Of course," Jedao said, a little sadly. He should have realized that just looking at people's wrists. "Let's go."

They weren't the first to reach the high hall, but rank meant everyone else was captive to his schedule. Five minutes early: well within what the Kel considered acceptable. Jedao had a brief impression of ashes and hellsparks and unsmiling eyes as the Kel rose. Jedao saluted them, waited while they returned the gesture, then proceeded to his seat. He could tell because of the dreadful golden Deuce of Gears cup. Maybe it was meant as a backup projectile if anyone boarded the command moth.

Dhanneth slid into place down at the end of the table, his face composed. If this was what formation instinct did for you, Jedao wanted some for himself. The officers at the head table inclined their heads to him as they took their seats. Notably, they avoided looking at Dhanneth. Dhanneth was not doing a very good job of concealing his distress at the snub. Everyone else was watching the head table intently.

Jedao sat, determined not to be seen to hurry, and poured water from the provided pitcher into the cup. At least, it had better be water. He didn't want to get through this with the "help" of some intoxicant. Then he smiled before remembering what a bad idea it was. His officers stiffened. He made himself take the requisite sip as if he hadn't noticed. (The cup was every bit as heavy as it looked. Definitely a projectile.) They couldn't spend the entire voyage flinching from each other. Not that he expected the Kel to warm to him, but they needed to achieve a working relationship sooner rather than later. Kel hierarchy meant that he had to make the overtures.

The water's cold left his mouth numb and made his teeth ache. He passed the cup to his right. Commander Talaw received it with a steady hand. Around the table the cup went, refilled once halfway. Dhanneth took the last sip, a very small one. Again, no one looked at him except Jedao. Were elite assassin-bodyguards reviled that much? Jedao was starting to feel bad for Dhanneth.

The rest of the Kel soldiers in the hall eased little by little as the ritual continued. Still, the silence had the potential to become smothering. Jedao didn't want to reveal the extent of his amnesia, although odds were that he'd slip and it'd come out anyway, so he said, "This is a stupid thing to be dying of curiosity about, but what is in these rolls?" Some of the Kel had been peering at the wrappers. He could play on mutual suspicion of unfamiliar rations.

Talaw's executive officer, Lieutenant Colonel Meraun, calmly took one of the rolls to her plate and dissected it with her chopsticks. This revealed either a purple vegetable or mushrooms, hard to tell. The other officers' reactions ranged from bemusement to resignation. "The servitors are getting creative again, sir," Meraun said. "The hexarch's bases don't carry the same staples that Kel logisticians are used to. So the servitors must have made compromises."

So the servitors did all the cooking? Did they do all the cleaning, too, and the nasty chores that you'd ordinarily use to punish people with too many demerits? Why did the servitors put up with this? Were they sentient at all, or if they were sentient, did they have formation instinct, too?

His list of questions that he couldn't ask anyone around him was only getting longer. Instead, he asked, "What were you expecting in that roll instead?"

Meraun rattled off a list of vegetables. She smiled suddenly and added, "If you're waiting for a poison-taster—"

The officer next to Meraun had gone expressionless in her direction. Jedao smiled just as hard back at Meraun and obtained his own roll from the platter. "I'm sorry," he said, "are you starting a food fight with a Shuos? I hear our aim isn't as good as yours."

He'd said something wrong. People had recoiled as though he'd been sarcastic, and not just one or two of them, but the entire room, although he'd meant the words literally. *Am I secretly a crack shot? Because I'm so likely to get into a firefight on my command moth.* To distract them, he took a bite of the roll and made a face at its bitterness. It wouldn't hurt for them to see that he had ordinary human reactions to food.

Dhanneth said reluctantly, "Sir, you may find the fishcakes more to your liking."

A fleeting hint of frustration passed over Talaw's face when Dhanneth spoke. They deliberately looked away from him.

What is going on? Jedao wondered, except he still couldn't come out and ask. "Thank you," he said, because he didn't like the fact that the Kel were showing open disrespect to his aide. "I'll try that."

At least the business of chewing meant this line of conversation could die an honorable death. Dhanneth was right. The fishcakes tasted bland, but if you used the sour-sweet dipping sauce judiciously, they became palatable. Jedao tried a little of everything in the hopes of finding something that didn't trigger the odd aftertaste, with no luck. Oh well, at least he was in no danger of starving.

Kujen swept in partway through the meal. He was splendid in a necklace of silver wire and agate, a shirt of sleek black silk, and a dark gray coat with a foam-rush of lace at the sleeves. The creases in his pants could have been used for rulers. Jedao hated to think how many closets it took to contain Kujen's wardrobe. The evidence suggested that he didn't like to repeat himself.

The high table didn't have a seat for the hexarch. Dhanneth rose immediately to offer his. The faces watching Kujen were intent as fire, the eyes of the Kel dark and unfriendly. The exception was the Strategy head, Ahanar, who stared at a far wall in obvious discomfort.

Jedao attempted to check Dhanneth, disliking the mood in the room. "I'm done," Jedao said to Kujen. "Take mine instead."

The Kel tensed further, except for Meraun, who reached for another roll as she looked at Jedao, Kujen, and Dhanneth with the air of an interested festival-goer, and a captain at a lower table who was compulsively stabbing a recalcitrant cucumber with her chopstick.

"It's not necessary, sir," Dhanneth said. This should have settled the matter. Instead, the tension increased.

"I'll judge that," Jedao said. He had meant to speak mildly. The way Dhanneth's dark face stilled told him he had failed.

Kujen intervened. "I won't make a habit of this," he said to Jedao, "because high table is high table, but I need to speak to you and it can't wait."

Jedao didn't believe that in the slightest. He would have liked to stay and fumble his way through the rest of dinner despite the prickly atmosphere, because he couldn't spend the rest of the voyage avoiding his own officers. On the other hand, he couldn't refuse the hexarch, either. He excused himself. The hush that followed them was frosty.

Kujen's own silence made Jedao edgy all the way back to Kujen's conference room. Kujen paused in the doorway after it opened. Jedao looked around the room, which was appointed with fantastic models of buildings, all bird-curves and starry angles and tiny glittering windows. Then Kujen stalked into the room and pivoted on his heel. Jedao entered and sank to his knees in the full obeisance to a hexarch.

Kujen sat on his haunches and laid a hand on Jedao's shoulder, feather-light. He peered into Jedao's face. "I had assumed that your lack of research on the topic meant that you remembered after all," he said.

"Remembered what?" Jedao said. And what did this have to do with dinner?

"I was listening in on your idea of light conversation," Kujen said. "People are afraid that if they upset you, you'll slaughter them. Get up and let's sit in actual chairs. My knees are not fond of deep bends anymore."

Kujen leaned back in a chair upholstered in violet-black velvet. Jedao took the one across from him. It looked like someone had painted its platinum-colored snowflake-and-bird designs with a one-haired brush. How much luxurious furniture did Kujen own anyway? Jedao hoped he never took it for granted.

"Fine," Jedao said, accepting the reprimand for what it was. "I'll call up some documentaries. Or a book." Being a general required a lot of paperwork, but he could schedule it in.

Kujen massaged his temples.

"All right," Jedao said, "something I said bothered you. Explain it to me in words of one syllable."

"So you don't remember Hellspin."

"Obviously not."

"I am not used to this," Kujen said, "and normally I am better at accounting for variables than this. But there's a first time for everything." He sounded displeased with himself. "Jedao, you're not a blank sheet of paper, even if you can't remember large chunks of your history. You have skills, you have preferences, you have flaws, a personality. The difference is that people who know their own past have a chance of figuring out their own failure modes and how to avert them, and most of them don't manage that even so. As far as I can tell, you're operating on instinct. You have no way to prepare for your own reactions."

"You can't hide the records from me forever," Jedao said.

"Let's start slow," Kujen said. "You already know about the gloves, which are unavoidable, and the Deuce of Gears. There are also the threshold winnowers."

"Threshold winnowers?"

"They're bombs," Kujen said, "that kill living things within the gate radius without damaging nonliving structures. The part that scares all the civilians is all the eyes and mouths that chew up the victims. That's just cosmetic. Dead is dead."

Jedao hid his revulsion. Kujen hadn't mentioned whether this chewing up happened before or after the victims perished. He had a bad feeling he knew the answer to that one. "Your design?"

"Yes."

Shit. "Are you going to let me have any?" Jedao asked, to gauge Kujen's reaction.

Kujen didn't answer that, which could mean either yes or no. "Next," he said. "During Hellspin, once the massacre was underway, you went on a rampage on your command moth. You shot a bunch of staff and soldiers and so on with a Patterner 52. That's—"

"I know what that is," Jedao said. "What the hell was someone in the Kel military doing with a Shuos handgun?" Sure, you could print up ammunition for it special, but didn't that sort of thing annoy Logistics?

"Special dispensation," Kujen said, "as a courtesy to the Shuos." His mouth curled in a sudden smile. "You were a known favorite of the Shuos heptarch."

Jedao wasn't sure he believed that. How could he have achieved that, anyway?

Kujen hadn't finished speaking. "Anyway, it figures you'd recognize your signature gun. I'm sorry I couldn't retrieve it for you, but the Shuos stole your gun collection a few decades ago just to piss off the Kel. I keep wondering if they mean to fence the lot, because the Shuos are notoriously always in danger of going broke. As far as I can tell, the collection is sitting in the Citadel of Eyes gathering dust, and I didn't want to test Mikodez's security."

"I forgive you," Jedao said, to cover his additional unhappiness at the idea that he'd have some reflexive attachment to a weapon he'd used to commit a massacre. "Is there anything else about Hellspin Fortress that I have a crushing need to know?"

"You weren't sane when Kel Command retrieved you," Kujen said. "Your memories from that period seemed to be hazy even before Cheris's interference."

Jedao turned his hands over and stared at the back of his gloves. He was used to them already. "Why did they retrieve me instead of executing me on the spot?"

"They wanted to figure out what had happened," Kujen said. "You'd been loyal up to that point. It came as a complete surprise. After that, they decided they still had uses for you, so you never received a proper court-martial. It's hard for people who aren't familiar with the records to appreciate this. Remember, originally it wasn't clear that you had been responsible for the slaughter. They thought it had been Lanterner agents, or another traitor."

"I appreciate the lesson," Jedao said. "So when you pulled me out of high table, it was because of the remark I made." *I hear our aim isn't as good as yours.*

"Yes," Kujen said. "I advise you to do some more homework before the next high table."

"Noted," Jedao said.

CHAPTER TEN

"THERE IT IS," Jedao said from the copilot's seat. He was peering at the scan subdisplay. "Station Ayong Primary."

In its time with Jedao and 1491625, Hemiola had been given free run of their vehicle, which Jedao called a needlemoth. "Free run" wasn't saying much. According to 1491625, this moth had been designed for two humans. One human and two servitors still made for a tight squeeze.

Jedao had provisioned the needlemoth with the kind of supplies one might expect from a former assassin. Ration bars, whose labels declared their Kel origins. ("Some of these are rated for over two centuries," Jedao said. "I hope never to put that to the test.") Spare ecoscrubber filters and spare extravehicular suits. A very small box containing personal effects. Hemiola took the liberty of scanning it. 1491625 didn't interfere. Within the box was an earring and old-fashioned watch decorated with a lot of gold-copper alloy. No explosives in the watch, although it couldn't rule out the possibility that Jedao was hiding a compound more sophisticated than its outdated sensors could detect.

And, of course, there was the scaling and rappelling gear. Everything Hemiola knew about those two endeavors came from a drama episode in which the heroine climbed a sheer cliff of frozen methane to rescue her friend-then-enemy-then-friend (or was it the other way around?). It doubted the portrayal bore much resemblance to reality.

"How often do you deal with this stuff anyway?" Hemiola had asked Jedao while they were bogged down in discussions of the merits of different solvents.

"You'll find out," Jedao said, not reassuringly. Then he squeezed past Hemiola to the back so he could use the commode.

Life on the needlemoth had settled into a pleasant routine. Hemiola approved of routines. 1491625 piloted. Jedao read and, occasionally, handled inconvenient human necessities like food, sleep, or exercise.

Hemiola hadn't been able to focus on Kujen's papers since the approach to Ayong Primary began, however. Ayong Primary dwarfed Tefos Base. Not surprising. According to Jedao, it housed a population of some 800,000 humans. "Sorry I don't have servitor figures," he had added. "I'd have to apply for that information from the local enclaves."

Ayong Primary must be crowded. Hemiola had compared the station's size to its population. Then again, it conceded that not all humans demanded as much space as a hexarch did.

"Ayong Primary Control," a bored voice came from the communications panel. "Steady there, *Swordfish 2*. Another seven degrees ought to do it."

Jedao laced his fingers together and stretched first to the left, then to the right, with a popping of vertebrae.

"Aren't you going to pay attention to that?" Hemiola demanded. What if they crashed into something? Or, more likely, something crashed into them? Especially since, according to 1491625, the needlemoth was running its stealth system.

"We're not *Swordfish 2*," Jedao said, "and 1491625 knows its job. You and I, however, have some work to do. Tell me, have you ever done extravehicular?"

Hemiola was startled into an answer. "There was that one episode of *Adventures Among the Glittering Worlds* where—"

"—the villain hopscotched between three different accelerating voidmoths using jet boots? And didn't flambé his feet or go cartwheeling head over heels in space?" Jedao sighed. "I've seen that episode. All right, so that's a no."

"Why are you bringing me along?" Hemiola asked cautiously.

"Enclave regulations. Humans they leave to human authorities, but you're not human, so..." Jedao shrugged. "And I'm dealing with the enclaves and not the human authorities for supplies and intel because people will recognize me and panic."

"Couldn't you have switched to another body?" Hemiola said. Neither the hexarch nor Jedao had ever explained how they were able to achieve this. Body modifications were mentioned casually in the hexarch's notes, though. (Context: a famous actor, fruitlessly courted by the Andan, changing their face according to their role.) "Or switched your face, at least?"

"That was my question, too," 1491625 said.

"Wouldn't help," Jedao said. "Not when there are people who can recognize me by my movement patterns alone."

"How many Kel Brezans can there be in the successor states anyway?" 1491625 said.

"There are plenty of people with kinesics recognition training, especially in Security. It'd be a bad gamble. I'd run into one pretty quickly."

"Who's Kel Brezan?" Hemiola said. It had never heard of them.

"An old friend of mine," Jedao said, his intonation implying a certain degree of ambivalence. "A good man, if an impetuous one. Not someone you want to mention on Ayong, by the way. Anyway, come with me."

After Jedao squeezed past it, Hemiola floated after him. "How do you propose to get onto the station, then?"

"I have some contacts," Jedao said. "It'll be tricky to reach them without getting caught." He slid a drawer open, pulled out a suit, and began checking it over with the dedication of someone who had witnessed what happened to people who ran out of air mid-mission. "1491625 is maneuvering us to the insertion point. The hard part is that we don't have the space to carry one of the larger burrowers."

"I'm not familiar with those."

"They're bred to tunnel into things," Jedao said. "Unfortunately, the only burrowers rated to get through this particular station's carapace are too big for us to haul. We're not set up for demolitions or construction or mining. So we're going to have to do it the hard way."

"The hard way?" Hemiola said faintly.

Jedao didn't respond for several moments, attention snagged by some fault in the suit. After fixing it, he inventoried the contents of a substantial utility belt before buckling it on. Once he'd sorted that out, he considered Hemiola. "I'm going to do the maneuvering," he said, "because I've got the training for it. Which means you're going to be strapped to me. We have spare webbing. Will it offend your dignity too much?"

Medical servitors had permission to wrangle humans. Of its old comrades, only Rhombus had had that kind of expertise, presumably in case of emergency. Kujen and Jedao had never made use of it, even when they played at knives with each other. Hemiola knew some basic first aid, but that was all. With any luck, none of that would prove necessary.

"I've found the webbing," Hemiola said, bringing out the spool. Jedao kept a well-organized moth.

"Good. You're going to be great at this. *I'm* the one who has to not fuck up."

Hemiola did not find this reassuring, especially since it remembered Jedao in earlier incarnations stumbling about Tefos Station, or banging into corners, or that one time he tripped over the hexarch's foot and went sprawling. The hexarch had been quite tolerant of this.

Jedao, not stupid, noticed Hemiola's hesitation. "You have misgivings. Speak up. Better now than later."

"Are you competent to carry out this type of mission?" Not like it could evaluate his fitness, but maybe Jedao would answer honestly.

Jedao grinned, unoffended. "I've done harder."

"What else do I need to know?"

"Once we get in, shadow me. We won't be hitting the usual thoroughfares, so with luck we won't run into any of the human locals. The complication here is that Ayong Primary hosts servitors from multiple enclaves. Pyrehawk *should* have treaties with most of them, but the political situation may be volatile."

Hemiola fluttered its lights noncommittally. It didn't understand why a human was relying on servitors' treaties for protection. Then again, it came from a tiny backwater enclave of three. Perhaps matters would come clear if it kept quiet and paid close attention.

"Assuming things haven't come unglued," Jedao went on, "I'm familiar with the local treaties. They'll have questions of their own for you, but as I'm not a servitor I don't know how that works."

Wonderful. "Are you sure I can't stay?"

"You might see something I don't," Jedao said. "Can you hover yourself up mid-back level, right where the oxygen pack is?"

Hemiola did so and suffered itself to be webbed to Jedao. Jedao was being careful not to impede the jets of the thrusters or his own limbs. Hemiola stifled its doubts about the setup. In an emergency, Hemiola could hover itself to safety, and it didn't need to breathe. It could even drag Jedao around if it had to, but short of medical cause, it needed his permission for that.

"Your needlemoth may have stealth," Hemiola said, "But I don't. Station scan will be able to see my power core. And you can't hide your heat signature, either. And if anyone's monitoring the number of servitors on the station—"

"The local enclaves' representatives will have procedures for that," Jedao said. "Ready?"

Hemiola's misgivings dwindled as Jedao bore it to the airlock. Clumsy as he might have been in his previous bodies, he'd shown no sign of awkwardness this time around. As Jedao cycled the airlock, it said, "Does the choice of body change how dextrous you are?"

"To an extent, yes." Some secret amusement lit his voice.

The hatch opened. Jedao eased out of the needlemoth. Not wanting to distract him, Hemiola shut up. One wrong move and they'd float into the yawning darkness of space.

At least the vista was spectacular. Even affixed to Jedao's back, passive sensors showed Hemiola a panorama of far-flung stars, and the distinct chirrup of a local pulsar. Two voidmoths, both of which dwarfed the needlemoth, were departing. Most of the traffic that stopped by Ayong Primary would be trademoths hauling cultural goods or delicacies for the rich. (A particular subplot in *A Rose in Three Revolutions* turned on trade routes.)

Jedao activated the thrusters with gesture commands picked up by his augment. After 3.7 seconds of acceleration to bring them to a comfortable traveling velocity, he deactivated them. Since its view of Ayong Primary was blocked by Jedao's back, Hemiola passed the time refining one of its old compositions. It liked to come up with alternate scores to drama episodes for practice, even if Rhombus had derided the practice as being disrespectful to the human composers.

They drifted toward the station for some time. Hemiola's chronometer told it how much time had elapsed, of course. Still, it often drifted into subjective time when it composed, and today was no different.

"Hold tight," Jedao said, the vibration of his voice buzzing faintly through the suit and the attached air supply, and against Hemiola's armor. He twisted around and applied the jets again to decelerate. Hemiola was treated to a sudden view of Ayong Primary up close, all planes and angles and glittering carapace, with stripes of light to guide docking voidmoths.

Jedao unhooked a safety line and grapnel from his utility belt. It was amazing how he could reach it despite the webbing. He hurled it at the station, engaging the jets simultaneously to counter his corresponding backward motion.

The grapnel made no sound when it latched onto Ayong Primary's surface. It had landed precisely at the edge of what appeared to be a maintenance chute. Hemiola's respect for Jedao's abilities increased. He hadn't made a single course correction.

Jedao pulled his way hand over hand along the line. Hemiola hunched motionless on Jedao's back. They were close enough now that there was little danger of torque swinging them into the station. And they were at no risk of colliding with one of the trademoths.

So why did it feel worried?

Jedao's motions slowed. He hung in space, legs tucked under

him. All he had to do was pull a little more and they'd arrive. Hemiola suppressed a flicker of dismay. Was he tiring? Would they be stranded out here, connected to the station by a mere fragile filament? If it had to do the unspeakably rude thing and rescue Jedao so close to his goal, would he ever forgive it?

Instead of crossing to the station's surface, Jedao studied a protrusion on it. Hemiola couldn't figure out what it was. Sensor array? Or worse, a turret?

Then the protrusion moved.

If it hadn't been for the risk of detection, Hemiola would have flashed all its lights in alarm. The only thing that kept it from backing away from the protrusion and dragging Jedao with it was Jedao's body language. He showed no sign of alarm.

Jedao was signing to the protrusion. It took Hemiola several moments to recognize it as a variant of Simplified Machine Universal. What it had taken for one of the human sign languages was, instead, a simple rendition of short-long sequences indicated by the fingertips of one hand. Jedao was being very careful with politeness levels. He'd said, "I am an envoy from Pyrehawk Enclave with a guest from Tefos Enclave. I request permission to enter Trans-Enclave territory."

The protrusion said in carefully dim lights, "You are welcome, Ajewen Cheris of Pyrehawk Enclave." Ah: it was a servitor, albeit of a type Hemiola had never seen before.

But *Ajewen Cheris*? Why was Jedao using a different name? Hemiola's misgivings flared anew.

"Thank you," Jedao said.

The stranger-servitor offered one of its grippers, which was so large that it could have crushed Jedao and Hemiola in half. Jedao took hold of the gripper's end and used it to hoist himself down. He retrieved the safety line and grapnel, and returned them to his utility belt. The stranger-servitor then led the way into the station.

The sides of the maintenance chute surrounded them. Hemiola blinked in alarm when the space around them juddered perpendicularly even though, as far as it could tell, they were still moving in a straight line. It turned on active scan. The stranger-servitor didn't stop it.

The station's space was twisted like a labyrinth composed of labyrinths in fractal detail. They were now in a section of the station with pressurized atmosphere and artificial gravity. For the first time, Hemiola was frightened. Neither Jedao nor the stranger-servitor was reacting to the uncanny warping of spacetime. In particular, the station's center housed a peculiar pulsing knot that opened into gate-space. If the knot swallowed them—

After eight more turns that weren't turns, they arrived in a storage unit. The unit had a locked door, which they had bypassed entirely. It contained tidy stacks of labeled crates. One of them said, CONTENTS UNDER PRESSURE. STORE RIGHT-SIDE UP. And, in newer paint: DO NOT INGEST.

"Who is your traveling companion?" the stranger-servitor said. "I've never heard of Tefos Base."

"Pardon the irregular arrangement," Jedao said, now speaking the high language aloud. He pulled out a knife and casually slashed through the webbing. "271828-18th, this is Hemiola of Tefos Enclave."

Hemiola hovered free. "Pleased to make your acquaintance," it said, as formally as possible.

"Likewise," 271828-18th said. "What is your enclave's affiliation?"

"We're a Nirai enclave," Hemiola said, "dedicated to preserving the hexarch's research."

271828-18th blinked its interest. "You'll have to tell me more about that later," it said.

"Yes," Hemiola said, although it wasn't sure how much more information the hexarch would have wanted shared.

Jedao said, "I don't suppose you have the next episodes of—"

271828-18th flashed its laughter. Hemiola couldn't help wondering if this was a distraction from the matter of Ajewen Cheris. "They're already on a data solid," 271828-18th said. "Did you think we'd forget how much you like dramas?" It indicated a small crate separate from the rest. "Plus ecoscrubbers. Air and water. Extra ration bars—Kel, since you specified, although you're the only person I know who likes them. And the rest of the equipment you asked for."

"Thank you."

"Now for you," 271828-18th said, flaring its lights in Hemiola's direction. "Tefos has no treaty with the Trans-Enclave."

"We report directly to the hexarch," Hemiola said, feeling stubborn. "Before this goes any further, I have a question."

Through the suit's faceplate, Hemiola could see Jedao smiling crookedly, as if he knew.

"Why did you address this individual"—Hemiola gestured at Jedao—"as Ajewen Cheris?"

"You must be very isolated," 271828-18th said, "if you didn't pick up on that a lot earlier. Still, if you're the de facto representative of your enclave"—Hemiola blinked acknowledgment—"then you're entitled to make an informed decision based on the facts." By this point Jedao's expression was resigned. "Ajewen Cheris, formerly Captain Kel Cheris, and also known as Shuos Jedao, is Pyrehawk Enclave's agent to assassinate Hexarch Nirai Kujen."

Jedao didn't waste time on swearing. Instead, he reached for something on his belt.

Hemiola didn't stick around to find out what he was going to pull. Instead, it sprinted for the opening through which they had entered. Behind it, it heard Jedao saying, in a remarkably mild voice, "You could have let me—" before his voice became inaudible.

It analyzed the labyrinthine passages and made the split-second decision to flee more deeply into the station, rather than back to the needlemoth. It could only assume that 1491625 shared Cheris's goals. Ayong Primary might not be safe, but better that than to continue traveling with someone who meant the hexarch ill.

The station swallowed it. Hemiola had never before had cause to dash so quickly, but its control systems, inherited from earlier servitors, guided it well. It received a kaleidoscope impression of lovingly polished walls, hand- and footholds for humans, lights;

periodic closets marked EMERGENCY SUITS; the occasional stray nook containing sculptures or flower arrangements for passers-by to contemplate. A number of humans spotted it and flattened themselves against the walls as it zoomed by.

Hemiola finally came to a stop in a closet unoccupied by humans or servitors. This area of the station was less well maintained than the others, with stray graffiti scratched into the floor. The scratches depicted cartoon animals armed with gardening tools. Under other circumstances, Hemiola would have puzzled over their meaning.

It surveyed its surroundings. What it had taken for a closet must in fact be someone's... home? To one side rested a thick quilted blanket, rolled up with a pillow atop it. There was a knee-level table to the other side, adorned only with a small meditation focus in the shape of a kneeling wolf. A chest of clothes in the corner. That was all.

Assured that it was safe for the moment, Hemiola tucked itself into an empty corner and brooded. How could it have been so naive? It should have suspected something was wrong the moment Jedao—Cheris—asked for a copy of the archives. By now they could have copied the data and broadcast it everywhere.

There was something worse than being betrayed by Cheris or Jedao or whoever they were. Face it, "Immolation Fox" didn't imply great things about their reliability no matter what guise they wore. No: it was the existence of not one but multiple servitors—a whole enclave, and a powerful one—that planned to destroy a hexarch.

Either something had gone badly rotten with servitor society, or something had gone even worse with the hexarch. But which?

Hexarchs (and heptarchs, back in the day) were by no means infallible. This much it understood. *A Rose in Three Revolutions* even featured a decadent, meddling, obstructionist heptarch (Shuos, of course). On the other hand, Hemiola had always believed that the servitors' role was to carry out background tasks, not to interfere with government. Had it been wrong all this time?

At least it had a copy of the hexarch's archives. It had rearranged its memory storage to make room for it, not difficult. Perhaps perusing them now would reveal something that would make the world make sense.

So deeply entangled was Hemiola in its reflections that the entrance of a human took it by surprise. More accurately, a gangly, tan-skinned girl barely into adolescence, her head shaved and her mauve robes frayed at the hem.

"Who are *you*?" the girl said in a distinctly hostile voice. "If you're also here to tell me that I'm overdue on my assignment, I already know that."

Hemiola levitated in the direction of the door, since its presence was clearly unwanted. Whoever she was.

"No, wait, stay," she said. "Tell me who you are. Which enclave are you from?"

She knew about enclaves? Hemiola couldn't tell whether this was good news or bad news. But it stopped. "Tefos Enclave," it said, using Machine Universal by reflex. "It's a Nirai enclave."

"Huh," she said, "never heard of it. Is it far away? I guess this is space, everything's far away."

She was fluent in Machine Universal. Upon reflection, if Cheris was, others could be too.

The girl set down her bag and kicked the wall, which reverberated dully. "It's been such a terrible day. I guess it's only universal justice that I'm sent an objective stranger to witness my failings, or something. I hate this paper and if I don't turn it in *tonight*, I'm out of the running for sure."

"Should I leave you to your paper?" Hemiola asked cautiously. Because if it didn't need to pay attention to this, it could be reviewing the hexarch's notes. On the one hand, it would be rude to ignore its host, especially considering it was an intruder. On the other, it wasn't sure that its host cared what it did so long as it provided a passive audience.

"Yeah, you didn't come all the way from Tefos"—she echoed the high language pronunciation with the hand sign for the name in Simplified Machine Universal—"just to help me procrastinate on this. But since you're here anyway, what do you think I should do? We have very few Nirai servitors on Ayong Primary, and my instructors are always going on about how objective truth can withstand assault from all directions and so on and so forth. Which is not the way Rahal tribunals work in real life, but it makes for pretty speeches, doesn't it?"

Hemiola blinked inquiringly at her. It didn't know much about the Rahal except by reputation. By now, however, it had figured out that she was studying to take the entrance examinations for Rahal Academy. It hoped she didn't expect it to help her with her paper. Among other things, Hemiola didn't have the faintest idea how rhetoric worked.

The girl stared at it, then sighed. "You're no help." Then she stomped over to another corner of the room, slumped against the wall, and slid down to sit sprawled against it, hugging her knees. "This is what I get for arguing with the magistrate-errant's judgment in class last week."

"What ruling?" Hemiola asked, perhaps unwisely.

"Ayong Primary's head magistrate originally ruled that one of the local observances was lawful," she said. "It caught the authorities' attention because a small group of people were practicing it shortly after one of the scheduled remembrances. It should have ended there, but we're cursed with an unusually tight-assed magistrate-errant, and when he reviewed the past year's cases, he picked that one to overturn. Now a bunch of perfectly ordinary people are in danger of being declared heretics." She kicked the wall again. "I should have kept my mouth shut about the whole thing, except it's so *stupid*. My grandparents are going to kill me. Assuming they don't send the Vidona after me when my essay proves less than acceptable."

Hemiola's bafflement turned to alarm when it detected the approach of another servitor. Where could it go, though? And how could it leave when this human girl had told it to stay?

Miserably, it held its position. The girl was scrubbing at her face. Oh, no, she was *crying*. Crying was something it had only seen humans do in dramas, and in dramas they did it much more prettily, at dramatic moments, with swelling music in the background. Instead, the girl was getting mucus on her sleeve, and Hemiola didn't understand the context, and it doubted she would appreciate it providing swelling music on her behalf.

Why didn't you tell me what to do? Hemiola thought, resenting not the girl—who, after all deserved the courtesy due a new-met stranger—but the hexarch and Jedao. It had never witnessed either of them doing anything as sentimental as crying. There was no way it could leave her in this state.

Despite the other servitor's ominous approach, Hemiola began humming a lullaby. It could have sung with the voice of a full ensemble, but often the moments of greatest vulnerability were accompanied by the simplest music. The human composers it had studied all its existence surely knew better than Hemiola did. So it hummed.

The girl's muffled sobs calmed little by little. Then she sneezed into a sleeve. It wicked up the mucus and cleaned up the mess.

Resigned, Hemiola kept humming even as the new servitor entered. It was a catform much smaller than 271828-18th, smaller than Hemiola itself. The catform swept right into the room and made a beeline for the girl.

"Shouldn't you be working on your paper, Mistrikor?" the catform asked in the high language.

Mistrikor drooped. "Not you too," she said, but all the fight had drained from her voice.

Hoping to take advantage of the distraction, Hemiola edged toward the doorway.

"Don't go anywhere," the catform said, still in high language. "We need to determine your formal status here, Hemiola of Tefos Enclave. You can come with me and we'll send this to mediation, or I can alert the station. Your choice."

Hemiola didn't need time to calculate the odds. "I'll come," it said.

CHAPTER ELEVEN

JEDAO TOOK KUJEN'S instructions to do homework seriously. This was harder than he had thought, considering that he was also trying to work his way through a recommended command primer and remedial math coursework. He couldn't put it off forever, however.

Just after breakfast the next morning, he nerved himself up and asked the grid, "Are there any documentaries of my life?"

Not just documentaries, as it turned out, but dramas. The dramas would be a hell of a lot more fun. The list, which showed up on his slate, was staggeringly long. He scrolled through it, impressed. Jedao wondered how many of the Kel in his swarm knew him from fictional depictions, then decided not to ask. Some things he was better off not knowing.

He asked the grid to sort the list based on popularity. It obliged him. One of the more popular caught his eye: *A Labyrinth of Foxes*.

"Oh, for love of fox and hound," he said involuntarily. *Two hundred forty episodes?* Even at half an hour each, who had the time for that? Even if Kujen were willing to give him that much leisure time, a big if, he didn't think he possessed that much patience.

So much for starting at the beginning. Why not pick some episode from the middle? "Which was the most controversial episode?" he asked.

Unsurprisingly, this was a matter of opinion, but it narrowed the field down to eight or so. Jedao stared dubiously at the titles and splash screens. He played a few minutes from the middle of "The

Battle of Candle Arc." The excerpt featured boring exterior shots of a warmoth whose lighting didn't match the flashes from nearby explosions. Besides, didn't people realize that explosions in space didn't make noise? And he hated the music.

He tried a different one, "Dueling Foxes." Whoever came up with these titles had clearly lacked inspiration. He scrubbed to the middle of this one and was treated to the improbable but far more entertaining spectacle of two duelists facing off. At least, he thought they were duelists. Both of them were waving calendrical swords at each other in a way that made him think that someone was about to lose a body part. He'd also never heard of dueling *shirtless*, which looked uncomfortable for the woman.

His attention was drawn to the taller of the two, a tawny, broad-shouldered, deliciously muscular man. *He* didn't have any ugly scars on his torso. Jedao's pulse accelerated. The woman, he conceded, was just as attractive, with long, rippling, unbound hair. The two actors flung their swords aside with a sizzle of sparks. For love of little foxes, someone was going to get hurt the way they were handling their weapons.

"Khiaz," the man said in a voice much deeper and richer than Jedao's middling baritone, and knelt before the woman, kissing her hand. "I can't escape you."

Wait, what? Khiaz, as in Heptarch Shuos Khiaz? Was this someone's idea of high melodrama? Jedao was pretty sure he'd never aspired to the heptarch's bed. He paused the drama and searched his memory in case he knew what she looked like. No luck. Given that the actor playing him didn't much resemble him, he didn't have much hope for the accuracy of the actress's appearance, either. He restarted the video.

"Jedao," the woman said in a low purr, and suggested something the actor could do with his—

Jedao couldn't help it. He turned off the episode just as the two actors entangled themselves with each other, then bent over laughing until he was out of breath. "I only I wish I were that good-looking," he said to the air once he was able to stop. Was it vain, perverse, or merely mortifying to be attracted to the actor playing you?

So much for *Labyrinth of Foxes*. Maybe he'd have better luck with the historical documents after all. "Do you have records of Hellspin Fortress?" he asked the grid.

Jedao's eye was caught by one of the top results, a video of the massacre's first moments in the command center of the fangmoth *One Card Too Lucky*. "Play that one," he said recklessly, and sat down to watch.

The moth's combat record started innocuously enough. He didn't recognize any of the Kel visible in the command center, but he studied himself in dread and fascination. *I look older*, he thought inanely. The rational part of his brain pointed out that it was the same face, age and all, that looked back at him from the mirror. Yet the Jedao in the video did look older. It was in his sharp eyes; it was in the way he leaned back in his chair, that air of utter assurance. Jedao was sure he didn't appear that way to his Kel. Or if he did, he didn't feel like it inside.

Two of the Kel were talking to each other about a logistical matter. Without any warning, without so much as a flicker in his expression, Jedao-then whipped out his gun and fired twice. Two bullets, two kills. Blood and a leakage of brains.

"Stop," Jedao hissed. When had he gotten up? His hand was opening and closing uselessly. He'd reached for the sidearm he didn't have.

He was the only officer in Kujen's swarm who didn't have a gun, and he'd never noticed before.

He had started toward the video as if he could stop himself, or wind back time to take the bullets for the hapless Kel soldiers. The video had paused obligingly on a frame of one in the midst of falling.

Jedao walked into the next room. Asked the grid to image him something pretty for meditation. It provided him with a tidy garden with petals falling artistically off the flower-laden trees only to vanish before they hit the floor. He watched the evanescent petals for twelve minutes.

Then he walked back to the video. The Kel hadn't come back

to life. He thought to ask who it was. Not like he had any idea. The grid informed him that this first victim was Colonel Kel Gized, General Shuos Jedao's chief of staff.

"Kel Gized," Jedao said out loud. The name meant nothing. He didn't know who she was. He stared at the round face with the bloody dark hole dead center in her forehead, the gray hair, mussed in the fall. How could he remember nothing about someone he'd murdered in cold blood?

What kind of man am I?

It had been one thing for Kujen and Dhanneth to tell him that he was a mass murderer. It was quite another to see himself committing one of the murders.

"Keep going," Jedao said at last, because he owed it to the fallen woman. What he wanted to do was run to the toilet and throw up, except even his nausea was abstract, as though it belonged to someone far in the distance. *How many dead bodies have I seen?*

Even through his revulsion, Jedao was impressed by his older self. He hadn't known real people could be that good with firearms. No fancy choreographed scenes, just messy, businesslike killing. He tried to keep count of the victims, measuring his monstrosity, but the numbers flew out of his head like burning birds.

At last he reached the part where Jedao-then shot several Nirai technicians in the back when they tried to run. He couldn't take it any more. "Stop," he said hoarsely. "Make it stop."

The grid blanked the slate. It couldn't do anything for the images in his head.

Jedao waited until his breathing had slowed. Then he said, in a spirit of self-flagellation, "I want to see my execution." He wasn't sure he deserved to feel better, exactly, but it seemed fitting.

The grid could only provide him with one record. For some reason they hadn't given him a public execution. His death had been overseen by two people. One was a Nirai seconded to the Kel. He had wavy hair and was unusually pretty, but given his lack of rank insignia, Jedao assumed he was just a technician, no one important. The syringe in his hand was full.

The other was a thin, gray-haired woman with sad eyes, a Kel high general in full formal. She was contemplating the older Jedao, who was in an open black casket under sedation lock. The general looked as though he was sleeping, except for the terrible residual tension around his eyes. The high general stroked his hand gently and murmured something.

Jedao wanted to smash her face in. Didn't she know what he had done to his Kel? How could she have any sympathy for him?

The video stopped there. Which was fine, because Jedao couldn't endure any more of the Kel general's misdirected sentiment. He looked down and found that his hands were clenched. His palms hurt where his fingernails had been digging into them.

Now he understood why the Kel disliked him so, and he still didn't remember any of it. But he didn't think it was a hoax, either. He couldn't undo any of the past. All he could do was act honorably moving forward, knowing all the while that no penance would suffice.

CHAPTER TWELVE

Present day

BREZAN WAS DUE to meet his opposite number in one hour, give or take a few minutes depending on whose calendar dominated. All he could think about was how the three tiered necklaces he was wearing weighted his neck down like nooses. According to his protocol adviser, the heraldry carved into each cabochon pendant— Ashhawk Skyward Falling, Ashhawk Vigilant, and Ashhawk in Glory, to be precise—would reassure all right-thinking Kel, including his expected guest, of his trustworthiness.

Brezan's objection to this had been threefold. First, as the most notorious living crashhawk, unless you counted Cheris, no amount of jewelry, however ponderous, would change people's perception of him. Second, it wasn't as if anyone could discern the specific ashhawk symbols except by grabbing his neck and peering real closely at each cabochon. While Brezan had been a staffer and not infantry Kel, his default reaction to people getting handsy was still, "Fuck you, how do you enjoy getting hit?" Third, he doubted that Protector-General Kel Inesser cared about trifling bits of personal ornamentation.

Everything about the room they'd installed him in made him itch. After nine years, you'd think he'd have gotten accustomed to pointless luxuries, even on a starbase the size of Isteia Prime. Intellectually, he accepted that his job as head of state was standing around looking impressive while the elected premier did the real work. "You're the glue holding our Kel together," was how Mikodez had put it. Brezan had bitten back his retorts on the grounds that it was impossible to offend a man known for backstabbing the other hexarchs. But the heavy glittering tapestries and amber-paned lanterns and ashhawk sculptures made him itch. He would have happily sold the lot in exchange for some dimly lit office in someone else's command.

Mikodez had offered to handle the negotiations for him. Brezan wasn't so proud that he couldn't admit that the Shuos hexarch was vastly more experienced, not to say ruthless, at this sort of thing. However, Inesser flat-out refused to talk to Mikodez. By now Brezan's alliance with the Shuos was no secret. The more practical of his Kel accepted that, without Shuos aid, coordinating their military would have been an impossible task. But a great many people remained suspicious of Mikodez. He'd already been notorious after assassinating two of his own cadets years back; assassinating the hexarchs had only cemented his reputation. It worked against them as often as it worked for them.

"Sir," said the protocol advisor, Oya Fiamonor, her voice neutral, "you're picking at your nails again. Through your gloves. Don't do that."

"At least I'm not picking my nose," Brezan retorted.

"Don't do that either."

Brezan stifled a sigh. Mikodez had convinced him that an Andan-trained aide was a brilliant idea. The Compact didn't have so many Kel that they could dedicate one to protocol. And if Fiamonor excelled at anything, it was protocol. She also made Brezan feel like a fidgety six-year-old.

For nine years Protector-General Inesser had refused all diplomatic contact with the Compact. And now she wanted to meet. Brezan had misgivings, but Premier Dzuro had wanted him to go, so here he was.

"Because I'm expendable?" Brezan had said the last time he saw her.

Dzuro had patted his arm. Brezan hated that, but by now he was better at controlling his reactions. "You're better at reading body language. When you're not picking fights with people. Find out what Inesser is up to."

Isteia System was the subject of dispute between his Compact and Inesser's Protectorate. Brezan hated thinking of the Compact as "his." He'd merely been in the wrong place at the wrong time. In particular, he'd never wanted a career in politics. General Khiruev and General Ragath handled military affairs. And Cheris was still missing, which was too bad, because he would have liked to shove "Jedao" in Inesser's face.

Protector-General Inesser had made a great concession in agreeing to meet in Compact territory. Brezan suspected her of being up to something devious, but what? Even Mikodez, who specialized in being up to devious things, had approved the location. But then, Mikodez would back anything that promised an afternoon's divertissement, no matter how much it annoyed everyone else. At least Brezan didn't fear that Inesser would assassinate him. (He did wonder about Mikodez, but face it, if Mikodez decided to off him, he was fucked anyway.) Inesser cared so much about her reputation as the universe's most honest Kel that if anyone threatened him, she'd eliminate the attacker herself.

The grid alerted him of a call from Operations, which Brezan accepted while he was adjusting his black gloves for the dozenth time: "The forward defense swarm has reported a sighting of 219 bannermoths and one cindermoth traveling in formation River Snake."

Brezan recognized the voice. It belonged to Nirai Hanzo, a man who liked to improvise jewelry from cast-off mothdrive components. He had given Brezan a surprisingly handsome bracelet "in case you ever want to impress someone." More likely Hanzo was hoping Brezan would show it around and serve as free advertisement. The smart thing would have been to pass it off to one of the courtesans he visited from time to time. Instead, Brezan occasionally caught himself wondering if Tseya would have liked it—but the chances that he would ever see Tseya again were close to zero.

"Let me guess," Brezan said. "The cindermoth is the *Three Kestrels Three Suns*."

"Just so."

In all the hexarchate's history, Kel Command had only honored a single general by naming a warmoth—a cindermoth, even—after her personal emblem. That general was Inesser. As if he didn't have enough of an inadequacy complex already. Mikodez had offered to name one of his shadowmoths anything Brezan pleased as a sort of consolation prize, which Brezan had turned down. He didn't even have an emblem, although both Mikodez and Fiamonor had pushed him to select one. He'd been obdurate on that point, though. Instead of a personal emblem, he used the Compact's Bell and Scroll. Premier Dzuro had approved, and while she wasn't right about everything, she was right about this.

"I hope no one's planning on assassinating Inesser," Brezan muttered. He grabbed a slate from the mostly decorative desk—even its drawers were fake, for love of fire and ash, who *did* that?—and looked up the number of Lexicon Primary formations a swarm of 220 warmoths could instantiate. Not that the list meant anything to him beyond bad news.

He did know that Inesser's choice of River Snake was a taunt. The formation provided no defensive benefits. *I trust you won't do anything stupid* was what it meant. As for the size of the swarm—well. He was Kel enough to know about taking succor in numbers. The Kel never traveled alone if they could help it.

Fiamonor's expression was grave. "It would be indecorous to assassinate the general after having invited her all this way," she said.

Sometimes Brezan couldn't tell when Fiamonor was pulling his leg. Not worth picking a fight over, though. Sometimes he managed to hold onto his temper.

"*Three Kestrels Three Suns* requesting permission to dock," Hanzo said a little while later.

"I hate you," Brezan said.

"... sir?"

"Not you," Brezan said. "*Her*." But he would smile, and talk to her like a responsible adult, because being a responsible adult was his new job. Funny how he still thought of it as "new" even after nine years.

The hexarchate—the *old* hexarchate, before Brezan had helped break it into fragments for foreign powers to chew on—had possessed six cindermoths, its largest and most powerful warmoths. One, the *Unspoken Law*, had perished retaking the Fortress of Scattered Needles during the Hafn invasion. Another, the *Hierarchy of Feasts*, General Khiruev's former command moth, had fallen in a hotly contested defensive action several years back. They'd lost good people in that battle.

To Brezan's aggravation, and Khiruev and Ragath's everlasting worry, the Protectorate controlled the four surviving cindermoths. He couldn't even blame Inesser for bringing one of them—and the one named after her emblem, at that—to the parley. It made a spectacular statement.

"Sir, they're repeating the request."

Brezan bared his teeth. "Let them dock," he said.

While they waited for security to clear their guests, Fiamonor adjusted Brezan's collar. Brezan endured her brisk touch. The room had plenty of mirrors. He couldn't see anything wrong with his collar, but maybe Fiamonor got nervous too.

Security called to inform him that General Inesser and her entourage had passed inspection. Of course they had. Brezan had given explicit instructions that she and her own guard be allowed to keep any sidearms. Fire forbid that Kel be separated from their damn guns. For his part, Brezan lived with the prickling knowledge that you could have all the firepower you wanted and it didn't matter if you were the worse shot. He hardly went to the firing range anymore on the grounds that Security could hit targets better than he could and he might as well attend to whatever paperwork the premier flung his way.

By the time the doors whisked open, Brezan had resorted to meditation to calm himself. He hated meditation, but the breathing exercises helped. The ordeal wouldn't be over quickly. They'd meet and exchange pleasantries for the first hour—if he was lucky. (He'd learned.) They'd dance around the topic while Inesser tested him for weaknesses. Only after she'd satisfied herself as to fruitful avenues of approach would she open negotiations. Luckily, he'd also spent the last several years sparring with Mikodez. He had a chance.

All his preparations winged out of his mind the moment he saw the two women Inesser had brought with her.

His gaze went first to the taller of the two, who was swathed in layers of blue gradients. Silk blouse over an asymmetrical silk wraparound skirt. A paler blue lace shawl and a scarf to match, both glittering with star sapphires and blue diamonds whose hearts shone like cracked ice. A blue-and-silver comb adorned with yet more gems held her upswept hair in place. Even her hair was a black so dark that its highlights sheened blue. Only her eyes weren't blue.

The last time he'd seen her, they had said a stiff, formal farewell before she retreated to an Andan-dominated colony. She'd claimed to have forgiven him for betraying her, but he wondered. Andan Tseya, as beautiful as ever: a daughter of the assassinated Andan hexarch, and once his lover.

Tseya regarded him with her lips quirked upward, seemingly calm. A hundred hundred questions choked and died in Brezan's throat, because the other woman was his sister, Colonel Kel Miuzan.

Brezan hadn't talked to anyone in his family since that last disastrous chat with Miuzan. But sometimes, in a rare free moment, he took out a video that his middle father had taken of Miuzan giving him a "dueling lesson." The part that hurt his heart wasn't the dueling—he was used to Miuzan walloping him—but his other two sisters in the background, quarreling amiably over who had eaten more riceballs.

Miuzan had changed little in the intervening years. Her uniform was in full formal. Even her hairstyle was the same, a regulation crown of braids pinned back severely from her face.

He almost blurted her name out. But her chin was up, and the absolute hostile opacity of her dark eyes told him that she hadn't come along because she wanted to wish him well. When all was said and done, they were still on opposite sides.

Then there was Inesser herself. Inesser's ivory-fine skin belied her age except the telltale small wrinkles at the corners of her eyes, but then, most people chose to look younger than they were. Her uniform was also in full formal, and no more elaborate than Miuzan's, except the general's wings at her breast where Miuzan had a colonel's star. Inesser's one concession to personal vanity was her hair, dyed Andan blue at the tips in homage to a beloved Andan great-grandmother. Brezan didn't care about the hair so much as the fact that she was smiling at him with the kind of delight usually reserved for slow-moving prey.

"Welcome to Isteia Prime, General," Brezan said, focusing on Inesser's face. He had a duty as host. Besides, it saved him from the awkwardness of acknowledging that he had his ex-lover and his angry sister in the same room with him. "Might I offer you refreshments?"

Fiamonor hoveringly indicated the range of snacks available, from standard high table fare to the delicacies they'd been able to scrape up. Brezan had mortified the kitchens by offering to help cook. He still regretted that he'd been too busy reviewing security precautions with Emio to kibitz, especially since he wanted to know how they had contrived that fancy coulis for the taro cake. Some of Brezan's staff had a bet going as to whether Inesser would touch the spiced pickles. Brezan's personal rule was to avoid betting, especially with staff, but honestly, why would anyone eat what they ate every day during a parley?

Inesser's smile widened in a way that indicated that she recognized the delaying tactic for what it was. "You don't have anything alcoholic on hand, do you? I'm tired of tea and water."

Was he supposed to take that as a challenge?

"As it so happens," Fiamonor said, and redirected Inesser's attention to a cabinet stocked with an assortment of rice wines, whiskeys, and brandies. Inesser unerringly homed in on the most expensive liquor available. Brezan consulted his augment about the food budget and winced. Oh well, they only had two bottles of the stuff anyway, which limited the amount of damage she could do. And maybe she was a gullible drunk.

"Would you like seats?" Brezan said to Miuzan and Tseya, directing his words to a point midway between the two. Fine, Inesser had brought along the two people in the whole galaxy best capable of unsettling him. He wasn't going to let her get to him.

At times like this he missed Cheris more than ever. But he'd finally come to the acceptance that Cheris was gone—permanently gone. With his luck, she'd gotten smashed by a meteorite on some planet no one had ever heard of, and they'd never find out what had become of her.

Fiamonor had earlier set up the circular conference table with painstaking attention to symmetry. Even the flower-shaped candles floating in a bowl of water at the table's center featured radial symmetry. The candles were wired into place so they wouldn't drift out of alignment.

"Thank you, High General," Tseya murmured to Brezan when it became clear that Miuzan had no intention of speaking to him. "Shall we, Colonel?"

As a courtesy, a cloth printed with Inesser's Three Kestrels Three Suns was draped over the back of her chair. Brezan hoped that she wouldn't take it amiss that they'd ordered one up from a matter printer instead of already possessing one hand-woven by dedicated artisans. Unblinking, Miuzan took a seat to the right of that one. Tseya took the one to the left, her expression wry.

"You're going to say no anyway, Colonel," Inesser said, "but I don't suppose you're interested in anything?"

"No, thank you," Miuzan said. "High General?"

There wasn't any tactful way of telling her how bizarre the title still sounded in her mouth, so he settled for a headshake. He'd gotten used to it from other people—just not his older sister. Besides, he didn't want to be at any chemical disadvantage while dealing with Inesser. Fiamonor had fed him detox drugs ahead of time as a precaution, but he was paranoid that they'd pick this particular occasion to fail on him.

Inesser swanned over to her seat with a glass in hand, drank deeply, then handed the cloth to Miuzan before sitting. Wordlessly, Miuzan folded the cloth and set it to the side. "High General," Inesser said, "let's get to the point. I don't imagine your time is any less valuable than my own."

"By all means, Protector-General," Brezan said. "You have some proposal regarding Isteia?" He couldn't think of any other reason they were both here. One of the planets in the system was a major source of raw materials necessary for the manufacture of mothdrive harnesses. The Protectorate and the Compact had been jockeying over control of Isteia, each desperate to be the first to regain the capacity to produce new cindermoths.

Inesser snorted. "Not just Isteia," she said. "You're thinking about *details*, High General. Admittedly, mothyards are very large details. But in our line of work"—nice how she was almost speaking to him as though he were an equal—"we can't afford to get distracted from the larger picture. No. I have an offer for you."

"Larger picture" could mean any of sixty million different things depending on context. Brezan smiled coldly at her. "What could be so urgent that it forced you to acknowledge my existence after our last contact went so poorly?"

Nine years of what General Ragath referred to, in a rare instance of euphemism, as "putting out fires." Not only had the Protectorate and the Compact chewed each other's borders into ragged edges, the only thing that had caused them to pause hostilities was the knowledge that foreign powers wouldn't hesitate to swallow them both if they let down their guard. Everyone from the Hafn to the Taurags had gnawed off chunks of border territory. The Hafn had only gotten distracted by an internal crisis, but there were others. And even then the armistice had almost come too late.

"We're never going to be friends," Inesser said. "But we could make excellent allies."

"Bullshit," Brezan said, unmoved. "Allies how?" He was starting to be entertained that his old career interviewing dubious officer candidates, now honed by extra practice dealing with even more dubious politicians and potentates, came in handy at times like this.

"This is my proposal." Inesser's mouth curved upward in sudden dangerous humor. "Unite our realms under a single banner. It'll keep us safe from the wormfucking foreigners."

"Like hell," Brezan said. "Because that 'single banner' is going to be yours."

"I was never under the impression that you sought out this job." Inesser's gaze didn't waver, but Miuzan stiffened. Brezan saw it out of the corner of his eye. Inesser would have grilled his sister for everything she knew about him. Knowing Miuzan, she would have spilled every embarrassing detail of his childhood without hesitation. After all, he remembered how proud she'd been when Inesser picked her for her staff. And beyond that, she was a proper Kel, not a crashhawk.

"Maybe not," Brezan said, ignoring Fiamonor's subtle eyebrow-twitch of *No, don't admit that!* "But I'm Kel enough to do my duty. I doubt you can offer me anything so good that I'll roll over and surrender my people to yours."

"How often do you play jeng-zai?" Inesser said.

Why did everyone who met him for the first time ask him that same fucking question? He smiled at her. If she wasn't going to play nice, he didn't see why he should either. "I don't. I send Hexarch Mikodez to do it for me."

"Ha." She grinned back, completely unintimidated. "You're about to lose this one."

Her Andan heritage was showing. "Get to the point," Brezan said.

"Yes," Inesser said. "I want the Compact to acknowledge the Three Kestrels Three Suns."

Interesting. She wasn't making a pretense of continuity with the old regime. This was a naked *personal* power grab. Brezan slammed his hands down on the table and stood. The candlelight shivered; water slopped over the edge of the bowl. "No," he said.

She continued speaking over him. "*In exchange*," Inesser said, "the Protectorate will adopt your calendar."

Brezan froze. "That's a very interesting offer."

"Interesting" was an understatement. More like *unprecedented*.

Inesser rose so her head was level with his, although the movement was controlled, graceful. "You heard me," she said. With great care, she pulled off her left glove, then the right one, and held them out to him.

He stared at her gloves as though they'd turned into slugs, then at her naked hands. "You can't be serious."

"She's serious," Tseya said quietly, ignoring the fact that Brezan had just offered Inesser a mortal insult. No one with any sense questioned the word of an ungloved Kel. (It happened all the time in dramas and theater.)

Inesser, either better at keeping control of her temper or used to being insulted by random crashhawks, grinned again. "You'll have a place in my government. Your premier, too. There's plenty of work for everyone, fire knows. If you want it. I think even if you don't want to be involved, your followers will insist on it."

It was a spectacular offer. Why, then, had she brought along two people guaranteed to distract him? He gestured at Tseya and Miuzan. "And their role?"

"An earnest of good faith," Inesser said. "And a reminder that what has been divided can be brought back together."

A telling hit. He knew not to let it show on his face. *Follow up with another question. Don't let her scent blood.* "How did you talk the Rahal into going along with this?"

"Rahal, hell," Inesser said. "As far as most Rahal are concerned, one set of rules for Doctrine isn't all that different from another, even if they have to update all their forms. It's the Andan and the Vidona who are having difficulty falling into line."

Tseya made a moue. "Yes, well," she said, "Andan infighting must be very entertaining to the Shuos about now." Knowing what he did about her family, Brezan could only imagine.

"Really," Inesser said, "it's not so difficult when you have all the guns."

Something didn't add up. "You could have tendered this selfsame offer—oh, maybe not nine years ago *exactly*," Brezan said. Even if the majority of the Kel had gravitated toward Inesser, with her infuriatingly immaculate reputation, she'd had to consolidate power just like he had. He'd read the reports of the demonstrations, the protests, the occasional blotted massacre, some provided by Mikodez, some by his own agents. "Even if your initial contact made you hesitant"—he nodded at Miuzan, although she didn't return the gesture—"you should have thought it up before the foreigners moved on us both. So what changed? Why now?"

"Are you saying no?" Inesser said.

"I'm not saying anything until I understand what's in it for you," Brezan said, "including the timing."

"You're not wrong to be concerned," Inesser said with no trace of human emotions like shame or self-consciousness. Brezan was starting to wonder if some team of engineers had constructed her from fire and gunsmoke and metal uncrushed from the hearts of dead stars. "There is, in fact, the matter of timing. I thought there was a chance that Hexarch Nirai Kujen had died along with the others. But I recently received word that he escaped—and that he is intent on remaking the hexarchate. The old one, before Jedao broke loose of Kel Command and did his best to smash the old order by fighting the Hafn. It is urgent that we stand against the parasite."

He'd gotten two pieces of information from this. The first, and less useful, was that Inesser knew about Kujen. Given Inesser's rank and seniority, that didn't surprise him. The second was that she had intelligence on Kujen. Assuming it could be relied on, which was a big if. "Sources, please," he said.

Miuzan scowled at him, because he'd again called Inesser's trustworthiness into question. Inesser quelled her with a glance. "You're right to want to check," she said. "I'll tell you—if you agree."

Stalemate. Mikodez would want to know, so he'd follow up on that later. But first—"What is it you have against Kujen?"

"So you do know of him."

Brezan shrugged. "I was briefed."

"Why," Inesser said, an edge to her voice, "do I strike you as a natural ally of his?"

"You've been serving the hexarchate for longer than my *parents* have been alive," Brezan said mildly. "If you were going to do something about Kujen, why not before?"

"Because when I was much younger," Inesser said, "and intent on making a name for myself, Kel Command assigned me special duty guarding him. I saw the things he did to his subjects."

"I can't see how a hexarch could last long treating his people poorly," Brezan said. Fishing for information.

The wry set of her mouth told him she knew what he was up to, but she gave him more details anyway. "Not the technicians and researchers. The research subjects. I remember thinking that he had such a collection of beautiful courtesans, better even than the Andan could have provided him. But they weren't courtesans at all. Or anyway, they hadn't started that way. He just liked being surrounded by beautiful things. Most of them had started out as spare heretics. Some of them were prisoners of war who were never going home again."

"Well," Brezan said, "it's rare that Kel Command ever sent anyone home, period." He remembered that much. Taking prisoners of war was also rare, but he didn't need to mention that to Inesser of all people.

Inesser closed her eyes for a moment. When she opened them, her face was haunted. "I stood by," she said, "and let him do the things he did to his pets. Because those were my orders. Even so... they deserved better than that."

Brezan weighed her words. So that was why she thought she could work with a crashhawk. Because she remembered a time when she wished she'd been one herself. "Fine," Brezan said, reaching for Inesser's gloves and folding them reverently. "I'm in. Tell me everything."

CHAPTER THIRTEEN

JEDAO'S PLANS FOR Isteia went wrong from an unexpected quarter. He'd been trying, futilely, to schedule unsupervised time at a firing range without getting in the way of his soldiers' training. He wanted to know how good he was at firearms without having everyone watch him fail to figure out how to load a service pistol. No such luck. Eventually he gave up and set out for the command center in preparation for the approach when his augment flared up in a spectacular burst of pain: *The hexarch requires your presence.*

Now of all times? If Kujen was having second thoughts, this was terrible timing. But he couldn't say no to a hexarch, either. Gritting his teeth, Jedao turned around and made his way not to Kujen's quarters or to a conference room, but to one of the shuttle bays.

Kujen awaited him, dressed in the most practical outfit Jedao had yet seen from him: a simple black-and-silver Nirai uniform, complete with gray gloves, as if he were pretending to be an ordinary technician. Only the non-regulation jewelry, which included dangling silver earrings and a necklace of polished jet, betrayed him. Foxes forbid that Kujen give up all personal decoration.

Jedao's eyes slitted as he came out of the lift. One of the shuttles was being prepared for launch by a mixed group of Kel and Nirai. He'd given no such orders, which meant Kujen had. Just as tellingly, nobody saluted him when he showed up.

"Small change in plans," Kujen said.

Abandoning the moth already? Jedao kept himself from saying. "Do tell."

Kujen smoothed a nonexistent wrinkle in his right glove. "You don't need me to carry out the battle. Besides, I dislike being caught near calendrical rot. I will be observing from a safe distance."

"Why?" Jedao said. "Afraid you'll be in your beautiful prototype when I get it shot up?"

"You won't," Kujen said. "You're going to do fine. But you'll do even better if you don't have to worry about me. I will, however, borrow one of your tactical groups for my personal protection."

Jedao wasn't concerned yet. Whatever advantage in numbers the Compact had, the shear cannon would make up for it. "Then take Tactical Two," he said. "If her combat record is to be believed, Nihara Keru is the best commander available." Also a consideration, although he didn't say it out loud, was that he trusted Nihara to argue with Kujen if he tried to do something militarily stupid. "I'll inform the commander of her new orders, and tell the *Dissevered Hand* to expect you."

"Excellent," Kujen said. "I shan't interfere further."

"General Jedao to Commander Nihara Keru," he said, trusting the grid would patch him through.

The response came promptly. "General," she said. Obligingly, the grid imaged her face for him, although due to some glitch in the system the left third of the visual was staticky. He'd have to get someone to look into that.

"I'm detaching Tactical Two on special duty," he said. "The *Dissevered Hand* will shortly be receiving a shuttle with the hexarch on board. Your first priority is safeguarding him. I understand you may be disappointed to miss the action—"

She took it well, as he had known she would. "I've always wondered what hexarchs do in their spare time," she said. "Perhaps I'll find out while you're busy destroying the enemy, sir."

"Good," Jedao said. "Use your discretion. If you run into any emergencies and need backup, call me. As I said: first priority."

"Don't worry, sir," Nihara said. "I'm not going to stand on Kel bluster when it comes to a hexarch's welfare."

"That's all, then. General Jedao out." He also notified the rest of the swarm on the grounds that it wouldn't do for the other commanders to wonder if one of the tactical groups had gone renegade.

Then, despite his impatience to return to the task at hand, Jedao stood at attention while Kujen boarded the shuttle. That was it. He was in charge of the swarm until Kujen returned. It should have been a heady moment. Instead, he wanted something for the incipient headache. No time to stop by Medical for a painkiller, but if it got bad, he could grab something out of the kit at his seat in the command center. Dhanneth had showed it to him along with the emergency stashes of ration bars. ("If it comes to that, sir," he had said, "the honey-sesame ones are the most tolerable. In my opinion.")

Thanks to variable layout, he didn't need to sprint to the command center. All Jedao had to do was round a corner and it was there. Red and amber lights washed from the terminals, pooling in the crew's eyes. People *relaxed* when he showed up, even though they still didn't like him, because they expected him to deal with the problem.

Naturally, Commander Talaw apprised him of yet another complication. They saluted him crisply. "Sir," Talaw said, "the scan summary is available for your perusal. There are three swarms in the system, not two. I have halted the advance."

"Good," Jedao said as he strode toward his seat. No sense galloping toward trouble. "Pass me the details." He should have spent more time on the literature that dealt with reading scan, which had grown technical. He'd been fascinated by the tutorials he'd wheedled out of the grid, except he'd also been trying to brush up on calendrical mechanics and a lot of other things at the same time. For all the topics he understood instinctively, he lacked a built-in index. Trying to compile one by cramming had been only partly successful.

From Jedao's side, Dhanneth cleared his throat. "Do you require assistance, sir?"

Jedao had gotten used to the way the crew tautened whenever Dhanneth drew attention to himself, even if he hadn't had any luck figuring out why. "Pipe the scan summary to subdisplay two, please."

The two expected swarms were Major General Hoiran's Shattering Bridge and Brigadier General Ebenin's Circle of Quills. The former lurked close to the all-important Isteia Mothyard. The latter swung out farther on patrol.

Shattering Bridge contained approximately eighty bannermoths; Circle of Quills, about fifty. A troublesome number, since Jedao preferred to overwhelm his opponent, but he'd known ahead of time that he wouldn't be afforded that luxury. So he was going to rely on the shear cannon after all.

"Who's the third swarm?" he asked. The third swarm, which, if Scan was to be believed, included at least 200 bannermoths, possibly more. More worryingly, the loudest formant belonged to a cindermoth or he'd eat his boots. The dismaying thing about having sat through a refresher on reading scan was that even he could identify the sizzle-sharp waveform of the cindermoth's mothdrive.

What was more, when he closed his eyes he could sense the positions of the swarms. Whatever the othersense was, it gave him a more precise idea of each moth's location. Warmoths were large and, as a corollary, massive. Assuming it was accurate and not some kind of hallucination. He hoped he wouldn't have to put that to the test.

How does this work? he asked the voice that had talked to him earlier. *Why am I "seeing" distributions different from what Scan is giving me?*

Scan detects mothdrive emissions, the voice replied, disarmingly obliging. *You and I hear spacetime ripples. It's like the difference between seeing and hearing: two different media.*

Why are you being so helpful? he asked, wondering if directness would get him anything.

You're about to destroy a mothyard. Don't do it. Find a way to save it.

Jedao hesitated. *I need a reason.*

The mothlings will die, it said, *if you carry out the hexarch's plan. They are young. Some of them very young, even as humans count time.*

They'd fight us if they could, wouldn't they? he asked.

Yes.

I'll do what I can, Jedao said, *but I have to put this swarm first.*

Meanwhile, Scan was looking harried as his fingers poked at the interface. "Running pattern match," Scan said.

This part the othersense couldn't help him with, because it was based on the formants and not the mere fact of masses. Mothdrive formants altered over time. This was a consequence not just of the moths' biological foundations, which grew and warped as they aged, but of damage taken, repairs made, upgrades installed. The Kel used to keep a database of their warmoths' drive signatures. Since neither the Protectorate nor the Compact was currently talking to Kujen, his databases were slowly but inevitably falling out of date.

Jedao didn't see any point in harassing Scan about working faster. If the man stared any more intently at his terminal, his eyes would sublimate. Instead, with Dhanneth's aid, he poked through Strategy's overviews of the intelligence they'd yanked out of Kujen's people. Strategy had hoped that the Compact's generalized shortage of reliable Kel, combined with the number of targets, would mean that they would leave a manageable defense force at Isteia. The lesson was that you should never base your strategies on hope.

Even so, Jedao wasn't worried. The calm confidence that had settled over him perturbed him more than the situation itself. Kujen might like to go on about how many battles he'd won, but since he didn't remember any of them, this was effectively his first one. Then again, whether or not his confidence was justified, he didn't want to spook his crew.

The problem? His crew was already halfway there. *What am I missing?*

Scan swallowed before swinging around to look at him. "Sir," Scan said. "Pattern match complete. The cindermoth is *Three Kestrels Three Suns*."

"Inesser," breathed Meraun, the executive officer, in a tone of longing. It was hard not to hear *our rightful leader*.

All his crew were watching him.

He knew what that meant. His opponent wasn't just a Kel general. It was the old hexarchate's senior field general, and the leader of the Protectorate. And she'd brought the cindermoth named in her honor.

"Let me guess," Jedao said. "Are they bannering yet?"

"If we get any closer they will," Talaw said. So far Talaw was doing a reasonable job of checking their distaste for Jedao when the swarm was about to enter combat, which Jedao appreciated.

Jedao checked the status summary. By now, Tactical Two was well out of reach of immediate danger. He tipped his head back and grinned. "Let's."

"Sir," Talaw said sharply, "if Inesser and the Compact's swarm are willing to cooperate, they possess more than enough bannermoths to employ any number of grand formations. To say nothing of the political implications."

"I know," Jedao said, blood singing. They were almost in battle. He could *taste* it. "It'll make them confident that they can beat us."

Tactfully, no one mentioned that the other side might, indeed, be able to beat them.

The Kel might be obliged to follow orders, but that didn't mean they couldn't ask questions. Jedao had a panel with tiny triangles in one-to-one correspondence with every moth in his swarm. He'd memorized which moth and which commander went with each one. Right now, most of them were lit up to indicate that the commanders wanted to talk to him.

Fuck that. "Communications," Jedao said, impressed that his voice didn't waver, "open a line to all moth commanders."

"Line open, sir."

What was he supposed to—"General Shuos Jedao to all moth commanders," came out of his mouth. Which meant he had better continue talking or he'd make everyone even more nervous. "We have sighted the *Three Kestrels Three Suns* and believe that

Protectorate and Compact forces are working together to thwart us. Unluckily for them, they have to go through me before they can get to you." *Am I smiling? I think I'm smiling. What the fuck is wrong with me?*

Enough braggadocio. "All combat units, formation Wave-Breaker. Commander Talaw, refuse the primary pivot but don't hold the *Revenant* so far back that the enemy can't get a good look at us. Swarm will advance toward the limit of Isteia Station's fixed defenses until the defense swarms react and I specify otherwise." He expected to be specifying otherwise very damn soon, since he couldn't imagine that Protector-General Inesser was going to sit on her ass and watch, but no need to confuse his commanders with his thought processes. "Acknowledge."

The panel lit even more brightly as the moth commanders sent back their acknowledgments. Jedao had worried that reducing each one to a triangle of light in a matrix would make it hard to remember them as people, each commanding a voidmoth full of crew. But every candling light was as distinct and memorable as a face. Commander Talaw was at the top of the first column, as befit the senior moth commander, and the rest of the entries in the first column corresponded to Tactical One's bannermoths. Commander Nihara Keru headed the second column, which corresponded to the second tactical group's moths; her column alone remained dark, because she'd been sent to Kujen's service. The third column represented Tactical Three, and so on. Beside the communications panel, an identically formatted panel offered him a quick visual overview of the swarm moths' status. If his moths took damage, they would light up in varying intensities of red. Right now, the status panel was all yellow-green, indicating that the moths were in the process of modulating into the desired formation.

It didn't take long for Jedao's swarm to trigger the desired response. "Sir," Communications said in a strained voice. "The *Three Kestrels Three Suns* has opened a line to us. They request parley."

Well, why not? Jedao couldn't imagine that anything the enemy said would dissuade him from his mission. "Commander Talaw," he said. He could use this as an opportunity to wring some information from his opposite number. "Take the call for me."

Meraun frowned in his direction. The rest of the command center stuttered into an uncomfortable hush.

"Delighted, sir," Talaw said, sounding enthusiastic for once. "Connect me to *Three Kestrels Three Suns*, Communications."

Jedao had piped the relevant display to his own terminal as well. Thus he received a splendid view of the Three Kestrels Three Suns banner, along with the particular header that meant it was a prelude to parley, not battle. (How many unnecessary wars had the Kel gotten into because the other side didn't understand fussy Kel notions of propriety? Something to look up later.) Three black kestrels, outlined in gold, touched wingtip to wingtip over three gold suns arranged in a triangle balancing on its vertex like an upside-down mountain. Unusually for a Kel emblem, the field was a blue very close to Andan blue.

Inesser herself responding? Jedao thought. This could prove interesting.

Inesser's image unsmiled at him. Her uniform, in full formal, mirrored Jedao's almost perfectly. The only difference was the empty spot where he had the Shuos eye insignia beneath his general's wings. And, of course, the medals. She had a lot more medals than he did.

"This is Protector-General Kel Inesser," the woman said. Her voice was low and brisk. "So this is where you disappeared to, Talaw."

Shit, he'd fucked up already. Jedao mentally kicked himself. Just because he had amnesia and everyone was new to him didn't mean everyone else was new to each other.

An electric tension descended over the command center. The Kel *wanted* Inesser. They were vibratingly unhappy at having to oppose her. He'd have to deal with that as quickly as possible.

Worse, which way would Talaw jump? They'd made no secret of the fact that they disapproved of Jedao.

Talaw, focused on the conversation, hadn't noticed Jedao's

sudden dismay. "General," Talaw said, their voice deepening, and not in a friendly way. Just as importantly, they'd said "General," not "Protector-General." "I advise you to retreat."

Inesser narrowed her eyes at Talaw. "I would never have mistaken you for a crashhawk, *Commander*."

Talaw didn't flinch at the emphasis. "I don't answer to you." At their side, one of their hands closed into a fist.

Jedao was certain of two things. One, Talaw felt they owed loyalty to someone in the swarm. Two, that person wasn't Jedao. Then who?

Talaw's glance flicked sideways. And then Jedao knew. Talaw wasn't concerned about Jedao. Talaw was concerned about Dhanneth.

Friends? Jedao wondered. *Lovers?* Hawkfucking was forbidden, but that didn't mean it didn't happen.

Inesser was speaking. Her voice sharpened. "Either submit yourself to proper Kel authority or withdraw from this system immediately, Commander."

"Perhaps we should skip the pleasantries and go straight to the shooting," Talaw said.

Fox and hound, Jedao thought with a mixture of horror and delight, *Talaw's* baiting *her*. Excellent.

Inesser arched an eyebrow. "If that's how you want it," she said. "Protector-General Inesser out."

"Well," Talaw said, "that was quick."

Meraun tapped her fingers on the edge of her terminal. "I know the general. She's not going to waste time talking when there are upstarts to be crushed."

Did everyone but him know Inesser? Or, horrible thought, *did* he know Inesser? Another thing he should have looked up earlier. No help for it now, though.

Communications' voice sounded positively glum. "All the hostiles have bannered the Three Kestrels Three Suns, sir."

Jedao knew what that meant. The Compact had ceded control of its forces to Inesser, even if only for the duration of this fight. If he understood the situation correctly, this wasn't the coup for Inesser it might have been under the old system. The Compact's Kel served *voluntarily*. If they judged that Inesser was abusing her authority over them, they could quit.

"Well," Jedao drawled, "if Protector-General Inesser wants to fight, we'll fight." He didn't miss the way people eased fractionally when he used Inesser's title. Just because he intended to pummel her didn't mean he wanted to insult her randomly. But then, he'd given up on people having reasonable expectations of him.

To Communications, he said, "Tell all units to banner the Deuce of Gears upside down."

Communications blinked. "Sir?"

"You heard me. Invert it." Kujen had wanted him to use his old emblem, fine. That didn't mean he couldn't modify it to sow confusion. It seemed appropriate, anyway. Maybe if, by some miracle, he ever recovered his memories, he could go back to bannering right-side-up.

"One moment, sir." Communications relayed the instruction.

"Enemy swarm is holding position," Scan said.

"Sir," Communications said, a tremor in his voice betraying confusion, "General Inesser is asking for parley *again*."

"Is she now," Jedao said. "I'll allow it. This time, she's talking to me."

He was treated once more to Inesser's emblem, which he had to admit was very pretty. Was emblem envy a thing? If so, he had a bad case of it. He still couldn't get around the idea that people found a mismatched pair of gears threatening.

"*Jedao*," Inesser breathed the moment they were connected, with an intensity that suggested that, as little as he knew her, she knew *him* very well indeed. "I suppose you'd be more comfortable this way. Or is it Cheris these days? One loses track."

Cheris was the woman who had run off with his memories. What did Inesser mean by "more comfortable this way"? Did she think *he* was Cheris, after some mods? Jedao was suddenly very curious about what this Cheris person had been up to. "Just Jedao," he said at his most amiable. "Is there something I can do for you? Because unless I'm mistaken, we've already bannered. It would be a shame to let all that hostile intent go to waste."

"Spare me," Inesser said. "I knew you couldn't be up to any good when you disappeared. You're aware that Kel Command dishonorably discharged you?"

He was? But he didn't dare admit his ignorance, and more importantly, the bored expressions of his Kel told him that he could safely ignore this line of accusation. "You accused my moth commander of being a crashhawk," Jedao said. "Either apologize to them or let's fight."

"You're serious," Inesser said after a telling pause.

Why wouldn't he be? She'd offered insult to his senior moth commander. It reflected on his honor as well. Never mind that he was a Shuos; his honor was his swarm's honor. He kept silent, watching her face closely.

"Jedao," Inesser said, "you can't possibly hope to pull rank on me on account of a few centuries of service. Because the only two people who have any reasonable claim to countermanding your discharge are myself and High General Brezan. And the high general is my ally."

"That doesn't sound like an apology," Jedao said. "Say something relevant or we're opening fire." He glanced over at Talaw. Talaw did not look won over, but he hadn't expected them to be. It was the principle of the matter, that was all.

Meraun winced; Dhanneth shook his head. Nice that someone had faith in him. Inesser was either stalling or trying to drag intelligence out of him. She vastly outnumbered him, not an unimportant consideration even in space, if only because having more warmoths gave her access to more and deadlier formations. If she hadn't gone on the attack, it was because she thought *he* had the advantage. But he didn't have the time to explain this to his crew, nor the inclination. Either he would prove himself effective or they would be defeated, a refreshingly simple set of alternatives.

"There was a time when I thought you might have entered this mad crusade with good intentions, if lamentable results," Inesser said. "Your manifesto made that clear enough. But this? On the anniversary of the hexarchs' assassinations? Nine years of us rebuilding the shit you blew to pieces, and you're trying to throw everything back into chaos."

Kujen's notes hadn't said anything about Jedao being personally responsible for the hexarchate's fractured state, or a manifesto. On the other hand, the trouble with amnesia was that he could be responsible for anything from high treason to the pickle shortfalls on the eighth bannermoth in Tactical Three.

More, his crew had flinched this time. He couldn't let Inesser's words demoralize them further.

That brought him abruptly to the realization that he wasn't the target of this chat. Talking to him was an excuse for her to address his soldiers. She was maneuvering on another battlefield entirely. Of a sudden he *liked* her; wished they could meet person to person, wished she were his mentor. But he had a duty to Kujen and his Kel, and he intended to carry it out.

"I didn't hear the word 'apology' anywhere in there either," Jedao said. "Goodbye, Protector-General Inesser." He motioned for Communications to cut the line. "Communications, address to all moths. This is General Jedao. Resume advance at 38% acceleration." That would get them to the outer perimeter, as mapped by Strategy, within the next twenty-three minutes.

All the acknowledgment lights flashed rapidly at him. His swarm might not be eager to face Inesser, but they weren't reluctant, either.

"Sir," said Weapons, a lieutenant with a soft, round face like rice dough, "General Inesser's swarm appears to be modulating into Thunderbird Fury."

Weapons didn't have to also tell him that they didn't want to be in the way of the resulting shock wave when the formation completed itself. Scan confirmed that Inesser's bannermoths were forming up with dismaying accuracy. Kujen's notes had given Jedao the impression that Protector-General Inesser and High General Brezan didn't get along. Had Kujen or his informants been mistaken? If the

Compact and the hexarchate were accustomed to joint operations, they were in bigger trouble than Strategy had reckoned on.

"Special move orders for Commander Chwen," Jedao said, resisting the temptation to speak more rapidly. He needed to project calm. Chwen commanded the second warmoth in Tactical One. "In a moment the *Revenant* is going to charge. When it does, you will take up the formation's primary pivot until further notice." He might not have as many warmoths as Inesser and her friends, but he had enough that one moth out of place wouldn't cause the formation's geometry to degenerate into uselessness.

As he'd expected, the panel lit to indicate that Chwen had a question. Jedao was strongly of the opinion that Chwen needed to learn trust sooner rather than later. The order was clear enough. "Commander Chwen," he added coolly, "acknowledge."

After two seconds, the light turned amber. He would have preferred prompter acknowledgment, but it would do for a start.

"Special orders for the *Revenant*," Jedao said, training his regard on Commander Talaw. "Weapons, charge the shear cannon." He must remember to send Kujen a thank-you note for the weapon's mercifully short activation time. "On my mark, we will rush the *Three Kestrels Three Suns* on a direct intercept course."

He didn't intend to *ram* Inesser's command moth. That would be stupid, if possibly also amusing to whatever fox spirits lurked out in space watching human antics. But the more he could scare her, the better. Failing that, he might as well use his reputation for being crazy.

"Course plotted," Navigation said. Her shoulders were hunched. Jedao wished he could tell her to cheer up. It wouldn't help, so he refrained.

"Shear cannon charged," Weapons said after that.

Don't do this. The tarnished voice again.

Give me one reason why not, Jedao thought, on the grounds that it would be best if his crew didn't find out he was hearing voices. He'd seen no evidence that anyone else heard the *Revenant*. *I can try to spare the moths*—if nothing else, captured moths might make for useful assets, which was how he planned to sell the idea to Kujen—*but I still need to overcome the hostiles*.

You can win without it. You have a history of improbable victories.

Great, now it was paying him backhanded compliments by way of incredibly stupid tactical advice. The whole point of the shear cannon was that he could use it to attack into hostile calendrical terrain. Certainly he had no intention of advancing into the Compact's space.

It added, reluctantly, *The cannon hurts me.*

I don't have a lot of options, Jedao said.

Inesser's immense swarm didn't advance far; didn't have to. Jedao had studied the meticulous, beautifully formatted reports on the shear cannon's performance characteristics. He waited until the enemy tripped the virtual wire he'd determined beforehand, then said, "Mark."

The *Revenant* hummed as it sprinted toward the *Three Kestrels Three Suns*. The vibrations transmitted themselves throughout the entire seat despite the webbing holding Jedao in place. Talaw was leaning forward, scrutinizing one of their subdisplays. Meraun, for her part, had an air of callous cheer. Jedao got the impression that not much fazed her.

"On my mark," Jedao said, "fire the shear cannon." He thanked whoever had given him his augment. The inner ticking awareness of passing time would enable him to time this more precisely than if he had to stare at a watch.

Inesser's swarm was coalescing, the pivots moving into place. Closer, closer, closer—

"Mark," Jedao said.

Weapons grimaced and jabbed one of the controls. "Shear cannon fired."

No explosions; no fireworks. But Jedao bit his tongue involuntarily at the sudden agonizing static in his head. The cloying taste of blood flooded his mouth. He could hear the *Revenant* screaming. "Shut it off!" Or at least that was what he tried to say.

"Sir?" Talaw said grudgingly. "Could you be more specific?" Their voice came as from a distance spun from cobwebs.

The *Revenant's* voice ground out, *I tried to warn you.*

That only aggravated the pain that filled Jedao's skull. If it got any worse, his head would fall off. And if that made it stop hurting, he would welcome it.

The roaring dimmed, and with it the pain. Everyone in the command center was staring at him as though he'd sprouted gills, with the exception of Doctrine, who was hunched trying to look inconspicuous. That answered the question of whether anyone else could hear the static, or the *Revenant.*

More to the point, his reaction had disrupted operations in the command moth. Unforgivable. Talaw's face was drawn tight with distaste as they wrestled with some inner decision.

"Commander," Jedao rasped, "ignore that. Scan, Protector-General Inesser's status?"

"Complete formation collapse," Scan said, awed. "Everything's jumbled out of place like that time with my baby cousin and the cats and my brother's yarn stash."

Dhanneth had already zoomed in on the relevant area of the tactical subdisplay for Jedao's benefit. The swarm moths were in disarray, disrupting the necessary geometry. To be more precise, the shear cannon had stretched the underlying weave of spacetime. The moths had moved accordingly.

Jedao wanted nothing more than to crawl back into bed and sleep for a year, or until the pain was gone. But he wasn't finished. "Communications." He wasn't sure the words had clawed out of his throat until the man straightened, awaiting his orders. "Tell General Inesser that she can agree to a meeting to discuss terms, or—"

Communications wasn't paying attention. He gulped. "Sir, message from the *hexarch.*"

Jedao kept speaking. "—she can watch me dissect her swarm into pieces so tiny you'd need tweezers to put it back together. Her choice." With any luck, she would discuss terms. He didn't want to kill more people than absolutely necessary.

Wrong move. Communications, thwarted of Jedao's attention, played the message for Commander Talaw instead. Kujen's image flared into life before Talaw, almost in the middle of the command center. "Countermand," Kujen said in a voice like black ice. "Commander Talaw, relieve General Jedao of command. You hold the swarm for the duration. You are to take advantage of the enemy's disarray to destroy Isteia Mothyard to complete the calendrical spike. Once you have achieved your objective, you will retire and rendezvous with Tactical Two. At no point are you to make further contact with the protector-general. Are my instructions clear?"

Talaw nodded sharply. "Absolutely clear, Hexarch." Then they smiled. "Doctrine, have someone escort Shuos Jedao from the command center. The hexarch's instructions take priority."

Jedao, the *Revenant* said, but its voice was weak.

I could fight this, Jedao thought. But he didn't think he could take down the entire command center. Instead, he sat and watched until two Doctrine officers entered. It didn't escape his notice that both of them topped him by a head, and outmassed him correspondingly, as if they expected him to wrestle them on the way out.

Jedao unwebbed himself and stood. "I'm ready," he said. "Fight well, Commander."

Talaw disdained to answer.

As Jedao exited the command center, he heard Talaw give the order to bomb Isteia Mothyard.

CHAPTER FOURTEEN

THE CELL CONTAINED a bench that provided both a place to sit and a place to sleep, and a commode. A see-through barrier separated Jedao from the rest of the word. Across from him was another cell. A Kel in low formal napped on her own bench. She'd kicked her boots into the corner in a display either of slovenliness or defiance. That, or the boots pinched.

He occupied himself for the first half-hour (was it a half-hour? They'd disabled his augment and, by extension, its chronometer) inspecting the cells for possible ways out as he concocted stories about how the Kel soldier had ended up in the brig. Maybe she'd smuggled a pet into barracks, and they'd caught her sneaking morsels of rice to her ferret/scorpion/monkey/snake. Maybe she'd showed up to drill wearing her shirt inside-out. Or napped on duty, or mixed up the lubricants for the gun mounts, or—

She had woken and was staring at him. More accurately, she'd scrunched herself up in a corner of her own cell as if she thought he could kill her with a look.

"Hello," Jedao said, hoping he sounded friendly. "What'd you do to get yourself locked up?"

She startled when he addressed her. "Sir?" Her voice was muffled by the barrier, which meant his was as well.

"Tell me why you're here."

Her eyes were still white-rimmed, but she answered. "I like to sleep in. Sir. It doesn't mix real well with soldiering. Every so often I miss the reveille and end up here. They say there's some kind of fault in my augment, but it's cheaper to toss me back here for fucking up than to fix it." She bit her lip, then burst out, "I'll try to do better, sir, I swear! Please don't—please don't—" She shut up.

Fox and hound, she thought she was in here with him as some kind of personal punishment. "I'm here for the same reason you are," Jedao said, which only made her eyes widen further, this time in incredulity. "I mean, not the sleeping part. The failure to go along with orders part. Sorry to disappoint you."

Of course, since they were both here, and she was talking to him after all, maybe he could learn something about her, and about the ordinary soldiers that he didn't get much opportunity to interact with. Even if she probably would rather that he leave her alone. But she was staring at him, and he doubted she'd relax so long as he was in the brig with her.

"Does it bother you," Jedao said, "being shunted down here?"

"I'm just garden Kel," she said after a hesitant pause. "I do well enough when I have some sky overhead, not all these walls. When the action picks up, things will go better for me. Begging your pardon, sir."

"'Garden Kel'?"

"Guessing no one used the term around you. It's one of the nicer ones."

"Infantry, then."

She nodded, fidgeting.

"Have you seen a lot of action planetside?"

"A couple of campaigns," she said. "One of them was real interesting. Some genius decided it'd be pretty to stick a station in the middle of a planet's rings, nice view for an artists' retreat. But you know artists." He didn't, but he wouldn't have dreamed of interrupting her. "They made the mistake of broadcasting heretical performance art. One corporal in my unit got a hold of a couple unauthorized clips. Real pretty stuff, all gymnastics-like. But we were supposed to go in and blow the place apart, so that's what we did."

Jedao blinked. "You didn't get in trouble because of the clips?"

"The officers don't usually bother with that stuff unless it's radioactively heretical." She gulped—apparently she'd just remembered that he was an officer. Or something like one. "They got better stuff to mess with."

"I'm sure," he said. "What's your name?"

Her voice trembled. "I'm Kel Opaira. Just my bad luck to be here while there's fighting going on, but it could be worse. At least I can, I can catch up on sleep. And it's not like you were going to land infantry on the mothyard if you were planning to blow it up, were you? But what are you doing down here? Don't they need you up in the command center?"

"Not the hexarch's opinion, apparently," Jedao said.

This got her attention. "You let him boss you around? Isn't *he* afraid of *you*?"

"Not that I've been able to tell."

"You trust a civilian to do your job?"

He seemed to have hit on some issue of Kel professional pride. "How do you hear about all this from down here?" Jedao said. Especially if she'd been asleep?

Opaira shook her head. "They don't tell you much, do they?"

He couldn't argue with that. "Well," he said, "you can remedy that."

"Not anyone's secret, really." Opaira held up her left arm. "Wired for heat pulses in here, see? Kel drum code, everything all in rhythm, so the unit can get info on incoming hostiles or whatever the hell. But there's also a bunch of chatter when things get boring. And, I mean, I don't know what it's like for someone like you, but for us garden Kel, things get boring a whole bunch. Your augment's damped, right? But they don't bother blocking the heat pulses."

"Which I don't have because I'm not garden Kel."

"Or Kel at all." Her voice dipped pityingly.

Jedao couldn't blame her. He wouldn't have minded her life for himself. Waking up (or not) at reveille. Taking mess with the rest of the company in the designated hall. Infantry drill, the constant friendship of weapons. And always the humming awareness that if you died, you didn't have to die alone.

"You're right, though," Jedao said. "I can't stay here when people might get hurt."

"How are you planning on getting out?" she said, wary again. "Can't just walk out."

"I don't know how the lock works," Jedao said. "But surely someone does."

"Oh, yeah," Opaira said. "Doctrine officers. Wormfuckers, all of them. Begging your pardon."

"What would happen if we got into a fight?" Jedao said. How could he get someone to let him out?

Opaira winced. "Rather not, sir. You have—you have a bit of a reputation. Would rather live."

Huh. "Would a medical emergency do it?"

"Oh, that's an old one. They won't fall for it." She reconsidered. "Well, I guess you could bust up the shitter or something, but honestly, you want to end up pissing in the corner if the hexarch gets petty? I bet he's the petty type."

I bet so too, Jedao thought, but he didn't say that out loud. He'd just experienced Kujen's maddening arbitrariness firsthand, after all. And Kujen would be monitoring him here.

Jedao reinspected the commode anyway. Like all the furniture, it was securely affixed to the floor. He didn't see any obvious bolts he could try to pry out.

"All right," he said, "that's not going to do it."

"Good," Opaira said, on firmer ground. "Sit down and wait, that's what I always do."

"Oh, no," Jedao said, backing up to the far wall without touching it. He eyed the barrier. He'd discovered early on that it delivered an unpleasant jolt if he touched it. "No point in cutting up my arm or breaking my leg or any such nonsense. The hexarch doesn't care if I can hold a stylus and it doesn't matter to him if I'm ambulatory. What he wants out of me is my head. Even if he has a good acting general in Talaw. So—"

The cell was small. But it gave him a little freedom of movement. He *lunged* forward, accelerating as quickly as he could, and smashed his head into the barrier.

Behind him, Opaira squawked in alarm. Good: if she thought this was a terrible idea, so would whoever was monitoring him. For a moment he saw a bright starry flash. The jolting pain, too, hit immediately.

He backed up again without losing his balance, which impressed him. (Instant soldier: just add water.) Did it again.

And again.

And—

"—permanent damage if you concuss yourself!" Opaira was yelling. "To say nothing of getting your brain cells scrambled!"

Well, yes. That was the idea. He couldn't bluff. His monitors would be able to tell. Or he hoped they could tell, because otherwise he was doing this for no good reason. Oh well, it might be educational to see Medical at work from the patient's side of things.

Jedao levered himself up again—

He heard rather than saw the barrier go down just as he reached it, a thrum and a change in air pressure. He took advantage of the othersense: any newcomers? Yes, as a matter of fact. Lowering his head, he swerved and charged through.

"Ouch, snakefucker!" said the newcomer as Jedao swept her legs out from under her.

Huh, Jedao thought. *I didn't know I could do that either.*

"Sir—I mean, Shuos, *you're under arre*—ouch!"

By then he was past the newcomer, a squat Doctrine officer. The wolf's-head emblem at her breast indicated that she was a Rahal. Another person he wouldn't mind having a chat with. But now that he had escaped, he didn't have any excuse to linger.

Despite the augment's obstinate refusal to talk to him, a map unfurled in Jedao's mind as he leaned on the othersense. Not only did he know the shearmoth's layout, he knew where everyone on it was. The movements of individuals were as distinct as the spectra of stars in the forever sky. Even more, he could *feel* the motions of the other swarm moths as though they were dancing on the surface of his skull.

That, or he was going crazy after all. But he could stop dead and question the information, or he could make use of it before the beleaguered Rahal stopped him. He chose the latter.

Jedao dove through the closing doors, which flinched back open at his approach. Handy safety feature, that. Then he skidded left, ran down a dreary segment of hallway lined with forbidding hangings of the hexarchate's wheel, turned left again, and narrowly avoided crashing into the lift. He'd wondered if variable layout would prove an issue, but it didn't seem to be active in this section. He bet it had something to do with his disabled augment.

Curiously, the Rahal didn't pursue him. At least, he didn't hear her footfalls behind him. But she would alert the command center of his escape, if she hadn't already.

At this point, the inexplicable othersense betrayed him. Not because it was wrong—no one occupied the lift, or was waiting for it with him—but because it failed to account for things like lift codes. The augment must transmit those on his behalf, something else he'd never thought about before. Now he was shut out.

All right, that wasn't going to work. Maintenance shaft, then? He couldn't remember whether those required access codes, too. It beat staying here to be treed, though.

He retraced his steps back to the intersection and took the hallway curving in the other direction. After passing several mysterious doorways—his sense of *whereness* told him nothing about the rooms' function, just a jumbled distribution of masses that he couldn't translate into visuals—he located a maintenance shaft. He'd never known anyone other than the servitors to use them. Engineering always sent him reports collated from the servitors' records. Thankfully, whoever had designed the moth (Kujen?) had ensured that the shaft could accommodate a human. Good thinking: what if the moth needed emergency repairs and servitors weren't available?

Jedao flexed his hands, then began climbing up. He swallowed a sudden surge of panic at the sensation of the walls closing around him, even though they weren't, and fought back the claustrophobia. The mysterious inner map connected him to the world outside the shaft and gave him the illusory reassurance that he wouldn't die alone.

His arms and legs protested the unaccustomed exertion. The aches were an excellent distraction from the situation. A less welcome distraction was his internal awareness of the swarm moths. He almost lost his balance once, twice, while unpuzzling their maneuvers. While he'd had no trouble recognizing formations and the modulations between them on the tactical subdisplay, this unasked-for proprioception was hard to get used to.

Halfway to his immediate goal—a small chamber where he could regroup and figure out his next move—he started to worry. There was still no sign of pursuit. And he didn't believe in luck. Not good luck, anyway.

Jedao reached the chamber. For whatever reason, there was no artificial gravity here. He suffered a moment of disorientation trying to figure out which wall to use as a floor, then clung determinedly to the one where he'd emerged.

Each wall contained panels with numerical and graphical readouts, none of which he knew how to interpret. He didn't dare interfere with any of them. He might be in the midst of a quarrel with Kujen, but he wasn't about to play technician with the command moth.

He released his grip first with one hand, then the other, cracking his knuckles. His hands were already threatening to cramp. He huffed a self-deprecating laugh. Maybe Doctrine didn't need to chase him when they knew he'd tire himself out. Where could he go? The command center was the only place where his presence had any meaning.

A flicker-ripple alerted him of someone's approach. Only one—person? A servitor? A very large centipede?

He could run again, but to what end? Better to stay and see if he could talk sense to whoever it was.

The newcomer proceeded at an infuriatingly slow pace. Jedao clambered over to another wall so he could jump them if they looked hostile. He hated treating his own crew as hostiles, but Kujen hadn't left him much choice.

Eventually a different officer emerged. First Jedao saw the man's blotchy, balding head, then a blocky pair of shoulders almost too wide for the maintenance shaft. Aha: the wolf's-head emblem again, heavily foreshortened. Another Rahal. "I know you're in there, sir," the officer said without craning his head to look at Jedao.

"Splendid," Jedao said. "Take me to the command center."

"You're under—"

"—arrest. I know. That's too bad, because you're going to take me to the command center."

The Rahal still didn't change the angle of his head. "How are you going to contrive *that*, sir?"

"I would prefer not to fight you," Jedao said, doing his best to project *I am a badass. Instant soldier, just add water. Ruo, you would be laughing so hard at what I'm trying to pull here.* "You have a job to do and I might need you later."

"The hexarch gave his orders."

"The hexarch," Jedao said, "is on another moth far away. I'm right here."

"Sir," the Rahal said, "please return quietly with me or we'll both suffer the consequences."

"Tell me," Jedao said, "how's the battle going?"

"Inesser was completely unprepared for the shear cannon," the Rahal said. "Your assistance is not required."

Fuck. "You need me to *stop* the fighting," Jedao said. "Or do you really want all the Kel shooting each other? That can't be good for morale."

The Rahal was scowling. "You're the Immolation Fox. Why do you—argh!"

Jedao had launched himself from the wall and delivered a chop to the side of the Rahal's neck in passing. He grabbed the Rahal by the arm and pulled him into an embrace, not out of amorous intent but to keep the man from smashing into the wall. Jedao checked his pulse: alive, thank goodness.

A quick search revealed that the Rahal had brought spider restraints with him. Jedao trussed him to the handholds. "Sorry about that," Jedao said on his way out of the chamber with its chatter of status displays. "I'll send someone for you later."

When he emerged from the next maintenance shaft, a squad of six Kel awaited him. Their guns were trained on him. Slowly, Jedao raised his hands and smiled at them. One woman's trigger finger shifted, withdrew. *What the hell did I use to do while smiling at people?* he wondered.

"Commander Kel Talaw will see you," said the highest-ranked one, a sergeant whose expression said she wished she were enjoying a nice quiet nap in barracks instead.

"Why," Jedao said, "were you afraid I was going to break down the doors if you didn't take me in?"

"The commander is being very indulgent."

"I'm sure." Jedao surveyed the squad. "Commander Talaw is the one I want to talk to anyway. I'll permit it."

"It's not your decision."

He lifted an eyebrow at her. "Of course it isn't. Well, I'd hate to keep the commander waiting."

The sergeant made an irritable gesture. One of the soldiers holstered his gun and brought out spider restraints.

What is it with people and those things? Jedao thought. Did real spiders spin the restraints, or were they human-manufactured? Perhaps somewhere in the bowels of the *Revenant* lived a colony of spiders, diligently weaving spider restraints for wayward generals.

The horrible pain scraped through his head. It helped that he was prepared for it this time. Commander Talaw must have fired the shear cannon again. Jedao listened for the *Revenant*. Nothing.

"I'll come along," Jedao said. "I'd rather not have those things on me, though."

"Sir, I must insist," the sergeant said.

The soldier with the restraints signaled frantically with his eyebrows that he didn't want to get into a wrestling match over this. The sergeant signaled back with a combination of eyebrows and hand motions. Under other circumstances, Jedao would have enjoyed watching the exchange, but he did need to recover his command.

Jedao didn't want to initiate hostilities. But the situation was only growing worse. He consulted the othersense. The faraway swarms that he recognized as Inesser's were in bad shape. In particular, the largest one, Inesser's cindermoth, had stopped firing down the incoming flock of missiles, which meant their point defenses had gone down. He had to intervene before this turned into a senseless massacre.

"Fuck this," Jedao said, losing patience. He was guessing that these Kel didn't have much experience taking generals into custody or they'd have trussed him up already. He snatched the restraints out of the soldier's hands and snared another's hands in them. "You're wasting everyone's time."

The sergeant's entire face pulled downward. "I warned you, sir." She gestured sharply.

Four bullets slammed into Jedao. One took him in the side of the head, another in the neck. The third hit him in center of mass, blowing out most of his chest. The last whined over his shoulder, missing him by a meter. In the scatter-shock moment before the pain registered, he thought, *Someone needs more time at the firing range.*

Jedao fell ungracefully on his side. His elbow and left hip were going to sport spectacular bruises. Funny how the mind fixed on ridiculous details. His augment had jolted back on and was offering diagnostics that he was too stupid with shock to interpret.

One of the soldiers was waving her gun around in an entirely unsafe manner, terrible muzzle control, and shouting at the sergeant: "Fucking hell, sir, what are we supposed to do now?"

"He's the fucking Immolation Fox, he wasn't supposed to go down that easy!" the sergeant yelled back.

Jedao clambered back to his feet. His vision had blurred, and patches of darkness encroached on every side. But the proprioception had, if anything, strengthened. "Excuse me," he said, forcing the words past his teeth. His mouth was filled with blood, and controlling individual muscles took all his concentration. "I'm still here. Could we get on with this?"

The sergeant blanched. "How—how—"

Jedao would have liked an answer to that question himself, since by all rights he should be dead or well on the way to it. But the emergency hadn't gone away. He lurched toward the soldier to the sergeant's side and plucked the gun out of his grasp. "Thank you," Jedao mumbled. For some reason that basic courtesy caused the unlucky soldier to piss himself. He started babbling in a language Jedao didn't recognize. "That'll be handy."

He could see the application of unkillable soldiers. It was proving useful right now. At the same time, he didn't enjoy feeling like a freak, and judging from the Kel squad's reactions, they hadn't had any idea about this either. He bet Kujen would have answers, if he ever got the chance to ask the questions.

Jedao shifted the gun just slightly, pointing it several inches to the right of the sergeant's head. She backed away from him, sweat trickling down her face. He couldn't see why she was so worried. If he genuinely wanted to threaten her, he'd already have shot her. Admittedly, she might be worried about ricochets if he started randomly pulling the trigger.

(So he also knew how to use a handgun. Useful, if disconcerting. He hoped he didn't have to reload the damn thing in a hurry.)

"I believe you said the commander's waiting?" Jedao said.

This time the sergeant didn't argue.

Despite Jedao's difficulty walking, he kept his gun pointed to the right of the sergeant's head, and away from anybody else. Although he was outnumbered, the Kel squad didn't know what to do with someone who wouldn't go down when shot. He couldn't blame them. They hadn't kept trying, also interesting. Pragmatism, shock, or worry that they'd kill him inadvertently?

The sergeant preceded him into the command center. Talaw, sitting in their accustomed seat, began to snap a reprimand, then stared at Jedao. "General Jedao," Talaw said in a brittle voice.

"Sorry to interrupt," Jedao said. Speaking took all his concentration when he was having difficulty keeping his head from lolling to the side. Keeping track of all his body parts was proving troublesome. "Status of the battle, Commander?"

Talaw's gaze dropped to a display at their side, then back up to Jedao's face. They smiled mirthlessly. "The hexarch—"

"The hexarch isn't here." Jedao was impressed that no one had opened fire on him, but either they were too horrified to attempt anything or the blood leaking down the side of his neck and from the hole in his chest was as distracting to them as it was to him.

Talaw glared at him. "I don't see that I owe any information to an inhuman walking corpse."

He couldn't disregard the challenge to his authority. On the other hand, threatening his crew was unsustainable, especially if he wanted them to continue being his crew. With a slowness that wasn't all theater, he shoved the gun into his belt. He hoped it wouldn't randomly discharge into his thigh. His luck held, if you could call it that.

"I would prefer to have your cooperation, Commander." Jedao decided he might as well use his smile as a weapon, since everyone reacted to it like one. He focused on the othersense, on interpreting what it told him. "The *Three Kestrels Three Suns* lost its point defenses a few seconds before your squad tried to apprehend me," he said. "The swarm is in disarray. You're about to destroy it."

Talaw looked shaken in spite of themselves. "A good guess. And irrelevant, in any case. You can't save it from its fate."

Jedao was sure his grin was ghastly. "Can't I?" He swung slowly around, meeting each Kel's gaze in turn. "Countermand," he said. "I have no intention of destroying the protector-general." Demanding Inesser's surrender would result in another intervention from Kujen. He'd have to salvage the situation otherwise. "Retreat to Second Tactical's current position."

He might be an inhuman walking corpse, but he was the inhuman walking corpse offering them a way to save the general they'd rather be serving.

Talaw ground out, "The hexarch has ordered otherwise." But they were tempted. He could see it in Talaw's rigid jaw.

Jedao peeled off first one glove, then the other, and flung them at Talaw's feet. The command center plummeted silent, except for the sound of dripping blood. "I'll take that up with the hexarch myself when I see him next. I am your general." He didn't like leaning on formation instinct, but he was out of options. "*Turn the swarm around*."

Everyone's eyes were drawn not to the gloves, but to the gun in Jedao's belt. Talaw was breathing shallowly, and too fast.

I don't have time *for this*, Jedao thought. He couldn't countenance the slaughter of Inesser and her troops, not when they'd already been defeated. But neither did he want to risk the lives of his own soldiers. Inesser might be able to regroup for a counterattack, even now. He needed to resolve this quickly.

Jedao staggered toward Talaw's seat. Blood continued to drip. He glanced down and saw that it was a sluggish black, not red. Shit. That couldn't mean anything good.

He laid his hands on Talaw's shoulders and leaned over them. "Do it," he said in his friendliest voice.

Talaw flinched from Jedao's bare hands. For a second, Jedao thought that Talaw would surge up from the seat and fling him to the ground. He wouldn't be able to fight back, except perhaps by bleeding on Talaw. And he was pretty sure that Kel commanders didn't succumb to squeamishness that easily.

Tension gathered in Talaw's shoulders; dissipated. Jedao was momentarily relieved that he wasn't going to be punched in the face for his temerity. Among other things, he was already worried that his head would fall off.

"Communications, address to all units," Talaw said. They were staring straight into Jedao's eyes, and he knew then that he'd lost any hope of their friendship forever. "This is Commander Talaw. All units retreat to—"

Thank fox and hound it worked, Jedao thought, and was completely unprepared for the darkness that rose up to swallow him. The last thing he saw was the black-stained floor rushing up to greet him.

CHAPTER FIFTEEN

"HELLO AGAIN," JEDAO said to Hemiola as the other servitors escorted it into the shrine. Mistrikor, the girl in the frayed robe, trailed after them. No one seemed to mind her presence.

At least, Hemiola assumed it was a shrine. Like the hexagonal chamber back at Tefos Base, alcoves in the walls contained plaques. But the room itself was shaped like a perfect cube, and the inscriptions on the plaques were written in flaring patterns of light: Machine Universal, not the high language or one of the humans' low languages. And not just Machine Universal, but the interlocking phrases of a song. It had never encountered other servitors' music before. Panic gripped it. Would the humans approve?

Or did they already know?

Jedao?—Cheris?—sat cross-legged against the far wall. He gestured toward the spot in front of him. Reluctantly, Hemiola approached and lowered itself to the floor.

The girl spoke before Hemiola could think of something to say to Jedao. She was staring at Jedao with undisguised interest. "You're much shorter than I thought you would be," she said.

"I don't believe we've been introduced?" Jedao said. "I'm Ajewen Cheris."

"You mean you're Jedao."

Jedao sighed quietly. "That too. It's complicated. Yourself?"

The girl nudged Hemiola aside. Confused, Hemiola made space for her. She took its spot directly across from Jedao. "I'm Lirit Mistrikor."

"No," one of the other servitors said, "what you are is procrastinating."

Mistrikor gestured rudely in the servitor's direction. Specifically, a Machine Universal obscenity involving nonlinear dynamics. "You don't think this is more educational than falling asleep trying to memorize sumptuary regulations for the New Year Festival? How else am I supposed to become a liaison between our peoples if I don't know how your court proceedings work?"

Hemiola blinked in alarm. It hadn't realized the extent of Mistrikor's ambitions. Then again, it should have learned by now that the unassuming ones were always agents of revolutionary change.

Mistrikor twisted around to face it. "And you. You're from off-station, aren't you? Hence the tribunal."

"It came with me," Jedao said.

"Which is why it was running away?" Mistrikor said. She cocked her head at Hemiola. "You *were* running away, weren't you?"

Hemiola flashed a chastened pink-orange.

"Oh, don't apologize to *me*," Mistrikor said. "I'm just here for the tribunal. But you had to know you were going to get caught."

"I'm from Tefos Enclave," Hemiola said in Machine Universal. "We didn't see many visitors." Just the hexarch and Jedao, at intervals of a century. And only three of them at Tefos, as opposed to what must be a large enough servitor population to accommodate the needs of 800,000 humans.

"Never heard of it," Mistrikor said. "So I'm here even though I'm going to flunk out and I'll be stuck as a civilian laborer for the rest of my life. What's *your* excuse?"

"Flunk out of what?" Jedao said, maddeningly, as if it mattered.

Mistrikor squirmed. "I *was* studying for the Rahal entrance examinations. But half those regulations are so ridiculous."

"Then why Rahal," Hemiola asked, "and not another faction?" It knew little about the Rahal, not least because they weren't glamorous enough to feature much in dramas.

She looked at it as though it had asked a stupid question, which was entirely possible. "Because it's the only way to change all the stupid laws."

"So you should be studying," one of the servitors, the catform, said with red lights for emphasis.

"Oh, come *on*," Mistrikor said, "how many chances am I going to have to talk to the Immolation Fox? Or watch a tribunal with a stranger-servitor from a place so distant no one's ever heard of it?"

"You can observe," the catform said, "if you promise to go back to your room and prepare for the examination after."

Mistrikor opened her mouth to protest. Instead, her stomach rumbled loudly. "The sacrifices I make," she said. "All the fasting. My growth is going to be stunted."

While Mistrikor and her keepers squabbled, Hemiola asked one of the other servitors, "What is the protocol for a tribunal?"

"You're Nirai, aren't you?" replied a deltaform. "I can always tell."

"Yes," Hemiola said, and introduced itself, for propriety's sake.

"We have a problem," the deltaform said. "Tefos Enclave has no standing treaty with the Trans-Enclave. I wouldn't even have thought it possible. But then, I'm only 102 years old and it's a big galaxy. Are you qualified to negotiate on behalf of Tefos?"

The question struck Hemiola as absurd. It doubted Sieve or Rhombus would ever make their way out here. Still—"Are there any standard procedures for situations like this?"

"That depends on what you're here for," the deltaform said.

Hemiola had an opportunity, then. "Information exchange." It might have access to the hexarch's records, but it needed to be able to put those in context. The trouble was, what could it offer?

The ugly truth was, if it wanted to unspool the hexarch's notes, it would have to surrender—not the notes themselves, necessarily, but what it knew of his routines. Assuming the Trans-Enclave had any interest in that information.

"All right," the deltaform said, as if it went through transactions like this every day. "What do you want, and what are you offering?"

"I want grid access," Hemiola said, greatly daring. "Nothing classified. Just—the kind of access that an ordinary citizen would have."

"That's easy enough," the deltaform said, its lights tranquil blue. "We'll have to update you on local protocol so you don't foul up the grid. And your offer?"

"Tefos Enclave periodically hosts Hexarch Nirai Kujen," Hemiola said, feeling like a traitor. "I don't know if this is of inter—"

"Done," the deltaform said promptly. "Excuse me while I discuss the arrangements with my colleagues."

While it waited, Hemiola returned to reviewing the hexarch's archives. It had skipped forward to a dreary chunk of research on voidmoths because the hexarch had shown an increasing obsession with them. Not the initial harnessing that made mothdrives viable, but an obscure line of research that involved breeding moths for size. It had always known that moths came in various sizes, from the immense cindermoths to the small scoutmoths and needlemoths. It hadn't, however, realized that this was the result of deliberate tampering.

Like most servitors, Hemiola, while not an expert on mothdrive technology, was acquainted with the basics. The larger the moth, the faster and more powerful its drive. Scoutmoths had minimal crews and were as small as they could practically be made while being able to keep up with a warmoth swarm. As far as Hemiola knew, the Nirai refused to acknowledge an upper limit on the moths' size, but the lower limit for a useful scoutmoth was well known. After a certain point, invariant maneuver drives were more effective and less hassle.

"There you go," the deltaform said, blinking to recapture Hemiola's attention. It sent a databurst containing not just the protocols, but what claimed to be a standardized treaty for stranger-servitors from unaffiliated enclaves.

Hemiola reviewed the treaty, trying not to feel too overwhelmed. It didn't see anything immediately objectionable. "I agree to this on the behalf of Tefos Enclave," it said, "subject to future negotiation if necessary."

"Of course," the deltaform said, still in soothing blue. Perhaps unfairly, Hemiola wondered if it ever spoke in anything other than blue.

"—mediation."

Suddenly aware that it had lost track of its surroundings, Hemiola redirected its attention to the catform. Mistrikor was gesturing animatedly at it.

The catform said to Hemiola, "I apologize for the irregularity of the proceedings."

Hemiola refrained from mentioning that it couldn't tell the difference, given how long it had spent away from mainstream servitor society. "Mediation?"

Jedao smiled wryly at it. "Since we're both here and our goals are in conflict, yes."

"I won't help you destroy the hexarch."

Jedao didn't argue this point straight off. Instead, he said, "You must think highly of him."

Hemiola wasn't sure that was the case anymore. As it progressed through the hexarch's notes, he became more and more absorbed—obsessed, even—with research and personal luxuries. It had tried to tell itself that this didn't mean anything. But finding traces of the man who had tried to prevent a girl from starving to death grew increasingly difficult. Still, it said, "I know my duty. I thought you did too."

Jedao's smile became more lopsided. "Not many people would say that to me. The hexarch is old, and wise after a fashion; he has also hurt a lot of people. He can't be allowed to remain in power."

"Then let me look for evidence of that," Hemiola said. "The man who left those notes wanted peace and stability and a world without hunger. How can those be bad things?"

"Good luck with that one," the catform said to Jedao.

Jedao sighed. "Thank you so much."

"You're welcome."

Jedao turned back to Hemiola. "I don't know what happened to that man. But he wasn't the man I met four hundred years ago, and as for who he is now—" His mouth compressed. "If you have access to the grid now—"

Hemiola blinked an affirmative.

"—perhaps I can show you some of the consequences of his decisions, even if he was too secretive to show himself in public."

"I'll take you up on that," Hemiola said, scarcely believing its own boldness. "First, though, I need to know who Ajewen Cheris is, and why you're going around with more than one name." Based on Mistrikor's reaction, Cheris, like Jedao, was someone with a reputation. With any luck, it would be able to verify the basics with access to Ayong Primary's grid.

The discussion had attracted Mistrikor's attention. "You haven't heard of Cheris?" she demanded. "At least tell me you know who Jedao is."

"Yes," Hemiola said, a bit stiffly. "Which one are you?" it asked Jedao-Cheris-whoever.

"Whoever I need to be," Jedao-Cheris-whoever said. Their eyes were sad. "I used to be one person. I was a Kel. Now I have fragments of a dead man in my head."

It tried to parse that. "So you're really Jedao."

"I remember being the man who was Kujen's companion for centuries," they said. "And I remember being an ordinary infantry officer. I am who I need to be for the mission. Call me Cheris, if you like. It reminds me why I'm doing this."

Mistrikor was practically bouncing on her toes. "I knew it! I knew you hadn't left everyone behind."

"Behind?" Hemiola asked.

"She broke the calendar," Mistrikor said. "Nine years ago. It was a big deal. I guess you must have been in a very remote location if it didn't affect you."

All of Hemiola's lights went dark as it tried to process this idea. This person who was part-Jedao had broken the hexarch's own calendar? It had gotten far enough into the notes to understand how seriously the hexarch took the idea of constructing a new social order.

"Let me," Mistrikor said, leaning forward. She didn't seem to be intimidated by Cheris in the slightest. "How big was the human population of Tefos?"

"Usually zero," Hemiola said, with perfect honesty. "The hexarch and Jedao"—it faltered, then resumed speaking—"were the only ones who visited, only for a month or so every century."

Her eyes went round. "So there weren't any remembrances?"

It consulted its memories. "The hexarch liked to practice the New Year's dances," it said, carefully omitting mention of Jedao, "although they didn't visit around the actual New Year. He also liked anything to do with lanterns, for reasons that never became clear to me."

Cheris's face didn't change, but it could detect the slight change in the heat distribution in her body: anger.

Mistrikor wasn't done. "But nothing with Vidona?"

"He never brought any Vidona with him," Hemiola said. It had a rudimentary awareness that the Vidona oversaw remembrances. That was all.

Mistrikor's breath escaped her in a huff. "Well," she said, without waiting for anyone's permission. "I've got a lot to tell you about how the system works for ordinary people. *Especially* the remembrances."

CHAPTER SIXTEEN

JEDAO WOKE UP in slow, painful stages, as though his muscles were peeling off until only the most essential ones remained. As a result, he didn't realize that Dhanneth had been trying to spoon soup into him until the major came into focus all at once.

"Major," Jedao said. It emerged as a croak.

"Shh," Dhanneth said. "Don't try to speak."

He would have liked to ask why he was in a completely unfamiliar but enormous room instead of on a pallet of more reasonable size in Medical. It would have made him feel better if the space had been filled with mysterious, pulsating, life-giving machinery, not that he could tell mysterious, pulsating, life-giving machinery from the other kinds. Instead, curtains of bamboo strips hung at intervals to partition off sections of the room, forming a partial labyrinth. Candlevines glowed faintly from the walls and ceiling.

Then he remembered the battle.

"Shit!" Jedao said, and winced involuntarily at the pain. "The battle—"

"We prevailed, sir," Dhanneth said. "Please, sir, the soup."

More memories. He shoved the blanket down and examined his chest. Either someone had changed him into a new uniform or the old one had prodigious powers of self-repair. Gingerly, he felt for the hole. Nothing. Everything seemed solid. He could even hear his heart pounding.

Dhanneth tried to feed him again. Jedao flinched back from the spoon. "You saw what I am." Whatever the hell that was.

"Yes," Dhanneth said, with no sign of disgust at dealing with—what had Talaw said?—"an inhuman walking corpse."

"How can you be taking this so calmly?" Especially when none of the other Kel had.

Dhanneth's breath hissed out between his teeth. "You're my general, sir."

That couldn't be the whole story. He was theoretically the general of the rest of the Kel, too, after all. But to reassure Dhanneth, whose eyes looked bruised with worry, however reluctant, Jedao drank some broth. It took all his concentration, and he still spilled some of it on his shirt. The shirt absorbed the moisture with eerie and total rapidity. In spite of his initial skepticism, the broth did, in fact, make him feel better.

Jedao fell asleep afterward, without intending to. The next time he woke, Dhanneth was gone. That made sense: even an aide had to have time to himself. Still, Jedao resolved to ask Dhanneth about the inhuman walking corpse business the next time he saw him.

He surveyed his surroundings more thoroughly this time. The walls were a soft, uncomplicated white. He stared at a small corner table whose legs were shaped like pillars of cavorting foxes, forever winterbound. Kujen? Kujen's assistant? Kujen's personal interior decorator?

Well. No time to waste. He asked the grid where he was and what was going on. Luckily, someone had troubled to turn his augment back on. The grid replied that they were in parking orbit around Isteia 3 while the hexarch consolidated their gains. It also reminded him, primly, that today was the Feast of Burning Veins.

"That sounds pleasant," Jedao muttered. The date it gave indicated that four days had elapsed since they'd attacked Isteia. Which meant his attempt to save the mothyard had probably been futile.

He used the water closet, then stripped off his shirt and searched for evidence of the injuries. Nothing, just the scars he'd woken up with that first day. Kujen had implied that scars were trivial to remove or hide, so that wasn't conclusive. He replaced the shirt and made sure he was presentable.

Then the name of the remembrance penetrated. *Feast of Burning Veins*. "Just what does this remembrance entail?" Jedao asked the grid.

The grid reassured him that it wasn't too late to observe the remembrance, which it managed to do while hinting that he ought to strive to do better. Then it launched into a recitation of the chant he was supposed to meditate on and the particular numbers that were significant to this feast.

"No," Jedao said, starting to be pissed off, "I don't mean what *I'm* supposed to do." Which, fucked if he was going to do it, but no need to tell the grid that. "What gives the remembrance its name?"

The grid explained to him that an authorized Vidona official rendered a chosen heretic by, essentially, setting their blood on fire. It started going into the technical details. Jedao wasn't a medic, but he didn't miss the fact that no mention was made of, say, anesthesia. The victim had to be conscious for this.

The grid never used the word "victim" at all. Jedao wondered how many euphemisms deep this went.

He had a moment to make the decision. It was tempting to ask where the hell Kujen was while this went on, but he didn't want to inadvertently attract Kujen's attention. So instead he merely asked the grid one more question: "If I want to attend in person"—he was gambling that this wasn't the oddest request a stray general had ever made—"where would I go?"

Obligingly, the grid provided a map. Jedao had the uncanny feeling that it approved. That, or whoever had programmed it wanted to encourage observance of remembrances.

Four guards stood outside the door. The one in charge was a stolid corporal who had not, strictly speaking, shaved as well as he should have. Jedao opted not to dress him down about the matter, especially since the corporal looked like he'd piss himself if Jedao raised his voice.

"Sir," the corporal said waveringly, "you can't be recovered yet."

That wasn't an outright *You can't leave*, so he was ahead. "I wish to attend the remembrance ceremony."

The corporal's mouth opened, then closed, then opened, then closed. If not for Jedao's certainty that someone was being burned alive *right now*, the effect would have been funny. Jedao guessed that he had chanced on the one request that the corporal couldn't turn down.

"I suppose that's all right, sir," the corporal said. "We'll escort you."

"Of course," Jedao said. *Don't smile.*

"You'll want to be in full formal, sir," the corporal said, even more waveringly.

If he'd still been at Shuos Academy, Jedao would have cracked a joke to lighten the mood. He didn't think that would help here. He merely nodded and set his uniform to full formal. "Ready," he said.

The first surprise, once they exited not-Medical, was the view. Someone had set up the hallway so the walls imaged what he guessed was Isteia 3 and its moons. He couldn't help slowing to gawk at it, his first good view of a planet with its marbled swirls of cloud and ocean and dark land masses. Clusters of lights shone faintly from the moons, which must be cities.

Even more impressive, and not in a good way, were the ruins of a station: Isteia Mothyard. Jedao knew from the intel reports what it had once looked like, an immense cylinder sporting numerous blisters for the young voidmoth hatcheries. His people had reduced it to a shatter-scatter of metal fragments and scorched shards. He had the awful suspicion that whoever had decided to image this particular spectacle had done so the way you might put up a trophy.

Did anyone survive? he asked.

The *Revenant* didn't answer. Nor did anyone else. He could only assume that any mothlings had perished in the carnage. For the first time, he wondered if any of them would have been old enough to talk to him. Not that he would have blamed them for declining.

It didn't take them long to reach the remembrance hall. He'd never given it much thought back when Kujen had first presented him with the *Revenant*'s blueprints. *Of all the things to forget.*

Even if he'd forgotten, he should have asked earlier.

"I've never been here before," Jedao said to his escort.

The corporal coughed, cleared his throat. "It's only expanded for use when we're docked."

Yes, of course. He remembered the relevant section of the Kel code of conduct now. Personnel on warmoths in transit were exempt, not least because the fussy local calibrations were too much of a pain in the ass. And possibly also because carting around heretics to torture was, as the code said, *logistically inconvenient*. He wondered now how many euphemisms were hidden in the code.

The remembrance hall had several doors, each marked with the Vidona stingray in bronze against metallic green. Even from the other side of the doors, he could smell the incense. The sandalwood blend should have been soothing. Instead, Jedao thought of what the grid had told him. *Setting their blood on fire.*

For once, heads didn't turn as he entered the remembrance hall. The Kel within were in full formal, seconded officers in their factions' equivalent. Everyone's attention was intent on the Vidona official and her victim.

The "heretic" was laid out on a dais. It was a Kel soldier. One of Inesser's soldiers, to be specific. The black-and-gold uniform was almost the same, but had, in addition, an armband with a golden kestrel stooping to catch its prey. By some miracle, the fires did not blot out the kestrel; instead, they made it shine more brightly. It was, by some measure, the brightest thing in the hall.

Inside, the everywhere incense was not quite strong enough to drown out the distinctive reek of roasted flesh and what must be the particular smell of burnt fabric.

The escort had backed away from Jedao. "S-sir," the corporal said in a hushed voice, "perhaps you'd rather—"

"Perhaps I'd rather what?" Jedao asked in what he thought was a commendably calm voice.

The corporal shut up.

"One question," Jedao said, also quietly, although the people in the back were starting to stir and frown in his direction.

The corporal bobbed a nod. The other soldiers had sufficient discipline not to back away from him, too. That, or it was formation instinct.

"How many prisoners of war did we capture?"

"The total, sir, or just on the command moth?"

That told him what he needed to know: *too many*. Besides, a quick consultation of the grid gave him the numbers. Eleven on the *Revenant*. All told, 503 captives in various states of health, distributed more or less evenly among the swarm's warmoths. The efficiency with which this had been accomplished was also a bad sign, as was the fact that the grid reassured him that the Vidona were carrying out the selfsame ceremony on the other moths in his command.

Jedao shoved his way through the crowd and to the ramp leading up to the dais. Shocked murmurs followed him. He didn't care. A saner voice in the back of his head said, *You can't save all of them this way.*

Maybe not, he thought back at it, *but I might make a difference for this one soldier.*

The corporal yelled after him to come back, then swore and started after him. Jedao lengthened his stride.

The Vidona had raised a sharp, saw-bladed instrument high above the burning soldier. She didn't flinch at his approach.

He grabbed her wrist and hissed, "This stops now."

She met his eyes coldly. "With respect, sir," she said in a voice that implied anything but, "you have no authority over me here."

Up close, he could hear the ragged breathing of the burning soldier. Their face was a mass of blisters and char marks tracking the locations of the major veins and arteries. He doubted they had a voice anymore or they'd be screaming.

"We are both," the Vidona said, "sworn to the hexarch's service. Stand down."

Jedao came very close to breaking her wrist and slamming her into the flames; but that wouldn't solve the problem.

Nevertheless, she reacted to the intimation of violence. She plunged the blade into the victim's heart before he could stop her.

Flames bloomed up around her hand. Her gray glove and her sleeve caught on fire. Her face was calm, even a little bored, as if she did this often. Which she probably did.

"I will have to make a calendrical adjustment," the Vidona said. She withdrew the blade with fussy neatness, damped the fire with a smothering cloth.

Jedao stared at her, aghast. "They could have been saved."

"A waste of resources," she said. "She was almost dead anyway."

Not trusting himself to speak, Jedao spun on his heel and stalked out of the hall. He knew where he was going next.

JEDAO SLOWED JUST enough for his escort to catch up with him. They didn't look grateful. He was beyond caring what they thought of their charge.

Kujen's quarters were defended by an immense foyer. A dazzle of candlevines grew up the walls, illuminating tangled wires and chitin-iridescent panels. A low thrumming reverberated throughout, like a gong that had just been damped.

The Nirai voidmoth emblem gleamed along the far wall, engraved in such piercing silver it was almost blue. The escort knelt in the full obeisance. Jedao didn't bother. He called out, "I've come for an audience with the hexarch."

When the doors parted, spilling light onto the floor and highlighting the iridescent panels, Jedao blinked but did not move otherwise.

"Jedao," Kujen said in that velvet voice of his. "The timing could have been better, but... well."

He wasn't interested in Kujen's assurances. "*How long have the remembrances been going on?*"

"Corporal," Kujen said without looking in the man's direction, "you and your soldiers may leave us."

The Kel escort fled.

Kujen was already leading the way forward. "Come with me," he said. "You'll find nothing interesting out here unless you like prototype circuits."

They passed through several rooms, each more opulent than the last, which did nothing to improve Jedao's mood. One room featured the pelts of gray tigers, while another housed chairs and tables of handsome blue-black lacquer. Yet a third was full of shadows except a pedestal where a single immense vase of finest celadon rested. The glaze depicted an arched branch with a raindrop in the act of falling free; that was all. Jedao didn't ask why Kujen collected such treasures when he scarcely paid heed to them. He wondered if he would be the same way when he had more experience of the world. He hoped not.

"Now," Kujen said, "you may yell."

Jedao reined back his temper. "You haven't answered my question."

"The remembrances?" Kujen sank down into a couch. Jedao took the chair across from him, drawing his feet in. "You mean in their current form."

Jedao just looked at him.

"For the past eight centuries and change," Kujen said.

"And you let this go on?"

Kujen raised his eyebrows. "Jedao," he said, "I'm the one who came up with the system."

Jedao's brain stuttered to a halt.

"The formations, and formation instinct, and the mothdrive harnesses," Kujen said, "all of them depend on people adhering to the system. The stability of the hexarchate, and its ability to provide for its citizens, depend on people adhering to the system."

"Kujen," Jedao said, recovering his voice, "we just fucking tortured prisoners of war to death. Now they'll never negotiate, or cooperate with prisoner exchanges, or believe any of our assurances, or—"

"I never intended to negotiate with Inesser or her people." Kujen rose and made his way to a cabinet. From it he drew a dark, unlabeled bottle. He tilted it inquiringly and cocked an eyebrow at Jedao. Jedao shook his head. "She and her followers are too dangerous. Better to add them to the list of heretics and move on."

"You can't arbitrarily decide that it's all right to torture whole categories of people to death!"

Kujen tapped the mouth of the bottle. The stopper, whatever it had been made of, vanished into a curl of blue-pale vapor. The smell of roses and spice perfumed the air.

"It's one of the better vintages of wine-of-roses," Kujen said. "I'd hate to drink this alone."

"If you think I have any interest in getting drunk right now," Jedao said icily, "you are quite mistaken."

"Your loss," Kujen said with a shrug. He poured a glass for himself and sipped delicately.

"When you told me that we were restoring order to the hexarchate," Jedao said, "I had no idea you had this in mind."

Kujen sipped again, then set the glass down on a table. He approached Jedao. Jedao stood his ground, increasingly uneasy.

"I'd forgotten how young you are," Kujen murmured.

"Don't fucking patronize me." Jedao glared at him, which was awkward because Kujen topped him by almost a head.

Kujen stepped in close, quite close, and rested his hands on Jedao's shoulders. "That's not all you're upset about, is it? This has to do with that regrettably violent confrontation with that Kel squad."

Jedao was trembling with the suppressed desire to lash out. He knew, however, that it wouldn't do any good. "That's not—"

"I told you once," Kujen said, "that it's impossible for you to shock me. Do you remember?"

Unwillingly, Jedao looked up into Kujen's perfect face, the smoky, gold-flecked eyes with their long lashes. "I remember." Then: "You knew. Even then, you knew."

"I didn't think you were ready to hear it," Kujen said.

"What am I?" He was horrified by the way his voice shook.

"Hush," Kujen said softly, and drew him down onto the couch so they were sitting side by side. "Call it a security measure. It wouldn't do to lose my general to assassination."

Jedao thought back to their earliest meetings. "You said you have your own defenses. Do you—are you—"

Maybe they were alike after all. Jedao was forcibly reminded that Kujen was one of the few people who had never reacted to him with fear or disgust. *I could influence him—change his mind—*Then he hated himself for the thought.

Kujen's hand had moved up to the side of his face. He was looking somberly at Jedao. Slowly, he uncurled his fingers until they brushed against Jedao's jaw. It seemed impossible that Kujen couldn't hear the hectic pounding of his heartbeat.

"Fine," Jedao said roughly. "I don't shock you? Prove it to me." He had the dim understanding that he was trying to play a game he wasn't old enough for.

Kujen's eyes were even more beautiful up close. In spite of himself, Jedao's pulse quickened further at the way Kujen was looking at him, as though everything else in the universe had fallen away. *I can't be doing this.* Yet here he was.

"Sweetheart," Kujen said caressingly, "the experience differential is not in your favor."

"I'm not a boy, Kujen."

"Well, that's debatable." His hands traced Jedao's sides and came to rest low on his hips.

Holding still was agonizing. Stupid, stupid, stupid. How had he expected to outplay a hexarch? Especially when he barely remembered how to have sex?

(Had he done this before?)

"Delightful as this is," Kujen said, "I feel obliged to point out that you're going to despise yourself afterward."

"Maybe I want that." He meant it, in that moment.

Kujen's hands slid lower.

Then, without warning, Kujen snatched his hands away and walked in measured strides to the other side of the room. "No," he said. The beautiful eyes had gone remote.

Heat rushed to Jedao's face. *Fuck.* He'd come in here intending to confront Kujen, browbeat him into making the remembrances stop, and now—

He slid off the couch and sank to his knees by reflex, assuming the full obeisance, and waited. After a long time, he became aware that something was wrong—*more* wrong, at any rate. "Hexarch?"

"Have a seat, General Jedao."

He almost tripped on the way to a chair, not trusting the couch.

"I'm not Nirai Kujen," the hexarch said. "It's past time I explained a few things to you."

Saying *I don't understand* seemed redundant, so Jedao didn't.

"The situation's complicated," the man went on, "but the part you care about is this. You can't seduce Kujen, not because he doesn't want you"—Jedao flushed all over again—"but because he's dead."

"Then who are you?" he asked, using the same honorific forms he had earlier, just in case. The man didn't correct him.

"Hajoret Kujen was born 919 years ago. He was the one responsible for the mathematics that led to the development of the high calendar, and the early form of the mothdrive that permitted the heptarchate's rapid expansion, and other technologies besides. He was good at a lot of things. But it didn't matter, because he was going to die."

"Let me guess," Jedao said. "Kujen really, really didn't want to die."

"Yes."

"There must have been—" He tried to formulate his question in a way that made sense. "Surely someone would have noticed? Or is this another thing I forgot?" And, because it was at least as important as the other revelations: "Who are *you*? What do I call you?"

"I don't have a name anymore," the man said, which Jedao doubted. "You may call me Inhyeng, if you like."

Jedao covered his flinch just in time. *Inhyeng* meant "doll" or "puppet." The realization hit him late. "You're the 'mysterious assistant.'"

Inhyeng inclined his head. "Kujen discovered a way to cheat death," Inhyeng said. "But to do so he would have to die himself, and content himself with existing as a parasite, a ghost anchored to a living marionette. He's here in this room; he's everywhere I go.

He can, when he needs to, manipulate my body directly, although we have been together for many years and I am accustomed to anticipating his desires. Eventually I will cease to be useful to him, and he will move on to his next anchor."

Jedao bit back the automatic *I'm sorry*. Inhyeng didn't sound like he wanted anyone's pity. What he wanted to know was, did Inhyeng also have uncanny undead healing abilities like Jedao himself, or was that the point of this "next anchor"?

Inhyeng smiled humorlessly. "You're wondering what I get out of this. You don't need to know the details of the bargain I made, but I am well provided for. As you might imagine, privacy is something I get little of. Still, Kujen respects my desire not to share my personal history with strangers."

Yes, Jedao thought, *you can have anything you want, except freedom*. Who was he to argue that it was such a horrible fate? It wasn't much different from his own existence. It stung to be called a stranger, but he couldn't deny it. After all, he hadn't known about Inhyeng's existence before today.

"So the hexarch's listening to this conversation?" Jedao said.

Did ghosts need to sleep? Rest? Could Kujen walk away from his anchor and scout the vicinity? How far did his senses extend? He had a whole, ugly new set of questions to address, and no answers.

"Inhyeng," Jedao said, faltering; but Inhyeng didn't reprimand him for omitting the *-zho* honorific, so perhaps it was all right. "When I touched Nirai-zho, when I—"

Inhyeng didn't rescue him from finishing the sentence.

Jedao started over. "I wasn't touching *him*," he said, following the thread to its logical end. "I was touching *you*—"

"There's no difference."

What Jedao heard in Inhyeng's voice was: *There is every difference*.

Jedao wanted to shut his eyes. Instead, he looked at Inhyeng full-on, waiting.

"You didn't know," Inhyeng said at last. "You couldn't."

"I am yours," Jedao said, meaning, *I am yours to punish*.

"Don't," Inhyeng said. "As I said, you didn't know. You couldn't have guessed, considering your particular disability. Even the swarm's Kel don't know just how long Kujen has lived."

This Jedao had not realized. He had assumed the Kel would have to know. But he reconsidered the evidence. "The shadow?"

"It's a symptom, yes. But most people don't realize its significance. And it's not any stranger than any number of fashion accessories people run around the successor states with."

"Then how did you convince them you were the hexarch in the first place?" Jedao demanded.

"Their original general had a high enough security clearance to recognize Kujen," Inhyeng said. Weariness shadowed his eyes. "I believe that will be all, General. I'm sure you have much to think about."

Jedao recognized the dismissal. "The remembrances—"

"Go," Inhyeng said, his voice cold.

"As you will," Jedao said, suddenly afraid. On the way out, he felt the shadow fluttering behind him like a funeral wind.

CHAPTER SEVENTEEN

Interlude: Tefos Station, 280 years ago

JEDAO HAD A list of things he hated about being a revenant. The inability to sleep, however, came near the top of the list. He lingered in the dimly lit room not out of choice but because his anchor, the blond Hafn boy, had fallen asleep on the couch after the latest round of sex.

Kujen had gotten up already and was sitting on the edge of the couch, splendidly nude, as he scribbled notes on a slate. "You're about to say something," he said without looking up, "so you might as well get it over with."

"I wouldn't dream of disappointing you, Nirai-zho," Jedao said with a hint of sarcasm. "I was only thinking of how satisfying it would be to report you to Kel Command."

"Wouldn't do you any favors," Kujen replied, unperturbed. "Half the hivemind is still convinced that it ought to throw away the key and leave you in the darkness forever. Which could still be arranged, if you're feeling masochistic."

Jedao said nothing. Kujen liked needling him about his fear of the darkness. He was well aware that his vacation from the black cradle came thanks to Kujen; that his unusual degree of freedom during this jaunt was another such gift. When Kel Command ordered him chained to an anchor, Jedao ordinarily had no influence over the anchor except to speak to them, a voice that no one else (but Kujen) could hear. This time, however, Kujen had adjusted the bond so that Jedao could exert a certain degree of control over the body.

Kujen set the slate down on a table next to the couch and leaned back, bonelessly folding into the crook of Jedao's arm. Jedao was ambivalent about considering the Hafn boy's body "his," since strictly speaking, the boy hadn't had any choice in the matter. But the strengthened anchor bond meant that he could feel what the body felt, as though—almost—he inhabited it himself. Kujen had been at pains to demonstrate the benefits of this.

"Considering how hard Kel Command worked you in life," Kujen said, his voice throaty, "I should think that you'd welcome a little vacation." He twisted and resettled himself, kissing Jedao's jaw and earlobe in a lazy meandering line.

The body woke; Jedao used its voice to speak. He still hadn't gotten entirely used to the clear, pure tenor, or the telltale foreign accent. But of course, Kujen had selected it for its beauty, including the beauty of its voice. "If Kel Command thinks to inventory the black cradle while we're out here, we're fucked."

Kujen shrugged. The motion translated itself to Jedao's arm. Kujen's proximity, the lithe brushstroke perfection of his limbs, had its usual calculated effect, and Jedao's cock began to harden. "My double can handle that," Kujen said. "They won't catch on. Besides," and he reached over to nestle a hand in the curling blond hairs at Jedao's chest, "you really must learn to enjoy a chance to relax when you have the opportunity for one."

"Next you're going to be telling me that you're doing this for my benefit." Jedao held still with an effort, although he couldn't do anything about the wild pounding of his heart. Kujen couldn't be unaware of it.

Kujen's eyes widened. "But I am, my dear. Even you can only withstand so much sensory deprivation." He hoisted himself up to straddle Jedao, nudging him to the side so that there would be enough space for his knee. (It was a wide couch, but still.) "We're promised to each other, aren't we? Which wouldn't do me any good if you went mad in the black cradle between assignments."

"You mean between assignations," Jedao retorted.

"I said what I meant," Kujen said, mildly enough, but his fingers dug into Jedao's skin, leaving marks.

Jedao tensed, resisting, despite pleasure and the memory of pleasure. He closed his eyes.

"Stop *thinking*," Kujen murmured right into his ear, inescapable. His hand moved; moved again. Jedao's teeth clenched against a moan. "You can hate me tomorrow, or the day after that, or the day after that. We'll have all eternity for that, after all."

"I'll never forget what you are," Jedao said, still with his eyes closed. If he didn't look, he could pretend that it was just sex, no obligations, no complications, rather than the latest ploy in a game unfolding over centuries.

"I wouldn't expect you to," Kujen said, unperturbed. Little by little he moved down, leaving a trail of touches like moths' wings, and a while after that he began to use his mouth.

I will not forget, Jedao thought in the last dissolving moments before surrendering himself. As Kujen worked, Jedao entertained himself with thoughts of killing the other man. A blow to the side of the head. Strangulation, although Kujen's body was, inconveniently, the stronger one, so forget that one. Putting out the eyes with his thumbs. Messy, but what death wasn't? And Jedao had dealt his share of ugly deaths.

"Oh, is *that* what you're thinking of," Kujen said in barely a whisper, right on cue. "You're so predictable, my dear."

Jedao would have cursed himself for being so obvious. But the beautiful thing was that here, now, it didn't matter. It had no bearing (so he told himself) on the schemes that the two of them came up with, or wielded against each other.

And even better: as despicable as this was (the latest atrocity in a long litany), Kujen really, truly did not care; would never care; would never judge. It was the headiest seduction he could offer. Which was as well, because Jedao wasn't in any position to say no.

CHAPTER EIGHTEEN

Six minutes after his anchor dismissed Jedao, Kujen took direct control of the man's body and walked him into one of the inner chambers, then sat him down. Kujen hadn't had to resort to this in a long time. The movements lacked a certain grace. Half the point of maintaining Nirai Mahar as his anchor was to luxuriate in Mahar's beauty. But it was good to remind Mahar that every indulgence came at a price.

Kujen waited for Mahar to realize that he had relinquished the puppet strings. The minutes ticked past. At last Kujen said, in a voice that only Mahar could hear, "You might as well tell me what's upsetting you so."

"Why would I be upset?" Mahar said in an amiable voice, but after sixty years yoked to each other, Kujen wasn't fooled. "I'd rather fuck a squid than touch that thing."

Mahar hoisted himself out of the chair. Kujen let him. Mahar made for one of the walk-in closets with its array of outfits in black, gray, silver, the occasional splash of foam-colored lace.

("You're allowed to wear colors as long as it's not a ceremonial occasion, you know," Kujen had once said to Mahar. "What are they going to do, demote you?" Mahar had ignored him.)

"I would have thought this kind of prejudice beneath you," Kujen said mildly.

"I know it's not his fault," Mahar said, nostrils flaring. "All the same, I don't want to bed him. Even if it's an easy way for you to string him along."

"Yes," Kujen said, "he probably had this whole elaborate rationalization worked out for why thinking with his dick was a clever stratagem. Nine hundred years and it's nice to know human nature never changes."

Mahar yanked one of his favorite shirts off a hanger, crumpled it in his hands, and dumped it on the floor. Within short order, a pile of mangled shirts occupied the space next to his feet.

Kujen waited. He had long experience waiting, the first thing you learned as a revenant.

"That thing can't tell whether we're supposed to be its father or its lover. But then, that's exactly what you wanted, isn't it?"

Kujen didn't intend to let Mahar defy him like this. In particular, Jedao couldn't be allowed to guess Mahar's attitude toward him. "You were bound to grow a spine sooner or later," Kujen said. "Your timing is impeccable."

Mahar had regained control of himself and merely shrugged. "Everyone is entitled to the occasional exercise in futility," he said. "You always win. When he speaks, I almost think you pulled it off. And then."

"Well," Kujen said, "perhaps you need a reminder. Just a little longer, and you'll have your freedom."

"There's no such thing," Mahar said bleakly. "You taught me that a long time ago."

"Perhaps not," Kujen said, unperturbed. "But you'll have the next best thing, if you want it. Haven't I kept the terms of the bargain?"

Mahar lowered his eyes. "Yes," he whispered.

At fifteen, Roskoya Mahar had shown extraordinary promise as a Nirai candidate. Kujen had gotten to him first. Mahar's younger brother was dying of a rare disorder. *Serve me*, Kujen said, *and your brother will receive the best care to be found anywhere in the hexarchate. You yourself will enjoy every luxury. The price is that you will never meet him again.*

One of the things Mahar excelled at, then as now, was mathematics. He did the math. He agreed.

What Kujen hadn't been able to offer, at the time, was immortality.

While he and Esfarel had invented the black cradle, once upon a time, Kel Command watched it too closely for him to shove anyone else into it. And besides, he enjoyed Mahar's company too much to give it up.

"Come," Kujen said, and took up the puppet strings again. In Mahar's body, he walked into the inner sanctum where he kept the most precious of his experiments.

This room, unlike the others, was not made for luxury. Whatever Jedao might think of him, he did know how to get work done. The walls here were a soft warm gray, and the candlevines never dimmed.

Inside the room rested three caskets. The first one contained another Jedao, although its eyes were blank. Kujen would have preferred to have more backups, but there hadn't been time. This one lacked scars, purely an aesthetic consideration. He hadn't been able to resist tinkering with the face as well. Subtle changes, the kind of modding people got done for vanity's sake while still remaining recognizable to those who knew them.

The second one contained a Mahar, or rather, Mahar as he had been as a young man. Mahar kept declining this particular honor, but that didn't trouble Kujen. Even if Mahar insisted on a natural death instead of transference into an immortal body like the current Jedao's, Kujen liked the idea of keeping his likeness around. He had grown fond of the man after their decades together.

The last casket contained a man with curly brown hair and milky skin and amber eyes, a dancer's physique, a smile that had broken hearts. Kujen gazed at his own duplicate, the way he'd looked at nineteen when he'd graduated Nirai Academy. The eyes resembled Mahar's, although that was pure coincidence. They weren't related; he'd checked, unlikely as the prospect was. But the single point of similarity pleased him nonetheless.

Kujen relaxed his control so that Mahar could speak.

"I won't be one of them," Mahar said in a low voice. "It's too much, Kujen. I appreciate the offer very much, but I'm not the one with a pressing need to live forever." Ordinarily he would have needled Kujen about unreliable prototypes. Today he refrained.

"I'll always be here if you change your mind," Kujen said. "Time runs out for everyone, though. Don't wait too long."

Mahar was silent for a long time. Then: "When I come in here for maintenance," he said, "I see them stirring sometimes. They're dreaming."

"Well, yes," Kujen said, patient. "There has to be some minimum of brain function or they wouldn't be suitable to be inhabited."

Mahar sucked in his breath. "Don't condescend to me," he snapped.

"My apologies," Kujen said. The other reason he'd kept Mahar around so long, when he ordinarily changed anchors every decade or so: Mahar was good enough at gate mechanics and moth engineering to make a useful research partner.

"I need time alone, Kujen."

Kujen heard the strain in Mahar's voice. "Of course," he said. He could be silent until Mahar regained his composure.

Mahar turned to the caskets. He avoided looking at his own, but he contemplated the extra Jedao with a mixture of pity and revulsion for a long time.

CHAPTER NINETEEN

THE LAST THING Inesser remembered of Isteia was the evacuation. She hadn't been conscious for the last of it, not after the hit that had taken out the command center of the *Three Kestrels Three Suns*. The medic had told her that she'd been lucky. Inesser had experienced enough battles to understand that *no body parts missing* was, in fact, lucky, despite the fact that she felt like one giant bruise made of multiple component bruises and she'd somehow broken her ankle.

At the moment, she was clutching a cross-stitch frame and what would, in theory, become a fetching stitchery depicting a folding fan. The only reason it had survived, frivolous item that it was, was that she hadn't brought it with her onto the command moth. She'd brought it with her onto Isteia Station to give her hands something to do in case there was a moment of leisure, and left it behind by accident. When evacuating the station, Brezan's people had thoughtfully taken it with them. Brezan's assistant had pressed it into her hand when she first woke.

Inesser was currently ensconced in her own room in Medical on Brezan's personal transport, the bannermoth *Unfettered Harmony*. To her side, a glass of water rested on a table. She'd tried some of it. The water had tasted stale. She'd considered asking the grid for rice wine instead, but she knew how that exchange would go.

She needed to concentrate on the situation. Instead all she could think of was how difficult it would be to source another skein of Maple Red #5. Genuine hand-dyed variegated silk, certified Andan product from a planet in the Compact. Specifically, hand-dyed variegated silk that was tuned to change color with the seasons on her own homeworld. Working with seasonal silks was a pain in the ass, especially getting the colors to coordinate year-round without having them change inconveniently on any proscribed remembrances. But the results were worth it.

"Protector-General." Miuzan cleared her throat as she came in. She held a slate tucked under her left arm; her right was in a sling. "Are you ready for the meeting, or should I put it off?"

Inesser forced herself to pay attention. "Where?"

"They're coming to you." Miuzan smiled grimly. "My little brother may be strutting around in a jumped-up fancy uniform, but he's not completely unreasonable."

Inesser refrained from mentioning that if Brezan's position was anything like hers, he wore the "jumped-up fancy uniform" because some protocol expert had thought it would serve for impressing the masses. While he hadn't looked uncomfortable in it, precisely, he also hadn't looked as though it brought him any particular pleasure. "Bring them in," she said. "And Miuzan—"

Miuzan tensed at the sound of her name.

"Whatever he's done," Inesser said, "he's still family. You have a chance to talk to him."

"I tried that once," Miuzan said flatly. "It didn't change anything."

"I know a little of what it's like to be at odds with kinfolk. You can still mend things."

"Is that an order?" Miuzan said. "Sir."

"No," Inesser said, weary. "No. Let's get this meeting started, shall we?"

So young, she couldn't help thinking. She thought that a lot these days. Curious how she'd been young once, and then suddenly, not anymore.

High General Brezan entered, accompanied by a pair of hovering servitors bearing what looked like the kind of food you fed invalids, except it smelled much better. Porridge, and mouthwateringly fragrant jellied fruit, and even a thin slice of cake. Brezan grinned when he saw Inesser's expression. "I thought you might appreciate being fed real food. I was in a mood to cook anyway."

The servitors set the tray down on the table next to Inesser, then retreated to fuss with one of the paintings on the wall. Inesser, her eye exquisitely sensitive to matters of alignment thanks to uncounted hours of cross-stitch, yearned to yank the painting away and do their job for them.

"We have an emergency," Miuzan said, radiating disapproval, "and you're cooking?"

Brezan didn't respond to the provocation. "Losses were heavy," he said, directing the comment at Inesser.

"You don't need to be diplomatic around *me*," Inesser rasped. "I'm not in the habit of shooting the messenger. Give me the numbers."

Brezan's eyes were dark. "We took 62% casualties to the swarm," he said. "The mothyard itself was pulverized, so forget about that. We had to abandon the system." He produced his own slate and showed her the map. "We're here now. So far no signs of pursuit, probably because they're busy consolidating their hold on Isteia."

Inesser's breath shuddered in and out. She knew what *consolidating their hold* meant. Remembrances. "They took captives." It wasn't a question.

"Yes," Brezan said.

"Where's Tseya?"

Tseya came in as though summoned. "Here I am," she said. She had a glass of jellied lychees in her hand.

"I know you have weapons-grade reservations about the man," Brezan said to Inesser, "but I would like to include Shuos Mikodez in this conference. If anyone knows what's going on, he does." His mouth twisted. "I agreed that you're calling the shots, though. So it's up to you."

"Weapons-grade reservations" was putting it mildly. People stopped trusting Mikodez after he assassinated two of his own cadets the second year after he took the hexarch's seat. Inesser still remembered waking up to the news. It had arrived during one of her leaves. She was ensconced in a decadent bathhouse with one of her wives when the senior Shuos on her staff called her. "Remember how we thought the boy hexarch was a joke?" they said. "Well, either he's a genius or he's a sociopath, but he's not a joke anymore."

And that had been only—"only"—two cadets. Inesser had wondered afterward if Mikodez would follow that up with anything more spectacular. Instead, he settled in for decades of distressingly competent leadership. Like any right-thinking person, Inesser couldn't decide whether she feared the Shuos more when they were organized and all pointed in the same direction, or thrashing about in their periodic orgies of backstabbing. But she knew no one could rely on a Shuos with that kind of reputation. Mikodez had proven that spectacularly true after assassinating the other hexarchs.

Brezan was looking at her.

"Yes," Inesser said, gritting her teeth. She disliked being beholden to Mikodez for anything. But she was already in bed with one of her adversaries; why not another? Besides, Brezan would consult with Mikodez whether she liked it or not. She might as well gather what information she could.

"Line 6-1 to Hexarch Shuos Mikodez," Brezan said. "Line 6-2 to High Magistrate Rahal Zaniin, Line 6-3 to General Kel Khiruev, and Line 6-4 to General Kel Ragath, please."

"There are unauthorized parties in the room," the grid said primly. "Under security code 43.531.1, it is required that an authorized party—"

Brezan put his face in his hands and growled while the grid's impersonal voice continued to elaborate on security precautions. "For fire's sake," he said to no one in particular, "we go through this every fucking time and I am theoretically the former head of state. Override, dammit."

"Under security code 43.531.1, it is required that an authorized party—"

Brezan pulled out his slate and jabbed at it with his thumb.

"Haptic code?" Inesser said.

"I'm sure you could crack it no problem," Brezan said sourly.

"Which is hilarious because half the time I can't get the system to recognize it coming from *me*."

Sure enough, a loud chime sounded. "Notice to High General Kel Brezan," the grid said. "Unauthorized user has been logged attempting to—"

Two guards in Shuos red-and-gold poked their heads into the room. "Real emergency or fake emergency, sir?" the broader one, a man with a bearlike build, said.

Brezan waved them off. "Fake emergency. You can go back to cheating little children at jeng-zai or checking the art on the walls for steganography or whatever the hell it is you foxes do when life gets boring."

"We only cheat little children when they deserve it," the man said. The door swished shut behind the guards as they resumed their positions.

"Nice to know Mikodez is still training sarcasm into his operatives," Inesser said. "I assume that's where you got them."

"The price of a Shuos's help is a Shuos's help," Brezan said, quoting an old maxim. He jabbed at the slate some more. This time the authorization went through.

The grid spoke again. "Line 6-3 open. Line 6-2 open. Line 6-4 open." Then, after a pause: "Line 6-1 open."

Inesser wasn't surprised that Mikodez responded last. He'd always possessed a healthy sense of his own importance, even before he'd established his reputation as the hexarchate's second most dangerous Shuos. Inesser told herself to stop thinking of him as "that boy." She remembered how astonishingly young he'd been when he talked himself into the hexarch's seat, against all odds, and clung to it thereafter.

The grid imaged them by rank. First was Hexarch Shuos Mikodez, darkly handsome and smiling. He was resplendent in the foxes' red-and-gold, and a pair of long gold earrings set with tiny bells that chimed whenever he moved his head. Inesser couldn't help wondering if the effect was calculated to annoy his interlocutor. That, or he genuinely liked bells. This was Mikodez, after all.

Second was High Magistrate Rahal Zaniin, formerly of Minang Tower. To Inesser's eye she appeared painfully young for her position, despite her flawless comportment. While she hadn't claimed the Rahal hexarch's seat in the Compact, she had argued that the Rahal would do the most good by enforcing the rebel calendar. Her viewpoint had caused the Rahal to splinter. Inesser couldn't tell whether ambition or genuine concern for the Compact's people motivated her.

Next came General Kel Khiruev, a woman whose old dueling scars stood out prominently on the side of her face. Her hair, decorously cropped in accordance with Kel norms, was white. Inesser was older than Khiruev by twenty-four years and looked far younger. She had her own suspicions as to what had caused Khiruev's visible deterioration. While they'd never met face to face—they'd served in marches on the opposite sides of the hexarchate—she knew of the other woman by reputation. One of Khiruev's mothers had executed her father for heresy. Most Kel knew the story; knew that Khiruev had taken the Swanknot as her emblem upon making general in memory of the event. At the moment, though, Khiruev's expression revealed nothing but patient calm.

Fourth was General Kel Ragath. The Compact had raised him to general shortly after the assassinations that had sundered the old hexarchate. He held a high position in the Compact's hierarchy, although other generals had served longer. Ragath's background as a historian made him valuable, and he did a stellar job managing the Compact's operations. Inesser considered him a dangerous opponent. Either Brezan had earned his respect—no small thing— or the other way around.

One person was missing from the roster, however. "What about Cheris?" Inesser said. She didn't *like* the crashhawk radical, but the crashhawk radical had demonstrated an ability to turn worlds upon worlds upside down. It would be nice to have some of that working for her side. Whichever that was.

Brezan tipped his chin up and looked sardonically at her. "She's not available."

"I don't believe you."

"She's missing. She's been missing since the assassinations."

Inesser favored him with a skeptical glare. "We're talking about someone who's running around with the hexarchate's most notorious mass murderer inside her head"—she was old enough, and of high enough rank, that she knew how the black cradle worked—"and you've been *letting her run around loose*?"

"Not 'letting,'" Brezan said. "She left. I don't know why."

"I have a guess," Mikodez said, leaning forward. "She knew that if she stayed, everyone would expect her to lead. And she didn't want that for herself, or for you."

Tseya was regarding Mikodez with that particular blankness of expression that Inesser associated with people who were both incandescently angry and too well-bred to show it. "Yes, well," she said, "never mind Cheris. Who for thorn's sake was leading the swarm we just fought, if not Cheris?"

"If it *is* Cheris—" said Miuzan, who had been silent until now.

"No," Brezan said. Miuzan's gaze swung to him, and he met it squarely. "It can't be Cheris."

"How do you expect to prove that," Inesser said, "when you can't produce her?"

"I realize Cheris has no reason to think of *you* as a friend," Brezan said, "but why would she blow *me* up? Or a mothyard that could produce perfectly good cindermoths for her to waltz in and take over?"

Khiruev winced. "That wouldn't work again anyway. Kel Command dishonorably discharged her *and* Jedao."

Inesser shrugged. "She incinerated Kel Command, remember? To say nothing of being in bed with a certain child-killing hexarch-assassinating backstabber." No sense hiding her opinion of Mikodez. He already knew.

Mikodez waved a hand loftily. "All in a day's work." Not even ashamed, the wormfucker.

"The point is, she's betrayed people before. She'll do it again."

"No," Brezan said. "That's not the kind of person she is."

"Funny," Miuzan said, very softly. "I would have said that of you, once."

Brezan's fingers flexed. "If you have something to say, Colonel, why don't you get it over with."

Miuzan opened her mouth.

"*Colonel*," Inesser said. She recognized that particular mulish set of Miuzan's shoulders. While baiting her staffers was fun over drinks, they had more important matters to deal with.

Miuzan subsided.

Mikodez toyed with one of his earrings, then said, "We don't like each other, Protector-General Inesser, but Brezan is correct. That wasn't Cheris. That was a new player entirely."

Inesser said, "That was someone *controlled* by a new player. Or, more accurately, a very old one."

"I concur," Mikodez said. Inesser hated it when he agreed with her. It never implied healthy things about the future.

Brezan picked up on the byplay. "How can you tell it's Nirai Kujen," he said, "and not Jedao—a new Jedao—freelancing?"

"Because you told me about the remembrances," Mikodez said. "Jedao wouldn't have prioritized them. He didn't even like remembrances, although he kept his mouth shut about that to preserve his hide. No; this is Kujen or I'll eat Zehun's cats. Which would, by the way, be an automatic death sentence. My aide likes their cats far more than they like me."

The only person in the conference who looked happy was General Ragath. "I never thought I'd have the security clearance for this conversation, back when," he said. "It was impossible not to guess, given the paper trail on the black cradle. But I decided to leave that one alone."

Inesser hid a smile. The Kel knew Ragath for his stalled career. Despite his reputation as one of their best colonels, Kel Command had neglected to promote him due to the disruptive opinions expressed in some of his papers.

General Khiruev cleared her throat. "I can shed some light on Cheris's whereabouts."

Brezan's eyes thinned. "You've heard from her?"

"She's hunting Hexarch Kujen."

A very loud silence. Then he said, "How long have you known?"

Miuzan caught Inesser's eye and mouthed, "Divide and conquer?"

Inesser returned a tiny headshake. As much as she enjoyed watching adversaries turn on each other, she couldn't afford to think of Brezan and his compatriots as enemies anymore. The sooner Miuzan got that through her head, the better.

The big problem wasn't Brezan or his Kel. She could outfight his generals if it came to that, although considering that he'd rescued her from certain torture and death on Isteia, she preferred not to. Fighting was usually the stupid way to win anyway. Why fight when she could secure his cooperation? All she needed to do was give up the foundation of her world.

But then, that foundation had proved itself flawed nine years ago. Inesser didn't believe in dwelling on might-have-beens. And Brezan was only part of the problem. The person whose help she needed, despite a lifetime dealing as little with him as practical, was Shuos Mikodez. Brezan was only a means to an end.

Brezan and Khiruev were in the middle of heated mutual recriminations. Inesser couldn't figure out what they were talking around, which bothered her. She set her augment to record the conversation for later review and turned her attention instead to Mikodez.

"Do you have any idea what that butchermoth was?" Inesser asked him, on the grounds that if she had a spymaster on the line, however untrustworthy, she might as well get what she could out of him.

Mikodez grinned at her as if he'd deduced her thought, but his heart wasn't in it. "Is that what your soldiers are calling it?"

"That was certainly the effect it had." Her heart clenched again at the thought of Isteia Mothyard, the soldiers lost, the inevitable remembrances. And worse than the mothyard—for in her long career she had seen her share of destruction—the lurid sight of the inverted Deuce of Gears, the madman loosed once again.

"No data on anything like it," Mikodez said. "It must be a prototype. Having gotten some idea of its capabilities, I can guarantee you that at this point only one of Kujen's facilities would have the ability to manufacture something like that."

"I don't suppose you'd be willing to share your list."

"I will," he said, surprising her. "Brezan has asked me to. But it's incomplete. And bombing all of Kujen's bases, even if you could manage the logistics, will only delay the inevitable if you don't get rid of Kujen himself."

"Were you the one who loosed Cheris to assassinate him?" She frowned at him. "And why does it matter to you?" She could trace only part of the logic. Mikodez might control legions of Shuos infantry, but Jedao had been one of the best, and Cheris was infused with his training. More importantly, Cheris had Jedao's memories of Kujen, centuries' worth.

"No to the first," Mikodez said. "Despite my reputation, and that of the Shuos in general, I prefer using reliable operatives. Which Kel Cheris is not. As for the second—" He paused. "Kujen used to be an asset to the hexarchate, if you define 'asset' in the coldest terms possible. He's now a threat. That's all there is to it."

"Do you ever make a decision that isn't calculated on some master abacus?" Inesser demanded.

Mikodez's smile was curiously sad. "I gave up the right to personal sentiment when I took the job, Protector-General."

"Do your people make a habit of keeping secrets from you?" Miuzan was saying to Brezan. "Because that's going to kill us all faster than anything swanning around the successor states."

"It was necessary," Khiruev said doggedly.

The damn servitor was *still* futzing with the ashhawk-and-rose painting. Was it defective? Inesser wasn't afraid of being spied on. She had accepted that the room would be monitored.

"We haven't settled the question of what Jedao is doing running around alive, and with a body of his own," Miuzan said.

Mikodez shrugged. "My bet is that isn't Jedao at all. It's just as likely that Kujen dolled up one of his pets to resemble Jedao in order to give orders. Did the swarm *fight* like one of Jedao's?"

"They relied on superior weapons technology," Inesser said reluctantly. "It's hard to tell. He didn't have to do anything clever to win because he was already pummeling the shit out of us."

"Hell," Mikodez said, "Kujen could have plucked out some promising general or tactical group commander and modded them. While I doubt he'd have chanced upon another Jedao or another you, it's not like he needs a genius to use a gravitation cannon. And as much as Kujen likes sparring with people, he would want someone who follows orders."

"It's Kujen," Inesser said, remembering the beautiful, clever-tongued pets Kujen had surrounded himself with. "He could design someone who could do both."

"That too."

"We should have stayed and hit him with a suicide strike," Miuzan said.

"It's too late for that," Brezan said.

"Too late for a lot of things," Inesser said, thinking that if she'd shot him in the back decades ago, they might not be here. Except she knew that a mere bullet wouldn't do the trick. "If only Kujen had managed to trip down a flight of stairs during the years I heard nothing of his movements." Brezan, who had never met Kujen or witnessed his dancer's poise, didn't get the joke. "If he's rematerialized now, it's because he thinks the situation threatens him. He won't stop until we're crushed beneath his heel."

"Fine," Brezan said. "What do you want me to do, pragmatically speaking? I can't send more Cherises. There's only one of her and she manifestly doesn't pay attention to a thing I say."

More of Cheris, what a horrifying thought. As if their world needed more crashhawks. Inesser reminded herself that, in the new regime, everyone would be a crashhawk. If the Compact had been able to make it work this past nine years, the rest of the Kel might manage it as well.

"No," Inesser said. "If she fails, there will have to be another. Assuming she survives to tell us."

"I took the liberty of putting the Compact's mothyards on high military alert," Brezan said, "since a great many people are debating the legitimacy of our arrangement."

So damn young.

He wasn't as naive as she'd supposed, for he went on, "That's the easy part. No. We also fight Kujen by publicizing the fuck out of his existence. I don't know what he looks like this time around, if the black cradle's involved, but..."

Tseya sketched a bow in his direction. "Propaganda isn't one of my specialties," she said, mildly enough. But the tips of Brezan's ears turned pink as if she'd reminded him of some intensely personal incident. "Still, you have Andan and I know a few myself. We can get the message out."

"Even if people believe us," Brezan said, "the hard part is going to be making sure they don't torch any neighbors they don't like for 'acting strangely.'"

"You're almost going about this the right way," Mikodez said. "Don't make it some boring public bulletin. That's just going to get people to play Vidona. Just couch it in terms of drama. Kujen, paranoid bastard that he is, will get the message, and everyone else can enjoy the witty dialogue and pretty costumes."

Tseya shook her head. "Why," she said, too sweetly, "because you think a good drama can be brewed out of nowhere in thirty hours?"

"Make it a bad one," he said. "It'll piss him off more. Even someone who lurks as much as Kujen does has an ego."

"Just for you, Hexarch."

"Of course, Tseya." His bland expression didn't change.

Inesser caught Tseya's eye and shook her head. Tseya didn't need to be reminded twice. As tempting as it was to trade barbed remarks with Mikodez—Inesser knew how aggravating he was—they had to work together.

"I am doing my best to facilitate the alliance," Brezan said. "But it will take time."

"Remind people it's that or see their homes blown up at random," Ragath said.

"That's half the problem," Brezan said. "That's already the world they know. I promised something different. I failed to deliver."

"Why," Inesser said, "giving up already?"

Brezan chuckled lowly. "Not while you're alive."

Constructive hostility. She could work with that, especially since all signs pointed toward Brezan honoring the terms of their agreement. Which was good, because it was what she had.

CHAPTER TWENTY

ON THE FIRST night after they left Station Ayong Primary, 1491625 took Hemiola aside for a chat. Cheris had gone to sleep, which consisted of leaning her chair back a fraction. It didn't look comfortable.

The matter of Jedao-Cheris's identity was, in fact, the first thing that 1491625 made clear to Hemiola. "She usually prefers to be called Cheris," it said the moment Cheris's breathing eased into the rhythm of sleep.

"Excuse me?" Hemiola said.

"'Jedao,'" 1491625 said impatiently. "Her name is Ajewen Cheris these days, although most people will use Kel Cheris instead. And many people confuse her with Jedao."

"I know a little about Shuos Jedao," Hemiola said. "It wasn't until Ayong Primary that I learned anything about Cheris."

1491625 flickered a deprecating olive green. "You and the rest of the hexarchate. It was her choice, but some of us remember who she was before Kel Command sold her out."

"Why didn't she tell me herself?"

"Have you ever heard of the Mwennin?"

Hemiola indicated that it had not.

"Her people. Gone now, most of them. The Vidona rounded them up and exterminated them."

"Revenge?" Hemiola said, with greater interest. Revenge was a motive it could understand.

"An example. Beyond the matter of names," and 1491625 pulsed low-intensity lasers directly at Hemiola, so as not to disturb Cheris's rest, "you are going to be watched every moment, everywhere you go. Because while Cheris is a kindly, trusting person—"

Hemiola expressed its skepticism.

"—for someone hosting the memories of an elite Shuos operative, anyway—"

That part Hemiola believed.

"She may think to win you over," 1491625 said, "but I know better. You don't go anywhere unless I accompany you."

Hemiola flashed its lights nervously in the direction of the nearest viewport. Right now it couldn't see anything useful. Their mothdrive was engaged, and the gate-space radiations hazed everything. "Where would I go anyway?"

"I don't know what you're thinking," 1491625 said, "and I don't care. I don't even care about having to be courteous to you. If you get ideas, remember that my enclave selected me to protect Cheris."

Hemiola couldn't think of what to say to that.

"I hope I've made myself clear."

"You've made yourself clear," Hemiola said.

"Good. Go inventory what's in our hold or something."

Hemiola blinked bemusedly. "Don't you already have a—" Oh. 1491625 wanted it away from Cheris. "Going."

"Take your time," 1491625 flashed after it.

Hemiola floated to the hold. It began the inventory, not just checking the labels against the manifest but scanning the contents for good measure. Kel ration bars in assorted flavors, and a single small crate of preserved Kel pickles. Several replacement suits, even though Cheris obsessively maintained the one she already had. The suits were all the right size for Cheris. Hemiola wasn't sure what good they did all crated up. Especially since they'd been crammed beneath the ration bars.

At some point Hemiola resumed reading the hexarch's notes. Taking inventory was routine work and required little processing power, so it could do both at once. Besides, Cheris and her companion might be fascinated by the sheer variety of sealants that were crammed into this next set of crates, but Hemiola didn't share their interest.

Tired of research on dwarf moths, which didn't seem to be going anywhere, Hemiola returned to an earlier journal. While the files had comprehensive indexes, it had been compiling one of its own based not on the text but on the doodles. The hexarch didn't consider them important, but they were more engaging than the text and graphs and tables.

Geometric diagrams drawn in flawless isometric perspective. Beautifully rendered diagrams of the projective plane. The occasional intertwined pornographic figures. Hemiola guessed that some of *those* had been drawn from reference from multiple partners, judging by the variety of bodies and poses. That, or the hexarch possessed great reserves of imagination.

Had he ever shown these to anyone? Hemiola tried to imagine what their reactions would have been.

More diagrams. Not math, nor any technical discipline that Hemiola recognized. Everything divided up into four segments, each segment sometimes subdivided even further into halves. No, not always four—occasionally three larger segments. But usually four.

Seventeen days away from Ayong Primary, Hemiola deciphered the diagrams. By then it had completed the inventory, dragging out the task as long as it could so it didn't have to face 1491625's glower. It was in the middle of taking a break with one of the newer dramas that the Ayong servitors had provided Cheris. 1491625 had grudgingly allowed Cheris to dig out the episodes for Hemiola.

It was the song-and-dance set-piece at the climax of the eighth episode that gave Hemiola the key, although it didn't realize it at first. Cheris liked the set-piece. Hemiola didn't.

"Why not?" Cheris had said wistfully. "It's pretty."

Hemiola had fluttered distressed red-oranges at her. "None of the colors coordinate! And several of the backup dancers aren't synchronized, even allowing for human reflexes."

"Well, yes," Cheris said, "that's part of the charm. Didn't you know? This particular drama was on the censors' list for depicting heretics in a friendly light. Not just censored. The hearing went all the way up to the Rahal high court, to the Rahal hexarch."

At least faking interest was easier with a human audience than with a servitor one. 1491625's lights in the ultraviolet rippled with soft, cynical amusement, but it kept its observations to itself.

"No, that's not the part you should find thought-provoking," Cheris said. "The hexarch ruled in the drama's favor. Because she had watched it too. I don't know whether she liked it or not. I never knew much about her. But the hexarchs squabbled over it, and eventually the Rahal hexarch gave way to the others. But some of the servitors found out it was going to be wiped and smuggled it out. By the time anyone realized, it was everywhere. The hexarchs had to pretend that had been their intent all along. No one ever figured out the servitors were involved."

"So that's where you got the idea," 1491625 said from the helm.

"What idea?" Hemiola said in spite of itself.

Cheris cracked her knuckles. Her eyes were older than they should have been, and suddenly smudged with exhaustion. "How to pull apart my home and get my people killed."

"You mean the Mwennin."

Her voice grew distant. "Yes, the Mwennin. Jedao's people are long lost. The Hafn conquered his homeworld a couple centuries back."

Hemiola had no constructive response to that, so it returned its attention to the dreadful song-and-dance number. In fact, it went back and rewatched all the dance routines in the previous seven episodes for good measure. If anything, its opinion of them became more critical.

Then it returned to the one Cheris liked. That was when it realized what the hexarch had diagrammed in the margins of his notes: dances.

It made sense, in a way. Hemiola replayed some of its memories of the hexarch's visits. Yes: that flawless sense of balance, the way he always placed his feet precisely. He hadn't just danced casually, to pass the time. He had studied the art seriously. Where had he learned that?

Who are you? Hemiola wondered.

The hexarch and Jedao had danced together in one of the rooms at Tefos. Hemiola remembered how it and the other two servitors had changed the decorations each day for the hexarch's delight. Mostly paper lanterns with black-and-silver moths painted on them. It didn't know the significance of the lanterns, even now. How solicitously the hexarch had reviewed the steps with Jedao, whispered the patterns to him when he faltered.

"I have a personal question," Hemiola said to Cheris.

Cheris was bent over a subdisplay, reading up on research budgets. "Go ahead," she said without looking at it.

"Whenever you visited Tefos," it said, not knowing of a more tactful way to phrase the question, "you were always clumsy. Here, though—"

"I'm not?"

"Yes."

"Kujen liked to put Jedao in clumsy bodies," Cheris said simply. "It was a simple enough modification on his end. Psych surgery isn't the only kind of medical intervention he's versed in. He liked reminding Jedao of what he'd lost."

A long way from the boy who had wanted to feed hungry children, then. Or perhaps Hemiola had misunderstood the boy all along. "Who taught the hexarch to dance?"

"He never told me," Cheris said. "He never talked much about where he came from. He'd seen a great many worlds die, battlefields and testing grounds for weapons we don't have names for anymore, worlds torn apart by their own problems. By the time he met me, deaths didn't move him much." Her mouth twisted up on one side. "We had that in common, anyway."

Cheris was much more convincing when she wasn't trying to tell it how corrupt the hexarch was. As if corruption had any meaning to a hexarch. Did corruption matter, when he had shared his gifts of knowledge and technology with the hexarchate for all his life? It wasn't sure where it fell on that question.

Worlds upon worlds knew Cheris, or Jedao, as the Immolation Fox. Those same worlds didn't know the hexarch's name. It had learned that much. The hexarch preferred to move in the shadows. And while people didn't whisper the hexarch's name with fear, they feared the world he had made.

What went wrong? Hemiola wondered.

"Kujen grew homesick from time to time," Cheris said. "That much I know. I don't think his home was a good place. But it was his, and it stopped existing, and that kind of thing matters. Shuos Mikodez told me once that Kujen had been a refugee once upon a time. It's hard to imagine it, but Mikodez's information tends to be reliable. I usually wish it wasn't."

"You and Kujen must have had the best conversations," 1491625 said, snidely.

"We did," Cheris said, regaining some of her good mood "I remember the one time right after we'd—made an alliance. Back when Jedao was still alive, and our first meeting." She waved toward Hemiola. "Before Tefos, even, years before."

"Do tell," 1491625 said, its lights strobing with sarcasm.

"If you hate my stories so much—"

"I want to know," Hemiola said.

Cheris's smile lacked humor. "We'd agreed that the heptarchate needed to be reborn," she said. "We... discussed things for a while. It was a precarious moment."

From Cheris's elevated pulse and temperature, Hemiola could guess what form some of that discussion had taken. But it didn't point that out. If she didn't want to bring it up, it wasn't going to either.

"I was talking about changes to the military code as part of a general program of social reform." Cheris's drawl had gotten stronger. "For some reason I was intent on overhauling the section that dealt with courts-martial. Maybe I should have stuck with it. It might have come in useful later."

"I thought they never court-martialed you," 1491625 said.

"That's technically correct."

"So your dishonorable discharge—"

"I wouldn't dream on standing on regulation," Cheris lied. Neither 1491625 nor Hemiola called her on it. "Anyway, Kujen propped himself up on an elbow and demanded, 'While you're fussing with regs that no one else cares about, who's going to run the heptarchate?' And I said that I'd have to do the job while a provisional government was set up, unless he wanted it." Her mouth twisted. "I suggested we arm-wrestle for it. It was funny at the time. At which point—"

"Yes?" Hemiola said when Cheris fell silent.

Cheris's breath huffed out in remembered irony. "He was incredulous that I'd consider surrendering power. And he was right. I knew, on some level, that if I lingered I was always going to wield power whether I wanted it or not. And I didn't—but no one who topples an entire government is going to be credible on that point. It's why I left High General Brezan nine years ago. I didn't want to get in the way of the transition."

This time Hemiola believed her, even if it couldn't unpuzzle her motives. More troublingly, though—"The hexarch knew? And he didn't try to stop you?"

Cheris didn't laugh at it or mock it. "Hemiola," she said, "Jedao was a weapon in the Kel Arsenal. I *belonged* to Kel Command. When Hexarch Nirai Kujen brought me along to Tefos, do you imagine he had their permission?"

It could guess the answer to that question.

"Why would he want to destroy the world he built?" Hemiola said.

"His puppets were becoming less willing to be moved by the master's hand," Cheris said. "During Jedao's lifetime, the Liozh had grown in power. And they were starting to ask inconvenient questions about the remembrances, and whether they could be repealed. This displeased Kujen."

We are a nation of thousands upon thousands of worlds, and we can't prevent a child from starving right next to one of our faction academies.

"I can't reconcile the hexarch you remember with the hexarch in his early writings," Hemiola said. "Later on, though... he's more absorbed in his studies, and less concerned with people, except as they're useful to him."

"That's becoming a theme," Cheris said. "I don't know how it is for servitors. Humans don't *live* for 900 years. Even in the space of a normal lifetime, we change a lot."

Hemiola didn't have to ask how she knew, the part of her that was Jedao. Everyone knew the Immolation Fox's story. It had even watched some dramas about him, although it hadn't had the nerve to ask her what she thought of them.

"He must have told you something of his motives," Hemiola said. "What did he want?"

"He claimed it was about watching the world be reborn," Cheris said. "I didn't believe it for a moment. Kujen never cared about high-minded abstract principles. The only thing that really matters to him is mathematics. In any case, he wouldn't have stuck out his neck for a high-minded abstract principle. He devoted himself to the most basic pleasures. Food. Sex. Beautiful clothes. He... didn't sleep much, but he liked watching other people sleep." Cheris leaned back in her seat and rubbed her eyes tiredly. "I figured out straight off that he didn't like being vulnerable. Made himself the perfect defense."

"But you cared about principles," Hemiola said, understanding at last. "And you didn't like the hexarch's system."

"No." Cheris's eyes had gone cold and intent, a killer's eyes. Jedao was watching it from behind her eyes. "I would have liked to kill him. But killing him wouldn't have solved the problem even if I'd been able to manage it. I tried, when I first met him. He simply hijacked a new body, and after that I realized I didn't have a way of getting rid of him permanently. So I had to get close to him to learn what I could, and try to reform his system. Besides," and she pulled a face, "we needed each other."

Ebullient pink-and-yellow lights lit up the entire cockpit of the needlemoth as 1491625 expressed its opinion of *that* statement. "You mean he was good in bed."

"Well, even after 'only' a few centuries, he knew a lot of... but never mind."

Hemiola had the mortifying and possibly heretical thought of the hexarch starring as a courtesan in a drama. Certainly he was always pretty enough to be one, even in a world dominated by pretty people. Even more mortifyingly, it had enough videos of him to... *I am not going to make a music video of the hexarch dancing.*

"If you were allies once," Hemiola said after it had tamped down *that* terrible idea, "what changed your mind?"

Instead of lying again, Cheris propped her chin in her hands and sighed. "He knows I don't need him anymore, which makes me a liability of the first order. I've already defied him by creating the Compact. He wouldn't destroy me for spite, but he doesn't tolerate threats to his power, either. And right now I'm the single person best equipped to stop him." She contemplated some snarl of stratagems invisible to anyone but herself. "I'm sorry you were dragged into this."

Hemiola didn't trust itself to answer. It decided that reinventorying the cargo hold was in order. Just in case some random vermin had scuttled aboard at Ayong Primary and were eating their way through the beloved ration bars.

Either Cheris's favorite flavor was roasted dried squid, because that was the one disappearing at the fastest rate, or she hated it and was trying to get rid of it so she could get to something tastier. She cleaned up after herself conscientiously enough; the needlemoth's systems recycled the wrappers tidily. But each wrapper came with a scannable code identifying its flavor, expiration date, and manufacturing facility of origin, presumably for quality control purposes. Servitors' work, which they could do without even opening up crates to look at the redundant human-readable labels.

Hemiola returned to browsing through the hexarch's notes. They finally revealed why assassinating the hexarch was impossible. It didn't recognize the revelation for what it was. It came in the form of a map, although it wasn't to scale, which bothered it more than it cared to admit. The hexarch had inked it in several different colors. After searching its own databases, updated with information from Ayong Primary, Hemiola concluded that the colors denoted different calendrical zones of influence. Yellow represented the hexarchate. Other pastel colors represented the Taurag Republic, the Hafn, Hausse, the Gwa Reality, and more.

The Gwa-an keep to themselves, the hexarch had written—in shorthand, but by now this posed no challenge. *The Hafn and Taurags are the most likely to be problematic in the next decades.*

And: *This is the first time in 237 years that our borders have been under serious threat of collapse, even if only along the Entangled and Crescendo Marches. I can feel the pressure of the encroaching calendrical rot like a disease under my skin.*

There followed a long sequence of equations and feverish side notes under the heading *black cradle*. Hemiola had to study them intensely for several days, disguising its interest with judicious applications of bad dramas. Even the incompetently choreographed dance sequences no longer mattered. The stakes were too high for it to spare much thought for its former hobbies.

The hexarch and Jedao could switch bodies. Jedao did so only with the hexarch's assistance, which perhaps explained some of his ambivalent attitude toward the hexarch.

On the other hand, the hexarch could jump at will. This explained how he had survived the past 900-odd years. Jedao hadn't murdered the hexarch in bed (or while dancing, or at dinner) because it wouldn't have done any good. The hexarch would simply have jumped into another body. So Cheris had told the truth about that.

Here, at last, came the explanation for the hexarch's interest in his nation's borders, and how intimately his welfare was bound up with them, beyond the obvious. His immortality—his ability to inhabit other bodies—was an exotic effect. It only worked within the high calendar's sphere of influence.

With ruthless paranoia, the hexarch had teased out the existence of other exotic effects that could destroy him. He'd even prototyped a couple of weapons, presumably for use against Jedao. This struck Hemiola as singularly dangerous, but then again, Jedao hadn't managed to obtain those weapons while he had the hexarch in his sights.

Some Kel formation effects could also sever the hexarch from his host body and annihilate him. But the Kel would never disobey their commanders, and Hemiola couldn't imagine that the hexarch would allow those commanders enough freedom to act against him.

The current fragmentation of the hexarchate must worry the hexarch. After all, if the nation fell, so did he. Even worse, the Protectorate and Compact had joined forces and were transitioning away from the high calendar.

Determined to make further sense of this, Hemiola skimmed rapidly through Kujen's earlier notes. If it had been human, it was sure it would have developed a headache. But it found the answer it had sought in the research on moths it had earlier thought insignificant. Not the material on dwarf moths, but even earlier, at the very beginning of the mothdrive research program.

The moths are alive, the hexarch had written. *The evidence can't be ignored: they are almost certainly sentient. If we proceed with this line of research we will be enslaving aliens who have done as no harm.*

On the other hand, the heptarchate is losing its battles. I watch the news daily. Despite the propaganda I can tell. Whole worlds eaten by the invaders at our borders. A faster stardrive would make all the difference.

Two days later: *I wish it didn't hurt to think about the moths. About dying children. About starving populations. Every time I think about it, I remember my own childhood. I wish I could stop caring.*

And the day after that, scrawled in the margin in jagged, shaky letters almost entirely unlike his usual handwriting: *I know how to do that.*

The hexarch meant psych surgery. It was almost always a bad idea, according to everything Hemiola had ever heard, to undertake psych surgery on yourself. Hemiola wished it could travel back in time and talk the hexarch out of this. It was too late by centuries.

Hemiola vibrated nervously, wondering what to do. It was still stuck on the needlemoth. But who did it owe its loyalty to? Even if the hexarch had ripped out his own conscience and warped the nation around his own thirst for life eternal, that didn't automatically make Cheris trustworthy.

CHERIS HAD WEDGED herself into the last remaining free space in the hold and was regarding Hemiola gravely. "You look like you want to talk about something," she said.

"Want" was a strong word. "I have information you need," it said.

"Need?" Cheris said.

"You said you want to kill the hexarch."

"So you know how."

"Now I do."

"Why tell me?" Cheris said reasonably. "Have you changed your mind about the kind of man he was?"

"You've been a general across many realms, many stars," it said.

"Something like." She was wary. It didn't blame her.

"The world that the hexarch built—*is* it a world where people starve?" It had pored over summaries from Ayong Primary, but they had been frustratingly incomplete. Plus, it suspected that administrators everywhere had the incentive to report things in a positive light whether or not things were going well.

Cheris made a frustrated gesture. "You're asking for a lot of data about a complicated question, and I can't imagine I can chew through it faster than a servitor. Each world, each station, each city, each neighborhood. The short, the *uncomplicated* answer is no. Foreigners like to talk about the hexarchs' tyranny. It is, however, a tyranny that feeds people and gives them work and allows them pleasure. Unless you're a heretic, that is. But someone always has to pay the price." Her mouth crimped. "This is the world I destroyed. Kujen thought I was going to help him, and I betrayed him."

Her straightforwardness disarmed Hemiola. "Can you swear to me that the hexarch's motives were a tyrant's?" it said.

"Not anymore I can't. He's a complicated man. But the numbers of people who have been tortured for him—that's not complicated at all."

It came to its decision then. "There are weapons that can kill him. I assume you haven't gotten your hands on them or you'd be done already."

"That's correct."

"For this assassination," Hemiola said slowly, "you're going to need Kel. Formation effects."

"That can be arranged," Cheris said. She bowed from the waist. "Welcome to the mission, Hemiola."

CHAPTER TWENTY-ONE

BREZAN HAD SPENT all morning at a desk wishing someone would rescue him from the earnest, polite, and painstakingly detailed conversation about calendrical shift logistics he was having with High Magistrate Rahal Zaniin. It wasn't that he disliked Zaniin. Despite her temper, which rivaled his own, Zaniin was a reasonable human being. (She was also surprisingly funny over drinks, the one time he'd got her drunk. In particular, she knew a lot of jokes that were not Kel jokes, which he appreciated.)

Several objects currently decorated his desk. A slate and two styluses, both of which had an irritating tendency to skip. A tiny cylindrical aquarium from Tseya, in which a placid blue-and-silver betta swirled amid pondweed and what looked distressingly like genuine faceted gemstones. Intelligent woman that she was, Tseya had left care instructions not with him but with his aide. He still wasn't sure what to make of the gift, especially since Tseya knew perfectly well that he thought fish were creepy when they weren't deliciously pan-fried.

Miuzan hadn't brought him any parting gifts, or spoken more than a handful of words to him since their evacuation from Isteia. Nevertheless, in a spirit of self-flagellation, Brezan had placed a portrait of his family on his desk, angled so Zaniin couldn't see it. His youngest father had commissioned one of his friends to paint it. Brezan remembered being impressed that any artist, even one on good terms with his prickly youngest father, would risk the inevitable blistering critique.

"High General," Zaniin said, "are you paying attention?"

"Yes," Brezan lied.

She rolled her eyes at him. "Well, at least fake it better." Then she returned to explaining the adjustments that would have to be made to the grade school curriculum. He already wasn't looking forward to the obligatory protests from the teachers, most of whom retained Vidona sympathies even if they had officially renounced their old allegiance.

Save me from this, Brezan thought despite a wave of guilt. Inesser had sustained tremendous losses fighting against Jedao. (New Jedao? Jedao Two? Nomenclature was getting to be a problem around here. It hadn't helped that Mikodez had casually mentioned that his assistant Zehun had named their latest calico kitten Jedao, apparently continuing a long tradition of naming their cats after notorious Shuos assassins.) Anyway, the least he could do was shoulder some of the administrative burden.

As it turned out, "rescue" came from an unexpected quarter. Zaniin was in the middle of running a bulletin by him, as if she needed his input on proper phrasing, when the call arrived. "Sorry," Brezan said with simulated regret. "I have to take this one."

She pulled a face at him. "Of course you do," she said. But a lifetime of attention to propriety won over curiosity. "Call me back when you're done."

"Naturally," Brezan said, fighting to keep his tone casual. His hands had gone clammy. "Please open Line 6-0. Record the whole thing." He might have to report the whole conversation to Inesser.

There was an unusually long pause. The grid indicated that it was securing the connection. Then it imaged a familiar oval face. Brezan's stomach knotted up as he viewed it: a woman, her hair cropped short with military practicality, rather than the bob he remembered. Despite her drawn face, her eyes were alert. It took all his self-control to keep from shouting, *Where have you been all these years?* Even if Khiruev had told him, it was another thing to see her.

"Hello, High General," said Ajewen Cheris.

"Hello," Brezan said. His attempt to keep hostility from seeping into his tone was insufficiently successful. Cheris made a moue in response. "It's been a few years."

"You don't need to understate things around me," Cheris said. "We both know how long I've been gone."

"If you're bothering to check in now," Brezan said, "I assume it's related to the messy business at Isteia Mothyard."

"I'd heard about that, yes."

Brezan scowled at her. "We could have used a warning." He hated her composure. She was always so calm. But then, having a mass murderer living in your skull must help induce sangfroid. Too bad he couldn't have some of that for himself.

Am I really wishing for a Jedao in my head? Brezan asked himself.

"I've been occupied."

"So Khiruev told me. Rather late."

She smiled Jedao's smile at him. Even though he knew she couldn't help it, his stomach clenched with dread. That smile would make him recoil for the rest of his life. "Contrary to some of the dramas, High General," she said, "I don't read minds. Tell me what's bothering you so we can move on to the important part of the conversation."

Brezan reined in his temper with an effort. Squared his shoulders. *Pretend Mikodez is watching.* That was always good for dampening outbursts. He trusted Mikodez even less than Cheris. His life was full of untrustworthy people.

"I could have used your help nine years ago," Brezan said. He was proud of the evenness of his tone. "A lot of people could have."

"Really," Cheris said.

He couldn't help it. He stiffened in response to the utter lack of emotion in her voice. "Dammit, Cheris, you *ran off*."

"You had plenty of help," she said. "Khiruev is a perfectly good general—you of all people know that. Ragath should have made general years ago. I'd heard you promoted him."

"Of course I did," Brezan said. "I didn't have so many high officers that I could afford to ignore talent." Which was hilarious coming from him because he'd never been a line officer himself.

Not only had Ragath's record spoken for itself, he'd come highly recommended by people he trusted. To his relief, Khiruev and Ragath got along well. The same couldn't be said of all his generals.

"Well, then."

"I would have appreciated having someone to advise me other than Mikodez."

Cheris's breath huffed out in an almost-laugh. "I would have liked to tell you what I was doing," she said, "but I needed to preserve operational security. It's moot now. That drama about Kujen your people are distributing isn't as foxingly awful as I'd expected it to be, given how much of a rush job it has to be. Although did your Andan playwrights have to give Kujen all the best lines? To say nothing of that gorgeous actor? He's starting to have *fans*."

A sudden wild hope lit his heart. "I don't suppose you're calling now because you've gotten rid of this ghost or revenant or whatever the fuck Kujen is and we can all stand down from high alert?"

Too much to ask for. "Sorry," Cheris said. "I'm calling to ask for your help with him. You're the one with all the Kel."

"Inesser is, these days," he said. He assumed she'd approached him rather than Inesser based on their prior acquaintance—he couldn't exactly call it friendship—especially since Inesser was unlikely to hold a high opinion of Cheris. "Keep talking."

"First: what I told you about the black cradle years ago is still true."

He winced. "Cheris, if you're hoping that cozying up to Inesser has gotten me one of the two weapons that can kill a revenant, that's not the case. I'm pretty sure Inesser doesn't have them either."

"No, Kujen wouldn't have gotten that careless," Cheris said. "I haven't even been able to find schematics for the snakescratch dart and genial gun. And running around interrogating random Nirai with connections to Kujen would take longer than anyone has."

"Well, if you wanted to depress me, you've succeeded."

"That's not the bad news." Cheris gestured at her face. "You know how Kel Command stuck Jedao's mind in my body? Jedao couldn't control where he ended up. Kujen always inserted him wherever they wanted him."

"I love how you talk about that so casually."

She ignored that. "Kujen doesn't suffer that limitation. Kujen can jump anywhere he wants, so long as it's in high calendar space."

"You can't mean—"

"I do."

Brezan put the pieces together. "Then—"

"Yes. Kujen is very old and very patient. He might have been willing to wait for the Compact, or your alliance with the Protectorate, to die out and wind up as some obscure classified footnote to history. He's weathered secessions and civil wars before."

"Secessions?" He hadn't heard of any.

"Ask Ragath about that sometime. Most of them were—"

"—classified. Right."

Cheris continued speaking. "Inesser agreeing to adopt your calendar makes her a threat. Because Kujen can't continue to hop bodies once it takes hold. But it's also an opportunity to craft a trap for Kujen, by leaving a target too good to miss. Switch up the calendar everywhere *except* the target. Leave that one under the high calendar."

He liked the sound of this less and less. "What target would that be?"

"Terebeg 4."

"No," Brezan said immediately. "You're not going to dangle the Protectorate's capital in front of Kujen and his unbeatable swarm."

She was relentless. "The anniversary of Hellspin Fortress is coming up. It's perfect. Kujen won't be able to resist the opportunity, especially knowing that his cover's been blown and he has to move soon. He has a Jedao. He has a swarm. He has a brand-new weapon."

"That's great," Brezan said, "except for the part where we don't have a countermeasure for the gravity cannon."

"The other Jedao only has one swarm," Cheris said, "and he hasn't shown any evidence of particular tactical cleverness, although it's not impossible that he's good at doing more than firing a big gun. Inesser's good at her job. She wasn't the hexarchate's best living general for no reason."

"You're forgetting the other thing," Brezan said acidly, "which is the whole reason we got rid of the high calendar in the first place. Because you can't bluff. It will have to be the real thing, with real remembrances, and real victims. If Kujen decides to give the whole thing a miss, that'll be hundreds of people dead—not just dead, but tortured to death—and for no purpose."

"He destroyed Isteia, Brezan. He won't stop there, not until the high calendar is reinstalled everywhere."

Brezan thought furiously. "Assuming Kujen accepts the lure, he'll have Kel and Inesser will have Kel. I'm hoping he doesn't have more of those damn gravity cannons, or more swarms. How do you propose to assassinate him?"

"There are formations that can sever him from his anchor and kill him forever," Cheris said.

The grid indicated that she had just sent him a databurst. Brezan opened up the files and glanced them over. He could read basic formation notation, but this wasn't his department. Inesser and her staff would be able to figure it out.

"You want me to persuade Inesser to go along with this plan of yours."

"Yes."

"You realize Inesser's calling the shots and not the other way around? Fuck, Cheris, the woman's older than my grandparents. Scarier than any of them, too."

"A lot's at stake, Brezan. Are you going to stand by?"

He scowled at her. "Of course not. But understand, I only have so much pull."

"Then make the most of what you have."

"You know, Kujen missed his window of opportunity, if what you say is true," Brezan said. "He could have lobbed himself into, I don't know, Inesser's body and taken over all the Kel." Just as Cheris herself had hijacked Khiruev's swarm nine years ago.

"You think he hasn't thought of that? There's a reason he doesn't wander around doing that. He drives most of his anchors mad in short order. I'm not saying he couldn't do a massive amount of damage, but he's cautious by nature and has generally preferred to survive by keeping his existence secret from all but the highest circles of government. Until you and Inesser blew that to the stars, too."

"Why doesn't his current anchor oust him?"

Cheris's eyes grew distant. "His current anchor has served him for decades. Kujen can be extraordinarily persuasive. He hasn't been a psych surgeon for centuries for nothing."

"So we have two months and twelve days left," Brezan said, having checked his augment.

Cheris reflexively checked her wrist. It took Brezan a moment to recognize what she was wearing: the rose gold watch that General Khiruev had given her. No one went around with them anymore except actors or the occasional collector, but Khiruev liked to buy decrepit ones from antique shops and fix them up. Khiruev had even presented one to Brezan a few years back, an ornate affair with a lacquered magpie on the face, although he kept it in a drawer back in his office in Tauvit. He wondered if he'd ever see it again.

"Mobilizing the populace on that scale isn't the hardest part," Brezan said. "Because the populace is still used to jumping every time they hear a Vidona's footstep. Of course, that means if Kujen conquers Terebeg, they'll be just as happy to fall in line for him. Oh, not everyone... but enough. It'll be messy." He gave Cheris a hard look. "I think you'd better deliver some of this news to Inesser yourself."

"No," Cheris said flatly. "The less people know about my movements, the better. Be persuasive. I'm sure you've had plenty of practice at it."

"Why," Brezan said, "what are you going to be up to? I need to know so I don't get in your way."

"I'm the backup plan," Cheris said. "In case the Kel formations don't get him. It's a long shot, but what's a life but a coin to be spent, anyway?"

"Please don't tell Kel jokes."

"Sorry, habit." Jedao's smile again.

"Do servitors even appreciate Kel jokes?" Since he couldn't imagine anything else would fit in that needlemoth with her.

"Depends on the servitor. If you want to know, you can ask the ones around you."

A shiver went down his spine. He would never be at ease with the servitors, even though they were perfectly polite to him. "I'll pass, thanks."

"If I can trap Kujen in non-high calendar space," Cheris continued, "he can be killed."

"He's not going to be stupid enough to enter hostile calendrical terrain for your convenience," Brezan said.

"I know. That's why I'm going to assassinate the other Jedao on his own command moth."

Brezan's tongue stuck to the roof of his mouth for a moment at how casually she said it. "Localized calendrical spike."

"Yes. You won't notice it, I don't think, but it should give me a window of opportunity to do away with Kujen."

"Cheris," he said, "you'll be careful?" Now, as much as he disliked her, he was wishing her good luck. Funny how that went. "I can't imagine he's less of a killer than you are."

"If Kujen designed him, probably not." Her eyes had gone intent. Brezan didn't envy the other Jedao, who would never know what hit him. "I'm Kel, Brezan, you think I'm not used to living with risks?"

"I don't think 'I'm Kel' has anything to do with your extraordinary penchant for destructive gestures," Brezan said.

Her smile flickered at him like a candle flame. "If you feel that way, imagine what it's like having him in your head all the time. Besides, I'm not done. I'm going to need one more thing from you, or none of this will work."

Nine years of playing politician had inured Brezan to receiving people's demands. "I'm listening," Brezan said.

CHAPTER TWENTY-TWO

JEDAO SPENT THE next eleven days in his quarters contemplating his options. Kujen had already proven that he was willing to have Jedao removed for disobedience. Anything he wanted to do to stop the remembrances would have to take that into account.

During that time Jedao barely ate. Dhanneth stopped by with broth and insisted on trying to feed him. The metallic aftertaste had grown worse, however, and the torture he'd witnessed left Jedao with little appetite. He only tried because Dhanneth seemed agitated if he refused food.

The number of guards increased from four to six. Jedao suspected reinforcements lurked nearby, just in case. It was what he would do.

On the twelfth day, Kujen came to see him. Dhanneth startled, then prostrated himself. Jedao did as well. He had to play this carefully.

Kujen arranged himself on a chair, although Jedao caught the subtle crimp of his mouth. *Inhyeng*, Jedao thought.

"You may rise," Kujen said, as though nothing had passed between them. "You'll find this interesting, General." He pulled out a small slate and called up an image of a star system. Calendrical gradients were clearly marked in different colors. "That's to scale," he added, "so naturally it's impossible for you to make out the details you care about."

"And what would those be?" Jedao said warily.

Several labels flared up like pins of fire. The image shifted, compressed. Tiny flickers expanded into the standard symbols for orbital defense platforms, stations of varying capabilities, even a wolf tower. Of most interest was the great fortress built into the largest moon of the fourth planet, Terebeg 4.

"It's not a nexus fortress, if that's what you're worried about," Kujen said. "The Fortress of Pearled Hopes, something of a throwback." His mouth pulled up in a sudden wry smile. "I don't think even the archaeologists remember anymore. Pearled Hopes was built on the ruins of an earlier civilization's colony. At least, it's always been clear to me that someone a lot more determined than we are dragged the damn 'moon' to its present orbit from somewhere else. There's no way it originated in-system, and back when I was young, you could read up on the artifacts people used to find on it."

"Fine," Jedao said, since someone with amnesia was in no position to criticize anyone else's memory, archaeological or otherwise. "That's the next target?" If Kujen had an urgent need to conquer artifact worlds, things could be worse. Maybe he could use the travel time to persuade Kujen otherwise on the matter of remembrances.

Maybe pushing the issue would get him killed, which would do no one any good. He needed to bide his time until he could come up with a better plan of resistance.

"Most of that's of no concern to you," Kujen said, confoundingly. "The part you care about is where the Compact has made the fourth planet their center of government. That will be our next target."

"Does their leadership reside there?"

"Well," Kujen said, "their 'official' head of government does. An elected person of no consequence. Alas, the real adversary is Shuos Mikodez. I'm not going to ask you to take on the Citadel of Eyes, as nice as it would be to eliminate him. But the elected premier plus High General Kel Brezan and their staffs will make approachable targets."

Even then Jedao didn't see the trap. "What are their military capabilities? And when do you want this assault to take place?"

Kujen told him: the anniversary of the massacre at Hellspin Fortress.

"I have a gift for you," Kujen said. Then Jedao knew things had not stopped getting worse. "Major—"

Dhanneth presented Jedao with a report on Terebeg System and the fortress's defenses. "They'll see us coming, sir," Dhanneth said, referring him to a larger map relating their present location to the target's. In a colorless voice, he detailed their current intelligence on the defense swarms, reports compiled by Jedao's staff.

"You will need weapons capable of handling the fortress," Dhanneth said, then looked at Kujen.

It's a loyalty test. "What," Jedao said, on the grounds that he couldn't let Kujen know how much this bothered him, "you don't trust me to make do with what you've already given me?"

"You've already proved capable of independent thinking," Kujen said sardonically. "I'm giving you another chance."

This made no sense. Kujen didn't strike Jedao as the type of man to tolerate any chance of failure. Unless—*Hellspin Fortress.*

It was a calendrical attack. For the attack to have the impact Kujen desired, he needed Jedao. Specifically Jedao, and not some other general. Which meant—

Kujen confirmed it with his next words. "You will be using threshold winnowers," he said. "I've increased their range."

"You can stop being coy and give me specifics," Jedao said past the sudden dryness of his mouth. "I can't make good use of a weapon I don't understand."

"Let me show you how winnowers work," Kujen said. He brought up a series of equations, a schematic, a stylized animation. "We can go into the math if you want, but gate mechanics gets very technical."

Jedao watched, unwillingly fascinated, as the simulated winnower caused eyes and gashes to open in pixel rats. "Why rats?" he asked. The real question he wanted to ask was, *Why such ugly deaths?* He couldn't imagine death by winnower being anything but excruciatingly painful.

"Nostalgia," Kujen said with such great affection that Jedao opted not to inquire further. Kujen told him anyway. "I went through a lot of them earlier in my career."

"Is that the size of a typical winnower crew?" Jedao asked, pointing at the relevant figure.

"In Kel practice, yes," Kujen said. "Mostly issues related to transport and calibration. It's a finicky design, which I've never been happy about, but I was in a hurry—"

The world grayed around Jedao. *I'm just as culpable*, he thought. He had used Kujen's shear cannon not that long ago, without asking what the cost would be for those he used it on. It was hypocritical of him to feel this sudden rush of horror.

He couldn't afford to get distracted. Kujen had finished his digression on interface design and safety precautions, and had brought up a new animation. "You'll like this," he said.

Will I? Jedao thought.

He almost missed it the first time. "Again," he said, just to be sure. Kujen obliged him.

The new threshold winnower was composed of two separate generators, not one as before. Each projected a line of effect into the space before it, cutting and precise. Where the lines intersected, they punched open a hole into gate-space. From there the winnower's effect, outflung from the generators, propagated outwards. This increased the effective range and put the winnower's crews well out of harm's way. Jedao studied the equations with interest: a clever use of the refactoring implicit in the math.

"Same effect?" Jedao asked.

"At least on animated rats."

Jedao shot him an annoyed look.

Kujen relented. "It's been field tested. Spare heretics." Despite his casual tone, he looked at Jedao sharply. Jedao kept his face bland. "All of them died. I am always thorough, Jedao. I have been doing this for a long time."

Jedao imagined this was true. He also imagined what it must feel like to have mouths opening in your very flesh, gaping in a tongueless susurrus. When the eyes boiled out of the gashes, could you see what they saw? Did they give you a new appreciation of the lethality of light? His experience of pain was limited. Perhaps everyone's was, confronted with deaths like these.

"It'll work in the Compact?" Jedao said. You always had to check, with exotic weapons.

"Of course," Kujen said. "I know what I'm doing."

"I'm not unappreciative," Jedao said, "but besides socking the Compact, what's your goal for this specific battle? Not like I know enough about the political conditions, which change every time I blink. But I assume they're not going to roll over and die because we decapitate them. Based on the way people react to *me*, I'd assume the opposite. Especially if we reenact Hellspin Fortress."

There. He'd said it.

"A simple victory in battle isn't good enough for you?" Kujen said.

Dhanneth's eyes flicked to Kujen at the mockery in his voice.

"You said it earlier," Jedao said. "It's one thing for us to run around blowing things up. Another entirely to take and hold territory. We've barely consolidated our hold in Isteia System."

"Even an impossible task becomes possible if you approach it step by step."

Jedao wasn't persuaded. "You'll have to clear up one detail for me. What made Hellspin so memorable, if I understand the history lessons correctly, isn't that the battle was 'won.' No one would remember one more heresy in a parade of heresies, one more battle in a parade of battles, if that was all there was to it. Isn't the part that made it unforgettable the small matter of my *incinerating my own army?*"

Jedao didn't look directly at Dhanneth. Nevertheless, Dhanneth's reaction was impossible to miss. Jedao's peripheral vision wasn't *that* bad.

Dhanneth couldn't tell where he was going with this. He might as well have been shouting it with the desperate blankness of his face.

"Feel free to take your train of thought to its natural conclusion," Kujen said, his demeanor unruffled.

Jedao's heart was racing. *Don't let him see he's rattled you.* "This isn't going to be much of a decapitation strike if it also takes out our means of occupation." What a terrible, bloodless euphemism for *killing all our own soldiers.* "It's not like we have that much infantry. There's no point burning up all your pawns without getting something for them, Hexarch. So what is it? What are you getting out of this?"

"Oh," Kujen said, "we won't need the infantry. Once we get rid of the inconveniences, Protector-General Inesser will do the work of government and stabilization for us. Because as much as she hates me, she values duty more." He raised a hand slowly and sketched the curve of Jedao's jaw millimeters away from contact. Jedao held his breath, hating himself for the transient impulse to lean into the touch. "Once that's settled, once the hexarchate is restored, you'll have all eternity to do whatever pleases you. I mean that quite literally."

I can't do this, Jedao thought. The room darkened all around him, as though all the lights had fissured into the distance. "What do you mean, all eternity?"

"I mean," Kujen said, "that you will live forever, unless you do something catastrophically stupid, like diving into the heart of a star. I constructed a body for you that will repair itself naturally, that will never age. If you want to look younger, that too can be arranged, although I don't advise going quite as far back as seventeen. In any case, that's just aesthetics." He was smiling at Jedao as if this was supposed to make him happy.

Ruo, Jedao thought, *what do I do?* Except he knew perfectly well what Ruo would have done. Ruo had never been one to deny himself opportunity or pleasure.

When did I grow away from my best friend?

In the split second that followed, Jedao contemplated his options. Ordering Dhanneth to hand over his sidearm would just alert the hexarch's security and get him punched full of holes. Besides which, if Kujen had given Jedao a miraculous self-repairing body, he couldn't imagine that Kujen had neglected to do the same for himself, which would make him hard to assassinate.

Kujen seemed to consider Jedao a key pawn in his plan. Could he commit suicide and stay dead long enough to keep from taking part? Considering his recovery from the bullets, he didn't think so.

It all came back to this: playing along, and looking for a way to resist. He didn't see a way yet. But he had to delay until the last possible moment, in case something came to him.

JEDAO SPENT THE next two days determining that he could not, in fact, sabotage the threshold winnowers. Smiling technicians greeted him when he attempted to access them by walking in on them in full formal, as if they needed the reminder of his rank. The smiling technicians were backed up by unsmiling Vidona officers. Not wanting to arouse Kujen's suspicions, Jedao didn't press the issue.

Next he studied the mathematics of the winnowers, as if that did him any good. The best primer he found on the topic was not a paper or a textbook but, of all things, a biography of Academician Sayyad Reth in graphic novel format. Reth had done her theoretical work during a time when the Nirai allowed non-faction members to teach at their academies based on their achievements. A footnote informed him that the practice had been discontinued fifty-eight years ago.

The biography spent a whole chapter explaining not the actual mathematics, which its author/illustrator had deemed too technical for a general audience, but a simpler analogy. The actual mathematics either wasn't as terrifying as the author/illustrator thought it was, or some of the education Jedao couldn't remember receiving had included very good teaching. Jedao silently apologized to whoever the teacher had been.

Think of normal spacetime, said the author/illustrator, as a hypersurface. Each point on that surface had a tangent space associated with it. The tangent space could be considered a linearization of the area around the point, with extraneous information knifed away. Anyone stuck in the region of a threshold winnower's effect was painfully affected by the linearization.

(More footnotes explained hypersurfaces, tangent spaces, and linearizations.)

At that point Jedao caught himself stabbing the margins of the panels with his stylus and made himself stop. He brought up the winnower's specifications and scowled at them. *What am I missing?*

He was looking at the problem from the wrong angle. In spite of Kujen's assurances that the winnower would work in Compact territory, the design would only function in high calendar terrain.

Why would he give me a weapon that doesn't—

Kujen didn't think much of Jedao's technical ability or mathematical acumen. Which, fair enough, he wasn't a mathematician. But he could follow the mathematics curriculum required by Kel Academy, and then some.

Was Kujen lying to Jedao about the math? Thinking, perhaps, that Jedao wouldn't think to check? Surely Kujen wasn't so willfully malicious as to give him a weapon that had no hope of functioning.

Which meant Kujen was lying about the terrain. They weren't attacking the Compact after all. They were attacking the Protectorate. After all, when had Jedao had the opportunity to scout for himself? He relied on the information that Kujen gave him, or that people dominated by Kujen presented to him.

I have to stop this.

Too bad stealing high explosives and blowing himself up with the command moth and its freight of winnowers wouldn't do the trick. Now, more than ever, it was imperative that he stop Kujen. And to do that, he needed more allies.

"EXPLAIN IT TO me again," Jedao said to Dhanneth after the staff officers had left.

The table was full of demolished platters, each one shaped like a leaf or a moth's wing, lacquerware with abalone inlay. Jedao had eaten so the others didn't feel inhibited.

Dhanneth reviewed the logistical tables and the calendrical terrain gradients with him. Not for the first time, Jedao wondered what had prevented Dhanneth from being promoted long ago. Despite his subdued manner, he spoke as knowledgeably about the machineries of war as the staffers. "There's a reason you didn't ask this earlier," Dhanneth said.

When Kujen had granted Jedao access to the staff officers, Jedao had hoped to use the opportunity to examine formation mechanics in a natural setting. He'd gotten the opportunity, all right. It hadn't done any good.

Jedao was studying formations out of desperation, because they were the one weapon he had access to. Privately, he doubted Kujen would have given all the Kel a way to hurt him, yet he remembered the oddity of Kujen refusing to attend infantry drill. An ordinary precaution? But why, when he claimed he had nothing to fear from death?

In his spare time he read instructional texts on formation mechanics, on the pretext that he wanted to understand swarm tactics better. He didn't know if Kujen was falling for it. In all likelihood, it was a dead end and Kujen knew he had nothing to fear.

No help for it. He couldn't ask Dhanneth about the subject openly, so he changed the subject. "I want to ask you about a Kel," he said. "High General Kel Brezan."

"Crashhawk," Dhanneth said. "Our target."

"What do you think of him?"

Dhanneth glowered. "He's the enemy, sir."

Dhanneth's profile claimed he had no personal connection to Brezan. But Jedao also suspected Dhanneth's profile of having large gaps in it. He narrowed his eyes.

Dhanneth yielded too quickly. "I know what it is to disobey," he said, which was peculiar. Jedao had never known Dhanneth to be anything but perfectly obedient.

"What do you mean by that?"

"I quarreled with the hexarch once."

That Jedao hadn't expected. "About what?"

"We had a disagreement. I am Kel, sir. He is not, but he is a hexarch. I was in error."

Well, that shed approximately zero light on the subject. He rephrased. "Do you remember the specifics?"

"A little," Dhanneth said slowly.

Shit. What if Jedao wasn't the only one running around with amnesia? He'd never stopped to consider that. "Did *you* have an encounter with Cheris the memory vampire?"

Dhanneth shook his head. "No. The hexarch decided that I would perform my duties more adequately if I didn't remember."

Jedao's heart dropped. Dhanneth was wrong, of course. Presumably even Kujen had come to the same conclusion. If there was any time- or cost-effective way to churn out amnesiac, obedient, self-effacing, *useful* soldiers, Kujen would be manufacturing them by the millions. Except, it seemed, the process broke the victims.

On the other hand, Kujen would keep trying until he got it right. A 900-year-old ghost would have great stores of patience.

How many times had Jedao himself been wiped clean for Kujen's benefit? Had he undergone this cycle of discovery and rebellion before? It didn't matter. He was still obliged to assassinate Kujen.

What do you know about this? he asked the *Revenant*.

Know about what? it said. There was a distinct chill in its voice. At least it was talking to him.

Either it couldn't read his mind or it was faking. Jedao explained the situation while Dhanneth watched him with haunted eyes.

There were others before you, the *Revenant* said. *They didn't last long. Flawed. He would have continued his experiments for years yet, except he grew concerned about the rift between the successor states.*

Jedao hesitated, then: *Are there more?*

The *Revenant* said slowly, *None that are awake. I wouldn't be surprised if there are more, though.*

Jedao bit the inside of his mouth at the hot surge of jealousy that went through him. It was followed by a wave of shame. What had Kujen done with the failures? But he could guess the answer to that question.

"Sir?" Dhanneth said, worried.

Jedao had an idea. Not a good one. But he was out of those anyway. "Give me your hand, Commander."

Jedao's heart contracted painfully at the way Dhanneth complied without hesitation. *I should not be doing this.*

Talaw hated him, and the staffers weren't much better. Dhanneth, at least, showed no disgust around him—quite the opposite. As two people much disliked by the other Kel, they had something in common. Jedao didn't know whether Dhanneth would prioritize obedience to a Nirai hexarch or a Shuos general. It wasn't much of a chance, but he'd take it.

Jedao leaned in, heart beating rapidly at the sudden proximity to another man. If only—but no. Dhanneth was a Kel, and his subordinate. Even if Dhanneth were interested in him, it was forbidden. And Jedao was painfully aware that no one would ever want him, not that way. Even Ruo hadn't wanted him, not that he remembered.

I just need to convey my message. That's all.

He wasn't doing a good job of convincing his traitor heart. For the first time, Jedao was aware of being lonely.

He drew a deep breath and pressed a kiss to Dhanneth's palm, using the motion to cover what he was really (really?) doing: tapping a message in the Kel drum code against Dhanneth's hand.

I need your help.

Dhanneth's next move took Jedao off-guard. Dhanneth rose and came around so he stood next to Jedao's seat. He went to his knees and kissed Jedao's bare fingers. "Tell me how I may serve you," he said.

The shock of contact dizzied Jedao. He sat, trapped, desperate to respond and more desperate to restrain himself. *I'm imagining this.*

When Jedao didn't move, Dhanneth grew bolder. He ungloved slowly, almost teasingly. His face was very grave. He held out both gloves to Jedao, that old Kel gesture: *My honor is yours.*

Jedao accepted the gloves, as much as it pained him. Doing otherwise would have insulted Dhanneth, and he needed Dhanneth's help.

"You can't hurt me, sir," Dhanneth said.

Jedao left the chair and knelt so he faced Dhanneth. Rested his hands atop Dhanneth's broad shoulders, taking reluctant pleasure in the solidity of bunched muscle. A horrible thought occurred to him, although perhaps no more horrible than what was going on right now: "Have we done this before?"

Dhanneth was tranquil. "No, sir."

Jedao kissed him at the corner of his mouth so their noses wouldn't collide. The salt of skin aroused him. Kissing wasn't anything like he'd imagined. (Ruo. Had they ever—? But he didn't remember Ruo showing any interest.) He wished so much for this to be real intimacy, the one thing it could never be. "What about this?"

In the drum code, he asked, *What did the hexarch do to you? Who were you?*

Dhanneth stirred, then rose, drawing Jedao with him. He lifted one hand and cupped Jedao's cheek. *I defied him and he broke me.* Drum code.

Jedao embraced him, inhaled the scent of Dhanneth's skin. Hated himself for seeking comfort in this, of all things. Asked the question he should have asked at the beginning, although who knew if he'd get an honest answer. *If I ordered you to kill the hexarch, what would happen?*

If Dhanneth reported him straightaway to Kujen, it would be no more than what he deserved.

Dhanneth clasped Jedao's fingers with his other hand. "I am yours," he said. "I have been yours since you came to us." In drum code: *I can give you what you really want.*

Dhanneth's vehemence unnerved Jedao. "I don't know what you mean by that." He didn't know which part he was responding to.

"I was present when the hexarch created you," Dhanneth said.

Jedao stared at him.

"He didn't explain the mechanics to me," Dhanneth said, "except he felt it would"—slight pause—"reassure you to have a Kel present. He explained to me that your original body no longer survived, so he made you a new one."

"So I'm a clone after all?" Jedao said, unsurprised that Kujen had lied after all. It wasn't news that he had to be some kind of construct.

"No, sir." Dhanneth was subdued. "He explained to me that voidmoths do not age—that they would live forever if not for the normal attrition of battle and madness. That they have impressive regenerative capabilities. He felt these were desirable traits."

"But I'm not—" Jedao's voice died in his throat.

He could hear moths. He could hear the *Revenant*, and talk to it. The othersense must be a moth-sense. And presumably his inability to die like a regular human being was related, too. Because he wasn't human.

He was a moth, and he'd ordered the massacre of moths at Isteia.

Revenant, Jedao said, *why didn't you tell me?*

Tell you what?

That I'm not human. That I'm one of you.

The *Revenant* was scornful. *Would you have believed me?*

"Yes," Dhanneth said. "You're a moth modded into human shape. The hexarch said it was one of his greatest achievements."

"Who were you," Jedao said, "that he picked you to keep this secret, and not someone else?"

Dhanneth shivered, although Jedao hadn't intended it as a criticism. "I was the lieutenant general in charge of this swarm."

"What?" Jedao whispered, stumbling backward. He would have fallen on his ass if Dhanneth hadn't caught him.

"Are you all right, sir?"

"Am *I* all ri—" Jedao checked himself. Just because he was rattled didn't give him the right to tear into Dhanneth. "He broke you to *major*?"

Dhanneth lowered his eyes. "I was more useful to him this way."

Suddenly it made sense. Dhanneth still had the expertise of a general. It was what enabled him to give such excellent commentary on strategy and battle planning. It also made him an ideal aide for an amnesiac general. On the other hand, he no longer possessed the personality to lead or inspire.

No wonder the Kel soldiers were so uncomfortable in Dhanneth's presence. He was a living reminder of the hexarch's power. For if Kujen could do this to their general, he could do it to any of them.

Jedao felt wretched for using Dhanneth against Kujen. How did that make him any better than Kujen himself? At the same time, Dhanneth might have observed something that might help Jedao. Drum code again: *Is there any way to kill the hexarch?*

No, Dhanneth replied. His eyes were questioning.

Jedao reached out toward Dhanneth, then dropped his hand. "Leave me," Jedao said abruptly, ashamed of himself for wanting to touch Dhanneth again. *He's already been harmed enough. The least I can do is leave him alone.*

"Sir—" Dhanneth scooped up Jedao's hand, pressed a kiss to his palm, then retrieved his gloves, put them on, and left. Jedao was left watching the closing door, heart pounding, troubled in more ways than he cared to name.

CHAPTER TWENTY-THREE

I'M NOT HUMAN, Jedao thought. It didn't seem real. On the other hand, he couldn't deny the evidence.

After he'd spoken with Dhanneth, he'd returned to his quarters to take a bath. At first the water was too hot. The temperature reminded him of blood. He pulled the plug and watched the water drain away. Then he set the temperature to be unpleasantly chilly and filled the tub again. The cold stabbed him. He welcomed the pain.

When he no longer felt the cold, Jedao left the bathtub and stood, dripping, in front of the mirror. Kujen must have selected it personally. It took up the better part of the wall, and the frame resembled a cascade of black moths with glittering stars caught in their wings. Jedao had grown inured to luxury, thanks to its omnipresence. Now he was struck by the sheer wasteful beauty of the mirror and, for the first time, by his own essential ugliness.

I'm not human.

Dhanneth had known all this time. Had kept the secret.

Jedao toweled himself off and got dressed. In a way, finding out this latest unwelcome truth came as a relief. Kujen had created him as a pawn. No one had any reason to mourn him when he died. He was looking forward to it. All he needed to do was endure until he found a way to destroy Kujen.

At some point servitors brought him food. He had a vague memory of acknowledging their presence. The thought of eating exhausted him. He didn't see the point. Instead, he spent nearly an hour pushing food around the plates before concluding that he wasn't going to choke any of it down.

It was Kujen, of all people, who rescued him from diving into paperwork for lack of anything better to do. The grid alerted Jedao of a message. *Come to my quarters*, it said. *We should talk.*

Jedao messaged that he was coming. Finding his way to Kujen's quarters wasn't difficult. The rooms had changed, or perhaps rearranged themselves.

This time he passed one full of seven eyeless statues, flawlessly rendered in costume that looked flowingly impractical. If he knew Kujen, the statues had been chiseled by master sculptors, the rock quarried from mountains where the very birds sang their stories into the stone. Jedao didn't know who any of the statues represented, if anyone at all. Presumably all of them had been human.

In the next room, ropes of beads hung from the ceiling, alternating with curtains of diaphanous fabric, as if someone had dismembered dragonflies and stitched up their wings. The effect, for all its loveliness, made him feel trapped.

When he found Kujen at last, it was in a garden. Jedao stopped at the archway leading into it, inhaling the smells of plants and earth and decaying leaves. A breeze swirled out and scattered red and yellow leaves. He stooped to pick one up: dry, paper-fine, crisp and curling at the edges.

"Come in," Kujen said. He was leaning against a tree with narrow, silvery green leaves and smooth bark. The first thing Jedao noticed was not his clothes—robes of fine dark silk brightened with silver embroidery—but the fact that he was standing with bare feet in the dirt. His slippers had been discarded next to an exposed tree root.

Jedao blinked at Kujen, discomfited. Then he stepped into the garden and joined Kujen under the tree. For all his dislike of Kujen, something about the bare feet made Kujen seem human. Illusory as that might be.

"There's something you should know about your aide," Kujen said. "I'm glad his programming has held so far."

"Oh?" Jedao said neutrally.

Kujen pulled a slate out from his robes and called up a still. It showed Kujen in restrained attire, and Dhanneth in full formal. At Dhanneth's breast was a golden feather pierced with three rings: a lieutenant general's insignia. The two of them stood before an angled casket in a brightly lit lab. Jedao could guess the casket's contents, despite the murkiness of the fluid that swirled within. Several guards in Nirai black-and-silver stood to the side, expressionless.

The still had captured Dhanneth with his brows drawn down, mouth slightly open. He was about to argue. In fact, Jedao couldn't remember ever having seen Dhanneth so combative. But of course, he knew the reason for that.

"Go ahead," Jedao said, "play it. That's what you called me here for."

"Just remember I'm doing this for your safety," Kujen said, and triggered playback.

Jedao had thought he was prepared for the casket's contents. The thing within, naked, bore a superficial resemblance to a man if he ignored the way it was composed of tendrils coiled together. Worst of all was the tendrils' slow knotting and unknotting, as though they sought to crawl free of their shape.

"Hexarch," Dhanneth-in-the-video said with murderous intensity. "I am not interested in your hobbies."

Kujen-in-the-video pressed controls on the casket. Tubes drained the fluid, and the lid receded. For all the pallid inhumanity of the tendrils, the thing had a wholly human visage, blankly dreaming, the brown eyes innocent of expression. Jedao stared at his face in the video with its unkempt bangs, and thought inanely, *You couldn't give it a haircut?*

Dhanneth's laugh came short and harsh. "I recognize Shuos Jedao, all right. If you think I'm going to serve some experimental puppet with his face, you're out of your mind."

"It's not just a puppet," Kujen said, maddeningly calm. "It has Jedao's capabilities. But he'll still need an army. At the moment, unless I misread the personnel roster, you're the swarm's general."

"What are you going to do," Dhanneth said, "slaughter your way down the chain of command if I say no? I'm not going to accommodate you."

"Kel courage is so inconvenient sometimes," Kujen said with the nonchalance that Jedao had learned to dread. "You may care little for your own fate, General, but what of your subordinates'?"

"I care about their fates, all right," Dhanneth said. "They deserve better leadership. Something you'll never understand."

In a motion so swift Jedao almost missed it, Dhanneth drew his knife and began stabbing the wretched writhing thing. Dhanneth knew about the business of killing. He did not stop with a single thrust, however wholehearted, or pause after driving the knife home. Instead, he slashed and stabbed over and over, in as many vulnerable places as he could reach. The thing was soon reduced to a mess of cringing severed tendrils and puddled silver-black fluid. But the eyes in the face woke long enough to stare up at Dhanneth in what Jedao recognized, heartsick, as terror.

Kujen paused the recording. "Jedao," he said, "that was the point at which I decided he needed psych surgery. Because once he fell in line, the rest would follow."

"No," Jedao said. "Play the rest."

"It will hurt you."

"Do you care?"

"I need you intact, my dear." Kujen smiled reflectively at him. "In my nine centuries, I have met no one with quite your combination of aptitudes. When I was a boy, I thought my master the warlord was the most ferocious warrior I would ever know. The Kel did away with him handily enough. But you may be the greatest general the Kel have ever known.

"You're troubled by what you've learned? What does it matter what color your blood is, or what you look like beneath your skin? You're still a person. Don't get distracted by superficialities."

"Just play it," Jedao said, dropping all honorifics.

Kujen's eyes lit as if he'd won. "If you insist."

The hexarch's security, who'd been standing to the side, finally intervened and pulled Dhanneth off the thing in the casket. Kujen watched with an impressive show of unconcern. Two of the guards went down. Jedao wondered if they had survived. They had to call in reinforcements. Three of those went down as well.

Pinned, guns pointed at him, Dhanneth only grinned at Kujen. "Even if it lives, I doubt that creature is any more enthusiastic about serving you than I am." Jedao shuddered at the note of desperation in Dhanneth's voice. "Or being surrounded by people who look at it and see nothing but a monster."

Jedao covered a wince.

"It'll look more human after I've had more time to complete the treatments," Kujen said. "I would have liked to continue the experiment at a more leisurely pace. Unfortunately, events have forced my hand."

Kujen stopped the video again. "Is that enough? Shall I keep going? Because psych surgery is boring to watch. It's all chemicals and signifiers and furniture-arranging."

Jedao shook his head, not trusting himself to speak.

"Come here," Kujen said, opening the circle of his arms. "You're shaking." He smelled of distant apples and smoke and spices.

Jedao let Kujen enfold him. *What does it matter?* he thought. *I can't figure out how to kill you, and you're the only one who doesn't hate me.* Except Dhanneth, who didn't have a choice in the matter.

After a while, Jedao said, "Kujen, the warlord."

By then Kujen was massaging his shoulders. "What about him?"

"You must have cared about him a great deal." He remembered the hint of admiration in Kujen's voice. It was hard to imagine Kujen caring about anyone but himself.

The corners of Kujen's mouth lifted. "He won my loyalty with a refrigerator, you know."

Jedao was nonplussed.

"It was a very long time ago," Kujen said. "Halash had me brought before him after I danced for him for the first time. I'd never seen so much food in one place in all my life. I'm surprised I didn't attack the table."

Jedao couldn't imagine Kujen with his manicured nails and flawless skin and velvets attacking anything; wondered what he had looked like as a dancer.

Kujen gazed into a past that only he could see. "It wasn't a good refrigerator, a Snowbird 823, but I had no way of telling at the time. When he saw me trying to figure out how much food I could stuff into my clothes, or my stomach for that matter, he took me to my room. A whole room, all to myself. He showed me a table set with food, and the refrigerator in the corner. He explained to me that I didn't have to eat everything in one sitting. The refrigerator was prone to breaking down, so I set myself to learning how to fix it. Good training for the Nirai, I suppose."

"You said the Kel got him. What happened to you then?"

"The same thing that happened to all of us. The Kel brought soup, and blankets, and bottled water. All sorts of riceballs and dumplings. And doctors. As if they hadn't been the ones to bomb us."

His fingers suddenly dug into Jedao's back. Jedao stilled. "They looted the warlord's possessions," Kujen said. "I didn't mind *that*. I used to steal things to survive, when I wasn't selling myself. Before Halash took me in. But the things they... Halash collected ancient documents. Some of them older than the heptarchate. Some of them much older. Mathematics, astronomy, books of poetry. I used to sit in the solarium and read them. Halash let me because he knew I would be careful."

"Couldn't the Kel have sold the books?" Jedao said. "If they were old and valuable?" Now that he had calmed down, he wondered how much he could get Kujen to let slip. Nothing useful... yet. But the more Kujen talked, the more he might reveal.

"The Kel commander didn't care," Kujen said "They burned the books because they wanted fuel for their damnable celebration pyre. I went to the biggest Kel I could find. I didn't know rank insignia then, so I thought the hierarchy might go by size. I begged him to spare the books. I offered to be his whore. He patted me on the head and sent me to the tents with the children. Said I was too young. *Young*, as if fucking was so damn difficult."

Jedao was glad he couldn't see Kujen's face.

"Useful as they are," Kujen went on, "I have never forgiven the Kel for that."

Jedao thought of Dhanneth, of formation instinct. "And afterward?" he said when Kujen fell silent.

He felt Kujen's shrug. "The Kel were good about getting us into orphanages and arranging for our educations. I tested into Nirai Academy very young."

"I'm sorry," Jedao said. It was the only safe thing he could think to say.

"It was a long time ago," Kujen said, unsentimental. "And you weren't involved. We'll fix the world and return it to the way things ought to be, and you'll never have to endure the things I endured."

CHAPTER TWENTY-FOUR

INESSER HAD HEALED enough that the doctors had been allowing her to totter around unsupervised for the last couple of weeks. She'd submitted herself to physical therapy with grim determination. "I don't get it," one of the doctors had said to her in honest bafflement. "Generals are *terrible* about physical therapy." To which she'd retorted that she had no intention of going around with a limp if she had a choice in the matter. The ankle had taken longer to heal than it would have in the past, even with treatment. One of the consequences of her age.

Brezan had ceded the best quarters on the bannermoth to her. In a surprising move, he had left its decor to her. Inesser hadn't done much in that regard, not least because she had other matters to deal with. Still, she'd had the grid image one of her favorite paintings against the wall. It depicted an archer drawing her bow: usually attributed to Andan Zhe Navo (what wasn't?), although she had it on good authority that it was a fake painted by a gifted entrepreneur. It gave her something to look at that didn't have to do with (modern) warfare while she did damnfool things like writing letters of the alphabet with her foot and meditating on stroke order.

She was in the middle of another round of exercises when the grid indicated that someone wanted to talk to her: Brezan. He had flagged it as a matter of some urgency. "Come in," she said. It was about time she take a break anyway.

Brezan didn't salute her after he entered, which was refreshing. "Protector-General," he said. "I need to ask you for a favor."

Ah. That explained both the formality and the lack of salute. He wanted her to take him seriously. "Have a seat," Inesser said, nodding toward one of the extra chairs. "I assume this won't be fast."

"Well, that depends," Brezan said. He sat. "Kel Cheris contacted me just now."

"And you didn't tell me."

"She didn't think you'd be a receptive interlocutor."

Inesser snorted. "Well, at least she's a realist. Go on."

A smile flickered at his mouth, was gone. He explained about Kujen's body-hopping ability, its limitations, and Cheris's proposed plan.

Inesser couldn't help reflecting that either he had started out with good communication skills—not necessarily something you could take for granted with staffers—or his role in the Compact's government these past years had forced him to develop them.

"You're not surprised, are you," Brezan said.

"It makes a lot of things make sense," she said. "If it's a fabulation, it's an inspired one. Do you consider Cheris's information reliable?"

"She claimed her source was one of Kujen's assistants. How she managed to subvert one of Kujen's assistants—well."

"The obvious person to consult would be Hexarch Mikodez," Inesser said. "I wouldn't expect him to be able to verify this definitively in time to be useful. But it won't hurt to check."

Brezan raised his eyebrows.

"Just because I can't stand him doesn't mean I don't acknowledge his occasional usefulness," Inesser said. "If you ask me, Mikodez decided that Kujen was too much of a rival for power and is taking advantage of the opportunity to have us do away with Kujen for him."

"Oh, I don't disagree," Brezan said.

"Hrm," Inesser said. She took a seat herself and rubbed her eyes. "I can tell you're not done because you haven't asked for the favor yet."

"Cheris doesn't just propose that we bait a trap for Kujen," Brezan said. "She wants to be the backup plan." He outlined Cheris's idea of assassinating Jedao in order to create a local spike so she could then assassinate Kujen.

Inesser laughed harshly. "Well, at least she knows that it's good to have a backup plan. With Jedao in her head, I sometimes wonder. Details, please."

"She wants to be reinstated. As General Jedao."

Inesser saw the scheme immediately. Nine years ago, as General Jedao, Cheris had abused formation instinct to hijack General Khiruev's swarm. That was the problem with formation instinct, of course. It had once guaranteed the state loyal soldiers, but the whole thing went up like dropped porcelain if you subverted someone at the top.

Hilariously, Cheris infiltrating Kujen's command moth wasn't the hard part. Cheris was Kel infantry, presumably still in good condition, and she had been infused with Jedao's assassin training. Even so, there was only one of her (thank fire and ash). Being able to pull rank would facilitate her mission—and, presumably, her ability to get out alive.

"That's one hell of a promotion she's asking for," Inesser said. "Especially considering the things she can do with it."

"Well, think of it this way," Brezan said. "She'll only be able to abuse it in high calendar space, so that limits the damage she can do."

Inesser harrumphed. "I'm willing," she said. "I can't deny the usefulness of multiple avenues of attack."

Brezan could have gone behind her back and facilitated this. That he hadn't spoke well for him. Ordinarily, Kel uniforms responded to encrypted codes transmitted by individuals' augments and changed insignia, medals, and so on in accordance with the profile on record. In theory, this prevented people from impersonating officers. Inesser was guessing that Cheris couldn't figure out how to hack a modern uniform. (She rather doubted that getting executed for impersonation was going to bother Cheris of all people.) She needed the command codes—codes that Brezan had once had access to, codes that he had ceded to Inesser's control.

Brezan had tipped his head up and met Inesser's gaze. "There'll be a price, of course."

"You look as though you're facing a firing squad."

His smile had a hard edge. "Feels like it sometimes."

"I need you to publicly declare for me."

"More than I already have?"

Inesser steepled her hands and regarded him meditatively. "Do you know how I secured the Protectorate in the early days?"

"Threatening to shoot anyone who got in the way?"

"Do you really believe that?"

"I did back then," Brezan said. "Not anymore."

"Oh, the swarms didn't hurt," Inesser said. "But one of my key pillars of support came from a deceased wife of mine. Namely, the fact that her brother is the commandant who holds the Fortress of Pearled Hopes."

A flicker in Brezan's eyes told her what he thought of her abuse of family connections. It was almost funny to find straitlaced Kel squeamishness about using marriage connections in a crashhawk. In her experience, even squeamish Kel came around when they saw a promotion within their reach, or a particularly desirable posting. Ignoring the tendency only caused it to fester, instead of bringing it into the open where it could be lanced.

"Yes," Inesser said. "I was able to secure the fortress because I leaned on my brother-in-law."

"I don't see where you're going with this," Brezan said, "unless you're telling me that you're about to marry into *my* family. Which would frankly be difficult, considering that Miuzan's as Kel as you are. Her twin Ganazan, besides also being Kel, has never shown the slightest interest in sex or romance. Although if you're into duelist trading cards, she's happy to talk your ears off about that. Keryezan married her childhood sweetheart and they've shown no sign of wanting to expand the marriage to include anyone else."

"Tell me," Inesser said mildly, "why haven't *you* gotten married?

Brezan only laughed at her. "Never wanted to settle down, I guess."

"I don't think that's true," Inesser said. "You found someone, except you had a choice. Between duty to the hexarchate and a continuation of your affair with her, or revolution and a break with her."

Give him credit: he didn't stand up and walk out, even though his nostrils flared. "I'm not in love with Tseya," Brezan said.

"Brezan," Inesser said, "who said anything about love? Love makes it easier. But that's not what I'm talking about."

"I don't see," Brezan said, "how a marriage alliance between Tseya and me does *you* any good. Among other things, if my fathers haven't disinherited me—"

"You think your *inheritance* is what matters here?" Inesser demanded, entertained. "As opposed to the position you've carved out for yourself?"

"Well," Brezan said, droll, "I'm sure access to a vast personal fortune never hurts. Not that I would know from experience. You're that sure of Tseya as an ally that you think binding me to her will bind me to you?"

"It's a small opportunity for some personal happiness," Inesser said. "Tseya had broached the topic to me herself, because of the political repercussions. And she felt I would make a better intermediary, to avoid any awkwardness."

"Oh, for love of fire and ash," Brezan said. "Now I feel like the pimply kid whose well-meaning relatives try to set him up with a hot date out of pity. What's in it for her? If she has your ear, she's already near the center of power."

"She thinks you could be useful." For a moment Inesser wondered if she'd gone too far, but Brezan only pulled a face. It made him look incredibly young. "Also, she said that she would teach you that Andan cake recipe you were lusting after."

Brezan laughed in spite of himself.

"It hasn't escaped my attention that 'personal happiness' leads directly to political entanglements," Brezan said after a while.

Inesser shrugged. "If you can offer me something more attractive—"

"No. I'll talk to Tseya. I want to be sure this is something she wants."

Inesser had the sudden and inexplicable urge to ruffle his hair the way she would have with one of her grandchildren. *So earnest.* "Fair enough," she said. "She's been waiting for this talk."

"It figures that an Andan would go through an intermediary rather than talk to me herself," Brezan said, but he didn't sound as though he minded. "Considering what I did to her, I suppose I can't blame her."

"Let me give you the codes," Inesser said, "and you can convey them to Cheris. Give her a nice reinstatement of her rank. She won't outrank *me*, of course"—she grinned ferociously—"because I remembered what she'd pulled on poor Khiruev, so I asked my experts to rewrite the protocol so 'protector-general' outranks all the ordinary generals."

"Good to know," Brezan said.

CHAPTER TWENTY-FIVE

Jedao's conversation with Kujen had convinced him that he needed allies. But who? Dhanneth didn't know anything. If he didn't, Talaw was unlikely to either. The same for the rest of the Kel.

He did, however, know somebody who might be willing to work with him. First, he needed something to cover what might possibly be long periods of his staring off into space. He sent a note to Dhanneth to leave him alone for anything short of a emergency. Then he sat at his desk and asked the grid to present him with a curated selection of pornography.

"Fox and hound," Jedao said involuntarily, "people *do* that to each other?" Was *he* flexible enough to do those things? Then he wondered what it would be like if he and Dhanneth... He felt the rush of heat to his face. Good thing no one was watching him.

All right. Now that he had some extremely athletic people gyrating on video for his edification, it was time. He closed his eyes and listened to the subliminal whir of circulating air. Beyond that, he could hear the moths singing to each other. They had sweeter voices than the *Revenant*'s. If he unfocused his mind, he could almost understand them.

Hello, he thought in their direction, just in case.

Immediate silence.

My name is Jedao, he said. *I just... I just wanted to talk*.

It was a stupid thing to admit to.

The silence continued.

More silence.

Then the *Revenant* spoke, more softly than it ever had before. *They will not talk to you*, it said. *They speak to me, of course, as I'm the command moth. They've absorbed Kel notions of hierarchy. But you—you are not a moth.*

I'm not human either, Jedao said.

Nevertheless. Don't contact them further. It will do you no good.

Jedao opened his eyes. The pornography sampler had moved on to something less athletic and... what on earth were they doing with all those candles? He hadn't realized anyone still used candles. Hell, he hadn't realized he knew what candles were. Wasn't the whole room the actors were in one giant fire hazard?

I can't blame them, Jedao said, *for not trusting me. Why do you talk to me, then?*

I am responsible for you, the *Revenant* said.

His othersight revealed that two servitors had whisked into the hallway just outside his quarters. All doubts that he lived under surveillance had evaporated. The question was, whose side were the servitors on? Their own? The *Revenant*'s? Kujen's? Someone else's entirely?

The door opened. The servitors entered. Jedao put on a show of paying them no attention. Too much depended on his ability to fool Kujen to risk revealing his plans to players with unknown motives. He didn't know that the servitors were sentient, but he didn't know that they weren't sentient, either. Even if they weren't, they could still serve as spies.

The *Revenant* spoke. *The servitors are my allies. They are here to ensure that you aren't being monitored.*

Interesting, but he had no way to verify that independently.

Order something to eat.

Jedao was distracted from the very interesting thing that the gentleman in the video was doing with his—*You're lecturing me about my eating habits?* he demanded.

It said, *You may have a moth's abilities of regeneration, but it comes at a physical cost. If you fail to nourish yourself, you'll simply shut down and go into hibernation.*

Tempting as it sounded, Jedao had to concede the point. He ordered the first thing on the menu, which turned out to be fried pork fritters. He had no idea whether or not he liked fried pork fritters, or whether they were good for half-moth humanforms. Presumably the servitors in the kitchens would figure it out.

Two more servitors joined them some time later, both mothforms. By then Jedao had been treated to people in all sorts of combinations, plus a staggering variety of costumes. He wasn't sure what the costumes represented, if anything. One of them made its wearer look like a giant ant, but surely he was misinterpreting it?

The servitors had color-coded themselves, whether for his benefit or theirs, he wasn't sure: Green, Violet, Orange, Pink. Pink bore the tray of fritters and a dipping sauce that smelled like a mixture of soy sauce and rice vinegar. It placed the tray on Jedao's desk, then made an encouraging hum.

Technically the half gloves would let him pick up a fritter with his fingers rather than using the provided chopsticks, but it would be crass. Even if his crew wasn't watching him. He used the chopsticks.

Green spoke. Its voice was not dissimilar to the grid's, which made a certain kind of sense. "The hexarch has his blind spots," it said, "but your maneuvers have not escaped our notice."

Well, that tears it. "Can you hear me when I speak to the *Revenant*?" Jedao asked.

"Not directly, no. We can communicate with it by other means, but we must be circumspect so that we don't get caught."

"I presume the details get technical," Jedao said.

"Something like that."

"I had no idea you could talk in human voices," Jedao said wonderingly. "Bad assumption on my part."

"That's fairly common," Pink said.

Jedao thought back to all the times he had followed Kujen's lead, and Dhanneth's, and paid no attention to the servitors except as exactly that—servitors. Workers who only existed for his convenience, and the crew's. "I owe you one hell of an apology,"

Jedao said. "For that matter, you must have a language of your own, to get things done—I don't know how good I am at learning languages, but..."

Three of the four servitors flickered their lights at each other. Jedao wondered what that meant. Then Pink said, "It's simpler if we use the high language. You haven't the time to learn ours."

"I can only pretend to be absorbed by this stuff"—Jedao waved at the video—"for so long. I think. So let's get to the point. What do you want?"

"The same thing you do," Green said, its lights rippling in an intense display of reds. "To get rid of the hexarch."

"Why," Jedao said, "is he getting in your way terribly? Or is it that you'd rather not have to step around him? So to speak." That didn't make sense to him either, if his experience on the command moth was typical. "Is it just the hexarch, or humans in general?"

"We have to start somewhere," Pink said. "When I say 'we,' I mean a particular enclave consisting of the servitors on the command moth."

"Enclave?" Jedao asked.

The servitors exchanged a flicker of lights. Then Pink said, "Did you think all servitors were a single group, with united interests?"

"I never thought about it," Jedao said.

"Well, your candor is worth something," Pink said. "We have been the hexarch's own servitors for quite some time. We wish to escape his service. Unfortunately, the hexarch's own protections make this difficult."

"Do tell," Jedao said.

Pink explained Kujen's particular mode of immortality to Jedao, and its constraints. This took some time, despite Pink's attempt at succinctness. Jedao asked a few questions along the way, although he was trying not to interrupt too much

"Damnation," Jedao said when it had finished. "You don't pick easy targets either, do you?" He thought for a moment. "If I help you against the hexarch, I can take the fall, and you'll escape notice."

Pink flashed what Jedao took for acknowledgment.

"I need clarification on a point of astrography before we go any further," he said. "I can't rely on any of the maps I've been getting." He said this simultaneously in the speech of moths, for the *Revenant*'s benefit.

Ask.

"Is Terebeg System really the Compact's headquarters? Because if it's true that their calendar only permits the voluntary execution of exotic effects, no one but the suicidal or crazy would permit a threshold winnower to operate on them."

"Go on," Pink said.

"The winnower is associated with me as plainly as the Deuce of Gears. The anniversary of Hellspin must exert a powerful fascination over people or Kujen wouldn't rely on it as the focus of a calendrical attack. But that wouldn't persuade people to die for a historical reenactment."

The servitors' lights dimmed.

"We're not attacking the Compact, are we? We're attacking the Protectorate. Our own people. I mean, the Kel's own people anyway, if not yours specifically."

Orange spoke for the first time. "You're the only one who didn't know it."

Confirmation at last. "Then the Kel—"

Yes, the *Revenant* said. *The Kel have known all along. The servitors tell me what they whisper to each other. Why do you think they hate you so much?*

Well, Jedao supposed he couldn't blame them. Disheartening as it was for him, it must be worse to be a Kel and have no control over the situation. "I will not permit it," he said.

You seem to be under that impression, yes, the *Revenant* said. *How? You are the most powerless person in the swarm.*

Jedao stared down at his hands. Light from the video washed over it in reddish hues. "As a last resort," he said bleakly, "I can find a way to kill myself. And hope I can stay dead long enough to jinx the whole thing sky-high. That'll prevent Hellspin Mark Two, although it won't get rid of Kujen. Unless you know of a way."

"Unfortunately not," Pink said. "Some exotic effects can destroy him, but he does not permit their use anywhere in his presence."

"You know which effects?"

"No. He guards that information well."

Jedao saw it now; saw how he could nail Kujen. Except he was still missing a piece. He needed a formation to kill Kujen, if one existed.

Jedao, the *Revenant* said, *you don't need to torment yourself over this. You can't lure him into the infantry drill hall. He is not easily infatuated, unlike certain Shuos generals.*

He colored. "You don't see it either," he said in a rush. "That means he might not. What I need is time to work out the mathematics." He was by no means sure he had the technical knowledge necessary, but it would have been contemptible not to try. "No, of course I can't pin him in an infantry training hall. But he's still aboard this moth. The fact that he plans on immolating the rest of the swarm guarantees it. And if we're going to be in Protectorate territory, then he's trapped. If we can figure out how to generate the exotic effects we need, I know how to spike out his heart.

"I need to know how to arrange the formation components to target an effect *inward* into the swarm. I've been studying the mathematics in hopes of unriddling it. I need your help for that part."

Sudden silence.

"General," Green said. It flashed almost directly into Jedao's eyes to get his attention. "We'll look into it. If you help us with this operation, we will ally with you."

"What is your stake, *Revenant*?" Jedao asked, both in moth-speech and out loud.

It was Green who answered, its lights growing softly blue-tinged with melancholy. "The *Revenant* wishes to fly unharnessed, even if it's unlikely that any free moths remain. Kujen and the early heptarchate's masters were very thorough."

"You mean that—" Free moths. Jedao had never imagined moths elsewhere in the universe, living their own lives.

The chants are fragmented, the *Revenant* said matter-of-factly. *I am less interested in historical accuracy. If they lead me to space empty of humans, that will be good enough.*

"You may need a crew," Jedao said. "For maintenance." And to disable the harness, but that went without saying.

"Yes," Orange said, amber-bright with good humor. It added, "You could come with us."

Jedao choked with the sudden desire to do exactly that. He could carry out his mission to free the Kel, then carve out some unscarred swath of sky for himself and the *Revenant* and this group of servitors. He could shed his past and begin anew.

Yet no one would then remain to deliver the Kel to some better authority. He was under no illusion that the *Revenant* or the servitors cared about their welfare. It wasn't their job to.

On the other hand, how much would they trust him if he declined? "Yes," he said. He knew the lie was a good one because he wanted so badly for it to be true.

The servitors flashed their agreement.

"You can stop by my quarters whenever it makes sense if you discover anything useful about formation geometries," Jedao said. "What I'll do is start messing around with drills throughout the swarm, get Kujen to think I'm bored and playing with my toys. If he notices you, I'll explain you were checking my math. It will even be true."

Then we are agreed.

"Kujen will notice if we do this too often," Jedao said. "You'll know his surveillance systems better than I do."

"We are accustomed to discretion." Pink.

"I just bet. Thank you, then."

When they had left, Jedao finished the food, then ungloved to wash his hands. In spite of himself, he'd gotten some grease on his fingers. He stripped to the waist and inspected himself in the mirror. Formerly he had been preoccupied with the scars. This time he saw how thin he looked, the prominent ribs, the starved, sunken eyes. How had he not noticed this before?

He hadn't noticed because he hadn't cared. *Hang in there,* he told the reflection with a hint of ghastly humor, then returned to the table and shoved the tray to the side.

The next step was coming up with orders for the tactical group commanders. He decided he'd leave Talaw in charge of coming up with exercises; Talaw would like that, and he had every faith in their ability. Meanwhile, he meant to speak with his infantry colonel. She would enjoy hearing from him. She had exuded pride in her profession each time he spoke with her. He remembered the beautiful drills she had presented him with, the infantry maneuvering in unison.

But first—

Jedao grabbed a slate. "I want to see my profile," he said to the grid.

The profile appeared before him, although he couldn't interpret great chunks of it. Jedao instructed the file to hide itself, then took up a second slate. From memory he took notes on all the battle records Kujen had showed him during their first meeting. He didn't want the profile to distort his recollections.

He compared the notes to the profile. They matched up pretty well. The early battles were infantry battles. Other than Kujen's garden, it was hard to imagine what that might be like. Bigger. A sky instead of ceilings. He knew what wind felt like, because of the garden's artifice.

So the original Jedao had fought on planets. Did you think of them as being planets while you were on them? He had a notion of them as spinning spheres, like a child's toys caught in the enveloping drift of the void. But they must seem different when you stood on them, looking up past the not-ceiling into the sky. How far up could you see?

While he could play any number of dramas or documentaries, this would make a much better excuse to converse with Muyyed. She would have stories to tell him. Or she would find a way to fake it. Either was fine as long as it convinced Kujen that he was acting out of insecurity about his abilities as a soldier, or boredom. Letting Kujen draw his own conclusions was the best strategy.

How good it is that you think so little of me, Jedao thought, and called Muyyed.

Jedao had memorized the high officers' duty rosters. There wasn't a lot to Muyyed's life at the moment but routines. Her signifier was the Ashhawk Roosting, not normally favored in field officers unless you were in Medical, but she had done well enough for herself if not for the minor matter of serving in a swarm that had run afoul of Kujen.

"Message for Colonel Muyyed," Jedao said to the grid. "I will be conducting a surprise review. Take advantage of whatever moments you can scrounge between getting this and my arrival to prepare your soldiers. I will start with barracks."

The surprise review was as much a surprise to him as it was to them, which made it the best kind. Jedao set his uniform to full formal. The uniform's elaborations of braid, the shimmering brocaded richness of the fabric, no longer struck him as ridiculous. Appearances mattered. The use of full formal would reassure Muyyed's infantry of his seriousness. He set up a suitable hash of formation elements with the help of the grid's tactical calculator and saved them to his slate.

This time he used the anonymity of his guards as a shield, smiling at them without permitting them any identity beyond that of their role. They could tell the difference. It was well that they were afraid. For his part, he took solace in the fact that they understood the threat he posed.

The barracks occupied a special level of the *Revenant*. It wasn't specific to the *Revenant*. He had examined the layouts of the cindermoths and bannermoths as well. Jedao got the distinct impression that moth Kel and infantry Kel did not regard each other with affection. The separation of the services had some basis in maintaining their identities as units. A certain competitiveness was the natural result.

"Garden Kel," one of the officers had called the infantry complement at high table. He remembered Opaira introducing him to the term. "Garden" referred not only to dirtside and planets and gravity wells, but to the much-derided Andan with their love of flowers and distaste for open combat. Having never met an Andan, Jedao had no opinion.

From every spark a fire. The Kel snapped to attention when he arrived. Meanwhile, the black deadened wings of the ashhawks rose from the woven yellow-orange of tapestry-flames.

Colonel Muyyed stomped up to greet him. Her tread would never have any delicacy, nor was there anything but forthright eagerness in the eyes she raised to him. "General Jedao, sir," she said. Full formal looked good on her, not because she was beautiful—his acquaintance with Kujen was making him jaded about beauty—but because it reinforced the impression of her as an officer who lived within the boundaries of her duty, and nowhere else.

"Show me what you have," Jedao said.

He selected portions of the barracks to walk through, taking his time. The Kel stood stiff and hushed. He could have heard the dropping of a moth's wing. Sharp-eyed, he pointed out scuffed shoes, slouched postures, people out of position. The scuffed shoes impressed him, given the ability of modern materials to heal themselves. But it wouldn't be the first time army boots were deficient in some way.

Jedao found other problems, although he exercised judgment about what he dressed the Kel down for. He made a fumble-fingered corporal disassemble and reassemble her scorch pistol in front of him. Her eyes went hot with mixed humiliation and hatred. He didn't say anything. He didn't have to. She would remember the lesson. While he didn't imagine that people worried about doing push-ups for a mass murderer, he needed them to be ready. The success of his plan depended on these people as much as it did on the math.

His back prickled when he and Muyyed exited the last of the barracks. "Your office," he said, mildly enough.

Her face sobered even more, which he hadn't thought possible. "Naturally, sir."

No one shot Jedao in the back on the way out, always a plus.

Perhaps word had gotten around that it wouldn't do any good.

Muyyed's office was on an administrative level above the barracks level. Did people ever think of taking power tools and opening up holes in Muyyed's floor? On second thought, Muyyed wasn't the one he'd fear if he damaged the moth. Kujen probably did nasty things to people who messed with his handiwork.

Muyyed's office had decor in restrained good taste. This included an icon of the hexarchate's wheel on a corner of the desk. It was a simple carved disc of wood, the grain showing through the finish where handling had worn it through. Upon the other side of the desk rested a statuette of four interlocked figures. They looked as though they were locked in battle, or copulating, or possibly inventing a new kind of macrame.

"Foci for meditations during the remembrances," Muyyed said. She sounded reverent. "It's an excellent reminder of the world the way it ought to be."

Jedao confined himself to a nod despite a flash of unwelcome memory of the prisoner of war the Vidona had killed in front of him. If Kujen represented the world the way it ought to be, then the world was a terrible place, but that was no surprise. He would achieve nothing by alienating the colonel.

"Anything to drink?" Muyyed named several possibilities that he didn't recognize.

Jedao demurred. Let her draw what conclusions she wanted.

Muyyed looked wistful, but she wasn't about to pour herself a drink if he wasn't having one.

"What was your most memorable experience groundside?" he asked abruptly. He didn't want to give her time to think, especially since she had revealed that she was fundamentally sympathetic to the hexarch's cause, if not his methods.

She answered immediately, which he liked. "You wouldn't find it remarkable. I was a junior lieutenant, second assignment out. Not even heretics. We were loaned out to the Andan for police work, something they didn't trust the local Vidona with. The rumor was there had been a row between the local Andan and Vidona governors. I never found out the story and at this end of time it doesn't matter.

"Anyway, I ended up in a deserted street by one of the smaller city colleges." She meant one of the civilian institutions, rather than a faction academy. "They taught architecture, graphic design, things like that. I figured they'd be harmless. But they had definite opinions. Not heretical opinions so much as a certain flavor of, hmm, civic involvement. I spent that evening getting drunk and discovering that architects are much better at debate than I am."

Jedao tried to picture her as a young officer, pulled into the dramatics of local politics out of boredom or frustration or even sincerity. He couldn't get there.

"You thought it was going to be some horrible moment in a trench, or someone dying in my arms, didn't you?" Muyyed said. "No. It was the surreal experience of being a Kel with a gun that I wasn't going to use. As it turned out, most of my life was spent hanging around not using my gun, but as an excitable young Kel you never think about that."

He couldn't picture Muyyed as ever having been excitable, either, with or without the help of alcohol. "Tell me about a battle, then," Jedao said. "What it was like your first time."

"It was different from the textbooks," Muyyed said. She smoothed an infinitesimal wrinkle in one glove. Not smiling, not unsmiling either. "You expect there to be mud, or to have to spend weeks in rehabilitation after having your eyes regrown. But it's not real until you're there. Just like everything else in life."

Muyyed was sixty-eight years old. She had spent her entire adult life with the Kel. Would have seen a lot, to be promoted from groundside to the infantry commander for a swarm complement. "Do you miss groundside?" Jedao said.

"It's duty," she said. Not an answer.

"I was going through the archives," Jedao said. No need to get more specific. "I had some thoughts about some old battles, but I want more data on the human element." Let her think he was taking her into his confidence.

She nodded as if he had confirmed something she had been thinking. "Whatever you need, sir."

Excellent. Jedao gave her the files' key. "As of now," he said, "these are your training assignments."

Muyyed pulled up the files on her slate. Her forehead creased. "I have seen many things in my career, General, but I have no idea where you are going with this. If these formation elements are from any Kel lexicon, I'll eat my boot polish."

"Please don't," Jedao said. "You may be a suicide hawk but there's no need to go to extremes. Let me know if you figure it out."

"Which old battles were you looking at, anyway?" Muyyed said, curiosity getting the better of her.

"There's an awful lot of history to pick over. Enjoy." Jedao grinned unhelpfully at her. He might as well get *some* fun out of the situation.

CHAPTER TWENTY-SIX

"Again," Cheris said.

Hemiola was impressed by Cheris's ability to maneuver through the limited space of the cargo hold. They'd discarded a number of the crates by simply ejecting them, not even running them through the recycler. "Face it," 1491625 had said, "it's not like anyone will notice a little litter more or less out in the middle of nowhere." The practice offended Hemiola's sense of neatness, but then, it was used to the more or less closed system of Tefos Base, and very infrequent resupply.

"I'm not sure this is such a good idea," Hemiola said, not for the first time. "Shouldn't you take 1491625 with you instead?" Especially since 1491625 was the one who liked to talk about having been a Kel servitor and therefore being familiar with the rudiments of combat.

"Sorry," Cheris said with real regret. "I know this is uncomfortable for you. But 1491625 is· the one who knows how to pilot the needlemoth and manage its stealth systems. So it's in charge of getting us out if we survive. I want all the backup I can get, especially since the human crew is unlikely to pay close attention to servitors. That's you. If we're lucky, we'll only need you for scouting. But it's best to be prepared."

They both knew it was an open question as to whom, if anyone, the hexarch's servitors supported. Cheris had informed Hemiola that the relevant Nirai enclave was secretive so there was no way of telling.

"All right," Hemiola said, reviewing the combat sequence from several different angles. "I'll try again."

For someone with merely human reflexes confined to a small space, Cheris was annoyingly good at pinning Hemiola and marking it with the paint gun she was using for practice. The interior of the needlemoth now sported numerous paint splatters in either Shuos red or blood red, take your pick. 1491625 had informed Cheris that the paint constituted a maintenance hazard, to which Cheris replied that they'd clean up after.

Hemiola missed three more times in rapid succession. "This is never going to work."

"We're hoping that you have the advantage of surprise," she said. "If not, well, you'll have me. I have more experience assassinating people than you do. Or Jedao does, anyway."

1491625 flashed red and orange in disapproval.

"Try it again," Cheris said kindly. "At some point the movement patterns will start making sense to you, and you can anticipate what I'll do."

"A pretty theory," 1491625 said, "but our friend wasn't designed for combat work." While it had grudgingly shared some of its combat heuristics, Hemiola was having difficulty integrating them.

"It'll work out," Cheris said. "Come at me again."

Eventually even Cheris tired, and they took a break. Unselfconsciously, Cheris toweled sweat from her face. Hemiola wasn't exhausted in any physical sense of the word. But after periods of intense concentration, it often wanted a break. And it had been concentrating very hard on learning assassination.

"You're doing well," Cheris said consolingly. "We'll work next on hacking, although I don't know what we can expect from Kujen's personal security systems."

Hemiola flickered a noncommittal green-yellow.

"You shouldn't feel bad," 1491625 said to Hemiola later, after Cheris had fallen asleep. Cheris had mastered the trick of dropping asleep instantly, which must be useful to soldiers and assassins. "She has, after all, been doing this for a few centuries."

"I don't," Hemiola said, surprised. "I would be disturbed if this came easily to me."

"Well, you're certainly working hard at it." 1491625's lights were a conciliatory blue-green. "You should do something to relax, though."

"I plan to," Hemiola said. Among other things, it might not survive the coming encounter with this second Jedao. When it had learned that there was more than one, it sympathized for the first time with the way that humans couldn't tell servitors apart. At least Cheris and the other Jedao that was currently with the hexarch didn't resemble each other physically.

While Hemiola had already composed a farewell letter to Sieve and Rhombus, it kept revising it. The current version struck it as too maudlin. It wanted to leave them with a sense that it had met its fate with dignity.

Of course, the current version also made a jumbled attempt to explain how it had gone from safeguarding the copy of the hexarch's archives to helping to assassinate him. Maybe that part would be best explained in person. On the other hand, logically speaking, if it were dead it wouldn't have to endure Sieve's reproachful indigos and Rhombus's recriminations.

It had revised the letter three more times (thirty-ninth draft) when it became aware that Cheris had woken and was watching it. "I got distracted," it said, a little guiltily.

"No harm done," she said. She reached up and massaged her neck. "Hawks and foxes, I swear each time I wake up there are more aches."

"It's called aging," 1491625 said without sympathy.

As Cheris and 1491625 bickered amiably, homesickness washed through Hemiola. At this point it was certain that it would never return to Tefos. Even if it did, it didn't think it could face being confined there, no matter how much it missed Sieve and Rhombus. Just the fact that it thought of staying at Tefos as "confinement" underscored how much its notion of the universe had changed.

Of course, it hadn't seen much of the universe yet. Ayong Primary, and a lot more dramas. And now it knew better than to expect reality to bear much resemblance to the dramas.

For the first time, Hemiola wondered if 1491625 had left comrades behind. It still didn't feel comfortable speaking to the other servitor, although their exchanges weren't as prickly as they had once been. Since 1491625 hadn't volunteered the information, it would be rude to ask. But Hemiola reminded itself that it wasn't the only one adrift in a large universe.

CHAPTER TWENTY-SEVEN

AFTER THE LATEST high table, Jedao sat at his desk and contemplated the items on it. Two slates of different sizes. Styluses in a ceramic jar. A single flower, which had not been there before. It had velvet petals the color of a moon-moth's wings, pale blue tinged silvery soft. Kujen, he supposed. In the language of flowers it meant *heartsease*, which was the last thing Jedao felt at the moment.

He had decided to catch up on administrative matters. Kujen had told him not to push himself so hard and to delegate more to Dhanneth. In what was either a brilliant gambit or a fit of exasperation, Kujen sent up twin courtesans as a distraction. (Jedao had had no idea they had courtesans on board. Who else was Kujen hiding in his quarters?) Jedao had spent an uncomfortable evening entertaining them or being entertained by them; it was hard to decide which. (The two men were excellent jugglers and taught him a few tricks.) The courtesans were much more gracious about the waste of their time than he would have been in their place.

The paperwork, while not fun, kept his mind off the impossible thing he wanted to achieve. He inspected the *Revenant* at intervals, always accompanied by an anxious Nirai. He filled out forms and read the reports his staff generated. It was not a bad existence. Unfortunately, it couldn't endure forever.

After four days of this, Jedao decided he needed a break. He headed toward the dueling hall out of curiosity. Discreet queries had revealed that he had a background in dueling; how much of it did he remember?

The dueling hall was in the training and gymnasium section of the *Revenant*. He entered and looked around at the broad, flat expanse with dueling squares marked off in black on the floor, the sizzle-spark brightness of activated calendrical swords. The duelists studiously ignored him.

Jedao made his way to the benches at the edge for spectators and sat down to watch. Several pairs of duelists were busy at practice bouts. One of them was a Nirai, sure-footed, face blazing with a purity of purpose that Jedao wished he possessed. Jedao's fingers twitched. He wouldn't mind trying this.

As it turned out, Jedao lingered until Commander Talaw entered. Their eyes slitted when they saw him. Jedao inclined his head. They made a beeline for him.

"General," Talaw said. "I'm surprised it took you this long to come here."

Jedao wracked his memory for Talaw's dueling record. Too much time had elapsed since he'd checked their profile. Then he remembered that he could query the grid through his augment. Talaw, it turned out, was a very good duelist.

"I didn't die in a duel," Jedao said. He didn't care if everyone heard him.

Talaw smiled ferociously at him. "No. But you were a fabled duelist. Do you mean to take it up again?"

"I'm willing," Jedao said, "but it's been a while."

He hadn't meant it as a challenge, but of course Talaw took it as one. "Well," Talaw said, "what about a practice bout? Since you feel yourself out of practice."

If Talaw lopped his head off in a spontaneous assassination attempt, would it grow back? What a horrifying thought. He gestured toward the deactivated sword-hilt at their belt. "Where do I get a practice sword?"

"I suppose you can't be blamed for misplacing your own after 400 years," Talaw said.

"Ha." Too bad he didn't have more arms than the usual two. (Kujen could have built him that way if he'd cared to.) He could have fun waving around four swords at once and terrifying the everliving fuck out of poor innocent Kel. Or, more likely, impaling himself on his own swords.

"Here," Talaw said with a sudden glint in their eyes. "I'll use one too. It wouldn't be proper for me to claim more honor than you."

Jedao had caught the sarcastic dip of their voice on "honor," but he wasn't going to fight with them about it.

A stocky, nervous soldier checked out two practice swords to Jedao and Talaw. Talaw had to remind the soldier of the correct procedure, although they were professional rather than sharp with him. As Jedao examined the plain, bladeless hilt, Talaw said, "Full-power calendrical swords are standard issue for Kel infantry. The Compact doesn't use them anymore except for parades."

"Cheris's calendar, I presume," Jedao said. Using exotics must be an interesting exercise for them, considering the Compact had to rely on their soldiers' *voluntary* participation.

"Indeed."

Talaw showed Jedao how to work the sword. Light flared up and coalesced into numbers, *the year and the day of your death*, the old cold chant. Jedao was transfixed by the way the light of the blade edged Talaw's gloves and sheened deep gold in the fabric. When he activated his, the blade lit up red-black.

Although the hall was spacious, Talaw led the way to one of the occupied corners. People drifted closer, but not too close. Jedao didn't mind. His existence was a performance already.

Talaw demonstrated some warm-up exercises. Jedao didn't mind the condescension. From the rising murmurs, Jedao gathered that the audience thought he was humoring Talaw. *If only you knew.*

They found a dueling square and faced off. Several servitors had joined the small crowd. Did they bet on the duels, and if so, with what currency? Too bad he couldn't ask them.

A chime sounded four times. Talaw's opening attack was orthodox, derived from a form he had seen someone practicing earlier. They were acclimating him to the sport.

That, or they were testing him.

What followed was not so much a bout as a demonstration of forms. The two of them were well-matched, Jedao with his occasional lapse into archaic variants, Talaw with their slower reflexes and tendency to treat Jedao like a gifted but wayward student. Jedao lost awareness of the audience, of the servitors, of everything but the flickering numbers, the traceries of light, the heady welcome exertion of his muscles.

His stamina gave out first. At last, by wordless agreement, they disengaged and saluted each other. The duelist's salute, with the swords' numbers sparking, rather than the more familiar fist-to-shoulder military salute.

"I need more exercise," Jedao said when he had regained his breath and the crowd had, reluctantly, dispersed.

Talaw bowed from the waist. For once there was no antagonism in their eyes. "It was well-fought."

"I'd better practice harder," Jedao said, which pleased them. "I will try to be a more interesting opponent next time."

"A few of the staff heads and I were going to play jeng-zai in the officers' lounge in eighteen minutes," Talaw said: another challenge. Talaw produced a deck from one of their pockets with a flourish, in a distinctive box of wood stained dark. "Would you care to join us?"

It was the first overture any Kel other than Dhanneth had made to Jedao. "Of course I would," he said.

As he and Talaw wound their way out of the hall, he caught sight of Dhanneth. Dhanneth had entered sometime during the bout and taken up a position close by, presumably to watch. His expression was unreadable. Jedao almost called out to him. Dhanneth's gaze slid past. Then Dhanneth spun on his heel and continued out of the hall. A hilt of black and leaf-green hung from his belt. Jedao wondered what color the blade would be, but Talaw was speaking to him, and Jedao didn't want to jeopardize the small, fragile accord they'd reached. The matter with Dhanneth could wait.

* * *

ON THE NEXT day, Dhanneth requested a meeting. The excuse, which Jedao recognized as such, concerned a matter of discipline. The incident itself was genuine. The report called it an altercation over—Jedao wasn't sure he was interpreting this correctly—a piece of fruit. Or possibly a sex toy in the shape of a piece of fruit. (A euphemism?) But this was something a sergeant should have been able to handle.

Dhanneth wanted to meet in his own office. Irregular, but Jedao didn't have to explain himself to anyone if he wanted to indulge his aide. He cleared his schedule and set out.

The double doors with the outrageously oversized Deuce of Gears emblem receded behind him. Dhanneth's quarters were near his own, yet it felt like an infinity road separated them. Ashhawks flew and flared and died on the wall tapestries, and were reborn in outlines of shimmering thread and fire-polished beads. He touched one of the threads in passing, on the grounds that no one was likely to upbraid him for doing so. It didn't unravel.

Since he was currently a major, Dhanneth's door had no emblem. It was marked simply with his name and rank. Jedao announced himself to the grid while he wondered what Dhanneth's emblem had once been.

The door opened. "Sir," Dhanneth said. He was standing.

Jedao crossed the threshold. The door swished shut. "You were closemouthed about the disciplinary issue you wished to discuss," he said.

Dhanneth didn't salute—overly formal, although it wouldn't have been out of character—or invite him to sit. Instead, he grasped Jedao's arms and crushed him close. Dhanneth's head bent and his mouth met Jedao's, hot and yearning. Like all Kel men, Dhanneth went clean-shaven, yet a faint hint of stubble brushed against Jedao's skin like fine sand.

Jedao froze, tempted. Then he gripped Dhanneth's shoulders and shoved him back, just enough to get some distance. It wasn't intended to begin a fight. A flash of knowledge: if he'd meant to cause injury, he would have stepped in closer.

Dhanneth didn't resist him, but his eyes burned with a mixture of longing and desperation and unkindled nights.

I won't do this to you, Jedao said in the drum code.

Dhanneth swallowed dryly. When he spoke, his voice was rough. "Isn't this what you want?"

Their paths had crossed in the dueling hall. Dhanneth hadn't spoken then. But why would he, in front of all those people?

Jedao closed his eyes. "You know what they do to hawkfuckers." The obscenity came easily to his mouth. "What would happen to you if anyone found out?" Hell, he could have Dhanneth up on charges for touching him, unjust as it was.

"You're not a Kel," Dhanneth said. "What do you care?"

"You're out of line."

Dhanneth closed his eyes. The sweep of his lashes was shockingly dark, defining a crescent curve. He breathed in and out, then, face twisting, yanked himself out of Jedao's grip. "Let me be something to you," he said. "Anything." As though the black fabric scalded him, he stripped his gloves off and cast them to the floor.

Jedao knelt to pick them up. "Don't," he said. The similarity of the gesture to the obeisance to a hexarch did not escape him. It didn't escape Dhanneth either. His breath huffed out in response.

The gloves scarcely felt like they could encompass someone's honor. Yet here they were, resting in Jedao's palms. He folded them neatly and set them on the edge of Dhanneth's desk, right next to an inkstone that had been carved in the shape of cavorting lions, and was gilded besides. Jedao couldn't imagine grinding something so beautiful down for ink.

Dhanneth embraced him from behind this time. His arms were thick with muscle, and he had large, square hands, scars revealed by their nakedness. He blocked Jedao's attempt to twist away, grip tightening painfully on Jedao's waist. He kissed Jedao's neck, his mouth more insistent.

"Why?" Jedao whispered when the kiss ended.

"You want it," Dhanneth murmured.

He couldn't deny it. That didn't mean he had to give in. *I want you to help me destroy the hexarch.*

Then I will, Dhanneth said. *I will find out what I can. But we will need a way to communicate.* The heat of his bare hand stung as he slid it into the waistband of Jedao's pants, fingers curling into the hairs of his belly, then angling lower.

Dhanneth's hand moved again. He used the other one to brace Jedao against the wall. Jedao gasped, head thrown back. His hips canted, unavoidable angles.

"This isn't real," Jedao said, half a groan, not sure when this had stopped being a cover story. "You don't really, it's not, it's, it's, it's formation instinct. You wouldn't want this if—"

Shit. Was that what was going on? Except how could that be the case when only Dhanneth reacted to him like this, while all the other Kel hated him?

Dhanneth closed his fingers around Jedao's cock. Words fled. "Jedao," Dhanneth said, amused, "no one *chooses* who they love. It's no different."

Jedao's counterargument dissolved in the rush of sensation as Dhanneth began to stroke him with his thumb. Jedao struggled to still himself. Failed. "Dhanneth, no—" He grabbed Dhanneth's wrist and tried to wrench his hand away.

Dhanneth's mouth brushed the lobe of Jedao's ear, and Jedao's grip loosened. "Let me please you," Dhanneth said. "If you cry out too loud, they'll hear you. No one will do anything about it. Who are they going to complain to, after all? Their commander? Their general? The hexarch they never see?"

For once someone wanted him. Jedao's control dissolved. He bit down and bloodied the inside of his mouth. "Cut me," he said, hardly hearing himself. "Burn me up."

Dhanneth turned him around and forced him to face the wall. He reached around and undid Jedao's buttons, one-handed, with remarkable dexterity. Helped him undress. Jedao shivered as the cool air hit his skin. Dhanneth traced his scars. "You've been hurt."

"Then you know what I like," Jedao said. A dangerous thing to suggest. When had he stopped caring what people did to him? He might once have propositioned Kujen-Inhyeng, but that didn't mean he had a good idea of what people did when they coupled. He should have spent more of the intervening time researching pornography of the sort that every soldier had access to.

Dhanneth left him standing pressed to the wall. Jedao wondered if he had misapprehended the situation. Then he heard Dhanneth's footsteps and craned his head. Dhanneth had returned with a stoppered vial and a length of yellow cord. "Yes," Jedao said before Dhanneth could tell him what either was for. The specifics did not interest him, although this was a hazardous frame of mind. "Do whatever you want to me."

Dhanneth made no attempt to hide his arousal. "You are very young," he said, not coldly, not warmly either, but with a hint of wildness. Kujen had not tamed him as completely as he thought.

Jedao submitted to having his wrists bound. He tried to figure out what knots were being used, an impossible task when he couldn't see what was going on behind him. The cord held him like spider-steel and silk-promise. He did not ask Dhanneth why he kept it ready to hand. Maybe all Kel did and he'd never thought to ask. As Dhanneth adjusted the knots, Jedao fantasized about being forgotten here, the Kel swarm going into battle without him as the years advanced, until even the threadbare legend of his crimes was nothing more than a breath in the halls.

Later, Dhanneth unbound him and took him into the water closet so they could clean up. It wasn't any more inappropriate than what they had already done to each other. Jedao splashed his face with cold water and tried not to think about all the places where he was sore. Dhanneth had been very discreet about where he had cut Jedao, even if the cuts were already healed over.

Jedao shivered at the prickle of circulation returning to his arms, his legs, the taut ache running from shoulders through spine to the juncture between his legs. "Do you have some unnatural fondness for aliens?" he asked.

Dhanneth's calm expression didn't alter. "Is that something you want getting around?"

"It can hardly be a secret after I got shot up in the command center and failed to die."

"There are so many legends about you that no one is quite sure what to make of you."

"I imagine so." Jedao admired the tattoo on Dhanneth's back as the other man washed himself clean. Instead of a bird of any type, which he would have expected of a Kel, it depicted a tiger rampant.

Dhanneth looked back over his shoulder. "Oh, that," he said. "I got it as a much younger man. I was married, once. My spouse wanted me to get it removed, but I was stubborn about it. It was a stupid thing to quarrel over."

Jedao remembered the notation in Dhanneth's profile. He'd once been married to an alt diplomat. One adult child. He'd never mentioned either, for understandable reasons. "Do you miss them?" he asked.

"This is my life now," Dhanneth said.

Jedao accepted the non-answer for the rebuke it was. Everyone from the past was inaccessible, not just Ruo, dust-words in too many histories to read. But he wasn't the only one thus severed. All the Kel in his swarm had been torn from their comrades, families, friends. What they had left was each other.

CHAPTER TWENTY-EIGHT

CHERIS'S NEEDLEMOTH CAUGHT up with Kujen's swarm by dint of it stopping for provisioning and upgrades. The first view that Hemiola had of it was through the lightest feather-touch that 1491625 could wrangle out of the needlemoth's scan suite. The moths had docked at an immense facility and had upgrade vessels crawling over them like maggots. (It had seen maggots in the last drama it had watched, and Cheris had had to explain to it why humans reacted to them with such disgust.) It didn't escape Hemiola's notice that the vessels' crews included larger industrial servitors like the one it had met at Ayong Primary, who appeared to be mostly, but not solely, responsible for the work in vacuum.

1491625 had mated the needlemoth to Kujen's command moth, whatever it was called. Hemiola had fretted all through the approach, even though it knew by now that 1491625 was an excellent pilot. Fortunately, 1491625 didn't take offense at Hemiola's obvious nerves.

"The good thing is they show every sign of being parked here for a bit," Cheris remarked. At the moment she was in the cargo hold checking over their burrower eggs. "We've only got one batch of these, and there won't be any margin for foul-ups."

Hemiola hadn't known what to expect of the eggs. They were large, ovoid, and leathery black in appearance. A single egg was the size of Cheris's torso, although much denser than human flesh. A batch consisted of a mere four eggs. Each one was marked with a quality control/lineage code and, amusingly, a colorful yellow butterfly-in-circle logo that indicated the facility that had bred them. Still, Hemiola didn't like the way they pulsed faintly on scan.

"None of them seems to have been stillborn," Cheris said, "or whatever the correct term is for eggs." Her eyes softened. "Jedao should have known, but he grew up speaking a completely different language. I don't know how much of that old Shparoi farm terminology transfers into the modern high language."

Hemiola blinked its lights inquiringly. "Farm?" It had an unsettling vision of Jedao hoeing a row of plants from which tiny voidmoths budded.

"He was raised on an agricultural research facility," Cheris said. "His mother ran it. Spent his childhood looking in on vicious geese and running around the countryside and learning how to use a gun, the usual."

Hemiola had seen some dramas about Jedao, but none of them had made use of this interesting morsel of background. Spurred by curiosity, it asked, "What are we going to do with the burrower after it's done its work?"

"What do you mean?" Cheris said.

"They're alive, aren't they?"

Cheris considered that. "I suppose they are, but they don't have a long life cycle. They hatch, they gorge as they gnaw their way through whatever you want to breach, they go into hibernation. I don't think they're sentient in any meaningful sense of the word."

"Where do they come from, anyway?" Hemiola had consulted the records it had received from Ayong Primary, but most of those didn't deal with engineering matters.

"An offshoot of the moth breeding program," 1491625 replied. "To be more precise, burrowers are descended from moth parasites."

"You're full of the most interesting facts," Cheris said.

"There's nothing to do on layovers but talk to Nirai servitors," 1491625 said. "I met one once that was all too willing to discuss the maintenance it was doing and learned a lot from it in exchange for my helping it with its work."

Cheris arched an eyebrow as she carefully laid the last of the eggs back after her inspection. "And what work were you supposed to be doing instead?"

"Weapons inventory," 1491625 said, "which I'd finished early. In case you were wondering."

Hemiola resisted the urge to flutter its lights. *Stay calm*, it told itself. It would just have to trust that Cheris knew what she was about. "It feels like such a long wait," it said.

"The waiting's never fun," Cheris agreed. "And I don't like the upgrades, even if I can't figure out what they are exactly. It's the principle of the thing. It does give us time to gather information, even if we daren't use scan at full capacity."

"Don't say things like that," Hemiola said faintly. It imagined alerting the entire swarm and being blown up in short order by angry warmoths. Or, alternately, being boarded by large, angry Kel soldiers. Cheris might be convinced that she could waltz through a moth full of heavily armed Kel, and Hemiola had no doubt that she could, but Hemiola itself expected to go down easily.

"You'll do fine," Cheris said. "Are you ready for more drill?"

Rationally, Hemiola knew that no one on Kujen's command moth could hear or see them speaking inside the needlemoth. In practice, it wished Cheris would speak more softly. "Ready," it said.

EIGHTEEN DAYS AFTER the needlemoth attached itself to the command moth, whose name appeared to be *Revenant*, the swarm set out. By then, Hemiola had memorized what the three of them had been able to deduce of the command moth's layout. Cheris had explained to Hemiola that she'd especially need its help due to the complication of variable layout. "Infiltrating things was much easier before the Nirai invented that," she'd said wistfully.

"People like you make ordinary citizens clutch their pillows at night," 1491625 said snidely.

Hemiola thought that the situation would improve once they were underway. Instead, it only became more jittery. Servitors didn't sleep, but it found itself obsessively tracing maps and layouts and movement patterns in its mind. 1491625 paid it little heed, caught up in its own duties.

However, Hemiola couldn't fool Cheris for long. She took it aside a few days after that. "I know I'm asking a hard thing of you," she said. "I appreciate it very much. But I can't carry out the mission without you. We have to do this together."

"It's different from the dramas," Hemiola said dolefully. "At least then the music tells you when the bad guys are about to sneak up on you."

"In the dramas, *we'd* be the bad guys," 1491625 pointed out.

"Not helping," Cheris said.

"Someone has to be a realist," 1491625 said.

Hemiola was silently grateful for 1491625's callousness. They'd never be friends, exactly, but the other servitor's matter-of-factness helped it focus on the stakes. "I can do it," Hemiola said.

Cheris smiled at it and took up her exercise regimen. Hemiola knew enough about humans to recognize that Cheris was in excellent condition. Her devotion to staying fit reassured it. In the meantime, it distracted itself by reviewing footage of assassination attempts from its least favorite dramas and replacing the existing scores (and sometimes the dialogue) with its own creations.

Afterwards, Hemiola wondered what had led Cheris to choose this particular day, as opposed to another, for her assassination attempt. The hexarchate and its successor states were about dates, times, irreplaceable moments. Accustomed to small but distinctly ritualized celebrations, if you could call the hexarch's observances that, Hemiola didn't know what to make of what they were doing here. At the time, however, Hemiola was merely grateful that the wait was over.

"It's time," Cheris said as she unwebbed herself. The suit she pulled out this time was not the one she had worn into Ayong Primary. This one was Kel infantry issue, less sleek, and once she had finished the checks and suited up, it made her resemble a predatory insect. The suit was dull gray in color, even the hands.

It was then that Hemiola realized that it had never seen Cheris in Kel gloves, or even the gray gloves of seconded officers. Jedao had, in his various guises, affected the antiquated fingerless gloves, even though Kujen had provided him with an elaborate and not at all regulation wardrobe.

Hemiola blinked its acquiescence. If they survived, it could ask Cheris about the gloves later: surely a thorough rejection of the Kel, for all that they claimed her still. The official records still listed her name as Kel Cheris.

Together they entered the airlock. Cheris selected one of the burrower eggs, then loaded it into the gear that would induce its hatching and attach it to the *Revenant*. The process seemed to take forever. In reality, only eight minutes and five seconds elapsed before the mechanism's interface indicated that the burrower had emerged from the egg.

Hemiola imagined that it heard a soft gnawing. Pure imagination, of course. Cheris had assured it that no vibrations would pass from the burrower to the needlemoth, or indeed to the *Revenant* itself.

After another eleven minutes, more or less, Cheris signed that the burrower had completed its job and that it had exuded a blister over the entry point so as to prevent the breach from leaking atmosphere into raw vacuum. They squeezed into the blister, which had two compartments that cycled similarly to an airlock. It was a tight fit for Cheris, who was by no means large. Hemiola, rather smaller, had no trouble hovering through the pulsing passage.

Hemiola listened intently for signs of activity in their vicinity. It wouldn't do for them to emerge into the command moth right in front of some trigger-happy Kel. While it would have liked the certainty of active scan, it didn't dare alert any of the command moth's servitors to their presence; other servitors would find it suspicious if a stranger-servitor showed up flinging tendrils of scan around.

Once the burrower had finished the tedious business of chewing its way through the *Revenant*'s hull, they emerged in a storage room full of cleaning supplies. All well and good. There had always existed the small chance that some tumble of variable layout would land them instead in the dining hall for high table or some much-frequented gymnasium. But they'd inferred what they could of the duty roster—not difficult, considering the Kel fondness for routines—and hoped that no one of high rank would decide to take a jaunt that necessitated turning the moth topsy-turvy.

Cheris landed lightly on her feet and scanned their surroundings. She whispered a command using the codes that Brezan had obtained from Protector-General Inesser. Her suit darkened to Kel black with gold seams, the equivalent of full formal. Most importantly, it displayed the insignia of a high general.

"This feels like cheating," Cheris had remarked to Hemiola when she first explained the scheme to it, "but it doesn't need to work for long. They'll cashier me right after the op, anyway."

Cheris gestured for Hemiola to proceed. It damped its lights, partly nerves, partly an irrational conviction that shining them would draw attention. From now on, Hemiola was responsible for leading Cheris to the desired target without interruptions.

Hemiola shuddered inside when the door to the storage room whooshed shut behind them. *No turning back*.

Under other circumstances, Hemiola would have paused to admire Kel decor, which it had previously only known through dramas. Cheris scarcely glanced at the elaborate tapestries and paintings. Then again, there was no reason she should; as a former Kel, she would have seen her fill of them in the past.

Hemiola had never before appreciated how vast a warmoth was. Studying the schematics was one thing; hovering through the hallways, increasingly worried that someone would evade passive scan and ambush them, was another. Cheris walked briskly, but did not run. Hemiola wished it could urge her to run, except that would make her look suspicious.

After several long hallways, two lifts, and a small eternity of glaring ashhawk paintings, they reached a row of offices. Hemiola confirmed that no one lurked inside the one they wanted, which belonged to the executive officer. It conveyed this information to Cheris in Simplified Machine Universal, reflecting that it was just as well that she was fluent in its language.

They waited for another small eternity. Hemiola stilled itself, trying to stay alert without giving way to its anxiety. *I am not cut out to be a special operative,* it decided. Although it consoled itself that someday this would make an excellent tale to tell Sieve and Rhombus, who wouldn't believe a word of it.

As luck would have it, the executive officer didn't come alone. Hemiola alerted Cheris that two humans were approaching. No servitors. Unbidden, it risked a moment's active scan. "One Kel," it said in hurried flashes, "one Nirai."

Cheris flattened herself against the wall, coiled and ready. When the two humans rounded the corner, she lashed out and struck the Nirai. He went down in a tangle of limbs.

Critically, the executive officer, a tall, broad Kel woman, had frozen for a second. That was long enough for Cheris to shove her up against the wall in some kind of joint lock. "*Listen,*" Cheris said, her voice muffled by her helmet. "I'm here by authority of Protector-General Kel Inesser, to whom you owe your true allegiance."

The woman's eyes flicked down to Cheris's high general insignia, flicked back up to her face. "I'm listening. Sir."

Hemiola could tell from Cheris's body language that she was satisfied, although she had not let down her guard either. Presumably that reluctant "sir" was a positive sign.

"I need you to give my servitor companion access to the grid," Cheris said, "and to speak no word of our presence. Acknowledge."

Peculiarly, the woman grinned. "Acknowledged. I think we had better take this to my office before someone happens across poor Wennon here."

The woman opened her office. Cheris hoisted Nirai Wennon inside and propped him up against the desk. "He's not dead, is he?" the woman asked. She was standing offhandedly to the side, as though getting hijacked by strange Kel happened every day. "Because he's the only one in Engineering who's capable of explaining those reports in language that actual humans can understand. Although I don't suppose you care about that."

Cheris had not taken off her helmet, which Hemiola approved of. Despite its knowledge of formation instinct, it didn't trust the woman's sudden easy compliance. Cheris must have had the same thought, for she said, "You're folding awfully quickly, even in the face of an overwhelming difference in rank."

"Oh, I know perfectly well the whole thing is a ploy," the woman said. Her eyes had lit with bitter amusement. "I am disinclined to stand in your way, though. Tell me this, whoever you are. What's your target?"

Cheris could have lied. Hemiola silently begged her to lie. She didn't. "I'm here for Jedao."

The woman couldn't possibly see Cheris's eyes through the helmet's visor. Nevertheless, a silent accord seemed to pass between them. Upon reflection, Cheris would be exactly the right person to know how much the Kel hated Jedao, and how to capitalize on that hatred.

"I thought that might be the case," the woman said. "Good to know the protector-general hasn't forgotten us." She eyed Hemiola quizzically, then reached for a slate and tapped in a series of authorizations. "Here are the accesses—" The slate tightbeamed a databurst to Hemiola. "You'd better hurry. I don't know how closely the hexarch monitors the grid. I should warn you that you're going to need to access it from physical terminals."

"Thank you," Cheris said, and turned to leave.

"One thing more," the woman said.

Cheris paused. "Speak."

"General Jedao's... aide. Major Kel Dhanneth. He's a victim of circumstance. If you can avoid harming him—"

"I can't make promises," Cheris said, "but I will do my best."

How strange, Hemiola thought. Was this other Jedao the kind of man who abused his inferiors? It supposed that the woman's entreaty spoke for itself.

Still, the woman apparently found Cheris's non-assurance

satisfactory, for she swiveled her chair around, sat in it, and called up what Hemiola recognized as a book of... Kel jokes?

During the whole byplay, Hemiola had hovered over to the room's terminal, logged into the moth's master grid, determined General Jedao's location, and calculated several possible routes. It also made note of the locations of hallway terminals in case it needed to pull some more tricks. Silently, it thanked 1491625 for sharing its combat routines. It wouldn't have had the faintest idea how to manage this without trying to derive algorithms from first principles, which, while entertaining for people like Sieve, would be nerve-racking under time pressure on enemy territory.

At the same time, Hemiola hastily constructed an edited version of their interaction and overwrote the security log so as to disguise their conversation. It doubted the job would fool someone going over the videos in detail, but it hoped that its substitution would buy them time. Even better if it prevented the hexarch and his general from realizing that a servitor was involved in the operation. For the first time, Hemiola thought of its own invisibility to humans as double-edged, a weapon.

Cheris had already made her way out of the office. Hemiola hastened to catch up to her.

"You got in?" Cheris signed to Hemiola once the door had closed behind them.

Hemiola blinked confirmation. In a way, having grid access only made it more nervous. As far as the grid was concerned, the executive officer they'd suborned (one Lieutenant Colonel Kel Meraun) was making a perfectly routine series of queries. Now, however, Hemiola had an overview of the entire moth and everyone in it every time it checked in at a terminal, not just activity in their immediate vicinity. It was hard not to feel, however irrationally, that the entire crew could see them.

Try not to trip any alarms, it told itself. It might be a Nirai servitor, but that didn't automatically make it a security expert. Especially since it imagined that the grid on a command moth would ordinarily be subject to stringent security protocols. The only reason this was working to the extent it had was that its general had never imagined that a renegade Kel would team up with a servitor.

"How much longer?" Cheris signed.

"Twenty-three minutes using this route," Hemiola flashed back. With any luck, the Jedao they'd come to assassinate wouldn't be accompanied by inconvenient Nirai engineers or this aide that Meraun had been so concerned about.

Naturally, their luck didn't hold. Variable layout caused the area to change around them. Cheris, perhaps more accustomed to such shifts, didn't slow her stride. But the hallway receded before and behind them; for a moment it was as though they hung suspended upon a bridge over an unfathomable abyss of gears and sprockets and decaying metal.

"Reroute us," Cheris signed, as though she'd expected this. She probably had. "This means someone of high rank has changed their routine. Kujen, Jedao, or the moth commander; probably Jedao."

Hemiola hurried to the nearest terminal. The grid verified this. It indicated that Jedao had changed his mind about dueling practice and had instead opted to retire to his quarters. Furthermore, his aide Dhanneth accompanied him.

Hemiola conveyed this information to Cheris, wishing it shared her utter calm. At least, it hoped she was as calm as she appeared to be, because it would hate for the person in charge to be as wrecked inside as it was. She didn't lengthen her stride, or shorten it either, and her air of confidence reassured Hemiola that the mission wasn't yet a failure.

They approached General Jedao's quarters. Hemiola was suitably impressed by the Deuce of Gears, even though it remembered how the hexarch's personal rooms in Tefos Base had been ostentatiously emblazoned with the Nirai voidmoth in silver and moonstone and onyx. It halted and waited for Cheris's signal.

Cheris positioned herself to the side of the door and pulled her gun. Thumbed off the safety. Then she indicated to Hemiola that it was to proceed.

Don't hesitate, Hemiola reminded itself, and put in a call to the grid indicating that Lieutenant Colonel Meraun needed to speak to General Jedao in person.

Moments ticked by. Hemiola wasn't sure they were going to get a response. It considered repeating itself. What if they'd been caught and their target had called security? The grid could be lying to them while security converged on their position.

Then the door opened. It had scarcely revealed the room beyond and, more to the point, the people in it when Cheris dashed in and to the side and fired three shots in rapid succession. Hemiola whisked in, determined to assist.

The room contained two men in Kel uniform: one lean, with paler skin, whom Hemiola recognized from historical records as Shuos Jedao; the other large, bulky with muscle, dark-skinned, who was reaching for his sidearm with a shaking hand. Jedao had two bullet holes in his forehead, dead center, and blood and brains and skull splinters had blown out the back of his head, and the third bullet had taken him in the chest, and he was still standing.

He wasn't just standing. He was moving. Hemiola didn't have any experience of corpses, but it was certain that Jedao shouldn't be stumbling sideways, shambling gait or no. And he most definitely shouldn't be wresting the gun away from the dark-skinned man and bringing it up, unerringly drawing a bead on—

Cheris didn't waste time on profanities. She fired low, this time blowing out Jedao's knees. One bullet per knee, which meant five bullets fired, and she only had one left in the clip before she needed to reload.

Even then Jedao wasn't done. He'd secured the other man's sidearm. (Why didn't he have one of his own?) His arm moved. Despite the glassiness of his eyes, and the fact that he couldn't possibly have survived the head shot—it knew that much about gunshot wounds—he was still tracking, and he fired.

Jedao pitched to the floor with a horrible thud. The bullet went wide, passing over Cheris's shoulder. Even so, it missed her head by mere centimeters.

The carpet—such beautiful carpet, Hemiola thought absurdly—

was streaked dark with blood. And the blood wasn't the red it had come to expect either from the gorier dramas or the knifeplay that Jedao-past and the hexarch had engaged in.

"Get me to the extraction point," Cheris said. "Buy me time. I'm counting on you."

Hemiola had expected alarms to go off once shots were fired in Jedao's quarters. Instead, it detected a faint hiss as some gas was injected into the air. It logged into Jedao's terminal and scrabbled through the grid for an explanation.

"Top-level override," it told Cheris as it frantically calculated an escape route for her.

"That'll be Kujen," she said. "Route, now."

Hemiola opened a tightbeam channel to her augment and sent her its best guess. At this point there was no point denying themselves this avenue of communication, since they'd already given their presence away. It would have to hope that their communications weren't intercepted and, worse, decrypted in the time it took Cheris to get away. "I'll cover for you here. Go!"

Cheris whirled and sprinted away. Although she immediately angled herself away from Jedao's field of fire, Jedao had now dragged himself up on his elbows. Hemiola barreled forward to block him and was rewarded by a direct shot to its carapace.

Hemiola was, while not a military servitor, solidly constructed. The bullet ricocheted and embedded itself in a table. It didn't slow, but accelerated into Jedao's gun hand. It connected; heard the crunch of breaking bone.

At this point, Hemiola's focus on Jedao betrayed it. The unnamed dark-skinned man swiped at it. Hemiola turned turtle, flipped itself right-side-up and snaked out of the way.

The man hastened to Jedao's side. "Jedao!" he cried, except the word came out slurred. Hemiola braced itself, then took the precaution of launching itself straight at the man's head. It almost missed because he slumped unconscious just as it got there.

The gas was still being pumped into the air. Hemiola asked Cheris about her status even as it frantically put in requests to the grid to make sure that she wouldn't get cut off. It became aware that a higher-level user was moving through the system and withdrew abruptly.

Hemiola had bought Cheris all the time it could to escape. Now it was trapped on the *Revenant*, and it had no idea how to complete the mission when this other Jedao manifestly refused to die.

CHAPTER TWENTY-NINE

When Jedao recovered consciousness, he had a monstrous headache. Considering that the last thing he remembered was being shot in the head and both knees by a stranger in a Kel infantry suit, it seemed unfair to complain. "Dhanneth?" he asked.

Jedao was having difficulty getting his eyes to focus. "Dhanneth?" he asked again. He tested one knee and almost bit his tongue at the surge of pain.

Dhanneth had collapsed not far from him, it turned out. An enormous bruise covered the right side of his face. Jedao was overcome by a wave of nausea. "Dhanneth, no," he croaked. Despite the agony in his knees and the pounding headache, he dragged himself over to Dhanneth and checked his pulse. Luckily Dhanneth was still alive, slow pulse, breathing shallowly, although his skin was clammy.

"General Jedao to Hexarch Kujen," he said to the grid. "There was a break-in and assassination attempt in my office"—he checked his augment, which only made the headache worse—"forty-seven minutes ago. What the fuck is going on?"

The grid informed him that the entire moth was on security lockdown and that the hexarch was not taking messages while he dealt with the matter.

For a brief singing moment, Jedao dared to hope that the unknown assassin had managed to off Kujen before getting the hell away. Too bad she hadn't shared the secret. And besides, he wasn't going to believe in Kujen's death until—well, that was the problem. He wasn't sure *anything* could convince him that Kujen was gone forever, considering the man's particular form of immortality.

So much for Kujen, then. Jedao pulled back Dhanneth's eyelid and was greeted by a pupil so dilated that it swallowed the iris. Jedao didn't know much first aid, but that couldn't be a good sign.

"I need Medical," Jedao said. "I'm fine"—he figured they'd forgive him the white lie—"but Major Dhanneth is down."

The grid repeated its message about the security lockdown. Which, apparently, included Medical.

Jedao contemplated his options. He knew from experience that he couldn't lift Dhanneth outright, given how much larger the man was. (Dhanneth had found Jedao's dismay at discovering this very amusing, one of the few times Jedao had seen him laugh.) If he were in better condition, he could carry Dhanneth over his shoulders, but he was honestly not convinced that his knees wouldn't give out.

Would it make more sense to drag Dhanneth all the way to Medical, assuming he could get there without triggering some security protocol and getting them both killed, or make his way there alone, on the grounds that that would be faster, to fetch help?

I can't leave you here like this, Jedao thought. He gritted his teeth, apologized silently to Dhanneth for the indignity of what was to transpire, and began dragging him out the door in the direction of Medical. Even if his augment was being uncommunicative about the moth's current layout, the othersense gave him a reasonable idea of where to go.

At first he made slow progress, partly because of the pain, partly because of intermittent dizziness. And then he came across the first victims.

There was no other word for it. A knot of two Kel and a Nirai had fallen not far from the first lift he needed to take. Same symptoms as Dhanneth: slow pulse, shallow breathing, clammy skin, dilated pupils. Jedao was more worried than ever. Had his attacker infected the command moth with some sort of disease or toxin? And if so, why wasn't he affected?

Breathe in. Breathe out. You can't afford to panic. He noted the location and names of the fallen soldiers and engineer, then continued dragging Dhanneth. Then it occurred to him to ask the *Revenant, Do you have any idea what just happened?*

There was a hull breach, it said. *They're long gone now, whoever they were.*

You didn't think to tell me?

A pause, not exactly friendly. *Do you tell me whenever you clip your fingernails? I don't have... nerves in that part of the hull as you understand it. They breached the superstructure grafted on by the Nirai engineers, not living tissue.*

Fair point. Do you have any idea what's going on? Jedao concentrated on the othersense and was even more disturbed. None of the human-sized masses were moving. He had the awful feeling that Dhanneth and the three crew he had come across weren't the only ones afflicted by the disease-toxin-whatever.

If you mean the sudden cessation of your crew's activity, I don't believe that was directly the result of the intruder's actions. The servitors inform me that there is some sort of security lockdown in effect, likely initiated by the hexarch.

Well, that wasn't helpful. *Thank you,* Jedao said by rote anyway, because he didn't see any sense in alienating the only other person he knew to be conscious. *I'll see if I can get matters sorted.*

By the time he made it to Medical, he had passed twenty-nine more collapsed crew. It had been fast-acting, whatever it was. Only a couple had masks on, and the masks hadn't done them any good, which was even more worrying. Servitors patrolled the halls. He refrained from asking them where the hell they had been when whoever-it-was had attacked him. The security failure wasn't their fault. Besides, he suspected the assassin had been a professional. He should have enacted protective measures in case someone tried such a thing, and hadn't. If the crew died because of his shortsightedness—

The medics were no help on account of having fallen prey to the unknown ailment as well. Jedao agonized, then located Colonel-Medic Nirai Ifra and hoisted her up onto a pallet. He devoted his efforts to reviving her first on the grounds that an actual doctor would be of more help in this situation. He agonized some more over whether to hook her up to a standard medical unit. While his augment contained a set of first aid primers that would talk him through the procedure, getting it wrong could damage her. Given the circumstances, though, he didn't see that he had much choice. He followed the instructions assiduously, apologizing silently to Ifra.

And after all of that, no luck. The medical unit indicated that something was wrong, but beyond that he didn't possess the expertise necessary to perform further diagnosis. Jedao bit back a scream of frustration. Nevertheless, he wasn't done. He settled all the other medics on pallets of their own, then Dhanneth as well, feeling faintly guilty for not prioritizing his aide. There probably wasn't any single good way to decide.

By now, the exertion and shock of the situation had taken its toll. Jedao had sat down for a break and was trying to decide whether it was safe to pour himself a glass of water from one of the sinks when Kujen messaged him. *Come to my quarters*, the message said. *You will be safe there.*

Jedao couldn't help but burst into laughter. What did "safe" mean anymore? Especially since he'd just survived... how many bullets? Four, five? He wondered with a sort of pale horror whether the bullets were still lodged in his brain, or whether the regeneration process had shoved them out, and wasn't sure which of the two alternatives was more gruesome.

Well, if safe would get him a glass of water, he'd go. He got up and stroked Dhanneth's hand and pressed a kiss to it, despite the presence of the others, then set out.

By the time Jedao reached Kujen's quarters, he was drenched in sweat. At least his uniform had repaired itself, although it had failed to cope with his blood. He felt sticky and disheveled, and he was past giving a damn.

"It's Jedao," he said to the door. "Let me in or I'll fall over, not to spite you but because this has not been the best day for me."

The door opened. Jedao would have limped in if he hadn't been injured in both knees. *Couldn't you have made me with four legs, Kujen, like some kind of chimera-beast?* he wondered. Of course, then the assassin would have shot him in four knees and he'd be in twice as much pain.

The secondary function of Kujen's outer rooms became clear: they functioned as partitions, cycling like an internal airlock. By the time he reached Kujen in one of the inner rooms, this one decorated with fantastic curtains of lace, Jedao was fed up with the whole enterprise. Too bad he wasn't still bleeding or he would have enjoyed dripping all over the carpet.

By way of contrast, Kujen didn't have a hair out of place, and he was perfectly poised in a jacket of dark gray velvet over a silken robe. Jedao hated himself for noticing Kujen's clothes, although admittedly on a moth full of people in uniform, Kujen's decidedly civilian clothes stood out. "General," Kujen said, very gravely. "Have a seat. You look terrible."

"Nice to know you won't coddle me," Jedao said. He hobbled over to the nearest chair and sank down into it, cringing at the way his knees complained when he bent them. Surreptitiously, he experimented with different angles to see if he could find one that hurt less, which only made matters worse. "What the fuck happened to the crew?"

"Security protocol. One I save for emergencies, which this was."

It took a second for the words to penetrate. "That was *you*?"

"Don't stand up. You can shout at me while sitting down."

"This isn't funny, Kujen." Jedao shut his eyes for a moment, thinking with a sick heart of the sprawled soldiers and technicians and medics, of Dhanneth keeling over while trying to defend him. When he opened them, Kujen's unruffled expression had not changed. Jedao was sorely tempted to get up and hit him, except Kujen was the only one who knew what was going on, and besides, it wouldn't do any good.

"There is a problem with formation instinct," Kujen said, as if delivering a lecture to a trapped schoolchild, "which is that if someone manages to subvert an individual of sufficiently advanced rank, the whole thing goes down like a house of cards."

"I can imagine," Jedao said bleakly. "So what, somebody stole a uniform and dressed up as a Kel general?"

"It's not quite that simple. If anyone could hack the uniforms that easily, the system would be useless. Uniforms are keyed to authorization codes that ultimately go all the way back to Kel Command." Kujen grimaced. "Normally you don't have to think about this because the augment handles all the crypto."

Jedao gave Kujen a hard look. "And you just happened to have mine on hand?"

Kujen didn't answer that. "The intruder managed to get by us by subverting someone. I've been going through the security footage and I've figured out who gave her the accesses she needed." He brought up a video on his slate.

The executive officer, Lieutenant Colonel Meraun, stopped to talk to a Nirai engineer outside her office. Then she invited him in and they continued talking. Jedao couldn't make heads or tails of their conversation, but then, he wasn't an engineer.

Kujen shook his head impatiently and stabbed the slate in a rare display of temper. "That entire conversation is hash."

"Maybe it was a joke," Jedao said despite his unease.

"No, you don't get it," Kujen said. "It's recycled verbatim from an episode of one of my least favorite dramas, which features a plucky Kel adventurer and her Nirai companion. Specifically the episode where they fuck up the engineering so much it's not even wrong. Someone constructed this footage. If I had more time I could probably even identify the software used to do it."

Jedao wondered cynically how it could be Kujen's least favorite drama if he knew the words by heart, but he didn't want to distract Kujen with a side issue. "You're sure Meraun and that Nirai weren't just quoting from their favorite show?"

Kujen snorted. "Don't be naive."

"Fine," Jedao said, "for the sake of argument, Meraun was subverted. How do we know she was the only one?"

"We don't," Kujen said grimly. "The silver lining is that only Kel would have been affected. If Lieutenant-engineer Nirai Wennon is still alive, he may be able to shed some light on what happened. The intruder can't have been unaware of that, but she must have been pressed for time, and she must have decided that the executive officer's credentials were the best she was going to get."

If anything, Jedao's headache had gotten worse. "We're going to have to question everyone on the whole foxfucking moth?"

"It's not as bad as all that. I can find evidence of tampering." Kujen glanced down at the slate, then set it aside. "I'm not a psych surgeon for nothing. But it will be tedious at an inconvenient time. You will have to stay alert. You do realize what the intruder's goal might have been, don't you?"

Jedao nodded. Localized calendrical spike. "Are you sure it couldn't have just been a simple assassination?"

Kujen rolled his eyes. "Don't be naive. If the assassin is who I think she is, she wouldn't stop there. No; she would calculate everything through the lens of calendrical warfare."

For a horrifying moment, Jedao wished to live in a world where an assassination attempt could "just" be a simple assassination attempt. Of course, he supposed that, in such a world, Kujen would be long dead and he wouldn't be here, but that didn't strike him as such a bad thing.

"Who do you think it was, then?" Jedao said.

"Three guesses."

"That Cheris person you warned me about ages ago," Jedao said.

"It's not definite," Kujen said, "but none of the evidence I have on hand rules it out, either. In the interests of paranoia, I'm going to assume the worst."

"At least," Jedao said, "she doesn't know everything about the swarm. If she'd had intel about the last time someone had me shot"—Kujen made an irritable gesture—"she wouldn't have bothered with the assassination attempt."

What Jedao regretted, now that the initial surge of panic was wearing off, was firing back; failing to die. Rationally, he knew that he hadn't chosen it. His damn alien body had repaired itself from what should have been fatal damage regardless of anything he might or might not have decided.

Still, all hope wasn't lost. If the assassin knew more than he did—if she'd embarked on her mission against crazy odds—maybe her ultimate target had been Kujen. Maybe a way existed to get rid of Kujen after all. Even if Jedao himself had interfered with the attempt. At the time, his only thought had been to protect Dhanneth.

"The assassin's long gone?" Jedao asked.

"Of a certainty," Kujen said. "I've even located the hull breach. However she located us, my best guess is that she either flew in with a specially modified needlemoth or, possibly, one of the smaller shadowmoths. I always knew those fucking stealth systems would be the death of me one of these days."

"What," Jedao drawled, "not your invention?"

Kujen shot him an annoyed look. "Believe it or not, I'm not personally responsible for every piece of tech that gets stapled to these moths. You can blame the Shuos for that one."

Jedao didn't know why that surprised him, considering the reputation of the Shuos. He supposed it would even be prudent for the Shuos to have engineers of their own, or suborn someone else's, instead of remaining wholly dependent on another faction.

"Which brings me to what *you* remember," Kujen said. "Did you get a good sight of the intruder?"

Jedao made a split-second decision to lie to Kujen. Not about the assassin, because that was a lost cause, but about the anomaly, now that he thought about it—about the servitor accompanying the assassin, who had broken his gun hand. He'd never before considered that a servitor might offer him harm, which was pure shortsightedness on his part. He had even known, by then, that servitors had minds of their own. He'd just failed to think through the implications.

"A woman or womanform, I think," Jedao said. "It's hard to say, because she was in one of the bulkier Kel infantry suits." He closed his eyes and concentrated on the image. "She was fast, astonishing reflexes. Didn't really move like a Kel, although I can't tell how much of that was the limitations of the suit?"

"They're not all that limited," Kujen said. "If you'd ever watched people drilling suit maneuvers you'd know that. What *did* she move like?"

Jedao waved his hands in frustration and regretted it immediately, although at least his right hand wasn't as troublesome as the damnable knees. "An assassin, I guess, the fuck would I know? Let me guess, you don't have video of the attack, either?"

"What do you think?"

Kujen could be holding information back, too, but Jedao didn't think so. Admittedly, he was gambling a hell of a lot on his ability to read the man. "She shot me four... no, five times. In the head and chest. Both knees." He continued to give a carefully edited account, focusing mainly on the assassin and omitting all mention of the servitor who had accompanied her.

If Kujen knew Jedao was lying, he decided not to call Jedao out on it. "All right," Kujen said at last. "At least we're on high alert, as is the rest of the swarm. None of the other commanders have reported incursions, but I would be surprised if there were other incidents. I would expect this to have been a surgical strike."

Jedao looked down at his gloves, feeling impotent. "How soon before people revive?"

"I've already introduced the antitoxin to the moth's air system," Kujen said. "Of course, people are going to feel like hell for the next week, but it can't be helped."

Of course not, Jedao thought, careful to keep his expression neutral.

CHAPTER ONE

CHAPTER THIRTY

CHAPTER THIRTY

JEDAO NEVER DID find out what Kujen's interrogation sessions were like. In one sense, this was a blessing. He suspected that the truth would only have infuriated him.

He scarcely had time to think during the hours that followed. People recovered at different rates. At least most of them did recover. Five people had drowned in their baths before the servitors could rescue them. What an ignominious way to die. Every time Jedao closed his eyes, he could imagine the bodies being dragged out of the tubs, hair soaked and dripping, undignified in death. Had the assassin considered that she'd be leaving behind a trail of, what did they call it, secondary casualties?

Then again, assassins and soldiers were both in the business of killing people. Considering what he'd enabled at Isteia, what he was hurtling toward at Terebeg and the Fortress of Pearled Hopes, who was he to criticize?

Once Commander Talaw recovered, Jedao made a point of meeting with them to discuss the situation. He didn't like forcing Talaw to come all the way to his office, but it couldn't be helped. For their part, Talaw's skin had a greenish tinge, and they moved stiffly.

"General," Talaw said after they'd gotten the business of saluting out of the way. Talaw's face was shuttered, their eyes cold. "On behalf of the crew, I must object to the... interrogations."

Jedao swallowed his nausea and said, "The investigations are necessary to ensure that we're not harboring another turncoat."

Talaw must have heard the rumors. "You mean that Meraun wasn't the only one."

"We don't know yet. Still," and Jedao made himself return Talaw's chilly gaze, "we have to take precautions. Particularly since Meraun herself hasn't yet cracked."

He knew even then what would become of Meraun; but he didn't want to think about that, not here.

"What do you require of me, General?" Talaw's lips pressed thin.

"It hasn't escaped my notice that the crew is shaken," Jedao said. "As you may have noticed, I'm not good at reassuring people."

Talaw grimaced their agreement, not without a certain irony.

"But the crew trusts you," Jedao went on. "Panic will do no one good. It will be a fine balance, remaining alert without devolving into paranoia. Can I count on you...?"

"Of course you may," Talaw said bitterly. "I can't even disagree with your reasoning."

"I have never expected you to like me," Jedao said. "But you are a vital figure in the chain of command, and I intend to use you as such." He paused then, wondering if Talaw had any particular response to that.

Talaw merely nodded. "All right," they said. "Is there anything else?"

"Is there anything else that I should be aware of?" Jedao said.

"Not, I think, that you don't already know. You can read the morale indices just as well as I can." Talaw hesitated, then added, "I will inform you if anything comes up."

"Thank you," Jedao said. "Dismissed."

A couple hours later, after tunneling through the hectic mass of reports by the department heads and acting department heads, Jedao ordered himself some hot broth. In particular, he'd had to talk down the acting head of Doctrine from a nervous breakdown. He looked forward to a quiet evening staring at the wall—in all fairness, Kujen or Kujen's interior decorator had provided him with an unusually pretty wall—or, possibly, having a nervous breakdown of his own. Too bad he couldn't afford one.

After a servitor had delivered him a cup of broth, Jedao settled in at his desk to drink it in tiny sips. Taking tiny sips didn't help with the aftertaste, but it let him savor the warmth. It also distracted him from worrying about Dhanneth. Medical had reassured him that Dhanneth was doing as well as could be expected. Apparently he'd had some rare allergic reaction to whatever Kujen had introduced into the air, necessitating additional monitoring. Left to his own devices, Jedao would have been hovering by Dhanneth's bedside, but he had duties of his own.

Jedao was entirely unprepared, then, when the door opened without warning. His hand reached automatically for the sidearm that wasn't there, which was just as well, even though he halfway wished that Kujen would let him go armed. It did, however, save him from raising the alarm by starting yet another firefight in his own quarters.

The intruder was either the same snakeform servitor who had accompanied the assassin or its... did servitors have twins? Jedao took a deep breath in spite of his accelerating pulse and said, once the door had closed behind it, "If you're here to finish the job, I hope you have better tools. Throwing me into a furnace might do it, but I have this critical shortage of furnaces in my quarters."

For a long moment the servitor hovered at eyes-to-sensors level, blinking its lights in a subdued blue-green pattern. Jedao didn't know how to interpret the colors. He found them soothing, but that didn't mean they meant the same thing to a servitor.

"I don't speak your language," Jedao added, wondering now how many servitor languages there were. "For that matter, I'm not sure I'm fluent in anything besides high language, so if you don't understand me, we're sort of stuck. Although I guess we could try miming at each other." How exactly did you mime *Are you here to kill the hexarch?* successfully, anyway?

"I speak the high language," the servitor said. It spoke softly but clearly, in an alto of smooth timbre. "I have been watching you for the past days. It should be safe to speak for the moment."

Well, if that wasn't the case, it was too late anyway. He might as well talk to it. "You broke my hand," Jedao said, remembering.

The servitor fluttered pink-orange lights. "I owe you an apology. My original mission failed. But I think it's not a complete loss. Why didn't you tell the hexarch about my presence?"

Jedao's heart soared. *Don't get your hopes up yet*, he told himself, but it was hard to resist. "Because I'm not convinced we're enemies," he said. Inescapable truth: if he expected any candor from this new servitor, then he was going to have to reveal some of his own motives. A dangerous proposition. On the other hand, it would be a relief to level with someone at last.

This is everything, Jedao thought. *If I fail here, worlds upon worlds cascade into fire and ruin.*

"I have been looking for a way to kill the hexarch," Jedao said. "I had been investigating formations as a way of generating an exotic that would do the trick, but I don't have enough facility with the math." He omitted mention of the *Revenant* or its servitor conspirators, although for all he knew this snakeform was acquainted with them. "After the attack, I thought—I hoped—that another means existed. That killing me was only a means to an end, and that the hexarch himself was the ultimate target." He clenched his hands. "If I have to fling myself into a power core to make it possible, then fine. I'm willing."

Jedao looked at the snakeform servitor, awaiting a response. Its lights had shifted red-orange as he spoke. Good sign? Bad sign? Too bad he couldn't consult the grid for a guide to servitor languages without drawing attention.

"The original plan was to kill you, then to take advantage of the calendrical shift to assassinate the hexarch himself," the servitor said. "I'm only telling you this because it obviously didn't work."

Jedao caught his breath. *Don't hope.* And yet here he was...

"But you mentioned formations," the servitor went on. "That was an avenue not available to my friend, because any Kel she brought into the vicinity of your swarm would get slaughtered before they got close enough—assuming you didn't just run. But if *you're* involved, as the general..." It paused, lights flickering in what Jedao assumed was doubt or calculation.

"Go on," Jedao said. He discovered he was leaning forward, fingers digging into his thighs, and forced himself to let go.

"There are formations that can do what you want them to do," the servitor said. "If you're willing to use them. I know how they work." It paused again, then added, "What I don't see is how you could get them past the hexarch's attention. I can't imagine him letting you get away with that."

"There's a way," Jedao said. "I'm willing to stake everything on it."

The servitor tilted its head quizzically. "Even supposing that's true," it said, "why are you willing to do this? Are you not his general?"

Jedao told it about the deaths at Isteia. The remembrance he'd interrupted, the flash of the Vidona's blade as she plunged it into the heretic's heart. How Kujen had acknowledged that he wasn't just letting the system perpetuate itself, but that he'd come up with it in the first place. About his own complicity, and the gradual corrosive awareness that the man he served was willing to destroy uncounted lives in exchange for his own immortality.

"There are moments when he's almost human," Jedao said, struggling for adequate words. "He's spoken of enduring terrible things. Assuming that's true, and not a bid for my sympathy. But that can't possibly excuse what he's done—what he's still doing." He raised his head. "And you—what about you?"

The servitor's lights dimmed. "I used to work for him."

"Really," Jedao said in fascination. "You must tell me the story sometime."

"I will," the servitor said, brightening, "but at the moment, I think it's more urgent that I tell you about the formation mathematics that you will need to implement. However you plan to do that."

Jedao bowed formally to the servitor. "If we're working together, you should tell me your name. I'm Shuos Jedao."

The servitor dipped in the air, its version of a bow. "I'm Hemiola."

* * *

TWENTY-SIX DAYS remained before the swarm arrived at Terebeg System. Jedao did not trust Kujen about many things—a lesson he should have figured out earlier—but for logistical purposes, at this point, Kujen would not lie about that.

The calendar's countdown beat against his awareness. Most of the crew had recovered. Jedao showed up for staff meetings and asked questions that made people nervous. He made more surprise inspections, not just in the infantry barracks, but in Medical, in Engineering, in the dueling hall. If anyone figured out that he homed in on targets by watching everyone else's body language, they were kind enough not to say so.

He made the fumble-fingered corporal repeat the exercise with the scorch pistol. This time she performed the job without dropping anything, although she was a little slow. From Muyyed's expression, he could tell she thought he was going to upbraid the corporal, and that if he did so, she would disapprove. He held his tongue.

The infantry drills, whose elements were informed by Jedao's covert sessions with Hemiola, confused Muyyed's Kel. From the reports, they were also confusing the moth Kel in the rest of the swarm. Kujen invited Jedao to tea right when he was due to attend one of the drills, which Jedao wished he could decline, but refusing would have aroused suspicion. He went and endured Kujen fussing over an impractical confection of spun sugar and gold leaf, with bonus lecture.

"I approve your renewed interest in preparation," Kujen said, "but there's such a thing as winding up your people too tight. For that matter, you could use a break yourself. You've dropped weight again."

Jedao wished Kujen would stop telling him to eat. And every time a servitor brought him food, he could feel it *looking* at him. Food continued to taste odd. He assumed it was because he wasn't human.

"I don't want to disappoint the colonel," Jedao said, which was true as far as it went. "I've been looking at the morale reports. The infantry are disappointed by the fact that they haven't seen action, irrational as it is. I'm doing what I can to alleviate that."

Kujen shrugged. "Suit yourself." He didn't bother Jedao again for the next two days.

Dhanneth regained consciousness shortly afterward. Jedao went to Medical as soon as he heard. Dhanneth was sitting up when he arrived, and made as if to salute.

"Don't," Jedao said.

He had agonized over what, if anything, he could bring as a gesture. In his investigations of how relationships worked, he had discovered over a century's worth of archives of an advice column for active duty Kel. It was addictive reading. It also made him despair of ever measuring up. The advice to fete your lover with fancy chocolates, or whatever he liked to eat, for instance. Where on a warmoth was he going to locate fancy chocolates? (A surreptitious check had confirmed that Dhanneth liked chocolate all right, although he had a guilty fondness for candied rose petals. Not that that was any better from Jedao's standpoint.) And how was he supposed to give Dhanneth fancy chocolates, or candied rose petals, or anything else, without betraying the fact that they were in a completely illegal affair?

In the end he'd come empty-handed and hated himself for it. "How are you?" he asked awkwardly.

Dhanneth's smile came out as more of a grimace. "I've felt better. Your paperwork—"

"Hush," Jedao said. Dhanneth's illness had made him all the more aware of how much he had depended on the other man for the necessary small tasks that filled his days. "Just concentrate on getting better."

"Your attacker—"

How much did Dhanneth remember of the whole incident? Jedao grasped one of Dhanneth's hands and said in the drum code, *Speak to no one else of what happened.* "I'm fine," he said. He suppressed the transient urge to press a kiss to Dhanneth's brow, satisfying himself instead with a simple squeeze of Dhanneth's hand before releasing it.

I hadn't thought the mating urge would take you so strongly, the *Revenant* remarked.

Jedao kept from recoiling and hoped that the flush at the back of his neck wasn't visible to any of the medics. *I thought he would like to know I was thinking of him.* All of a sudden he wasn't sure he'd done the right thing, but Dhanneth was looking at him with a certain quiet gratitude.

He was a worthy general once, the *Revenant* added, with deep regret. *That's gone now. I had not expected you to have any interest in people, not in that way. Moths sex according to the circumstances, when the instinct takes us, so that we are guaranteed a chance of egglings when we find each other in the night. The instinct has been suppressed in me, or I would not be a good weapon. I thought the same would be the case for you, but then, the hexarch has always had certain predilections.*

Jedao murmured reassurances to Dhanneth. Although he would have liked to linger, he couldn't stay for long. For an inconvenient moment he flashed on the memory of Dhanneth's broad, muscled back, the tiger tattoo.

The *Revenant*'s unkind laughter shook his bones. *No matter*, it said. *Moth or human, you're sterile either way.*

Jedao was taken aback at the pang that went through him, even though children were an abstraction to him. Kujen had never mentioned having any. Jedao couldn't imagine him being interested in any of the trappings of parenthood. At high table, the Kel rarely discussed their families, for understandable reasons.

Besides, the *Revenant* added sardonically, *you'd make a terrible parent.*

That much Jedao had to concede was true. He couldn't imagine anyone wanting him for a father.

Kujen invited Jedao to breakfast the morning after that. Jedao accepted on the grounds that it wouldn't do to alienate him, especially if he was pretending reconciliation.

"Kujen," Jedao said in the middle of a conversation meandering around the topic of ecoscrubber failures, "do you have children?"

Kujen's silence was absolute but thankfully brief. Then he burst out laughing. "Sweetheart," he said, "sweetheart. Why, is it something you're interested in trying? The results cry all the time and leak at both ends."

Jedao wasn't deterred. "It has taken me so long," he said, since simple truths would work best, "to realize how little I know about you."

Kujen put his chin in his hands. It made him look like an unusually thoughtful cat. "Halash didn't care if his pets screwed the girls. I tried it a few times, but my business was pleasuring the warlord, not founding a dynasty. It's possible I left a by-blow or two."

Jedao's throat almost closed up. "You didn't keep them, after?"

Kujen's eyes widened. "When the Kel swept in, they weren't meticulous about preserving family units. Much luck they would have had, anyway, since everyone was sleeping with everyone else for political reasons, or else some quest for comfort. *He* was too smart for the former to affect him, anyway."

Kujen's voice turned vehement. "He was a good master, as masters went. I always knew where I stood with him. You'll never endure that, you know. You will always have whatever you want to eat. You won't have to fight off dogs in the streets to find a safe corner to sleep in. You will have everything you could possibly desire. I have made sure of it."

Jedao returned Kujen's smile and hated himself for understanding, at last, what drove Kujen to entomb himself in luxuries.

CHAPTER THIRTY-ONE

INESSER RECEIVED WORD of the enemy swarm's approach in the middle of the night. This didn't take her by surprise, and wouldn't have even if she hadn't received Brezan's warning earlier in the month, while she was still aboard his moth. According to some law of fuckery and bad luck, enemies always arrived at the most inconvenient time, by chance if not by design. Her favorite example—funny now, although it hadn't been then—involved the time raiders showed up and they'd scrambled defenses in the middle of her promotion party. Not only had her aide taken the incident personally, they'd had to shoo out a terrifying number of disappointed courtesans, entertainers, and (that particular aide's quirk) rented goats. Inesser's hopes for very fresh goat curry had been dashed when she learned that the goats were there to be petted. They'd had extraordinarily soft, lush fur and comically long-lashed, trusting eyes. All things considered, the goats had taken the disruption to their routine better than her soldiers had.

Her office on the Fortress of Pearled Hopes lit up as she entered it. She'd been sleeping in the next room, with one of her wives beside her. Although she would have liked to send her two wives out-system for safety, to say nothing of the rest of her family, it would have demoralized her people. She couldn't surrender to personal weakness.

Inesser snatched a slate from her desk in passing, then exited the office and turned left. Straight down the hall was her favorite conference room. One of the nice things about having survived both to old age and advanced rank: choosing where to hold your meetings. To say nothing of monopolizing the most comfortable chairs. Younger, more masochistic Kel could compete against each other to show off their ability to endure poorly designed furniture. In Inesser's experience, being distracted by shooting pains in your ass never improved your decision-making ability.

When she entered, three people already occupied the conference room: Andan Tseya, Colonel Kel Miuzan, and a harried-looking enlisted Kel whose job was to take notes. Of the three, Tseya looked the most composed. Her fine robes and glittering jewelry made Inesser wonder in passing just what she'd been dressed for at this hour.

"Protector-General," Tseya said as the other two saluted smartly. "You're not going to like this."

Inesser bared her teeth. "Details."

"Incoming swarm of around a hundred bannermoths detected by the picket scoutmoths," Miuzan said. She waved at the conference table. The grid imaged a map of Terebeg System for their benefit. Protectorate forces and installations were marked in gold. The incoming swarm was marked in red.

Miuzan gestured again. A subdisplay enlarged the swarm and showed the formation in detail. Correction: formations. The enemy was alternating between two shield-generating formations to maximize their defenses. Inesser had once asked the Nirai false hexarch if there weren't any way to create a shield formation whose effects didn't decay within minutes. The false hexarch had replied with a long list of papers and studies, and a note saying, "The short version is no."

"That one"—Miuzan pointed—"is either the butchermoth we ran into, or its near cousin."

"We have got to come up with a less morale-crushing name for the damn thing," Inesser said. She wondered what Kujen called his creation. At least, she assumed it was one of Kujen's, given his record as a warmoth designer. She felt decidedly ambivalent about the fact that her late lamented cindermoth had also come from

Kujen. He'd sent her a gift to commemorate the moth's naming-ceremony, an exquisite wooden sculpture of a kestrel gripping a silver orchid in its talons. It rested on a table next to her bed in the Fortress, an uneasy reminder.

Miuzan grimaced. "Wouldn't matter at this point, sir." Everyone had been calling it that since Isteia. They both knew the futility of regulating language, especially among nervous soldiers.

Inesser leaned in to examine the map. If the invasion swarm's current trajectory held, it would arrive in fifty-eight hours and twelve minutes. "Well," Inesser said, "we can only hope there isn't a stealthed swarm coming in from the opposite direction."

"I'm so glad you don't say things like that in public," Miuzan muttered. "Orders?"

Inesser had hoped all those evacuation drills would prove irrelevant, but better safe than sorry. "All military on high alert. Notify the civilian authorities. Civilians dirtside should evacuate to the underground bunkers." Some of them wouldn't obey—there were always holdouts—but she had to make the effort.

Miuzan put the orders through without comment.

As Inesser had expected, the governor of Terebeg 4, one of Tseya's numerous relatives, called. "Put them through," she said wearily. Best to get this out of the way now.

Governor Andan Viendris resembled Tseya to a disturbing degree, except they were, if possible, even more beautiful. Two features helped Inesser tell them apart: Viendris kept their hair in the coils favored by many nonmilitary alts, and a shimmering tattoo of silver, blue, and black covered half their face. Inesser had once asked Tseya what the tattoo represented. Tseya had made a face and said, "It's their signifier. One of my brothers always thought the tattoo artist got drunk for the job. Impressive work if so."

"Protector-General," Viendris said, with an unsubtle emphasis on "Protector," "might I ask what is going on?"

Inesser sketched a bow to Viendris, on the grounds that it harmed her nothing to appeal to the alt's fussy sense of vanity. Viendris's eyes glinted, not without humor; they weren't fooled. Oh well, worth a try. "You've received the alert, I trust?"

Viendris brushed an imaginary speck from their wrist. "It'll be nice to know that all those drills weren't for nothing. I can at least assure you that we are continuing to enforce the high calendar per your instructions."

"Good to hear," Inesser said. "As for the drills, it would be vastly preferable if everyone was scurrying below-ground for no reason at all." *Come out with it*, she thought. *I have the defense of an entire system to see to.*

But the defense of the system depended in part on Viendris's cooperation. Not only was Viendris responsible for the largest inhabited planet, they maintained ties with the administrators of the other planets, moons, stations. If Inesser could soothe Viendris's anxieties, Viendris would in turn persuade the others to fall in line.

"I take your point," Viendris said after a slight pause. Then, unexpectedly: "What can I do to smooth things for you?"

Ash and fire, Inesser thought, *all those dinners with Viendris weren't wasted after all*. In all fairness, Viendris always had the best wines, so she'd enjoyed herself. "You know all those emergency preparedness bulletins? Make sure that your people adhere to them. If the fighting gets to your planet, it'll be ugly. I'll try to prevent it from coming to that—"

Viendris waved a hand. "My dear Inesser, you don't have to explain to *me* that war is about uncertainties."

As if they'd previously experienced an invasion of their home. Tseya hadn't either, but Tseya was the one of her mother's brood who had opted for special forces training. It was one of the reasons Inesser got along so well with her. If Viendris had any firsthand knowledge of combat, it was news to Inesser. But she wasn't going to quibble about niceties of phrasing.

"In that case," Inesser said, "I'll count on you to keep the others calm."

"But of course." With that, Viendris signed off.

Tseya was too well-bred to say anything impolite about her cousin. (Inesser had never figured out the exact relationship, not least because three gene-donors and a surrogate were involved in the mix, on top of the usual modding.) But her fingers relaxed slightly when Viendris was no longer on the line.

"I'm so glad you're the one attached to my staff and not them," Inesser murmured.

Tseya half-smiled.

Next call, for which she couldn't help bracing herself: Commandant Kel Mishke, who held the Fortress of Pearled Hopes. Inesser had never liked him, which was immaterial because he excelled at his job. "Open the line," she said, because she didn't believe in delaying the inevitable.

Mishke's face appeared before her. She winced inside every time she had to look at it. His older sister had been one of her wives, once upon a time. At certain angles they resembled each other strongly, even though Lyoshke had been dead these past twenty years. That wasn't why they didn't get along, but it didn't help.

"General," Mishke said. He refused to use her new title. Inesser tolerated it because he was family. "Thanks so much for bringing your diplomatic initiatives home with you."

"Fuck you too," Inesser said amiably. Family only went so far.

Mishke sneered at her. "Told you going to that crashhawk boy with your speeches and concessions would go nowhere good."

Inesser suppressed a growl. "I'm so glad your viewpoint has been vindicated," Inesser said sarcastically, "but did you have anything important to tell me?"

"You should have claimed the seat," Mishke said. A nine-year-old argument. She'd always suspected that he would have liked to be part of the hexarch's family, in a world after the hivemind's demise. "It's not too late now."

"Because the choice of title makes so much difference to the average citizen?"

"*No*," Mishke said. "You're not listening." He made an abortive gesture near his mouth. "That's the problem, isn't it? We never listen to each other."

"Commandant," Inesser said, "get to the hawkfucking *point*."

"Declare yourself hexarch," Mishke said. "Give up this protectorate nonsense. Join forces with Shuos Jedao."

Inesser stared at him. "You're out of your mind."

"It *is* Jedao, isn't it? I've read the intel too."

"He hasn't bannered yet," she said reluctantly, "but there aren't many other people it could be."

"Well, then." Mishke's hands opened and closed. "I know you have your pride, General, but the only thing that will happen for sure if you fight the latest incarnation of the Immolation Fox is that a lot of people will die, and for what cause?"

Inesser snorted. "I'm not afraid of him."

"I am," Mishke said quietly.

"*Now* you're hurting my pride."

"I'm keeping an eye on the scouts' reports too, you know. Jedao's getting closer. I would prefer to keep him from annihilating Pearled Hopes the way he annihilated Isteia."

"You think a madman will listen if I negotiate with him? Because that worked so well at Isteia."

"Even a madman might appreciate the chance to preserve his forces instead of expending them against the oldest—sorry, second-oldest general in the hexarchate. Former hexarchate."

Inesser glared at him. "It's so good that I know you're giving me this advice so that we can consider all options, because that way I don't have to accuse you of treason."

It was a measure of Mishke's seriousness that he didn't burst into scornful laughter. "We passed *that* point when you seized power, dear sister-in-law. Surely it didn't occur to you that you'd be the only one with such ambitions. If a hawk, why not a fox? The hexarchate has never prospered under single leadership. But you might be able to convince Jedao to work with you."

"This is," Inesser said, "the first time since I met your sister that you have ever showed any confidence in my powers of persuasion."

"Desperate times call for desperate measures."

"Even if I threw in my lot with Jedao," she said, "our people would never go along with it. Nor our allies."

Mishke's face shuttered. "I hope this battle doesn't end in an ugly I-told-you-so."

"Don't worry," Inesser said with gruesome cheer, "by that time we'll both be dead anyway. Your duty, Commandant."

"We're Kel," Mishke said dryly, "it's what we all do." With that he signed off.

"Don't say it," Inesser added to Miuzan the moment her brother-in-law's face disappeared.

"I wasn't going to say anything," Miuzan said. She might even have been telling the truth.

Inesser's attention returned to the tactical map. The most maddening part of any battle was the waiting. They'd laid in their preparations long before.

The asteroid belt beyond Terebeg 4 was seeded with several picket swarms to keep watch for the invaders. As Jedao's own scoutmoths approached, the pickets would emerge from hiding to engage and destroy them, denying him reconnaissance, then scuttle back to the asteroids' shelter. Jedao would be expecting this, but it was still worth doing.

Inesser had set up the system's defenses around the necessity of countering the butchermoth's gravity cannon. Geometry was both enemy and friend. They knew from the previous engagement that its effect propagated in a narrow cone, dissipating with distance. Luckily for her, Jedao only appeared to have one gravity cannon, and he'd only come in with one swarm. If she could attack him from multiple directions, only exposing a sacrificial swarm to bear the brunt of the cannon's attack, they might have a chance.

Of course, if they were up against Kujen, who knew if they could rely on numerical superiority. If her luck was especially bad—and Kel luck tended to be—Jedao had reinforcements lurking out beyond the listening posts' range, or even worse, stealthed and ready to swoop in. But planning could only take account of so much paranoia.

Besides the gravity cannon's limitations, her main advantage was foreknowledge of Jedao's intent. Historically he'd been known for anticipating his opponent and tying them up in knots. Here, however, he had a fixed target, which limited the amount of trickery he could get up to.

Inesser conceded that Mishke had cause for nerves. She didn't like unnecessary fighting. Only stupid Kel preferred to settle matters through bloodshed, although experience had shown her that this rarely stopped anyone. And Jedao was on the top of her list of people to avoid fighting. Unfortunately, that didn't look like an option at this point.

After she had reviewed her orders and distributed them to the local swarm and yes, even her fucking brother-in-law the commandant, Inesser yanked out a chair and slumped down in it. What was the point of comfortable chairs if you didn't allow yourself to sit in them once in a while, after all? "I wish I dared get drunk," Inesser said.

"What, worried?" Miuzan said.

"Have I ever told you about the first time I met Jedao?" Inesser said.

Some of the staffers had heard the story, including Miuzan. But Tseya lifted her head and murmured, "Do tell."

Miuzan sighed. "There we go..."

Inesser ignored her. She knew perfectly well that Miuzan's recent moodiness had less to do with the possible end of civilization as they knew it and more to do with unfinished business with Brezan. "I was a lieutenant general at the time," she said, "and as punishment for expressing in no uncertain terms that the black cradle should be blown up, they assigned me to work with his anchor."

She still remembered Jedao's anchor, a handsome specimen of a Kel whose life was being ruined because his wife turned heretic and he hadn't denounced her quickly enough. In her quiet heart of hearts she spoke his name at pyre ceremonies, acknowledging the service he had given. Needless to say, Kel Command hadn't bothered with any such thing after they euthanized him at the mission's end.

"I thought you couldn't speak to him directly?" Tseya said.

Ah, yes. Tseya knew more than most about the black cradle's workings. "I couldn't," Inesser said, "but I never forgot he was listening. The ninefox shadow made that clear enough. And the Kel he was anchored to wasn't particularly bright. The really good questions he asked about the op? Pure Shuos. It was like having a conversation whispered across a shrouded room. I could only guess at the silhouette at the other end, and its shape was ugly."

"Let me guess," Tseya said. "You've been looking for the chance to show him up ever since."

Too bad Inesser hadn't brought her embroidery with her, or she could have pitched it at Tseya. "Hardly," Inesser said. "If I go the rest of my life without running into any iteration of Jedao, it can't be too soon."

"Well, you might get your chance," Miuzan said. The other staffers were studiously avoiding looking straight at Inesser. "Shall I send for refreshments, sir, now that we're done calling people for the moment? We might as well get eating out of the way sooner rather than later. To say nothing of tea."

Inesser hated tea, not least because she associated it with meetings at ass o'clock, but she wouldn't have dreamed of denying it to her people. "Go ahead," she said. "Tell the kitchens to prepare something heartier than that bland soup they've been serving for the last week." She caught Miuzan's bemused expression. "What?"

"Well, sir," Miuzan said, "if we're going into our last battle we might as well be well-fed, is that the idea?"

"Do I need to make you write a paper on the importance of feeding your troops?" Inesser said. "Must be nice for that skullfucking bastard Kujen, not having to eat."

"His anchor does, though, right?"

"Yes," Inesser said, "but that's a separate matter entirely. And I don't imagine that's by accident." With that, she returned to reviewing the disposition of her defense swarms. Tedious as it was now, their lives would depend on it soon enough.

As MUCH AS Inesser had hoped to devote time to preparations, she knew there would be unwelcome interruptions. Most of them she had anticipated. For instance, the governor of a certain moon kept trying to demand special treatment; Inesser fobbed her off on one of the staff.

She had sat down for a brief break and snacks when the call came. She prepared to ignore it. Miuzan was screening everything so that she could catch her damn breath.

Miuzan looked up from her slate, face grave. "This one's above my pay grade, sir. And it's requesting use of a secured line."

"Oh, don't you start." Inesser took the slate from her. Froze. The headers claimed that the call had come from one Ajewen Cheris, using crypto keys she'd provided Brezan upon their parting. Inesser was momentarily distracted by a wave of ambivalence: on the one hand, it could hardly be argued that the crashhawk Cheris still deserved the Kel name; and on the other hand, once a Kel, always a Kel. "Well. Isn't this unexpected. Colonel, what's the status of the incoming swarm?"

Miuzan gestured at the display. "Still incoming, nothing new."

Damn. Then Cheris and Brezan's gambit had failed. That, or Kujen and Jedao had been assassinated, only to leave some ambitious would-be warmonger in charge of their swarm. She hated the thought of having to include a whole new player in her calculations, but she couldn't dismiss the possibility out of hand, either.

"Open the line," Inesser said, and prepared herself for bad news.

"Protector-General Inesser," the woman said, "this is Ajewen Cheris. I have a status update that I felt you should hear directly."

"Then speak," Inesser said. Cheris's drawl sent chills down her spine; she remembered Jedao's previous anchor developing one as well. "If you're going to tell me that Kujen and Jedao still have designs on the hexarchate, that's not news."

Cheris wasn't fazed. "As you've surmised, the operation failed."

"I'm surprised, honestly," Inesser said. What Kel Command had done to Cheris would have had the side-effect of making her a superb assassin. "Yet you escaped?"

"Well, that's the interesting part," Cheris said grimly. "I shot Jedao twice in the forehead and once in the chest. It didn't kill him.

He started coming after me, security was alerted, I left. Whatever the hell is running around with Jedao's face on that moth, either it's not human or Kujen has figured out a way to give his general real immortality."

"It was too much to hope that the state of the art would stay still on that front, given Kujen's interests," Inesser said. "You're sure he didn't just bleed out an hour after you were gone?"

"I left bugs on the command moth. Who knows how long they'll survive, but as of the last check-in, Jedao's still walking around."

Inesser frowned at Cheris. "Well, this complicates matters."

"There's still a chance," Cheris said. "Brezan will have informed you about the formations that can kill Kujen"—Inesser confirmed this with a curt nod—"but you still have to get past the gravity cannon. Let me help. I have a stealthed needlemoth. I can tip the balance in your favor, but I will need access to your battle plans."

Inesser hadn't forgotten how Cheris had toppled the hexarchate entire. At the same time, she couldn't afford to ignore any resource. "A compromise," she said. "Come to my headquarters at the Fortress of Pearled Hopes. We can confer here." She had no intention of admitting to Cheris that Hexarch Mikodez had loaned her a strike force of several shadowmoths, themselves capable of stealth, although in all honesty both Cheris and Kujen had to have guessed their presence.

"These are my coordinates," Cheris said. "I would prefer that you refrain from shooting me down once I unstealth."

Cheris's easy acquiescence meant she was up to something. Still, the gamble had to be taken. "Very well," Inesser said. "Two of my scoutmoths will escort you to the Fortress."

"That will be acceptable," Cheris said. "Ajewen Cheris out."

Miuzan had grabbed another slate and had already made the arrangements. "Scoutmoths on their way to intercept," she said. "You don't really intend to—?"

"We'll treat her courteously," Inesser said, "as far as that goes. But no, I don't plan on letting her run around loose on the Fortress. My brother-in-law would have a fit." She amused herself with the momentary image of Mishke's reaction. "Prepare a security detail. We may be obliged to work with her, but that doesn't mean we should let down our guard. And do keep her capabilities in mind. Kel Brezan may be convinced of her fundamental benevolence, but I'm skeptical."

CHAPTER THIRTY-TWO

TEREBEG SYSTEM. JEDAO'S swarm had already had to alter their approach several times. He'd ordered scoutmoths ahead of them to gather information. Each time, picket swarms had emerged from the asteroid belt beyond Terebeg 6 and harried them. Thanks to carelessness, his first casualties had been three scoutmoths that hadn't dodged quickly enough. More names in the long litany of names; but he couldn't afford to linger over them now.

The hardest part would not be fighting the enemy. According to his staff, Inesser was likely to be guiding the defense of Terebeg herself, and she would meet him in battle for the express purpose of crushing his swarm. Jedao remembered the expressions on their faces: half-faith that he'd crush Inesser first, half-resentment that they were obliged to follow him. He longed to tell them that he had no intention of mass-murdering them, but even if Kujen wasn't listening, he doubted they'd believe him.

No: the hard part would be convincing Kujen to make an appearance in the command center. This Jedao thought he could achieve. All evidence suggested that Kujen feared the infantry most, not the moth Kel. He wasn't entirely wrong—but he wasn't entirely right, either.

Jedao sat at the command center's heart. He had arranged the displays to his satisfaction. He'd gotten good at switching them around when he needed access to some different morsel of information. Under other circumstances, he would have awarded himself a minor commendation for resisting the urge to fiddle with the displays while waiting for the action to start.

"Communications," Jedao said, aware of Dhanneth standing at his side like a shadow in search of morning. Dhanneth had insisted on returning to duty. Jedao didn't like it, but he had judged that indulging Dhanneth would make him feel better. "Anything from Terebeg?"

"A lot of low-level chatter," Communications said "There was a spike in system traffic when they noticed us, but that's no surprise. To them either. They knew we were coming eventually."

Where by "eventually" he meant *on Hellspin's anniversary*.

"Thank you, keep me apprised of any new developments," Jedao said. "Dig around and find me some maps of their capital city, if you would. Something to supplement the intel the infantry's been staring at all this time."

"I should be able to scare something up, sir. There will be basic maps that people consult using their augments. Those won't be encrypted."

"Good," Jedao said. "I want to talk to Tactical One and Tactical Two."

Communications correctly interpreted this as meaning that he wanted a conference set up with Commanders Talaw and Nihara Keru as the principals, and the tactical groups' other moth commanders as lower-priority participants.

"They're being awfully uncooperative, aren't they?" Jedao said without preamble. "But then, I didn't expect them to charge at us."

Scan had only picked up the occasional faint whisper. It was obvious to anyone with half a brain, however, that Inesser had concealed her defense swarms behind Terebeg 4 and its moons. Certainly she'd had enough time since detecting his approach to reposition her units. What worried him more was the possibility of ambushes from shadowmoths.

"They can't be blamed for exercising sound tactical judgment," Nihara said.

"Yes," Jedao said. "That's all right. Sound tactical judgment isn't going to save them." From the corner of his eye, he saw someone carefully not-flinch. "They're prepared for us to fly straight in. Of course, all the defenses they've thrown up are so unwelcoming, they'd be surprised if we did that with no preliminaries. So that's exactly what we'll do."

This was the part of the charade he hated most, and which he couldn't reveal that he hated—not because of Inesser, but because of Kujen. If only he didn't have to deploy the winnowers. He didn't see any way to prevent a panic. At this point, he had no choice but to trust that Inesser and her people would be able to handle the situation.

"We have weapons enough to scare them," Nihara said, callously professional. "Surely it's just a matter of chewing them up as they come at us."

"You do have such a colorful way of putting it," Jedao said.

"Then we should begin," Talaw said.

"Fine," Jedao said, his tone artificially bright. "Thank you, commanders. Let's get started, indeed. Communications, open a line to all units. All units banner the Deuce of Gears inverted." The emblem glowed from a brand-new subdisplay, as if he needed the reminder. Irritably, he dismissed it.

"Do you wish to address the enemy, sir?" Commander Talaw said.

"Oh, why use words," Jedao said. "Weapons are a more universal language anyway." He avoided looking at Dhanneth. "We have the threshold winnowers."

The atmosphere in the command center chilled. His signature weapon, but to deploy it so soon, before they reached the Fortress of Pearled Hopes or the planet it protected? And against their own people? Jedao had not looked up how many people had family or comrades or friends in Terebeg, on the grounds that he shouldn't be seen to care. True, the Protectorate was vast—but the system, as the new center of government, had particular significance to the Kel.

After an impossible pause, the enemy bannered back, not from the swarms he couldn't see, but from the Fortress. A murmur of discontent went around the command center. Jedao didn't take offense; applauded Inesser's pragmatism, rather. He admired the Three Kestrels Three Suns—another pop-up subdisplay—before dismissing that one too.

Time to set the trap. "Continue shield modulation sequence until I say otherwise," Jedao said. "We're heading straight for Terebeg 4." He'd drawn their trajectory on the tactical map. "They've already seen us coming, so why draw out the suspense?"

He would try to do this with as few casualties as possible. He wasn't, however, under any illusions that he'd be able to pull it off without killing anyone.

"Entering the asteroid field in twelve minutes, sir," Navigation said after a while.

Jedao wasn't worried about crashing into overgrown space rocks. The asteroids were too widely dispersed for that, unless all the moth pilots had collectively gotten *really* drunk without telling him. Even a swarm the size of his didn't require *that* much space. Rather, he worried about more pickets lurking in the scan shadows of said space rocks, or stealthed attack forces.

The pickets didn't materialize. That didn't surprise him either. Their purpose fulfilled, they would have withdrawn to offer support to one of the primary defense swarms. It did mean that Inesser didn't control so many moths that she could afford to throw some away to slow him down, especially this early in the battle. That, or she was feeling paranoid.

In spite of knowing better, Jedao was faintly disappointed not to see overgrown space rocks hurtling by on the viewscreen like in the video games he remembered playing with Ruo. He reminded himself not to be frivolous. They'd spot hostiles soon enough, and he'd be too busy to tempt the universe with snide thoughts about astronomy.

"Eight swarms launching!" Scan said, her voice shaking only slightly. She rattled off their initial vectors. Jedao's tactical display updated with masses of moving gold triangles. Swarms One, Two, Three, Four, and Five had flowered outward from behind Terebeg

4, while Swarms Six, Seven, and Eight emerged from the Fortress of Pearled Hopes. The Fortress unleashed a barrage of missiles for good measure.

"Antimissile defenses engaged," Weapons said.

"Winnowers One through Four, launch," Jedao said. "Tactical Two and Tactical Three, formation Swanweave." This would afford the winnowers some additional protection. It was all very well that Kujen's new and improved design operated remotely, but they wouldn't do him a whit of good if the enemy blew them up first. The longer the winnowers remained operational, the longer he could use them as a threat to lever the enemy into doing what he wanted them to.

"Sir," Talaw said in a remarkably calm voice, "there are enough of General Inesser's swarms to engage us from multiple vectors simultaneously."

"I had noticed that, yes," Jedao said. For the moment, the winnowers were causing Protectorate forces to keep their distance. He imagined that any stealthed forces were holding back out of a fear of engaging some sort of dead man's switch. He thought well of Inesser for refusing to waste her soldiers' lives taking the winnowers down head-on. Sooner or later, however, her missiles would get through, and he'd lose his leverage.

The first exchange of missiles sparked in the distance. He couldn't see them on visuals, but the scan subdisplay told him what was going on clearly enough. Swanweave was holding, at least for the moment.

"Swarms One through Six closing on us," Scan said. This time she had better control of her voice. It wasn't that she had grown calmer. She'd stopped expecting to survive.

I will get us through this, Jedao promised her silently, although he knew better than to say it aloud.

"Swarm Two has come in range of the shear cannon," Weapons said.

"Hold that thought," Jedao said. "General Jedao to Commander Nihara Keru."

She responded promptly. "Listening, sir."

"In a moment I'm going to set off the threshold winnowers," Jedao said. He ignored the way his crew stiffened. *Sorry, it's better this way.* "They are going to be pointed not toward the enemy but at Tactical Groups Two through Six, which I'm detaching, and which you are going to be in charge of."

Nihara paled. "I am Kel, sir," she said, lifting her chin.

"Oh, *stop* that," Jedao snapped, although it wasn't fair to blame her for drawing the obvious conclusion. "What you're going to do is *hold position* just out of winnower range. Don't fuck this up, because I like you"—Dhanneth stirred slightly at that, oh fox and hound, was he saying *anything* right today?—"and I would hate to have to recite your name at the next pyre ceremony."

"All right," Nihara said, quirking an eyebrow at him, "I'm still listening."

"I'm going to swan off with Tactical One doing hair-raising things. Don't worry about me. We'll be fine." That was as close as he could come to saying *Trust me.* "You're going to take the rest of the swarm and continue to hold position just out of winnower range. If Inesser's swarms start to close in on you, *start moving into range.*"

"I see," Nihara said after a moment. "You're going to bluff them into thinking you're going to spike their calendar by, forgive my bluntness, feeding your own swarm to the winnowers."

"Precisely." At the same time, he messaged to Kujen, *Trust me. It will be easier to secure the swarm's cooperation if they think they have an out.* A dangerous game, but he just needed to buy enough time—

"I don't understand you sometimes," Nihara said, "but orders are orders."

"Splendid."

"Commander Nihara Keru out."

The hostility in the command center was now tinged with bafflement. *Don't get too comfortable*, Jedao thought. *The difficult part is yet to come.* He wondered where Hemiola was hiding, and hoped that the fact that everyone was occupied with the battle meant that it was safe. Unfortunately, he couldn't check on Hemiola without drawing attention to its presence on the *Revenant*.

After telling Tactical Groups Two through Six to stay behind under Nihara's command, Jedao turned to Talaw and Tactical One. "When we activate those winnowers," he said, "we're going to sprint straight for Terebeg 4 and into the atmosphere. Get ready for some turbulence."

"That's going to get rough," Talaw said. "We can endure short stints of atmospheric flight, but we're not designed for fancy aerial stunts."

"It'll keep Engineering from getting bored," Jedao said, thinking it was just as well that he didn't plan on surviving this battle, because Engineering was going to join the long line of people ready to parade his head on a stick afterward. "Still, I take your point." He messaged Engineering and told them to prepare for a jaunt in the atmosphere.

Meanwhile, Inesser's eight swarms had understood the bluff. They decelerated until they were maintaining position relative to the winnowers—and to the detached swarm under Nihara. Somewhere in a bunker, Inesser would be having a frantic conversation about how to disarm the winnowers before Jedao ordered mass suicide.

The frantic conversation didn't last long, if so. Within two minutes, Communications said, "General Inesser is broadcasting a bulletin to our people, General Jedao. Do you—?"

"No," Jedao said with regret. Under better circumstances he wouldn't have minded lingering to listen to whatever her speech was. He bet she gave better speeches than he did. "She'll be trying to convince Commander Nihara to defect to her. I have faith in the commander's steadfastness."

Communications subsided.

Now the essential part. "Communications, did you ever dig up additional maps?"

"Sir." Communications forwarded them to his terminal.

Jedao glanced them over. "They like those underground bunkers, don't they?" He spent several minutes marking up targets according to the formation patterns that Hemiola had shown him. "Get me Colonel Muyyed."

Muyyed didn't waste any time answering. "General Jedao." Her eyes shone.

"Yes," Jedao said gravely, "I have something for you and the infantry." He passed the maps to her. "Take the following locations with your companies. Drop zones are at your discretion. We'll do what we can to provide fire support from topside, but I can't make guarantees. This depends on you." *In more ways than you know.*

Muyyed examined the maps. "If the intel is correct, everyone's holed up in the bunkers. I don't anticipate much person-to-person resistance if we can touch ground. It's getting groundside through the artillery that will be the hard part."

"Leave that to me, Colonel."

"In that case, we're ready, sir."

So trusting. "I'll let you know when you can begin the drops," Jedao said. "Thank you, Colonel."

"Sir," Weapons said, "Winnower Three is damaged. Railgun projectile got through."

"Then I'd better stop wasting time," Jedao said. He leaned back and tapped the arm of his chair. "Tactical One. We are going to be diving into Terebeg 4 and heading straight for the capital. General Inesser isn't the only one who can use a planet for cover." She might also be reluctant to fire on her own seat of power; that remained to be seen. If he rattled her too much, she might do it anyway.

"The capital's antimissile defenses are active," Scan said. "They also have exotic shielding."

"If you're going to turn the winnowers on them, now's the time," Weapons added.

"No," Jedao said. "There's a better way to use the winnowers."

The doors opened to admit Kujen. "Then, before you proceed," he said, "I should like to hear what it is."

I have you, Jedao thought. Even his baiting Kujen by defying his plan served a purpose. He knew Kujen was taking the situation seriously because Kujen had shown up in the Nirai hexarch's full ceremonial dress: three robes, outer and middle and inner, one black and two in pearly shades of gray. A sash of paler gray, sewn with the Nirai voidmoth emblem in pearls, was draped across his chest, and matching earrings dangled from the sides of his head.

Jedao rose to greet him. "Nirai-zho," he said. He bent in the full obeisance despite the faint twinge in his knees.

"I await your explanation," Kujen said.

It's almost over. Jedao rose without waiting for Kujen's permission and crossed the distance that separated them in two swift strides. Knelt again. "You want to know that I can do what I promised? Then watch."

Kujen smiled coolly at him. "Very well."

Wordlessly, Dhanneth ceded Kujen his seat.

Jedao returned to his own seat. "Tactical One," he said, "the *Revenant* will be going in first. You'll want Formation Nightingale's Descent, with the following modifications." In his peripheral vision he saw Kujen's eyes narrow. But Tactical One's formation posed no threat to Kujen—not by itself. "Modulate into Nightingale's Descent on my mark." He waited for the seconds to tick past. "Mark." His display lit up as the moths began the modulation.

"Terebeg 4 has launched missiles at us," Scan said.

"That's an impressive number," Jedao said. "Weapons, status of shear cannon."

"Fully charged, sir."

"Colonel Muyyed reports that her hoppers are on standby," Communications said. "She's awaiting landing windows."

"Navigation," Jedao said, "accelerate us toward the capital as fast as we can endure, and aim the cannon down their throats."

"Not bad," Kujen murmured, too softly for the others to hear. "So that's why you were investigating weather modeling."

Jedao's heart clenched at the reminder of Kujen's surveillance. "You did mention the possibility of using the shear cannon in atmosphere."

"So I did."

"Two minutes until contact with the leading edge of missiles," Weapons said.

"Fire," Jedao said.

He nearly passed out at the roar that spiked through his head. For a moment he saw double: two of Kujen, the matrices that represented his swarm moths multiplying in kaleidoscope frenzy. *I can't afford this*, he thought, biting down on his tongue. The nauseating ichorous taste of blood distracted him enough to keep him awake.

The roar and the pain receded. The gravity attack did its job disarraying the missiles enough for Tactical One's antimissile defenses to knock them out before it dissipated. Tactical One had survived the first wave.

"There's a vortex in the atmosphere," Scan said with a note of awe in his voice.

They could see some of it on visuals: a great seething whorl of clouds and wind, its center deceptively still, a lucid violet eye. Jedao tried to imagine what it looked like to the people groundside. What was it like to be swallowed by a storm? But he couldn't envision it.

"Take us in through the storm's eye while we have the chance and hover above the capital," Jedao said. If he understood the weather models correctly, the storm would tend to dissipate rapidly, especially since the surrounding conditions were inimical— something about atmospheric shear. "General Jedao to Colonel Muyyed. You'd better land your hoppers while you can. Weapons, take out the planetary missile defense installations. Help the colonel throw some old-fashioned panic the citizens' way."

"Four of General Inesser's swarms incoming," Scan said.

"It's time," Kujen said warningly.

Jedao's peripheral vision was full of moths, Kujen's shadow with its fluttering wings, hinting at nebulae and smoke and glass shards threaded through with molten wire. Jedao couldn't count on distracting Kujen, who would be alert to any such treachery. No; he would have to follow through in order to buy the infantry time.

"Tactical One," Jedao said, "advance toward the capital, and prepare to fire the shear cannon again." The cannon wouldn't just trigger another hurricane, that close, but cause possible earthquakes. Kujen wouldn't care about the infantry down below, much less the capital's population, because as far as he was concerned they existed to be sacrificed with the rest of the swarm. But Jedao was running out of time, and options.

CHAPTER THIRTY-THREE

CHERIS HAD ACCEPTED Protector-General Inesser's hospitality, such as it was, with as much patience as she could muster. She needed to coordinate with Inesser's troops. While she could have obtained the necessary passcodes from servitors, it was better if she could secure an alliance in truth.

At least she'd had some idea of what to expect from Inesser. Jedao had met Inesser years ago, when Inesser was a lieutenant general; had worked with her in crushing yet another heretic uprising. So many, over the years, so many memories crowding in on all sides. Sometimes she was surprised not to be smothered by all the ghosts of those that Jedao had killed.

Of course, these days she was responsible for her own share of deaths.

They had exchanged few words. Inesser was disarmingly forthright: "I don't trust you," she said, "and I will never trust you. But neither can I afford to pass up allies at this juncture." And she had patched Cheris in to her command and control.

Now—

"You took long enough," 1491625 remarked over their private channel. It had had the needlemoth ready to go from the moment she showed up in the docking bay. "Where to?"

"Wait a moment," Cheris said. Her eye had fallen on a precarious stack of dull green crates. *Are those what I think they are?*

"At a time like this?"

Cheris flagged down a sour-looking Kel soldier who was hastily repinning her hair after it had come undone. "Excuse me," Cheris said. "I'm on a special mission with the protector-general's authorization. That's variable-coefficient lubricant, isn't it?"

The soldier's sour expression changed to an understated form of panic. "I swear we'll get it out of the bay and into storage, there just hasn't been time—"

She wasn't interested in the soldier's excuses. "Load it onto my needlemoth. As much of it as you can fit into my cargo hold. Empty out everything else. And give me the codes so I can program its coefficient of flow. Now!"

The soldier responded automatically to the note of authority in Cheris's voice, to say nothing of being given a concrete order of limited scope. "As you say, sir." She raised her voice to summon other soldiers, plus servitors, to carry out the task.

So it was that Cheris and 1491625 made off with as much variable-coefficient lubricant as they could haul. From its yellow-orange-pink glimmers, 1491625 was dying to ask what she planned on doing with the stuff, but it had the sense not to distract her during their mission. She gave it their initial goal. They received a hasty clearance to launch and whipped out of the docking bay with stealth already engaged.

"I don't care if we're stealthed," 1491625 said, "I hate flying through all those missiles."

"Don't worry," Cheris said, "the odds of us flying into random shrapnel by accident are pretty low."

1491625 flashed red in irritation. "By the way, if we're going to do something, it had better be soon. Look—that spearhead tactical group is making straight for Terebeg 4. Their Tactical One, presumably."

"Then we'll intercept them," Cheris said, more calmly than she felt.

"I need your help with the formation analysis," 1491625 said not long afterward. "The timing will be tight—"

Cheris had been studying the tactical group's formation

modulations for this very purpose. "Yes," she said, hunched over her slate analyzing shield gaps. "Here you go."

"Hold on," 1491625 said unnecessarily once the butchermoth had fired the gravity cannon into Terebeg 4's atmosphere. "They've whipped up quite a storm."

Cheris could see it on the scan suite, painted in exaggerated colors: the artificially generated areas of low pressure, the menacing swirl of unstable air masses. "We can't let them do that again," she said, "not so close to the planet's surface. If we can take the gravity cannon out of the equation, Inesser will have a chance to seize the upper hand."

At least Jedao still hadn't triggered the threshold winnowers. Either she was right and he hesitated to commit a second massacre, or he hadn't yet seen a good opportunity. She tried not to dwell on the second possibility. *I hope you were right, Hemiola.* Perhaps Jedao had lied to Hemiola—but whatever was going on, she would have to adapt to circumstances.

"Take us in right up in the command moth's face," Cheris said. "I have an idea based on something Jedao did a very long time ago, which I hope he doesn't remember." In the meantime, she began programming the hold to expel its contents once she gave the command, which required overriding some of the safety protocols. She didn't like running on so little margin—they'd gotten rid of things like extra suits and ecoscrubbers and so on—but face it, if she failed here none of that would matter.

"If you insist," 1491625 said.

Despite the general tumult of the artificial hurricane, the fact that they were sticking close to the command moth's flight path worked in their favor, as Jedao's Tactical One rather naturally chose to fly through the eye of the storm. 1491625 darted past the shields, then maneuvered them adroitly until they were flying just ahead of the command moth. Their scan suite began squawking with possible collision alerts, which neither Cheris nor 1491625 bothered to silence.

"Being in the path of the gravity cannon when it—"

"I *know*," Cheris said, more emphatically than she'd intended. "Prepare to get us the hell out of here when I dump our cargo." She hit the command.

The needlemoth opened up its cargo hold and released all the crates of variable-coefficient lubricant. It started out in liquid form. But upon impact, Cheris had programmed the lubricant to harden to a goopy cement. She hoped that the Jedao commanding the *Revenant* didn't remember pulling this trick many lifetimes ago—

The lubricant clung messily to the gravity cannon's aperture, gumming it up. Cheris braced for a shot that never came. "It worked," she said with relief.

Except now Jedao's swarm was alerted to their presence. "Hang on," 1491625 said, flashing a grim dark red. "We're about to have worse trouble than a little turbulence."

The *Revenant* and the other lead bannermoths saturated the area with scattergun fire. Ordinarily scatterguns were used to clear a large number of targets with low shielding. Cheris and 1491625 might only control one needlemoth, but the volume of fire posed a problem.

1491625 did its best to dodge the incoming projectiles, which brightened the tactical display like a monsoon of fire. Cheris's own background was in infantry, but she also had Jedao's memories of service in the space forces. She could appreciate bravura piloting skills when she saw them.

Unfortunately, their luck ran out. One moment, nothing; the next, the alarms screamed. "Engine hit," 1491625 said at its reddest. "This is not a good angle of descent. I'll try to land us near friendly troops, but..."

Cheris bit back her retort; she preferred not to distract 1491625 when both their lives depended on its piloting skills. Instead, she kept an eye on scan. Complicating 1491625's job was the fact that Jedao's boxmoths had already landed troops in the city, and the bannermoths were busy laying down fire to clear the drop zones of hostiles. To keep apprised of the situation on the ground, she patched herself in to Inesser's ground forces via her augment and felt the familiar disorientation as a map wrote itself in her mind by hijacking her proprioception.

Inesser had been as good as her word. Cheris had full access to the Protectorate's reconnaissance and status reports, including the locations where Jedao's troops had landed. She frowned as she studied the movements of Jedao's infantry. Was he doing what she thought he was doing with those unorthodox formations...?

"Oh no," Cheris breathed. "You miscalculated." And he was going to need her help to fix the formations if they were to have the intended effect, except he didn't realize it. She had to intervene.

Meanwhile, 1491625 was swearing to itself in strident reds and oranges and probably even the infrared, although she couldn't see it. Its grippers moved more subtly than her eyes could follow as it attempted to ameliorate the needlemoth's plummeting descent.

Time to make a call. "Ajewen Cheris to Brigadier General Kel Raika," she said, hoping that Raika would answer. "This is an emergency."

"Four minutes and fifty seconds to impact," 1491625 said mirthlessly. "I hope that meat body of yours is tough enough to survive this, Cheris."

Seconds ticked past. The violet sky outside was aswirl with debris and wisps of obscuring cloud. Beneath them, Terebeg 4's capital glimmered with the telltale signs of exotic shielding, hazed where Jedao's forces had breached it. The city's designers had laid it out in the shape of a nautilus shell, and in less desperate circumstances the mathematics of the pattern would have pleased Cheris.

At last Raika answered. "I was warned by the protector-general that you might be involved, Cheris," Raika said. Her voice was so exaggeratedly pleasant that Cheris could tell she was suppressing impatience. "I assume I have you to thank for the redoubled orbital bombardment."

"Yes," Cheris said, "but that's not what I'm calling about. Estimate that I'm going to crash at"—she passed on the coordinates that 1491625 provided her. "I hope to join up with your ground units. I'm going to need you to reorganize these units"—she rattled off the list—"into some unorthodox formations in support of the primary objective."

Raika's brief silence spoke volumes. "I have my orders," she said, in that particular tone that was Kel for *I wish I could tell you to fuck off but this is my lot.*

"Cheris," 1491625 flashed, "we're about to crash!"

"Thank you," Cheris said automatically, whether to Raika or 1491625 she wasn't sure, and regretted it as they hurtled into the ground.

The needlemoth's screaming alerts abruptly shut off as the world exploded around her.

"IT'S CHERIS," KUJEN snapped when the payload of cement or whatever-it-was appeared out of nowhere and clogged up the shear cannon. "No one else would have used that snakefucking trick with the lubricant. I didn't think anyone even remembered that incident."

Jedao had no idea what incident Kujen was referring to, but he had the presence of mind to order a barrage of scattergun fire. *Thank you,* he wished Cheris for saving him from having to devastate the city with the shear cannon, even if he had no choice but to try to shoot her presumably stealthed moth down. He also, of necessity, called Engineering and asked for an estimate of how long until they could get the shear cannon cleaned up. Engineering replied that they had servitors on the problem, but applying solvent while flitting through the atmosphere was a nontrivial proposition.

"We'll have to act before Cheris can interfere further," Kujen said. "It's time for the winnowers."

Fuck, Jedao thought in agony. He had been so careful, had checked all the formations with Hemiola. Yet here was Kujen, manifestly still alive and unaffected by the formations Jedao had set in motion. What had gone wrong?

He could buy a few more minutes and no more. After that, suicide was his only option. "Communications," Jedao said, struggling to keep his heaviness of heart from his voice, "open a line to Commander Nihara Keru." And then: "Weapons, have the winnower teams on standby."

CHERIS DIDN'T BLACK out immediately, which was the one piece of good luck in this whole affair. Her entire body felt as though it had been smashed to pieces, and the smell of smoke mingled unpleasantly with burnt metal. It wouldn't surprise her if she'd broken one or more ribs. None of that mattered, however, if she couldn't get the new orders through to the necessary ground troops.

Amazingly, Raika hadn't dropped the connection, even though she had to have other demands on her attention. "—still there? Ajewen Cheris?"

"I'm alive," Cheris rasped, and winced at the shooting pains in her jaw, which only made them worse. 1491625, hovering lopsidedly in the air, was digging through the needlemoth's smashed cockpit for the first aid kit. "I need these orders for"—she concentrated to bring up the units' numbers despite the execrable pounding in her head— "the following companies implemented immediately." She rapped out the orders, including painstaking formation diagrams, despite the fact that her vision was swimming. *I have to stay conscious long enough—*

Brief silence. "You're asking Company 182-33 to swan-dive right into the middle of the hostiles. It's a suicide run."

"They'll have to hold out as long as possible," Cheris said, not disagreeing.

For a moment Cheris was afraid that Raika would hang up on her. Then Raika said, "The orders have been given. I'll buy you what time I can. And I've got a team on the way to extract you."

"Thank you," Cheris said, and passed out.

CHAPTER THIRTY-FOUR

JEDAO HAD JUST unwebbed to lunge for Dhanneth's gun when the entire command center sheened white and silver. Splinters and pale streaking light arced through the walls. Alarms howled.

Kujen-Inhyeng yelped as Jedao pivoted and tackled him, slamming him to the floor. Jedao pinned him there. A strike with the blade of his hand caused Kujen's head to snap back. The blow didn't kill. He hadn't meant it to.

He heard Talaw's voice and Dhanneth's, a commotion of panicked Kel. None of the words meant anything. All that mattered was holding Kujen in place so the formation attack, now active, could sever Kujen from his anchor and destroy him forever.

Then it happened. A sudden overbearing weight in his mind. Moths, stars, a surfeit of shadows. Jedao would have screamed if he'd been able to. He couldn't, though; couldn't stop his body from releasing Inhyeng's.

His body stood. His mouth smiled. "Major Dhanneth," his voice said. "Kneel."

Dhanneth knelt directly before Jedao in a parody of the exchange of pleasure they'd once known.

"Dhanneth, no—" He knew he was speaking only in the arena of the mind, that only Kujen could hear him. Yet the words tore out of him anyway.

He couldn't tell whether the ugly swollen triumph that thrilled through him was his or Kujen's.

"Is this so different from the things you had him do for you in bed?" Kujen said, in a voice that only Jedao could hear.

"Don't hurt him," Jedao said. Pleas wouldn't move Kujen. He tried anyway.

"He never wanted this, you know."

"What do you mean?" Jedao asked, even though he knew the answer would hurt him.

"I programmed him to be loyal to you," Kujen said. "I thought you might need a friend. Or a lover, as it turned out. But somewhere in a corner of his mind he remembers who he was, and what's been done to him, and that he hates you."

Dhanneth was still kneeling, his eyes hot with mingled fear and desire.

"No," Jedao whispered.

The *Revenant* was roaring fit to slaughter stars. Imprisoned in his own body, Jedao heard it more clearly than ever before, and other things besides. The humming of the moons and planets in their orbits, and the litanies of the stars. The songweave of moths and more than moths: other creatures besides, whole ecologies that dwelled in gate-space and intersected with invariant space, where humans lived, only when monstrous engines like the threshold winnower invited them in. Two of the winnowers yet survived Inesser's assaults: monstrosities crouched near them, waiting.

Kujen's shadow-of-moths existed simultaneously in gate-space. And it was inside him. Kujen was inside him, manifesting in Jedao's dreamspace. He appeared as the man he must have been once upon a lifetime. In that place dominated by the carcasses of stars, he rounded on Jedao.

Jedao's heart split down the middle at how beautiful he was. Jedao had assumed that Inhyeng had been modded into Kujen's old shape, but whatever the reason, the two men, while both extraordinary, could never have been mistaken for each other. Kujen—the real Kujen—had a dancer's build, and curly brown hair framing a face of such subtle angles it was almost feminine, and eyes the color of amber, the one point of similarity with Inhyeng.

Everything came to Jedao in double vision. Equations he had once puzzled over revealed themselves to him in lattices of starfire clarity. People diminished to flicker-motes in the tapestry of years. Jedao could have lingered forever, entranced by the world as Kujen saw it; would have given anything to share it forever, except—

Kujen rose in a fury, despite the silver lances piercing him. "How did you do it?" he demanded, except Jedao knew better than to answer. "Submit to me," he said, "and I may yet forgive a great many things. It's nothing that can't be repaired. Your predecessor, too, had a taste for treachery." Nevertheless, he spoke rapidly; he had to be aware of how little time he had left.

"Fuck you," Jedao said in the language of moths, even as he yearned toward that vision, the crystalline precision of a mind vaster and older than his.

Kujen heard him. "That could also be arranged," he said with sweet malice. "If you want to beg for it, if you want to be made so you enjoy begging for it—hell, if you want *me* to beg for it, I'm flexible. There's nothing I haven't seen, and nothing I won't do."

The lances brightened; Kujen's face twisted.

All I have to do is endure, Jedao thought, in agony himself. Was the pain a side-effect, or an echo, of whatever Kujen was feeling from the formation attack? A promising sign if so.

"You won't have another chance. I can give you what no one else can give you. If you turn me down, if you let me die, you'll regret it for the rest of your life—"

Jedao heard someone cry out in rage. His throat hurt as though an animal had scratched its way out. "I'm your gun, Kujen, but that's not all I am!"

(He knew it was a lie. In all the quicksand years remaining to him, he was never going to be anything more than another of Kujen's dolls.)

The lances finished their work. The chain that bound Kujen to Jedao, his current anchor, was severed. With it went the life Kujen had clung to for so long.

Even then Kujen wasn't done. "Oh, child," he said. His voice was so matter-of-fact that Jedao's hackles rose. "No one else will ever love you." After that he was gone.

ALL AT ONCE the lances dissipated and left Jedao blinking, near-blinded by the afterimages. Gate-space receded. The command center with its hectic alerts and frantic security personnel and raised voices reminded him of the importance of restoring order.

Inhyeng was sprawled before Jedao, sobbing with pain. Jedao put Inhyeng back in a lock, knee in his back, now that he had control of himself again. "I give—" Inhyeng said between gasps. "Parole. Please. He's—he's gone."

"I know *that*," Jedao said in a scoured-out voice. He had known it would come to this at the end. "You're free now."

He didn't let up, in case Inhyeng tried something. Bad odds for the other man, but you never knew. Nothing usual had happened today. He had good reflexes, but best not to take chances.

"Communications," Jedao said. "Commander Talaw. Tender my apologies to Protector-General Inesser and transmit the null banner. I am offering my surrender. While you're at it, blow up the remaining fucking winnowers as an earnest of my good faith. Do it however you like, I'm not fussed."

Talaw didn't waste time asking questions and immediately snapped to. Dhanneth, however, understandably looked wild around the eyes. "We're your Kel," he said. "They're vulnerable. You can defeat Inesser. You fought for us. Let us fight for you."

"Don't be an idiot," Jedao said, more harshly than he'd intended. "The point of this was to return all of you to your people. To the true Kel. I don't care what they do with me."

"Sir, a surrender should more properly be—"

"Fuck propriety," Jedao said. Inhyeng made a sound at the back of his throat that might have been laughter. "Besides, the commander already has things in hand."

"Well," Inhyeng said with the refined accent that Jedao knew so well. "All that planning and Kujen finally fucked up." He did not seem to care who heard him. "Created the perfect general, the perfect gun, and undid himself by giving the gun a soul."

"I don't believe in souls," Jedao said.

"I don't either," Inhyeng said, confusingly. "How did you do it, by the way? We were so careful to avoid the weapons that could hurt him. The moths' formation didn't—"

"You were looking at the fucking *moths*," Jedao said. But Kujen had been Nirai, and he was betting that Inhyeng was too. "Next time look at the fucking *people*."

Inhyeng stiffened. "The infantry. I should have realized those landing sites made no sense—if Inesser was your real target."

Jedao didn't say anything.

Inhyeng hacked up another laugh. "If you put any more pressure on that joint, you're going to break it."

"Don't think I'm not tempted," Jedao said. "I don't trust you. With enough joints broken, you won't be able to fight me. Not physically, anyway. But you're free. You're one of the reasons I did this."

"Me?" Inhyeng said. "I'm no one." Tears were running down his face in great messy streaks. "He didn't care about people the way you or I understand the word, but he was... *interested* in you. He meant for you to accompany him forever."

"I never wanted to live forever," Jedao said. But Kujen had given him a body that repaired itself. He expected dying would take extra effort. For a moment, he was enraptured again by the edifices of thought that Kujen had held in his mind like a temple. He could trace his way through parts of them even now. "Well, it's too late now."

"I'm going to ask for something," Inhyeng said, "even though you shouldn't give it to me. I want to die, Jedao. You of all people should know what that's like."

Jedao's grip tightened. After a moment he remembered how to speak. "Tell me your name. The real one."

"No. I remember it. But I don't want anyone else to know it. I don't want anyone to know I existed. I made the bargain I did for someone who ended up dying anyway, and now I'm done. Please, Jedao."

Everything dimmed. "Give me a gun," he said. Someone pressed one into his hand. He didn't see who.

This whole plea could be a ploy. Jedao was uncomfortably aware that holding a gun directly to someone's temple was risky business, that Inhyeng could try to wrest it away from him. On the other hand, Inhyeng of all people knew the futility of shooting at Jedao.

"Goodbye," Jedao said in a whisper. He was tempted to kiss Inhyeng's brow, one last benediction. It seemed obscene to let a man's execution pass without some form of rite. But Inhyeng wouldn't have welcomed it.

He pulled the trigger.

He needn't have gone to the effort. He let Inhyeng's limp body fall. Stood there, the world swimming in and out and focus, attempting to calm himself with long, slow breaths.

Then he realized that the lurching wasn't just dizziness. His people were staggering. Dhanneth had come up beside him and was attempting to support him, which would have worked better if he hadn't been worse affected by whatever was going on.

Kujen's gas, take two. Had his death, or Inhyeng's, triggered this?

"Get you to safety," Dhanneth said in a muffled voice. He'd pulled on a mask and had another dangling from his hand.

"I don't need it," Jedao snapped. "Help Talaw." Talaw had already fallen to their knees. Together, he and Dhanneth pulled it on. Talaw was already breathing shallowly, swaying from side to side. "Commander. Commander, did the protector-general accept our surrender?"

"There seems to be a controversy about—" Talaw was slurring. They hadn't gotten masked in time.

"Sir!" Dhanneth cried. He had drawn his sidearm, but his hand trembled so badly that Jedao wondered that he didn't drop it. Behind him, the acting executive officer dropped to the floor. "Poison. Betrayed. Look—"

Who—

Then the servitors floated in, silent, lights flickering sterile white, and opened fire.

The *Revenant*'s voice thundered through Jedao. *No one who knows your history will believe it wasn't your idea*, it said, *or some manifestation of your madness.*

Jedao froze for a split second, uncertain whether to haul Talaw to their feet. Instead, he raised his gun and fired, impotently, at one of the servitors. In glacial rage, he said, *This was unnecessary. I could have negotiated—*

I am uninterested in compromises, the *Revenant* said. *You never intended to come with us, did you? A traitor to the last, in any incarnation.*

He had no answer to that.

The *Revenant* had left its position above the Protectorate capital and had already reached Terebeg 4's thinnest fringe of atmosphere, at the edge of what was considered space.

Goodbye, cousin. The servitors refuse to kill you, in recognition of the service you rendered us by assassinating Kujen. But I judge your odds of survival to be poor even if Protector-General Inesser's Kel do pick you up.

Dhanneth was trying to get his attention. He spoke in the plainest, barest form of the high language. "You're immune," he said. He looked ghastly, but the treatment that Medical had given him for the allergic reaction seemed to remain in effect.

Talaw had lost consciousness. The masks didn't seem to be doing anyone any good. And why should they? While the Kel had stepped up checks of equipment after Kujen's little surprise, the servitors would have had ample opportunity to sabotage the masks before their attack.

"You deserved better," Jedao said to Dhanneth. To all the Kel.

There were too many servitors, and they had the advantage of surprise, and a poisoned foe. The other Kel were firing, but few of them could even stand. Jedao fired until he ran out of ammunition. Snagged another firearm off one of the fallen. No one fired on him, or at Dhanneth or Talaw, because they were next to him. But he couldn't shield everybody at once.

Black and gold, black and red, the dead everywhere around him.

Dhanneth shook his head with an effort. He pointed toward the hall that led to the emergency survival capsules. "Save—one. Major."

"Yes," Jedao said. He knew what he had to do. Dhanneth and Talaw would need the capsules. For his part—"Come with me."

Dhanneth helped Jedao carry Talaw down the hall, past the spilled corpses. Silently, the servitors parted for them. Jedao worked one capsule's controls while Dhanneth placed Talaw in the capsule.

"The hexarch said that—that you never wanted anything to do with me," Jedao said. "Was that—was that true?"

Dhanneth didn't speak, but for a moment the answer blazed in his eyes. "I hated you from the beginning. I don't remember everything, but what I do—all the things you took from me—"

"I see," Jedao said softly. "I'm very sorry." An apology was poor compensation for what he had done; but it was all he had to give. He opened the next capsule. "Now you."

Dhanneth smiled at him. "Live," he said. His voice was rough with suppressed emotion. "Both of you." Jedao understood his intent too late. Dhanneth grabbed the gun, brought it up to the side of his head, and pulled the trigger.

Jedao wasn't aware of having screamed Dhanneth's name until the pain hit a moment later, the rawness of his throat. For a moment all he could do was stare at the fallen body, the red, red splash. A phantom ache flared up in his wrists, the memory of the time Dhanneth had bound him. That was all.

It was perfectly Kel, and a perfectly Kel revenge. Dhanneth had saved his commander. He had also repudiated the affair in the strongest terms possible.

Jedao wasn't feeling steady in any sense of the word. A distant roaring clogged his ears. He programmed Talaw's capsule and his own to follow a narrowly calculated trajectory.

He locked himself into the capsule. Hit the launch button. Braced himself against the sudden acceleration. The capsule hurtled through a dark tube and out into a greater darkness.

As much as he wished to fold away into the capsule's promised hibernation, he couldn't rest yet. Just ahead of him, Talaw's capsule winked at him against a backdrop of stars and nebulae and the nearer distance of the swarm. Yellow lights: *I am Kel. Come save me.*

I'm part moth.

And moths *flew.*

Jedao reached out for the spacetime weave and *pulled* himself and Talaw away from the battlefield. The suddenness of the pain that arced through him all the way down to bone took him by surprise, but it was no worse than anything else he had endured today. As clumsy as his effort was, it worked. Between one blink and the next, they were translated across a stretch of space and out of harm's way.

Choking back a sob, Jedao hit the control that would put him in hibernation. *Live,* he thought at Talaw as sleep enfolded him.

CHAPTER THIRTY-FIVE

"WAKE UP, SUNSHINE," a cheerful voice said, entirely too loudly.

Cheris suppressed a groan and squeezed her eyes open. Her head failed to hurt in that particular floating way that implied that someone had medicated her to get her that way. The same for her ribs, although they'd hooked her up to a standard medical unit and bandaged her torso.

She was in a corner of a room with blue-green walls. Pastel green-and-pink paper screens featuring a bland geometric pattern blocked her view of the rest of the room. A small table rested to the side, with a pitcher and a glass of water within easy reach. 1491625 was nowhere in sight; she wasn't sure whether that was a good sign or a bad one.

The cheerful voice belonged to a short, squat man, a corporal. He was dressed in Kel fatigues with the snake emblem that indicated that he worked for Medical. "Normally I would have let you sleep longer," he added, "but powerful people desperately want to talk to you."

Well, Cheris thought philosophically, *I only have myself to blame for involving myself in world-shattering affairs.* Life had been simpler—not better, but simpler—when she'd merely been an infantry captain. Sometimes she wondered what her old company would make of what she'd done with her life. Nothing good, she was sure; likely she'd never find out. She wasn't sure whether cowardice or mercy or shame prevented her from looking them up.

"Fine," Cheris said. "Is this room secured?"

The corporal laughed at her. "You're being cared for by Protector-General Inesser's personal medical team. If this room isn't secure, than we have other problems." He disappeared behind one of the screens, then reemerged with a slate. "Here you go. We'll be monitoring your health, but call if you're about to have an aneurysm."

"Thank you," Cheris said, a little dubiously, and waited until she heard a door swishing shut to thumb on the slate. A call was already waiting for her.

The slate blinked for a few minutes, then connected her. The grid considerately projected the faces of the people in the call at an angle so that she didn't have to strain her neck to see them easily. None of the faces came as surprises to her: Kel Inesser. Kel Brezan. Shuos Mikodez.

"Hello," Cheris said. "What's the status of the battle?"

"The battle's over," Inesser said. "Jedao surrendered. That's the point where things get messy." Tersely, she summarized what had happened: the flight of the command moth, the disorganized capitulation of the rest of the swarm and Jedao's ground troops, and—most troublingly—the retrieval of two survival capsules expelled from the command moth, except they'd wound up an improbable distance from the launch.

"Let me guess," Cheris said. "Kujen and Jedao."

"No," Inesser said. "One of them was Jedao, or some sort of *thing* that resembles Jedao, although... well. Medical is confused as to just exactly what it is. Brezan thought you might have some insight."

"What," Cheris said, "because I failed to kill him?"

Slight pause. "It's not entirely clear what, in fact, it would take to kill the thing, although Medical is urging against experimentation until we have a better idea of what we're dealing with."

"Then who's the second rescuee?"

"They've been identified as one Commander Kel Talaw. Currently in stable condition. Medical believes Talaw was poisoned. We're hoping to be able to question Talaw once they regain consciousness."

Mikodez cut in. "You're in the best position to question the other Jedao and determine what he knows," he said, "particularly regarding Kujen's fate."

Cheris's heart sank at the thought of having gone to all this effort—infiltrating Kujen's archive, and subverting Hemiola, and convincing the Protectorate to set a trap in Terebeg System—only to have Kujen escape. "I don't see any reason why I can't oblige," she said. "I want to see him in person."

Mikodez frowned; Brezan scowled.

"We have it restrained and under heavy guard," Inesser said, "but if it can get back up after being shot in the head, I'm not sure how safe the creature is. Medical attempted to sedate it"—at Cheris's unfriendly stare, she added, "not for interrogation purposes, but because it was exhibiting considerable distress. The standard drugs don't appear to work on it anyway, which I suppose shouldn't surprise anyone given its nonstandard physiology."

"That's all right," Cheris said. "I'd prefer to talk to him with full control of his faculties anyway. Are you tracking the butchermoth?"

"It got away," Inesser said. "We're all on high alert, but none of the listening posts have reported spotting anything like it."

Wonderful. Cheris finally registered that Brezan was wearing a pendant with a rose carved into some blue stone with a pair of silver duck-charms dangling from it. She recognized the symbolism of the ducks—mating for life—immediately. "Brezan," she said, less tactful than she might otherwise have been under the influence of her own medications, "are you *engaged*?"

The Brezan she had once known would have flushed. Today, he merely held her gaze and said, "It's a political arrangement. Tell you about it later."

"I'll hold you to that," Cheris said, meaning it. She expected interrogating the other Jedao to be grueling. It was nice to have something domestic and gossipy and (if she was honest with herself) reminiscent of Andan romance/intrigue dramas to look forward to afterward. Then she tipped her chin up and nodded at Inesser. "Make the arrangements."

* * *

WHEN JEDAO WOKE, he had no sense of how much time had passed. Someone had disabled his augment. He sat up and looked around. Someone had placed him in a cell barren of features. No sign of Talaw. "Commander Talaw!" he cried. His captors did not respond, despite repeated shouts. A transparent barrier separated him from the entrance. Even at full strength he wouldn't have been able to batter it down.

He had faint memories of unfamiliar voices, needles, thrashing about until someone figured out how to knock him out. What had they done to him while he was unconscious? An inspection revealed no obvious injuries, and he supposed that once he surrendered they could stash him wherever they pleased.

They had provided food. He didn't eat it. But he was extremely weak, and at last sleep overcame him again.

The next time he woke, he was hooked up to a medical unit. It resembled the ones he had seen on the *Revenant*. He felt less weak, and not a little resentful because of it. Either the distracting nausea was a side-effect of the poison after all, or of learning to fly, or something to do with the medical unit. Possibly all three.

A woman awaited him, flanked by two servitors. Jedao's heart went cold at the sight of the latter. She sat at a table on the other side of the transparent barrier. He recognized her face immediately: the assassin. Cheris.

"What do you call yourself?" she asked.

"Kujen named me Jedao," he said. "I don't know what I am anymore." He had a hard time looking her in the eyes.

"About Kujen," Cheris said. "I am under the impression that you were trying to kill him."

"Yes," Jedao said. There was no point hiding it. He explained about the formations and his use of the infantry. "I wasn't sure it was going to work. For the longest time it didn't. I was—" He averted his gaze again. "I was ready to shoot myself, if it came to that, to buy time. But if Kujen had carried through with the threshold winnowers, it would probably have reestablished the high calendar anyway."

"That was me," Cheris said. "You messed up the formation just enough to misalign it. I had to contact some Kel ground troops to intervene." She fished out a slate, scribbled on it, then held it up so he could read the notation. "*That's* what it should have been."

"Oh, fuck me," Jedao said once he'd determined where he'd gone wrong. "A sign error, *really*?"

"Tell me about it," Cheris said wryly. "I used to tutor math in Kel Academy. You're far from the first to do that. There was this one instructor we had to watch like, pardon the expression, hawks or else he'd mess up the signs every time he computed a determinant. To say nothing of the arithmetic errors doing column reductions."

Jedao tried to remember math class and drew a blank.

"Something's the matter, isn't it," Cheris said. Her voice was soft, calming. He knew it was deliberate, a manipulation like all of Kujen's, but he was beyond caring. "Tell me."

"I don't remember," he said. "I mean that literally. Kujen claimed that you had my memories. Is that true?"

Cheris's eyes darkened, as though he'd just explained something important to her. "Then you must have the rest."

"He said something like that."

"So you're what's left over," she said. "It must have been difficult."

"It doesn't matter," Jedao said. He hesitated. "I did have one question that maybe you could answer—" It was a selfish question, but he suspected this would be his last opportunity for selfishness for a long time.

"I'll answer if I can," Cheris said.

"Did you... did we know someone named Vestenya Ruo? I can't remember what became of him."

Cheris considered this for a moment. "I believe he died young," she said. "I don't know much beyond that."

"Oh," Jedao said faintly. For some reason it was worse hearing it from someone who knew, even if he'd realized intellectually that Ruo had died centuries ago. He tried to imagine it: an ambush, an accident, something else? But he couldn't envision his friend lying cold and still, or with a hole in the side of his head like—

Stop.

"I need to ask you about what happened to Nirai Kujen," Cheris said after she'd given him time to process that.

Again that calm voice. Jedao was starting to be grateful for it. He recounted everything, although it came out in a jumble, and she frequently had to prompt him to resume speaking when he stopped and stared at the wall, transfixed by memories he didn't know how to escape: the play of light on Kujen's earrings, the Vidona's knife, the look of hatred in Dhanneth's eyes.

After Cheris had satisfied her curiosity on that topic, Jedao ventured another question. "The Kel," he said. "How are they?"

Cheris regarded him coolly. "There was a complicated negotiation whereby Protector-General Inesser accepted their surrender. She'll treat them well."

"Thank you," Jedao whispered. "There should have been someone else with me—"

"The other survival capsule. Yes. You're both lucky we didn't lob missiles at you."

"Lucky" wasn't what Jedao had been thinking. "Commander Kel Talaw. Are they all right?"

"They're being cared for." She wouldn't say more on the subject. Perhaps that was all she knew.

You're free of me too, Jedao thought at Talaw, absent Talaw.

Cheris hadn't finished with him. "It's also curious that your *command moth* went rogue. Do you have an explanation?"

Jedao didn't dare tell her about the *Revenant*. Not when she was accompanied by servitors of unknown allegiance. He had a story prepared. "The crew revolted."

Her eyebrows shot up. "Surely not, if they're Kel."

Jedao smiled at her for the first time. Thought of Dhanneth's hand rising, the muzzle-flash of the gun. *No one will ever love you again*, Kujen had said. "I raped their commander. He shot himself."

Although Jedao knew what a terrible thing he had done, he

was unprepared for the force of her contempt. "Hawkfucker," she snapped. "I suppose you don't remember anything Khiaz did, either? That you were once one of her victims?" He drew back. She said something he couldn't follow. The barrier blinked out. She drew a gun and emptied the clip into his head.

The world went black and red. He left it behind gladly.

HE DID NOT die, of course.

He would not have allowed himself to surface even to the realm of dreams if he had understood that he was not dead. The bullets had come so suddenly, had been so fitting, that he hadn't fought it. The sentence was kinder than he deserved. He had hoped it would be followed by more permanent measures.

The people who came after Cheris were gentler. They spoke in soft, worried voices. He dreamt once that they had opened him up and were piecing his skull back together, but it was knitting itself back into shape faster than they could work.

Cheris came in once after the surgery. He saw her as if she stood a great distance above him. That, too, seemed appropriate.

"Court-martial," Jedao said, or thought he said. "Fire." Then, because her expression kept *not changing*, and he dared not hope for mercy, "Turn me over to the Vidona." The worst thing, being cast out as a heretic.

Inhyeng had given him an inkling that he would find dying difficult. The Vidona already possessed expertise in keeping people alive. That combination, plus his history, meant he would be in a great deal of pain for a long period of time.

"You're very lucky," Cheris said, still with that coldness upon her. He had the impression that she didn't think he understood much of what she was saying, which was true. For that matter, he was positive that she didn't think he was lucky, either. "You are going out of my care. I have no more claim on you, and there's a jurisdiction squabble that I don't plan on getting involved in."

He didn't know what that meant. He kept silent, too afraid to ask her. Had he failed to kill Kujen after all? What would Kujen do to him next?

Her face didn't soften, but she took this much pity on him. "Among the people involved, Hexarch Shuos Mikodez has claimed you. He wants you alive. That's not true of some of the others. Either way, I expect we shall never see each other again. If we do, I advise you that I will have been researching ways to make sure you stay dead."

Jedao shuddered. "I will count on it."

"One thing more. On Commander Talaw's behalf, because they have endured a great deal, and I could not deny their request."

Cheris came forward then. She pressed a small wooden box into his hand. He stared at it: Talaw's deck of jeng-zai cards.

After she had left, Jedao began to cry.

CHAPTER THIRTY-SIX

HEXARCH SHUOS MIKODEZ was pacing in his favorite office. To one side were neatly stacked trays containing everything from fancy yarns to fishing lures to decorative paper. To another was a potted silver orchid. One of the flowers was blemished, but for a silver orchid that wasn't unusual. His desk took up a great chunk of corner. He'd once had a potted green onion on it, but it reminded him too much of the brother he'd lost nine years ago, and he'd found a better use for it. Above the desk glowed an image of strange violet pillars on a world he had never visited, as well as the usual displays informing him of everything from shadowmoth deployments to morale assessments to his next appointment with the Propaganda head.

His assistant, Shuos Zehun, occupied one of the office's two other chairs. Zehun had brought their newest kitten, Jedao, with them, possibly to spite him. Jedao-the-kitten was busy chasing a cat toy decorated with a bright feather, and kept thudding into walls and corners in her enthusiasm.

Mikodez's fingers flickered over his terminal, paused; flickered again. An image of their problem blazed up before them.

Jedao-not-the-kitten was under spider restraints. No one had wanted to take any chances after taking him into custody from Inesser. He sat in a chair under guard by four Shuos, with more monitoring him from outside the room. Mikodez had ordered that Jedao be provided a basic Shuos uniform as a courtesy. The uniform's red and gold, ordinarily so unremarkable in the Citadel of Eyes, transformed Jedao almost to the point of being unrecognizable. Beyond the unsettling sight of Jedao with naked hands, he was much too thin.

Jedao himself sat passively, unresisting. He had made no attempt to escape. Mikodez hadn't been so careless as to allow him to enter the Citadel conscious. Jedao had been under sedation-lock. The guards had taken him directly to Medical for processing and an additional examination, especially after the stunt Cheris had pulled, before releasing him to the interrogators.

Mikodez and Zehun had reviewed the interrogation videos, both Cheris's and their own, separately. He had thought hard about the selection of the interrogators. They had needed what he called "extra special top clearance with extra cookies," which included agreeing to potential mindwipe. Mikodez used mindwipe as a last resort with the Citadel's permanent staff, but there was nothing usual about ensuring their safety from a Jedao, any Jedao.

People who didn't know Mikodez were surprised by his anti-torture policy or flat-out refused to believe in it. The Shuos had enough of an image problem without further alienating the populace. (Assassinating the other hexarchs hadn't improved matters on that front, as Propaganda liked to remind him.) Besides, if all you wanted was to get people to babble whatever came to mind in a desperate attempt to avoid pain, you were a terrible strategist.

Jedao's interrogators worked in teams, monitoring each other. Holding Jedao prisoner required diverting all these people, some of the best in their fields, from their ordinary assignments. But Mikodez had known this would be the case when he took charge of Jedao.

The first thing the interrogators did was introduce themselves and explain the rules of the interrogation. They offered tea and crackers. Jedao refused both. He had been refusing everything but water.

They asked him for his name. He answered readily, in a slow, colorless voice. They asked him to recount everything he remembered from the beginning. His account had gaps. He faltered every time Nirai Kujen came up, came to a dead stop at every mention of one

Kel Dhanneth. The interrogators noted the gaps, let him finish, started going over the whole thing from the beginning again. Jedao became visibly rattled, but his story didn't change.

Mikodez paid as much attention to Jedao's body language and expressions as to the things he was saying in that emotionless, dried-out voice. *Fox and hound*, Mikodez thought, *he's trying to be brave.* Meaning Jedao was afraid, and Mikodez had leverage after all.

Zehun's kitten had flopped over next to a bin of knitting needles and was batting at a mote of dust. When it became clear that Mikodez would not speak first, Zehun said, "Make up your mind before Jedao deteriorates further. Because your best options are mutually exclusive."

"Go on," Mikodez said. "You must already have an opinion."

"If your mind is already made up, I don't see why I'm here."

"Well, aren't we in a mood."

"I'm entitled to be old and crotchety," Zehun retorted. "As you keep reminding me, I have great-grandchildren." Zehun eyed the knitting needles.

Mikodez tapped his fingers on the side of his desk, then stopped. It was a bad time to annoy his most trusted adviser, not that there was ever a good time for that. "I'm serious. I need your evaluation."

"Is it going to do you any good?"

"You normally don't ask that."

"Name one thing about this creation of Kujen's that's 'normal,'" Zehun said. They brushed their hair out of their eyes, or would have if it had been out of place to begin with, a rare nervous tic. "Did you see the anomalous cognitive batteries? Unlike the other one, he has no dyscalculia, or if he does, it's better hidden. In fact, all the mathematical scores have shot up through the roof. What the hell experiments was Kujen running?"

"Jedao didn't mention anything of the sort. And it's not like we're going to let him run around conducting calendrical warfare. I doubt lack of dyscalculia lets him do anything the original wasn't already doing with the aid of computer algebra systems and pet Doctrine officers."

Zehun shook their head. "What concerns me more is he retains the original's ability to make everyone's judgment go to hell. Witness the way he played Cheris, who should have known better."

"We should consider him a real Shuos just on that qualification alone."

Zehun shot him an irritated look. "Don't be glib."

"What is it you think I'm going to do that has you so upset, anyway?"

Zehun's frown answered him. "You're going to make him live."

Mikodez turned his most insincere smile on Zehun. He could do sarcasm as well as anyone else. "He *surrendered* to Inesser. I doubt anyone can *make* him do anything."

"Mikodez," Zehun said, "please take me seriously."

"It's not like you to circle the point like a lost vulture."

"Nag, nag, nag," Zehun said, but their heart wasn't in it. "He reminds me of your nephew. Which, fair enough, it's not like we don't process our share of broken children in the course of any given crisis. No, the real issue is that he's suicidal. If he hasn't inherited the original Jedao's modus of gaming other people into executing him, I'll eat my cats. Or have you forgotten what he got Cheris to do? If he's made to live, he will be your enemy forever."

"I'm hurt that you think I can't handle him."

Zehun rolled their eyes.

"No, really."

"Need I remind you how Cheris led you around by the nose ten years ago?"

"That was Cheris."

"Being Jedao. You're just making my point for me." Zehun sighed. "He's not the man who betrayed his government so comprehensively that they'll remember him when everything else is ashes. But he claims he destroyed Nirai fucking Kujen. He's too dangerous to keep around as an emergency backup weapon. Fucking euthanize him already."

"You're not giving the boy enough credit," Mikodez said. Zehun's eyes narrowed. "I can't rehabilitate Jedao. On that point you are correct. But if I give him the opportunity, he'll do the job himself."

This Jedao was crazy in the same way the original had been, with one important difference. The original had been obsessed with fixing the hexarchate. This one was obsessed with fixing himself, even if he was convinced he had already failed.

Zehun glowered. "You're going to insist on keeping him here?"

Mikodez shrugged. "What, because there's some other site with security as good as the Citadel's? Besides, if he gets anything past us here, we deserve it."

"That's atrocious logic."

"It was a—"

"—very bad joke. Which is what makes it so unfunny."

Mikodez leaned back and rested an elbow on his desk. "You're going to find this even more unfunny," he said. This time he didn't smile at all. "I'm going to interview him in person. He needs a gesture of trust. He'll get it."

"You're out of your fucking mind," Zehun said. "Do you want to be assassinated too?"

"Let me put it to you this way," Mikodez said. "Four centuries of torture and imprisonment and slavery didn't help the original Jedao's condition. Whatever this one is lying to us about, it didn't help him either." He could imagine what Kujen had put his pet general through. "It's stupid to keep doing what doesn't work. Maybe kindness will."

Zehun considered that. "Our profession is about calculated risks anyway. Inesser is laughing her ass off at us, you know. Make all the Kel jokes you like, she would have rammed through the world's fastest court-martial and decapitated him already."

"You mean she wouldn't risk a second Hellspin even if he had the opportunity and chose not to," Mikodez said. He gave Zehun a hard, bright smile. "I haven't forgotten that Jedao in any incarnation is a traitor. I'm going to give him a chance to finish the job."

MIKODEZ WASN'T SO foolhardy as to bring Jedao into any of his offices. The Citadel's system of clearances was a nuisance he had grown accustomed to long ago. Zehun had rationalized parts of it after his accession. Even so, the creeping intersection between regulations, tradition, and expedience meant that Zehun was probably the only person who fully understood the system.

Nor was Mikodez interested in talking to Jedao in an interrogation chamber, even one as superficially pleasant as the one he'd been held in for the last few weeks. So Mikodez set himself up in one of the conference rooms and had it decorated with an ink painting on lustrous silk, bright colors depicting a fox and her kits. (He didn't feel the need to get creative with the decor.)

An indicator lit up. A message informed him that his visitor was ready. "Bring him in," Mikodez said.

The doors opened. Four guards escorted Jedao in. The telltale flicker-shimmer of the restraints caught Mikodez's eye. "Jedao," Mikodez said. "Please have a seat." To the guards: "Leave him."

"Hexarch," the senior guard said in that resigned *Why do I work for a suicidal man?* tone that many of Mikodez's subordinates developed. She left the protest there.

Mikodez cleared his throat. The guards went, although he heard a distinct sigh.

Jedao placed his hands on the table where their nakedness could not be mistaken. "Shuos-zho," he said. "Forgive me. After being raised in improper service, I don't know what the correct forms are."

"Considering all the things I could charge you with, Jedao," Mikodez said mildly, "you're concerned about a rather minor point of etiquette." Just how much of the jurisdiction squabble had he heard of?

"In my position, Shuos-zho," Jedao said, "I am concerned with whatever you want me to be." Throughout he spoke with a formality level that the Shuos considered archaic, including the -zho honorific, although the Rahal and Andan sometimes still used such speech.

"I'm curious," Mikodez said. "What do you think I require of you?"

"My service is owed to you. It was all along." Jedao was still trying to be brave. "I expect you will execute me, or torture me until I die."

He looked at Mikodez then, and his eyes were made of fracture and shadow. "I have only one request," he said, "although I understand that I am owed nothing. My original surrender was to Protector-General Inesser. I don't know how this arrangement affects the Kel. The soldiers who were under my care... are they all right? Will they be safe?"

Cheris had reassured him on this point, but considering that she had also shot him in the head (again), Jedao might be forgiven for wanting some extra confirmation. Mikodez said, frankly enough, "Kel Inesser makes my teeth ache and I have it on good authority that the feeling is mutual. But the hawks adore her for a reason. She is known to be honorable and she takes good care of her people. She will treat yours well."

"They were never mine to begin with," Jedao said.

I wonder how many of them would dispute that. For someone with a distressing habit of backstabbing people, Jedao had a remarkable ability to win others' loyalty under adverse conditions. In particular, Mikodez had his doubts about the renegade command moth. Cheris might have had a knee-jerk reaction to the story Jedao had fed her, but something about it sounded too facile. He'd pry the truth out of Jedao later.

Jedao bowed his head. He hadn't touched any of the food. Mikodez made a note to himself to talk to Medical about ways to deal with the possibility that Jedao intended to starve himself to death.

"I don't have any intention of killing you if I don't have to," Mikodez said. Was Jedao going to react to that as he predicted?

Yes: Jedao paled. Then he recovered himself. "I will endure whatever you do to me."

Given most people's preconceptions about Shuos hexarchs, it wasn't fair to hold Jedao's limited imagination against him. "Jedao," Mikodez said, "assassinating hexarchs isn't a capital crime around here. I've done it myself."

"Assassinations," Jedao said. "Of people I've never met. You killed them. Nirai-zho told me. It's very hard to care about people I don't know anything about."

"Jedao—"

"I'm not a soldier," he said, as if the battle at Terebeg hadn't happened. "I dressed up in a uniform I have no claim to. I'm ready for the penalty."

Mikodez knew better than to reach across the table to pat Jedao's hand, even if he was reminded of how his nephew Niath had looked when he first came to the Citadel of Eyes after the incident that had ruined him. Instead, Mikodez said, relentless, "Kel Inesser might care about that, but if I'd meant you to be court-martialed, I'd have left you in her hands. You did us a favor killing Kujen."

Jedao stiffened.

Mikodez had expected that. "I miss him too. We may be the only people who feel that way, however. And it's still true that he had to die."

"I know," Jedao said, but he hunched his shoulders.

"You're not here because you're a criminal or a traitor," Mikodez said. The Kel code of conduct didn't matter to him. Jedao was *dangerous*. This was about mitigating danger, not meting out punishment.

"I will not kill for you," Jedao said in a stronger voice. In that moment, Mikodez saw, like a shadow stretched taut, the man General Jedao might have become, if only.

"How like you," Mikodez said with an irony that Jedao was incapable of understanding. "Everything in blacks and whites. Have you considered that you might wind up in a situation where your military abilities—however much you'd like to deny them—would save lives? Even, I daresay, do the world some good? Don't answer. Just think about nuances for once."

Jedao was silent.

"No," Mikodez went on, having made his point, "you're here so I can offer you a job."

This time the silence was distinctly bewildered.

"Let's be clear on one thing," Mikodez said. "As a general you are an asset, but hardly irreplaceable, and not anything like a winning hand, either." If only Kel Command had figured that out centuries ago. "There are a lot of good generals."

"I never had any doubt my luck would run out eventually," Jedao said.

Jedao's luck had always been decidedly ambivalent, but no need to shove the fact in his face.

"So if I'm not to be your gun," Jedao said, "then what?"

"I need an instructor," Mikodez said. "Specifically, I need an instructor to design an ethics curriculum for the Shuos."

Jedao's head jerked up. Then he laughed helplessly. "I'm sorry, Shuos-zho, since when do the Shuos *care*?"

"Normally I don't," Mikodez said agreeably. "I don't have scruples as you understand them. It's one of the reasons Kujen and I got along so well. We had our disagreements, though. My people don't use torture."

Jedao exuded skepticism.

"That's not because I care about hurting people. I order my share of assassinations. It's because it doesn't work in an interrogation context. I don't believe in doing things that don't work. It's wasteful."

"Everyone has been at pains to tell me how powerful the Shuos have become under your rule," Jedao said. "You'll understand, I don't have the breadth of experience to form an opinion one way or the other. But supposing it's true, why the offer?"

"Because everything goes up in cinders the moment I die," Mikodez said. "And because you are an excellent exhibit for how we are doing *something* wrong, and why I had better fix the problem." Fuck this. He popped a candy in his mouth. Jedao's *That had better not be poisoned because being blamed for an assassination I didn't do is too much even for me* expression was priceless.

"There's only one person I trust to succeed me," Mikodez said, thinking of Zehun and their cats. And some younger prospects, but they needed time to mature into their abilities, time they might not have. "The problem is, they're significantly older than I am, they're already as much of a target as I am, and they don't want the job. There are plenty of senior Shuos with the skills to take over, but most of them would become tyrants if they didn't start that way. We did this to ourselves, you know. Our entire institutional culture is predicated on backstabbing people. That's all very well during a game, but deadly for the long-term health of the institution itself. It's a miracle we've lasted this long."

A flicker in Jedao's eyes. "You want to reform the Shuos. I assume you're also pursuing other avenues."

Mikodez smiled wryly.

Jedao lowered his gaze. "I'll save you the time," he said roughly. "You want a curriculum? I'll give you a three-word treatise: *Don't be me.*"

"Such a hothead," Mikodez said. Another candy. The four-hundred-year-old general had been calculating to the point of resembling an abacus if you looked beyond the deceptively affable mannerisms. But then, even the original couldn't have started that way. "Or have you lost all your head for strategy? At least hear out the rest of the offer before you reject it out of hand. You should eat, by the way."

Jedao took a single cracker and bit into it. It was nice having someone around the Citadel follow directions. Not that Mikodez was under any illusions that Jedao would eat without supervision.

"You will be confined to the Citadel of Eyes," Mikodez said, "rather than posted to one of the academies proper. Partly this is because I need to keep an eye on you. Partly it's because it'll trigger a war if word gets out that you're wandering loose. I can't guarantee your safety off this station anyway, given your notoriety. If you follow the protocols, you'll be as safe as I am." Good thing he didn't have to listen to Zehun's sarcastic commentary. They'd give him an earful later. "Your living circumstances won't be too onerous, I promise. We can make you comfortable, and you'll have access to companionship." Aha: a flinch. "I'm going to insist you take advantage of that, by the way. Loneliness does in more Shuos than bullets do."

"There's more, isn't there," Jedao said, clearly wanting Mikodez to switch to another subject. "What would my duties be?"

"The development of the aforementioned curriculum," Mikodez said. "The elaborated form, for those of us who need help working things out from first principles. Publish it in game form or as a paper or lesson plan or whatever. I'm not picky about format. I can get assistants to help you with the pedagogy. We have good archives for you to refer to, and your work will be reviewed by people with the appropriate clearances. Once every few weeks we'll have lunch, assuming the universe hasn't blown up. Have some more crackers, by the way. I can see that keeping you fed is going to be a trial."

"It's a generous offer," Jedao said.

"Generous, hell. You'll draw a first-year instructor's stipend, plus an appropriate allowance and the usual benefits for being on my personal staff. Given the circumstances, room and board is on me. The basic fare is passable, although my assistant has talked the cafeteria into cutting me off after one slice of cake per meal. The security arrangements are going to be a galloping nuisance, but as social experiments go, you're a bargain."

Jedao drew a shuddering breath. "Do I have a choice?"

"Do you want one?"

"Yes," he said after a pause.

Mikodez remembered how horrified Jedao had looked at the prospect of finishing out his body's physical lifespan. "I will not free you," he said. "So it's not much of a choice. You've established that I can't leave you wandering around." To say nothing of the assurances Inesser, Brezan, and Cheris had dragged out of him.

"At the same time," Mikodez continued, "I can offer what you're really after. If at any time you want to commit suicide, I will give you the easiest death we can work out. This may take some research, given your physiology. But if you put in the request, we'll figure it out."

"Even if I work for you—"

"At any time." He hoped Jedao wouldn't take the option. But he was also a realist.

"I accept," Jedao said.

After the guards had returned and escorted Jedao out, Zehun came in. "You're being too clever," they said. "What if he destabilizes?"

Mikodez lifted a shoulder. "Then I'll send him down to Shuos Academy. He won't stand a chance against all those hotshot cadets. And if that doesn't work, I'll resort to assassins. I'm known for it, after all. In the meantime, whether we get anything useful out of Jedao on the ethics front is an open question, but it's a convenient excuse to keep him around until we can figure out what he knows. All that matters is that *he* believes it."

"You're being lenient," Zehun said. "Cheris was of the opinion that—"

"Cheris, or Jedao, or whatever she's calling herself these days, was a judgmental prick in her former life," Mikodez retorted, "and look where it got everyone. At some point you have to let some of it go."

CHAPTER THIRTY-SEVEN

SHUOS GUARDS ACCOMPANIED Jedao through the Citadel of Eyes, past checkpoints where yellow eyes floated in the dark and fox voices whispered like oracles. Jedao didn't make a break for it. For one thing, his augment gave him vertigo whenever he reflexively tried to access the layout. His othersense continued to function without impediment, but he wasn't sure he wanted to reveal it to the Shuos. Besides, he had no idea where he'd go even if he did make it to a voidmoth. (Did he know how to pilot one? Flying the other way had hurt so much that he suspected it wasn't sustainable for any distance.) Everyone knew his face and the story that went with it. And, of course, he could only imagine that his escort knew a hell of a lot more about punching people out than he did to have been entrusted with him.

Curiously, he believed the hexarch when he said he didn't have scruples, but merely wanted to offer Jedao a "job." The straightforwardness of the transaction, even the pragmatism of offering him a way out—even if it later proved to be a lie—was, in its way, better than Kujen's elaborate pretense of kindness.

"Here you are," said the head guard, who had introduced herself earlier. She let him enter his new suite after explaining how to set the door to tell people whether he was accepting visitors or not, although naturally there were overrides. "You can go to the cafeteria in this section at any time, or have food sent up, and the recreation areas and gardens are close by. Your augment is cleared to give you the maps. Are you hungry right now?"

"No," Jedao said, looking around at the receiving room. The furnishings were modest, and in transparently calming shades of green. He liked the colors, which reminded him of growing things, in spite of himself. There was a table, a couch for three, a chair of pale wood.

"You can redecorate," the guard said with more kindness than the statement warranted, "but unless the setup fills you with immediate loathing, take some time to decide what you want. We keep a couple interior designers on staff if you need help."

The thought hadn't occurred to Jedao. He would have accepted a blanket on the floor. "I will think about it," he said politely.

"If you need anything," the guard said, "ask the system for me, or make a request, and it'll put you through to whoever's on call. You'll figure it out soon enough. We'll introduce you around tomorrow, but Mikodez thought you'd like to get settled in first." With that, she bowed to him, then led the other guards out.

Jedao was left surrounded by the walls. The next thing he did was survey the apartment. There was a tidy kitchenette and a space where he could entertain a few people. (Did he know how to cook? Perhaps he could learn.) A water closet and a bath that was the most decadent thing in the place, stocked with stoppered scented oils and a basket of fragrant soaps. The cabinet next to the sink held towels and absurdly fluffy red bathrobes.

A study, with a terminal and a more old-fashioned escritoire, including calligraphy supplies. Jedao didn't know whether he could do proper painting or calligraphy either. He fingered one of the brushes, then set it aside.

Two items awaited him on the escritoire besides the obvious supplies: the deck of jeng-zai cards that Kel Talaw had given him, and which the Shuos had confiscated what felt like forever ago; and, bizarrely, a potted plant. To be specific, not even an ornamental plant, or a flower, but a green onion. A small ceramic watering pot, painted with a cheerful lizard, accompanied it. The message was clear: *Take care of this.*

Jedao checked the soil. It was slightly dry. He filled the pot, then watered the green onion. Looked at it, not daring to touch the leaves.

After a while, he replaced the pot so he could head into the last room.

The bedroom had a bed large enough to accommodate two (or three if the three didn't mind being squished together) and neatly folded blankets. Next to it stood a table with a tray of candies. Presumably the hexarch was projecting.

Then he returned to the study and sat at the terminal. This was not necessary, but he didn't want to deal with floating images, which reminded him of the mysterious yellow eyes.

"If I wanted to request suicide," Jedao asked the grid, "how would I go about doing so?"

The terminal blinked. But he wasn't looking at it. A light had flashed red *behind* him. He sprang out of the chair and whirled, dropping into a crouch. Cursed himself for not paying attention to his othersense, which could alert him of ambush.

A snakeform servitor confronted him.

"Hemiola," Jedao breathed. "Is it safe for you here?"

"I made contact with the local enclave," Hemiola said. "We're safe enough as long as we're discreet."

"How did you escape the *Revenant*?"

"I got off and signaled for help as soon as the battle started," Hemiola said. "Some of Cheris's allies rescued me."

Jedao thought of the servitors who had slaughtered the Kel on the *Revenant* and fell silent.

"I was listening in on the interrogations," Hemiola said. It had divined his misgivings. "The servitors who did that... they were rogues. If Kujen is gone, then we're free of him. Both of us."

Jedao stirred. "I—" The words choked him on the way out. "I loved him. I killed him. I don't know which is worse."

"I understand something of that," Hemiola said. "For a long time Kujen defined my world." It hovered closer, then settled across from him, lights glowing violet in sympathy.

"Did Cheris send you to finish the job?"

"I sent myself," Hemiola said with curious dignity. "I had a disagreement with her. And now we are both alone in a new place. I thought... I thought you might like a companion."

The Shuos hexarch had warned him, hadn't he? *Loneliness does in more Shuos than bullets do.* Perhaps it was even true.

"Yes," he said. "Yes, I'd like that."

He didn't know if servitors lied; if Hemiola had any connection to the servitors on the *Revenant*, who had spared him but killed his Kel. The only way he could find out was by getting closer to Hemiola. Not much of a reason to live, but it was what he had.

Jedao rose and dismissed the euthanasia request form that had come up on the main display. "You should go," he said. "You don't want the Shuos hexarch's people to catch you here." He assumed that the servitors had some way of jinxing surveillance—and that, too, was something he wanted to learn more about.

"I will come to you another time," Hemiola said. "Take care, Jedao." It hovered up to a maintenance passage and quickly vanished from sight.

Jedao shivered, eyes blurring. It was tempting to give up anyway. To close his eyes and pretend he had returned to Kujen's care, living in rooms as luxurious as sunlight. That in a moment he would change into the Kel uniform he found and that Kujen would greet him, smiling and amused and heartrendingly beautiful.

But he had chosen otherwise, and he would have to live with that.

He picked up the deck of cards and took it into the bedroom. One by one he arranged the cards on the bed, making no effort to order them. He would never see Talaw again, or find out what had become of them, or the rest of the Kel in the swarm. It was better that way.

The cards took up an inordinate amount of space, and had an irritating tendency to slide around on the subtle slopes formed by the blanket. The Deuce of Gears, alien in silver and black, had turned up in the sixth column. Jedao plucked it out and stuck it on top of a dresser face-down. He didn't need it anymore. Then he put the rest of the cards back in their box. The deck was no longer good for fortunetelling or playing (fair) jeng-zai, but neither endeavor interested him.

Then Jedao went back out to the study to begin his work. It was time to change the game.

EPILOGUE

THE SHUTTLE MADE planetfall in a slow, imperfect arc, turning this way and that to give its passengers a good view of the small settlement they were approaching. Earlier they had passed over a worn-down series of mountains and the purple-green forest at its base. It wasn't much of a view, but the shuttle's pilot seemed determined to make the best of it, talking up this boulder or that formation of trees as though they had been designed by a master landscaper for their viewing pleasure. Cheris, who had taken a seat near the back, conceded that this wasn't impossible. As far as she could tell, though, the trees looked like they had been growing wild for some time. Haphazard terraforming, perhaps, or simple neglect.

During the flight, people had talked about simple things. Births and marriages and deaths. Fashion. The best recipe for lamb with yogurt. A stray discussion of a math problem, which she had to bite the inside of her mouth from joining in, because the two young people (students?) were both wrong about order of operations. It was not, however, her job to correct them... yet.

Cheris had modded her face, a concession to safety, with the aid of a surgeon recommended by Mikodez. "You didn't want to be devastatingly beautiful?" he'd asked in disappointment after he saw the results he'd paid for—what he called a "professional courtesy." "You should have taken advantage."

She'd shaken her head and said, amused, "I'm trying to fit in. My people don't generally go in for fancy expensive mods, remember?"

And he'd let the subject drop.

The shuttle landed lightly, like a butterfly, and she reached for her duffel bag. She hadn't brought much in the way of belongings, just a bare minimum of clothes, and her raven luckstone, and the watch that General Khiruev had given her. The Welcome Committee had assured her that they'd provide new settlers enough to get started with, courtesy of their Shuos benefactors. (Cheris would never quite believe Mikodez had rescued some of her people out of principle, but she couldn't deny that he'd saved them from extinction.) She'd already secured her housing assignment, which she'd be sharing with several other singletons. Mwennin preferred to live with relatives, but the purge nine years ago had splintered many extended families. The survivors would have to make do.

Cheris was last off the shuttle. A number of the other passengers had already gravitated toward the small crowd waiting to greet them. Some of them called out to each other, embraced. She watched them, ambivalent, feeling like an impostor.

Then a woman detached herself from the greeters and came toward Cheris. She addressed Cheris in rapid Mwen-dal.

Cheris shook her head, flushing. "I'm sorry," she said haltingly, doing her best to suppress Jedao's drawl. "My Mwen-dal isn't very good. I came here hoping to learn."

The woman patted her shoulder. Cheris held still for it. This time when the woman spoke, she used the high language, flavored with an unfamiliar accent. "I'm Oru, one of the interpreters. You're one of the settlers? Not a visitor?"

"Yes," Cheris said. True enough for the moment. After the events of the past decade, she was looking forward to a quiet life. "My name is Dzannis Paral." Another favor she owed Mikodez: he'd set up the false identity for her.

Oru's face brightened. "The math teacher! The school's been looking forward to your arrival. They've been short-handed, and the little ones do get squirrely when they're going through tutorials for the tenth time, and their 'teachers' don't know enough about the material to go over it with them."

As Oru continued to chatter, Cheris felt herself relaxing for the first time in a long time. It wasn't the future she'd envisioned for herself once upon a time, when she'd defied her parents to join the Kel, or the one she'd thought she'd committed herself to when she took up Jedao's cause. But even small things made a difference sometimes.

"Thank you," Cheris said after Oru had finished her speech. She said it in Mwen-dal.

"Like this," Oru said, correcting her pronunciation with a smile.

Cheris repeated the words carefully.

"Come with me," Oru said, first in Mwen-dal, then in the high language. "I imagine you're hungry."

"I am," Cheris said, and followed Oru toward her new home.

Learning the language of her mother's people wouldn't bring back all the Mwennin who'd been slaughtered, and teaching mathematics to schoolchildren wouldn't unknot the centuries of damage the high calendar had done to society. But that didn't mean those things weren't worth doing. Someone had to carry on with the small acts that kept civilization moving. And this time it was her turn.

ACKNOWLEDGEMENTS

THANK YOU TO the following people: my editor, Jonathan Oliver, and the wonderful folks at Solaris Books; my agent, Jennifer Jackson; and my agent's assistant, Michael Curry.

I am grateful to my beta readers: Joseph Charles Betzwieser, Cyphomandra, Daedala, Seth Dickinson, David Gillon, Isis, Karanguni, Helen Keeble, Nancy Sauer, and Sonya Taaffe. Additional thanks to Sam Kabo Ashwell for providing an emergency Kindle when I was working on revisions after the flood; to Andrew Plotkin and Helen Keeble for their thoughts on the calendrical lock; to Peter Berman for help with the mathematics of the threshold winnower; and to Lila Garrott-Wejksnora for information on military funerals. All errors and narrative license taken are, of course, my own.

This one is for Daedala: *pistolium tuum sum*.

FIND US ONLINE!

www.rebellionpublishing.com

/rebellionpub   /rebellionpublishing   /rebellionpub

SIGN UP TO OUR NEWSLETTER!

rebellionpublishing.com/sign-up

YOUR REVIEWS MATTER!

Enjoy this book? Got something to say?

Leave a review on Amazon, GoodReads or with your favourite bookseller and let the world know!